Over AND OVER AGAIN

COLE MCCADE

Cole McCade
blackmagic@blackmagicblues.com

Cover Artist: Les Solot
www.fiverr.com/germancreative

For my aneki, imouto, mija, and mei mei.

For chosen family, whose bonds run deeper than blood.

Table of Contents

1 1
2 4
3 8
4 16
5 21
6 29
7 34
8 38
9 42
10 48
11 57
12 63
13 68
14 77
15 82
16 87
17 94
18 97
19 101
20 106
21 109
22 115
23 122

24 130
25 139
26 146
27 150
28 154
29 158
30 163
31 172
32 183
33 188
34 192
35 195
36 198
37 205
38 206
39 208
40 213
41 216
42 220
43 226
44 234
45 243
46 248
47 258
48 262
49 268
50 271

51 277
52 290
53 292
54 299
55 302
56 304
57 305
58 314
59 316
60 337
61 349
62 362
63 382
64 389
65 397
66 398
67 413
68 426
69 450
70 454
71 459
72 465
73 471
74 479
75 488
76 492
77 499

78 503
79 507
80 512
81 524
82 530
83 541
84 546
85 554
Epilogue 564
Afterword 573
Acknowledgments 577
About the Author 579

Reading & Pronunciation Note

WHILE THIS STORY USES MOSTLY accurate British terminology in line with the setting, a few terms—such as "supper" vs. "tea" and "fence" or "fencewall" vs. "wall" (for a specific type of dry stone wall fencing)—have been adjusted to take into account a majority American reading audience for whom such terms have different enough meanings to be jarring. Most spellings are British, as well, but per the author's personal preference the use of "z" over "s" has been retained in certain spellings.

Also, while Imre's name can take on multiple pronunciations depending on the country of origin, in this case Imre uses the Hungarian pronunciation due to his family's Hungarian/Carpathian Roma roots. In simplified phonetics, the best approximation of each syllable is "Em" (rhyming with "him") and "ruh" (rhyming with "huh"), with a soft stress on the second syllable. Em-*ruh*.

Content Warning

WHILE OVER AND OVER AGAIN is definitely one of my sweeter, less trigger-laden stories, you may still want to be aware of specific content warnings for your reading comfort. Those content warnings include:

- May/December age gap.
- On-page, unprotected cis male/cis male penetrative anal and oral sex, including swallowing after oral sex.
- Self-harm through neglect.
- Depiction of sick farm animals.
- Discussion of animal euthanasia. (No animals are actually euthanized.)
- Recollection of a pet being struck by a car.
- Recollection of homophobic slurs used against a child by his peers.
- Alcohol consumption.
- Smoking.

As always, even if you may not understand why such things may be triggers for others, please respect that we all have different experiences and all respond to things differently. Some may be bothered by depictions of unprotected sex (while I myself have strong feelings about using fiction as a vehicle to allow queer men to explore unprotected sex without stigma as part of depicting a queer life without trauma); others may be sex-averse and may enjoy the romance, but not the explicit sexual descriptions. Some may have no problems dealing with self-harm, while for others even inadvertent self-harm through neglect may be immensely triggering.

Regardless of your feelings on these topics, be good to yourselves, always.

-C

1

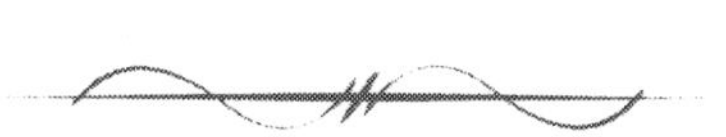

LUCA WARD'S PARENTS SAID GOODBYE to him at Sheffield Railway Station.

Luca didn't say it back.

They'd not even bothered coming inside the station with him. Instead they stood in front of that giant fucking urinal of a fountain in the square and made mealy-mouthed mumbles about seeing him in January, fresh farm air, it was for his own good, his Uncle Imre couldn't wait to see him.

"*He's not my uncle*," Luca hissed. "We're not even related. I haven't seen him in ten fucking years."

"But Luca—"

"Admit it. He's just some stranger you're foisting me off on, because you don't want to deal with me yourself."

His father hunched his narrow shoulders, sighing and fidgeting with his pencil-thin tie. His ties always made him look like he was choking, squeezing his neck too small until his head ballooned atop the willow lathe of his body.

"I don't know what to do with you anymore, Luca. I'm at the end of my rope."

"Try not shipping me off like some bloody criminal!"

His mother—his little golden apple of a mother, with her way of talking with her hands as though shaping flowing waves and moving clouds—reached for him. “Now don’t be dramatic, dear. You used to love the farm, and it’s beautiful out there in the Dales—”

“If you’re going to send me to the arsecrack of nowhere, it could’ve been Scarborough. At least they’ve proper beaches.”

His father’s lips thinned into a flat black dash. “This isn’t a vacation. This is punishment. This is discipline. You need to grow up.”

“I’m a fucking adult—”

“Adults don’t steal a bloody motorcycle and leave it crashed out in front of the Peter and Paul.”

Luca stared at his father. Marco Ward’s chest heaved, the colour spotted high in his cheeks, his eyes bright. His father was like that: a thin and sensitive man, wispy enough to blow away with the wind, quiet even in his anger. Yet that quiet was what made his fury so powerful, when he choked on his emotions and trembled as though he’d break down at any moment. Luca’s mother fretted between them with those wordless, helpless sounds she made when she wanted to knock their heads together, but meant to let them work it out for themselves. There was no hope Lucia Ward would step in and turn this wreck aside before it crashed.

Not when this had been her fucking idea, tossing him out like the trash.

His father sighed, shoulders sagging. “I’m out of options, son. You’re giving me no choice. The only alternative was to press charges, but I’m not ready to give up on you yet. It took fast talking to keep the church from prosecuting. If you want to be an adult, you can be tried as an adult. If you want to be reckless, you have to deal with how I choose to save your arse. But if you refuse to go, there’s nothing I can do but leave you to deal with your own consequences.”

Luca’s gut heaved, then turned cold. The threat didn’t need to be any clearer. He turned away.

"Whatever. I need a break from your dysfunctional horse shite anyway. Sort yourselves the fuck out, will you? You're a fucking disgrace."

He walked away from his parents, leaving them standing in the mid-September sun like Jack Sprat and his wife, two pins stuck in the Sheffield Station square and holding it in place.

"I love you, dearling!" his mother called. "Do try to dress warm!"

"We'll see you in January, son," his father added.

Luca tossed a middle finger over his shoulder, stuffed his earbuds in, turned up the White Stripes, and stepped into the shadow of the brick arches fronting the station's façade.

Whatever. They wanted to ship him off like a damned prisoner, they hated him so much they couldn't be arsed to drive to Harrogate themselves, they could go rot.

Would serve them right if he never came back at all.

2

IMRE CLAYBOURNE CROUCHED OVER A bag of seed, one knee planted in the cool earth beneath the shadow of the open barn door. With one hand he sifted a clover and alfalfa seed mix between his fingers, little green-gold kernels indistinguishable save for minor differentiations in shape and size. Their dusty, earthy scent wafted up with each handful that spilled back into the sack. His other hand steadied his cell phone, just barely catching it before it could slip from between his shoulder and ear, narrowly saving it from a swim in the seed bag.

"It's barely a minute to town, Marco," he said. "No bother at all. I'll nip right out, fetch him from the station, and be back afield within the hour."

On the other end of the line Marco Ward sighed, his breaths crackling against the speaker. "Thank you for this, Imre. I'm at my wit's end with that boy."

"He sounds a bit like you at that age."

"I never stole."

"Anything but your dad's rum."

Marco laughed, yet it was tired, strained. "I'd have let it go, even if I loved that bike—but the pol wanted to nab him for destruction of public property. He crashed the bloody thing into a church. If I'd not been friends with a few of the locals, he'd be in cuffs. The boy's on a fast track to hell at this rate."

"Let St. Peter worry about that when the time comes." Imre

chuckled. “He’s nineteen. Not a child. We still did daft things when we were nineteen. Uni worked out those wild oats well enough for both of us.”

“If he’d just *go* to uni, I’d be less worried. But he’s intent on making his gap year a gap life.”

Exhaling, Imre sank back on his haunches and checked his watch. Luca’s train would be pulling into Harrogate on the line North in about an hour and a half, and Imre still had an acre to till. Might just put it off until Luca was in and settled. Planting could wait another day. Alfalfa and clover grew quickly—and the herds would trim it down even faster, well before the frost set in.

Could just take the day off, he thought. Spend a little time with Luca. He’d be upset, no doubt. Luca had always been a brightly passionate boy, quick to smile, quick to cry. God knew what he was like now. Imre hadn’t seen Luca since he was a sober nine-year-old, one whose quick, brilliant smiles had already begun to disappear behind a careful silence and downcast eyes by the time the Wards had cast off and put Harrogate at their backs.

He’d hated to see it. Some people were born with a thick skin; some developed it over time. Luca had been born with skin like paper, and a crystal heart. He took everything into himself and transformed it into raw emotion that shone and bled from him in this vivid kaleidoscope of colour. Every love, every loss, every joy, every hurt. Back when Marco and Lucia had lived closer in Harrogate proper, they’d been out at Imre’s farm every other week; in those days Luca had been a pinwheel of animated energy, tumbling through the clover with soft white flowers dappled in the dark shock of his hair, his laughter echoing over the farm.

The problem with feeling things so deeply, though, was feeling them hard. Taking the wounds. And if those wounds had already made

Luca sober and quiet by the time the Wards had moved away to Sheffield ten years ago…

Imre worried what kind of seething, angry mass of scar tissue was about to show up on his doorstep as a grown man.

He straightened, brushing the dirt from the knees of his jeans, and leaned in the barn door, looking out over the fields. His goats—primarily spry, tooth-edged Alpines, a few Nubians scattered in the mix—milled in their walled pastures, gnawing at the last crop of alfalfa and clover, bleating and bouncing among themselves. The scent of fresh clover blooms was high and sweet; fat, furry bees swam through it, nearly drunk on the aroma. He couldn't help a faint smile. Luca used to bounce about just like the goats. Surely that vivid spirit couldn't be completely broken.

"It'll be all right, Marco," he murmured into the phone. "He just needs some time to cool off. Away from you. No doubt you're public enemy number one right now."

"God am I. No one told me when you had kids they'd love you until they hated you."

"He's just trying to assert himself as a separate person from you and Lucia. An adult."

"Then he shouldn't act like a damned boy."

Imre smiled to himself. "Give it time."

"You can say that. You don't have children of your own. You don't know what it's like."

"I suppose I don't." And Imre doubted Marco would want to hear much else. He didn't think Marco realized just how much he was like his own son—quiet and sensitive yet hot-headed and passionate, willing to listen to no law but his own. "I'd best go, if I'm to make it to the station on time. I'll take good care of Luca. You have my word."

"At this point I'd be grateful if you put a few stripes on his hide."

Marco groaned. “I don’t mean that. I don’t. Just…thank you, Imre. I know it’s an imposition.”

“It’s no such thing. I’ll let you know when he’s settled in.”

“Thank you. Lucia sends her love.”

“Send mine back,” Imre said, then ended the call with a swipe of his thumb, slipped his phone into his pocket, and folded his arms over his chest with a heavy sigh.

He’d said it was no trouble, but in truth he had no idea what to do with Luca Ward. The bright, laughing little boy he remembered wasn’t the man being dropped in his lap in disgrace. He didn’t know what to expect when he saw Luca again.

But as he watched the goats he remembered pale flower-flecks against a crown of dark hair, and thought perhaps he could welcome Luca not to a jail sentence…

But to a home.

3

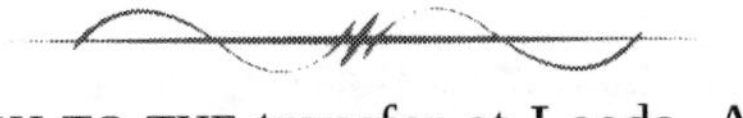

LUCA SLEPT THROUGH TO THE transfer at Leeds. At Leeds Station, he scrambled through the busy concourse, twice as large and crowded as Sheffield. He had ten minutes to make the second train from Leeds to Harrogate.

He was tempted to miss it.

Just…disappear into Leeds. It was a big enough city; he could vanish anywhere and everywhere. Sleep on park benches. Live wild. Survive on 50p cup noodles. Get a job as a barista or some such and find himself a tiny windowless flat in some shitehole back alley, miserable but *his.*

Stop being Luca Ward, and just…

Be Luca.

The idea shouldn't have such appeal, but he'd been thinking about it for months. Some days he felt like his heart was a bird with clipped wings, and flying was just a memory it was terrified of forgetting. That was what had been so beautiful about that moment on the motorcycle: hands up, hundreds of pounds of steel and burning petrol careening down the road, gravity gone and Luca weightless, flying, flying as if he could lift up on wings and send the bird of his heart soaring away.

But there was platform 17B, and the second train from Leeds to Harrogate already waiting. He double-checked his ticket, then hefted his heavy duffel and strode for the closest carriage, stretching his legs.

Ten-minute transfers were utter balls, but he scrambled on with a few minutes to spare. The carriage was half-empty, dotted with bored-looking people in plain, dull colours, scattered about like bits of seed strewn for pecking hens. A few glanced up at him, but didn't quite look at him—just dully registering his presence before returning blank stares to the windows, as if there was anything to see on an unmoving line.

He found a seat in the very back row, shoved his bag into the overhead bin, then slumped down in the bucket chair against the window with his earbuds shoved in. Leeds was so *noisy*, but Shawn Mendes crooned in Luca's ear, drowning it all out with aching pleas for someone to have mercy on him and his heart.

A few more seats filled in a shuffling of feet and luggage. The doors cranked closed. The train screamed out a shrill whistle and rumbled around him. A jerk of momentum jolted him as the carriage rolled forward, wheels grinding and squealing against the tracks. This was it. Last chance to turn tail and run slipping through his fingers, the doors locking and sealing him in. He rubbed at his chest, at the tight low pain there, rested his too-hot brow to the cool windowpane, and swallowed a breath that lodged in his throat. Leeds Station slid past slowly, then faster and faster until the train arrowed through bright flashes of morning sun off rooftops.

He wanted to go home already. He wanted his parents to just…let him *be*. He'd thought it would serve them right if he didn't come back, but they were probably glad to see him gone. He was someone else's problem now.

Maybe they'd be *happier* if he never came back.

His phone buzzed, cutting off the music track—and cutting off the prickle in his eyes before it could become anything more. He rummaged his phone from his pocket and swiped through the latest text. Xavier. Luca laughed under his breath. That motherfucker.

You there yet? Xav texted.

Luca dotted his thumb over the screen, Swyping out quick letters. ***Not yet. I almost didn't go at all. Could've run away in Leeds. At least it's a proper city.***

Harrogate's not so bad. Pretty, even.

Luca smiled, though he didn't really feel like it. That was how Xav had always been; bright side to everything. It had driven Luca through the roof during A-levels, and was the only thing that got him *through* A-levels: Xavier Laghari and his wide smile and bright black eyes in that pert brown face. Xavier was lucky. He was smart, charming, easygoing, and everyone *liked* him. Of course he could look at the bright side of everything; for him, every side was the bright side.

But it was Xavier's bright side that had made Luca's life tolerable, and now he didn't even have Xav when Luca's parents had just ripped him away from his friends, his life, everything he'd had in Sheffield.

Don't try to make me feel better, he texted back. ***It just pisses me off. I'm not even staying in Harrogate. I'm going to a farm somewhere in the backwoods.***

Maybe you can feed the ducks.

Luca scowled at the phone. ***You taking the piss?***

Always, Xav shot back. Luca could almost see that cheeky damned grin. ***Don't make too many friends there. I'll get jealous.***

Yeah. I'll make friends with all the fucking pigs, mucking around in the mud.

With a snort, Luca closed the text window and tapped play on his music again. The track skipped forward to *Bad Reputation* and he sighed, sinking down in his seat and letting his eyes half-close until the hard blue light of morning became a haze and the buildings streaked by in vague dashes of colour. He had a bad fucking reputation, all right. His father had probably called Imre already and filled his head with stories of what a degenerate reprobate Luca was. He flushed hotly and sank down deeper in his seat.

Unka Immie.

Though they weren't related by blood and Imre was just a friend of Luca's father from uni, for as long as Luca could remember he'd called him *Unka Immie*—until, around eight or so, he'd declared himself too old for such childish bon mots and begun pronouncing *Imre* so very gravely. He could hardly even remember what Imre looked like; he was more a collection of impressions than a solid mental image. Luca used to clamber all over him like a great, broad-limbed oak tree. To a tiny boy Imre had seemed a massive monolith, ten feet tall and broad as a mountain, with a thick nest of beard. Luca had always climbed in Imre's lap and tangled his fingers in that long, lustrously black scruff, stroking the soft strands and playing with the few tiny braids woven throughout, each tipped in small blue beads to match the slender, bead-tipped braids strung throughout the untamed mane of Imre's hair.

Those beads had been the same blue as Imre's eyes. That was his clearest memory: how startlingly clear a blue Imre's eyes were against his swarthy, weathered skin. That, and the kindness in his hands. He'd had massive hands, hands that could crush granite to dust, this great dark earthen god with the strength of stone, but he'd handled everything—from his tiny, bleating goat kids to the smallest clover flower to Luca himself—with a gentleness that flowed from his hands like water, imbued with a living warmth.

And Luca had been in love with him, the way only little boys could be.

He still remembered sitting on Imre's lap when he was five years old, snuggled in the heavy rocking chair before the living room fireplace at Imre's farm. Blue walls. The room had had deep blue walls, painted in varying shades over rough stone, turning the space into a dark blue night lit by the flicker of firelight, soft illumination shining like honey off the polished wood of the guitar propped on the mantle. Luca's parents had been tangled on the couch, wrapped up in each other and cuddling under a quilt stitched in patterns of zigzags and dots and knotted loops, drowsy yet so contentedly in love. Luca had curled up in Imre's lap like a puppy, clinging to his beard and his shirt, fighting off sleep though his eyes refused to stay open.

But he'd had a secret in his pocket, one he'd worked on all day, then hidden away in his jumper. And as the deep, heavy swelling of Imre's lazy sigh had moved his chest and stomach against Luca's cheek, Luca had opened his eyes, peeking at his parents to make sure they were really asleep, before rummaging in his pocket and pulling out his secret.

A ring, made of braided blades of grass.

He'd had to make it a whole eleventy-twelve times before it came out right, because the grass would break and splinter or one strand would be too short or it was just too *small* because Imre had hands big enough to hold the world. But now it was perfect, a thin flat band of interwoven strands making chevron patterns. He'd made it because that was what people did when they loved people, he'd thought. His parents had. They loved each other, so they had rings. So he'd made a ring too, smooth and pretty, and he'd tucked it away again and run his thumb over its textures before taking a deep breath and looking up at Imre.

"Immie?" he'd asked, biting his lip. His mouth tasted funny, like he'd been sucking on pennies.

Imre had rumbled a soft, curious sound and looked down at him with those eyes as gentle as his hands, surrounded by seams and folds that settled his gaze into a cradle of warmth, softening the forbidding crags of dark, heavy brows. "What is it, angyalka?" he'd asked, his deep, richly inflected English altering into something more melodious and smooth on the Hungarian word.

Luca had taken a breath so massive it tried to burst his chest, then announced, "I'm going to marry you one day."

Imre had blinked, then laughed low in his throat, the sound so large yet so quiet, shaking them both. "Are you, now? And why is that?"

"Because I love you." Luca had put as much conviction into the words as he could, more confidence than he'd felt when his ears burned and his bare toes curled until they caught in the denim over Imre's thighs. "Mummy and Daddy love each other and they got married. I love you, so I'm going to marry you."

Imre's gaze had softened, and he'd gently dropped one of those massive hands atop Luca's head, playing through his hair. "Five years old is very young to be so serious about marriage."

"I *mean* it." Luca had ducked his head, fidgeting his lower lip with his fingers, then gulped and pulled the ring from his pocket again. "I'm gonna grow up and I'm gonna be tall and handsome, and then you'll love me too and we'll get married."

Tilting his head, Imre had studied the ring solemnly. In the firelight, the edges of the ring had gleamed like spun gold fibre. "There's a problem with that."

Luca's heart had turned upside down. It was an awful feeling, a sick feeling, and he'd dropped his hands into his lap, staring down at the silly, pointless little ring. "Oh."

"The problem," Imre had said, catching his hand, swallowing it inside his own until Luca's fingers and the ring disappeared into a thick palm, "is that I already love you, angyalka."

A sharp breath had sucked into Luca's throat. Imre had uncurled his hand and gently grasped Luca's, and guided him—still gripping the ring so tight—to slip the ring over Imre's third finger on his left hand. It'd fit just right, sliding over his thickly ridged, scarred knuckle and settling into place nestled at the base of his finger. Luca had smiled so much his face hurt with it and flung his arms around Imre's shoulders, burying his face in his neck and his beard.

"I'm always gonna love you, Immie," he'd whispered, and Imre had chuckled again and wrapped his arms around him, holding him just tight enough.

"I know you will, angyalka. I know."

The memory of that night—the firelight in Imre's eyes, the sweet light flutters of Luca's heart—sank in his chest. He huddled down deeper in the train seat. He'd been such a ridiculous child. Imre had been kind to him, patiently indulging him and not crushing his five-year-old heart, but that had been fourteen years ago. Imre probably still saw him as that same earnest, simple little boy, full of nonsense ideas and making promises he'd never keep, unrealistic and completely confused.

He'd be right about one thing.

Luca was completely and utterly confused, and not sure what to do with himself. Not on that fucking farm, and not when Imre got sick of him and shipped him back home without a single damned thing having changed.

With a groan he leaned forward, thunking his forehead against the seat in front of him.

Why, of all people, did it have to be Imre?

"Hey," the man in the row before him barked. "Watch it back there."

"Sorry," Luca mumbled and curled in on himself, burying his face in his knees with a low moan. Fuck, he couldn't even manage a train ride without stirring up trouble.

The next four months would be miserable.

4

EVENTUALLY LUCA SETTLED INTO THE train's lull, the sound of the rails mingling with the pulse and rock and cadence of his music, hypnotizing him into a drifting thrall that wasn't quite sleep but wasn't quite awake. He snapped from it only long enough to show the conductor his ticket as she passed through before slipping into a trance again, silently mouthing lyrics and trying to ignore the heavy weight on his chest.

After passing beneath the castle-like arches and towers of the Bramhope Tunnel entrance, he drifted off fully. The darkness of the tunnel and the rhythmic flash of running lights eased him into a fitful doze, his phone clutched against his chest and his head resting against the window. He woke as the train shot from the tunnel and light splashed over him, searing through his eyelids and shocking him awake. He opened his eyes on a blaze of white, stabbing into his retinas and blinding him. With a wince he turned his face away and covered his eyes with his arm, blinking until he adjusted to the light.

The white haze cleared, replaced by green and gold and brilliant autumn fire: rolling fields that swooped up and down like the crests and troughs of waves, plunging high only to sweep gracefully low, stroked as smooth as the flick of a calligraphy brush. Deep pink and rich purple edged the green, catching the light in soft streaks, glimmering beneath a sky of endless blue and low, silver-bellied clouds. Tumbles of pale grey limestone pushed up through the grass like fragments of ancient ruins. The Yorkshire Dales swept past, segmented into fields by hedgerows, lines of trees, low fencing walls built of hand-stacked worn river stones in white and grey. Small blocky barns with white sides and peaked roofs scattered all about. At the peak of one hill, the sun shone in bursts through the legs of grazing cattle.

Luca's eyes widened. He pressed his fingers to the window, breathing in slowly. He'd never seen the Dales like this. During his childhood in Harrogate, the verdant acreage had been a close and ordinary thing. The last time he'd seen the Dales had been through a window, just a crevice of sky blocked off by stacks of moving boxes in the back of a truck. A heavy feeling struck hard in the pit of his stomach, at once sweet and swimming with a certain quiet, thrashing terror.

A feeling of coming *home*, when Harrogate hadn't been home for ten years.

He didn't even remember his old address, the house where they'd lived, as more than an afterimage of sunlight through overgrown trees his dad had always promised to trim from their tiny patch of back yard but never did. Everything else about Harrogate was just impressions: weekends on Imre's farm, weekdays running and playing with other children in the neighbourhood, all sticky fingers and red balloons and little legs pumping on bike pedals. Coming back now, ten years older and city wiser, made him feel like an impostor. He didn't belong here.

It may have been home once, but it couldn't be now.

But he still remembered the ugly, overly modern Harrogate Railway Station, sticking out like a raw sore against the town's graceful, historic architecture, villas, and tree-lined roadways. He groaned as the carriage pulled into the station, easing to a halt with a lurch and a grinding squeal of railway brakes. While the conductor called disembarkation stops and times, Luca dragged himself out of his seat, wincing when his body protested with shooters of pain lashing through his limbs and crawling up his spine.

He stretched it out, groaning as he pulled his muscles loose—then tugged his earbuds out, hauled his bag down from the bin, and slung it over his shoulder. His legs didn't want to work right; his body told him gravity swayed back and forth with the rhythm of inertial motion, but the train was at a standstill while he tripped over his feet like a puppy trying to figure out what to do with its oversized paws. He nearly tangled his boots together on the steps down to the platform, and barely caught himself from pitching forward by grabbing on to the doorframe.

Yet hands caught him before he even managed to grip the frame—large, warm hands, thick-fingered and gentle, radiating a familiar heat. He stiffened as those hands slowly drew him down the steps and set him to rights, handling him as if he were little more than dandelion fluff, light and spinning and wheeling as freely as his spinning, wheeling heart.

He'd thought he'd have to go searching for Imre. But as his feet came down to earth and settled on the platform, he stared up into clear, steady blue eyes he knew as well as he knew his own face.

Imre had come to him.

He was still tall even from Luca's higher perspective, well over six feet, and still broad—his shoulders the shoulders of mountains. His rough-hewn body was built of blocks of thick musculature, grace in the taper from shoulders to waist, strength in the hard press of sturdy thighs against worn jeans. But that wild mane of unruly hair and that thick, familiar beard had gone completely silver, soft as mist and in some places shimmering with streaks of pure white, shadowed to iron grey in others, a halo of shining moon-pale colour standing stark against naturally dark skin weathered even deeper by the sun. Those scattered braids in both beard and hair remained, the beads tipping them a darker blue now, some polished stone with black veins throughout and a luminous sheen.

The lines around Imre's eyes had deepened, shadowed by thick brows a darker shade of steely, sooty grey, and the creases around his mouth were starker—but the way he smiled was still the same. Just the slightest pull of a generous, sensitive mouth with full red lips and a precisely defined dip in the centre, a dip that softened and sweetened as that subtle smile tugged at it.

Imre's smile warmed as he steadied Luca with those large hands on his shoulders. "Luca," Imre murmured. His was a slow and measured way of speaking, and his voice—while deep and imbued with a quiet and rumbling authority—was always so *soft*, so coaxing, as if promising safety with every word. Imre was a man who never had to raise his voice to command attention, and he had Luca's attention entirely as he said, "It's good to see you."

Luca worked his lips incoherently. He hadn't expected Imre to *be* here, smiling like that, waiting for his unwanted burden right here on the train platform instead of impatiently tapping his foot in the car park. Luca didn't know what to say. He just stared up at Imre, his heart struggling to grow strange and beating wings, struggling to fly, as he took in how Imre had changed over the years. Older, yes, but still so vibrant, still simmering with a silent and undeniable strength.

And standing there with his silver hair dotted with flowers, dozens woven into a crown of soft, bursting white clover blossoms with their frothy round blooms and tiny petals interlaced with slender green stems.

Luca blinked.

Blinked again.

Tilted his head, and frowned.

"The *fuck* is that?" he demanded, and Imre burst into rough laughter that rolled as sweetly and smoothly as the sloping hills and valleys of the Dales. Luca just scowled.

Great. Not five minutes, and Imre was already laughing at him.

Just. Fucking. *Great.*

IMRE HADN'T CONSCIOUSLY REALIZED HE was still watching for a twig-thin sprout of a boy until a young man stepped off the train, and that *click* of recognition settled in like a lock sliding into a familiar home.

That tiny sprout had been replaced by a tall, graceful slip of a man who had just stepped past the cusp of adulthood: pale and smooth and slim as a lily, made up of sharp edges and sullenly beautiful angles. It was hard to see little Luca in that man, until he lifted his head and pale green eyes flashed from beneath a sideswept shag of ink-black hair. Those green eyes, light as new spring leaves and framed by a thick ring of black lashes, were still the same mirrors that reflected back every emotion he took into himself.

And right now they simmered with exhaustion, hurt, and a barely-suppressed and bubbling rage.

Until those emotions vanished, wiped away by shock and panic as his coltish legs tangled on the train carriage steps and he pitched forward under the heft of a bag that probably weighed more than he did.

Imre moved without thinking. Two steps and he was there, catching Luca under his arms and halting his fall. Luca probably could have caught himself, already reaching for the door frame, but Imre hadn't considered that. He'd just *reacted* and now he was standing here with his hands full of startled boy, the lines of Luca's body stiff under his touch, tension hardening lean sinew under the defensively black armour of his clothing.

Imre eased him down onto the concrete of the platform, then shifted his grip to his shoulders, holding loosely. Luca had the look of a trapped animal, ready to either attack or bolt, and Imre would prefer he did neither. And so no matter how he wanted to pull Luca into his arms and remind him he was home, he was *safe*, Imre would never hurt him…instead he only clasped his shoulders gently, giving Luca plenty of room to wiggle free and give himself whatever distance he needed.

No, this Luca certainly wasn't the bright-eyed, effusive boy he'd known. Luca the boy had been fragile, but Luca the man was completely broken. Lost. Hurting. Wounded, and struggling to cage all that unfettered emotion inside where he could protect it from others' sharp touches—yet still it burst from him at every seam, desperate to be free.

Not the Luca he'd known at all.

But still Luca, very much.

"Luca," he said. "It's good to see you."

Luca stared up at him, eyes wide, long lashes trembling. For a moment he looked lost, sweetly confused, before his brows knit together and he tilted his head.

"The *fuck* is that?"

Imre arched a brow, then realized Luca was staring at the flower crown on Imre's head. The sheer confused indignation sparking in Luca's eyes—as if the clover flowers had mortally offended him—roused a burst of laughter that rioted up from Imre's belly and past his lips before he could stop it.

Luca scowled. That sulky pink mouth twisted into a pout, and Luca lifted his pointed, utterly defiant chin and stepped out from under Imre's grasp, edging away from blocking the carriage exit and putting a few feet of distance between them. “What’s so bloody funny?”

“Nothing.” Imre let his laughter out on a slow breath, but couldn’t stop himself from smiling as he pulled the flower crown from his head and offered it to Luca, dangling from his fingertips. “I had made this to welcome you home, but if you don’t want it…”

Luca’s eyes widened, then narrowed. He jerked his face away, glaring across the platform, his scowl deepening so much his nose scrunched up. The tips of his ears and the point of his nose coloured a rather fetching shade of pink.

“Whatever,” he growled. “This isn’t home.”

“It’s my home. It used to be yours.”

Luca shot him a suspicious glare from the corner of his eye, then darted a look down at the flower crown, then back at Imre. Imre waited; he was content to wait him out as long as need be. He wasn’t certain what had happened to Luca in the ten years since he’d last seen him, but he was in no rush to force the defensive young man to bare his wounds. Imre had once had the trust of a little boy who loved anyone and everyone who treated him with the smallest bit of kindness. But that easy trust was as far gone as that boy, and didn’t seem to have any place inside this skittish, snarling man.

That was all right. Imre was patient. If Luca needed him to, Imre would take every small step needed to earn that trust again.

And he thought, right now, what Luca needed—more than the discipline his father wanted—was someone to trust.

After another wary look, Luca edged closer. Just close enough to snatch the flower crown from Imre’s fingers, before backing away again. He held his arms crossed close over his chest and hunched into them.

Yet he handled the flower crown delicately, the slim interwoven stems tangled carefully in his fingertips.

Imre studied him a moment longer, then looked away before he might make Luca uncomfortable with his scrutiny. "Do you have any other bags?"

"No. Just this one."

"It looks heavy."

Luca glowered. "I've got it."

"I only said it looks heavy." Imre shrugged. "I'd be happy to take it. You must be tired."

"I was barely on the train an hour and a half."

Imre chuckled. "I'm trying to be nice, Luca. You can counter with logic and facts if you like, but emotion doesn't listen to logic or facts."

"'Nice' isn't an emotion," Luca bit off, but he relaxed his death-grip on himself. Then unslung his bag from his shoulder.

Then, without looking at Imre—in fact, glaring pointedly away—he thrust the bag at him, but kept the crown of clovers clutched in his other hand.

Imre took the bag and hefted it over his shoulder. Something hard-edged inside dug into his back, but he ignored it and turned toward the doors leading into the concourse. "This way."

He led Luca from the platform and into the station proper—less busy at this time of day, when most of the commuters to and from Leeds were usually on the early morning or evening trains. A few gawking tourists stood about, too wrapped up in their maps and their iPhone photo galleries to step out of the main thoroughfares, but Imre navigated neatly around them with Luca on his heels, trailing in his wake as though he didn't want anyone to assume they were together. Imre kept his smile to himself and let the boy have his silence.

At least he wasn't running away. Imre had thought, the moment he turned his back, Luca would bolt and vanish into the brush with a last flicker of white like a deer's tail disappearing under the trees.

Luca held his silence, practically vibrating with it, fit to stab Imre with his fury until, as they stepped through the doors leading out to the station's main entrance, Luca caught up with him and angled into his path just enough to block him. Imre stopped, cocking his head. Luca stared down at his feet—bulky boots just like the post-punk anarchist chavs Imre and Marco had run with at Nottingham, back in their wilder days—that barely caged the rumpled bottoms of black jeans clinging to slim legs. He fiddled with the cord of his earbuds, tangling it with the flower crown, then blurted out,

"Listen, I'm sorry about this."

He chewed on the words like chewing nails. Imre could make a dozen guesses as to what he was apologizing for, but held his tongue and only asked, "About what?"

A mutinous shrug. "My dad's basically using you as an alternative to…I don't know. A therapist. Corrective school. Boot camp. Jail. Dumping me in the closest skip."

"Do you expect Lohere to be a prison?"

That flicker in Luca's eyes; so familiar. From the moment he could speak he'd always been curious about the little bits of Hungarian and Romungro peppered into Imre's speech, always asking what this or that word meant. *Lohere* was one of the first words Imre had taught him, and that familiar flicker said he recognized it and was trying to place the meaning. And just as he had when he was a tiny thing, Luca picked at his lower lip with his finger as he thought, tugging at the pink, soft curve and pinching it between his thumb and forefinger before something *clicked* in his gaze as he looked down at the clovers in his hand.

Lohere. Clover. Clover Farm, Imre's pride and joy, but it wasn't his farm that roused a spark of pride in this moment.

It was Luca, and that curiosity that remained alive even after years had dulled his brightness and fire.

But that curiosity faded, washed away by the troubled tides rolling across his features as Luca looked away again. “I don’t know what to expect,” Luca murmured. His voice, too, had changed as much as the rest of him: from an impish lisp to a husky tenor with a faint lyrical uplilt at the edges of his words, certain sounds catching in the back of his throat in a breathy burr. “This is so daft. He’s cranked off at me, so he sends me off to the farm like I’m still a kid. Like it’s some kind of object lesson about the value of hard work or some shite.” He grimaced. “Really, he just doesn’t want to look at me. But he can’t let me go, either.”

Imre caught the faint note of longing in Luca’s voice, lingered on how pale green eyes turned distant, far-seeing. “Is that what you want? To be let go?”

“Yeah.” Luca trailed into silence, his mouth soft and bitter in its twist, then added, “It’s time to cut the leash, but he won’t. Not until I’m properly trained to run the way he wants me to.”

“Luca.”

Imre considered, searching for the right words; words that wouldn’t send Luca running in the opposite direction. He hadn’t quite known what he was agreeing to when Marco called him in frustration, begging him to take Luca for a few months and keep him out of trouble. *Whip him into shape* had been the unspoken implication, but that wasn’t anything Imre had ever agreed to. What he’d agreed to, even if it hadn’t been explicitly stated, was to give Luca shelter—in whatever form that shelter might take, whatever form Luca might need.

And he was already realizing what Luca actually needed was a far cry from what his father *thought* he needed.

"I'm not your jailor," Imre said after careful thought. "I'm not the hand holding your leash. I'm not going to train you to do anything except help out on the farm, if you don't mind a little hard labour to make the days go by faster." He shifted the bag against his back. That hard edge was still digging into him fiercely, but he continued to ignore it. Luca—silent Luca, stiff Luca, Luca who still wouldn't look at him—was more important. "I understand why your father sent you here, but I've no agenda. This isn't any different from the weekends you used to spend at Lohere." He offered his hand, palm up. "No judgment. No punishment. I swear it."

But Luca only stared at him again, with that same look of baffled indignation as when he'd noticed the flower crown. Imre couldn't quite make out what was going on behind his eyes, with the strange way he stared at Imre as if he'd sprouted horns fit to mingle with his goats.

"What?" Imre asked.

"I…don't think I've ever heard you say that much out loud before."

"You're afraid. You seemed to need it."

Wrong thing to say; Imre knew it before the words were even fully out of his mouth. Luca's open, naked confusion slammed shut behind a door of fury, his expression twisting into a ferocious glare. "I'm not afraid," he spat, then turned away with a toss of messy hair, staring narrow-eyed across the street. "Just…just…let's go. I hate this place. It's noisy."

Imre sighed.

This might be more difficult than he'd thought.

He couldn't help being honest. Sometimes bluntly, terribly honest, whether people wanted to hear it or not. It had gotten him in trouble quite a bit in his younger days, and the only way he'd learned to temper it was with silence when he thought his honesty might be unwanted.

And he thought his honesty was very much unwanted, right now. So he only said "All right, Luca," and turned toward the car park, fishing in his pocket for his keys. "Come on, then. I'm parked this way."

Luca said nothing, just a wordless shadow skulking in Imre's wake.

6

LUCA COULD STILL SMELL IMRE.

It hadn't quite struck him at first, when Imre had caught him and for a moment they'd stood so close, Imre so overwhelming that all Luca could do was stare. That scent was so familiar it hadn't even registered on a conscious level: warm hay and sunlit clover fields, clean soft fur and the musk of a hard day's labour, a sweet undercurrent of honey and the tang of apples and something with a bit of mulled, creamy spice. Imre had always smelled of what he loved—and he smelled of Lohere Farm even now, of all the things that made up his home. That scent instinctively made Luca want to melt into it, melt into Imre, and it took everything in him not to press himself against Imre and beg him to make everything all right.

Make it stop hurting, the way only Imre could.

Like fuck. Luca was a grown damned man. Too old to be clinging to people and begging them to fix everything. Just because Imre still smelled like fond childhood memories didn't mean anything.

Yet that scent was even more pervasive in Imre's car: a battered flatbed Land Rover with its camper removed. Its paint had once hinted at green, or maybe that was Luca's faulty memory when it was nothing but a matte, washed-out grey now. The old, well-cared-for leather seats had soaked in that scent; it rose from the scatterings of hay left in the Land Rover's bed, crunching a little now and then when Luca's bag slid around the back as the jeep took the bumps and ruts in the road. Luca sank into the sun-warmed leather, closed his eyes, and let himself relax just a little into the scent filling the cab, while they rattled off the main roads of Harrogate and onto the smaller, dirt-paved farm roads leading out into the fields and dales.

Maybe he could treat this like being on holiday, instead of a punishment. Imre wasn't shouting at him, wasn't looking at him with Imre's brand of stern, quiet disappointment that was more effective than any raised voices or sharp words. Imre wasn't…*anything*. He was just a silent presence filling the Land Rover.

Luca couldn't stand it.

As a child he'd loved Imre's silence, loved how easy it was to just *sit* with him, each in their own private little worlds—but right now he'd give anything to know what was going on behind those calm, impenetrable blue eyes.

He'd give anything to know if Imre thought he was just some immature prat, and not the boy he'd promised to always love.

Luca's face flamed. He opened his eyes, glaring at the scratched and pitted roof of the car. Why was he even thinking about that right now? Why did it *matter*? Promises made to children didn't matter. They were promises made to different people. Luca might as well be a stranger, and it didn't matter what Imre thought of him. If he disapproved. If he felt anything at all. It sure as hell didn't matter if he still loved Luca. He didn't *want* Imre to still love him.

Not like that. Not like he was just a child to be coddled and indulged, even if he'd meant it with all his heart when he'd said *I'm always gonna love you, Immie.*

His breaths caught. His heart flipped. Oh—oh, fuck him in the ear. Was that why he was such a bollocky mess?

Was the five-year-old monster he used to be still naively in love with Imre?

No. Hell to the fucking no. The Imre he remembered was an idealized giant seen through the eyes of a child. This man was someone else entirely, as much a stranger as Luca.

"Something on your mind?" Imre asked mildly, his mouth curling at the corners. Luca jerked, flattening himself against the Land Rover's door. Guilt thumped through his heart in erratic rhythm.

"N-no." He huddled into himself and glared out the window as fields rolled past, dotted with cattle and round hillocks of hay. "Just pondering my next crime. Planning quite the spree. I've a reputation to uphold, don't you fucking know."

"Right regular criminal now, are you?"

"Oh yeah. Can't even talk to you without a witness in the room."

"Pity. You'd make for such scintillating conversation over tea."

Luca wrinkled his nose and stuck his tongue out at Imre. Imre chuckled, glancing at him sidelong.

"So what *have* you been doing to get Marco into such a snit?"

"I don't even know." Sighing, Luca thunked his head back against the seat. "I mean I know he told you about the whole…motorbike…*thing*, but he's been acting like I'm some kind of degenerate since way before that. Like I'm wasting my life drinking, smoking, and nothing else."

"Do you drink and smoke?"

"A little, yeah. But that's not all I do," Luca shot back. "If you're going to lecture me, I don't want to hear it."

"What would I have to lecture you about?"

"Not going to uni. Not having a job. Being a foul-mouthed prat. Crashing Dad's bike."

Imre's brows rose briefly, before he turned his eyes—those damned neutral, unreadable eyes that told Luca *nothing*—back to the road. "Do you think you need lecturing about any of those things?"

"No. What, you think I'm ashamed or something?"

"I don't think anything," Imre said softly.

That's the problem! Luca wanted to shout. *Show me something. Anything.*

Show me what you think of me.

Show me how you feel.

Show me that you see me, and not some tot to pat on the head and send on his way.

But Imre said nothing else. He sat languid in the driver's seat, his shoulders relaxed against the leather, one long, brawny arm stretched between their seats, the other hand casual on the steering wheel, narrow hips slouched forward and thickly muscled thighs spread. His faded, frayed dark grey henley was unbuttoned and open at the throat, the strong tendons of his neck leading down to a visible ticking pulse moving against the hollow of his clavicle. Luca caught himself staring at it and looked away sharply, hissing and hunching into himself again.

"Shut the fuck up, Imre."

Even as he said the words Luca wished he could reach out, pluck them from the air, and swallow them back down inside himself before they ever reached Imre. A stillness settled over the car, different from Imre's calm, easy silence. In that stillness floated things unsaid, things whispered in a language Luca couldn't understand, yet still they screamed their meaning inside him in echoes of guilt and wrongness that bounced off the walls of his heart.

"Please don't speak to me that way," Imre whispered, toneless and steady.

"Why?" Luca's hackles bristled, and *God* he wanted to shut up, but couldn't seem to stop his awful waspish frightened tongue. "You going to try to be my dad, too?"

"No," Imre answered simply. "It just hurts."

That frank, honest admission, spoken with neither recrimination nor shame, cut Luca's legs out from beneath him. He stared at Imre, but Imre only watched the road. Those clear, calm eyes were remote and strange, as if Imre were an island whose shore Luca could never reach, no matter how far he swam.

"Oh," Luca whispered, and shrank into himself. "I…I'm sorry."

Imre said nothing. He only shifted gears, as the long stone fencewalls of Lohere Farm came into view over the next rise in the road.

Luca huddled in the corner of the seat, looked out the window, and shut his awful, hateful mouth before it spat any more venom into the pool of acid misery eating away inside him.

7

LOHERE FARM WAS STILL AS Luca remembered it: a sprawling two-story stone house with connected extension and greenhouse, its peaked slate roof overshadowing walls festooned with climbing runners of honeysuckle, a few late showers of pale white and gold blooms spreading their horned mouths and soft fronded lips. Many other flowers littered the overgrown garden of a lawn in a carpet of fallen blossoms. Cathedral windows with cross-hatched interior framing bars peered through the showering leaves, making narrow gaps in the green completely covering the walls of the house.

One of those windows, the second from the right on the top floor, looked in on a room he remembered from childhood. There'd been a bed made up in that room just for him, covered in those quilts Imre seemed to have in infinite supply, with their bright zigzag and octagonal patterns and mandalas mixed with homey, earthy colours. There'd been a wall hanging, he remembered. A scarf in deep wine purple embroidered in gold, festooned with tiny silver bells. He'd loved to play with the bells until they shimmered with sound, and Imre had always stilled his hand gently and reminded him to be careful with it, to treat it with love.

But he'd never said why, when Luca had asked.

Against the backdrop of three massive white-walled barns and over seventeen acres of rolling land segmented into crop fields and pastures of grazing goats, the farmhouse still looked like a small, cosy cottage despite its size—and Luca remembered those blue walls throughout the house, each warm, close room filled with the comforting odds and ends of Imre's life. That pang struck Luca in the pit of his stomach again, that feeling of coming *home* when this wasn't home at all. He didn't have a home. Not when his parents didn't want him but wouldn't quite cut him loose to find a place of his own, and this place belonged to the man he'd told to shut the fuck up like Imre didn't have feelings and wouldn't care if Luca cut him open.

God, he was such a little shite. No wonder his parents didn't want him around, and banished him here. Maybe eating a handful of good farm dirt would clean his fucking sour mouth out.

He stole a glance at Imre as the Land Rover turned into the winding earth drive that circled the house and ran toward the closest barn. Imre kept his gaze straightforward; something about the set of his jaw said it might be better if Luca kept his mouth shut. Luca plucked at his lower lip, then looked away, dragging the high collar of his pullover up to cover the bottom half of his face, yanking the sleeves down over his hands, fidgeting with the hems. He stayed in his corner and made himself as small as possible, taking up as little of Imre's space as he could, until Imre pulled the Land Rover to a halt in the broad, flat expanse of swept earth in front of the closest barn.

Imre unbuckled his seatbelt and levered himself out of the driver's seat. After the door closed—hard enough to bounce the Land Rover on its tyres—Luca slowly uncurled himself, peering over the collar of his pullover to watch as Imre circled the truck on his long, smoothly prowling strides, that mane of silver hair flowing around his shoulders in tossing waves. He flicked a single glance at Luca as he passed the passenger's side window, then moved past to grip the straps of Luca's bag and heft it from the Land Rover's bed.

Luca winced and uncurled himself, then fumbled the seatbelt free and slunk out of the passenger's seat, flattening himself against the side of the truck to keep out of Imre's way. He reached for his bag.

"I'll take it," he mumbled, but Imre was already slinging it over his shoulder—and made no move to set it down, or into Luca's outstretched hand.

Luca let his hand fall. Imre looked away from him, gaze flicking over the house, the barns, the pastures, with the air of someone in control of his environment; the air of a fierce protector shepherding his herd, a half-domesticated wildling that still remembered the wolf he had once been. Then those thoughtful, searching eyes were on Luca again and Luca flinched back, dropping his gaze to his feet and pulling even harder at his sleeves.

"If you have to smoke," Imre said, "do it in the kitchen. The smell will upset the animals if you do it outside. The slightest spark, especially in a drier autumn, could send the fields or stores up in flames, and could start a wildfire that would destroy this farm and hundreds of acres beyond."

"I won't. Smoke, that is." Luca shook his head quickly, then lifted his head enough to peek at Imre. "Imre…I'm sorry. I really am. I'm mad at my dad, and taking it out on you. That was unfair of me."

Imre's subtly expressive mouth tightened, then softened. Those shielded eyes warmed, the creases around them easing, losing their stiffness. "I used to call you angyalka," he murmured.

"Angel," Luca repeated in a whisper. The soft nickname in Hungarian twisted up inside him, lacing its fingers into the chambers of his heart. He swallowed. "I remember."

He couldn't look at Imre. Not when Imre watched him as if he expected something, as if searching for the bright-eyed angel Luca used to be. Luca stared at the barn, with its painted blue doors the same shade he'd remembered from so long ago. His eyes prickled, and he took a shaky breath.

“I’m not an angel,” he said. “Not anymore.”

“Oh? You think so?”

“Just ask anyone,” Luca choked, and shrugged stiff shoulders. “Anyone with an opinion will tell you.”

“I didn’t ask anyone’s opinion.” A soft scuff of a booted foot in the dirt, and Imre’s scent drew closer, a more concentrated blend of the scents of this entire place—laced with the heady, heavy aroma of honeysuckle flowers decaying into the soil and releasing their fermented fragrance to colour the cool, biting early autumn air. “I asked yours.”

Luca shook his head, pulling back. He couldn’t handle Imre so close, asking him that. He edged from between the man and the Land Rover, backing toward the barn. “I don’t know. I’m not the little boy you used to know.”

But eyes as blue as the barn doors followed him, refusing to let him escape. “No. You’re not,” Imre said.

Then stepped forward and brushed past him, the broad muscles of his back flexing hard against his shirt as he hefted Luca’s bag against his shoulders and led him toward the house. Luca stared after him, his stomach tight. If he wasn’t that boy to Imre anymore, then…

Who was he?

8

LUCA'S HABIT OF TOYING WITH his lower lip, Imre discovered, was entirely distracting.

Luca was doing it right now, as he followed Imre toward the side entrance to the house—accessible via a broad grass-lined pathway between the rear of the barn and the wall of the house. Luca just kept playing at his mouth, pressing his fingertip into the peak of his upper lip, tugging out his full lower lip, pushing it in until it yielded and swelled his mouth into an overripe raspberry, gleaming and soft.

Imre snorted under his breath and lengthened his stride so it wasn't so easy to glance over and watch Luca toying and plucking at his lip with such utter innocence. Nineteen was no age. Technically a man, but still too much a boy.

Luca needed Imre's protection, his support. Nothing had made that more obvious than his cruel and barbed tongue. Those thorns were defensive, protective, not aggressive, and it was Imre's job to shield him from more pain.

Nothing else.

If another man of Imre's age ever looked at Luca that way, Imre would nail him to the barn rafters. Imre would deserve no less, if he let his thoughts wander back to that ripe pink mouth for even half a moment.

He distracted himself by letting out a long, low whistle through his teeth, controlling it until it swooped up at the end. Then he paused, listening. A few moments later a series of soft yips came from over the hills: first three from the north, then three from the east. *All clear*, those yips said, and he nodded to himself. Good.

Luca paused mid-stride, inhaling softly and casting Imre a wide-eyed look, gaze brimming with hope and longing. “Ciri and Gull?”

Imre shook his head. “Cirikli passed away a few years ago, Gullo about a year after.”

“Oh.” Luca’s face fell, his eyes lowering. “I’m sorry.”

“They were loved, and lived well.”

But Imre couldn’t stand that look on Luca’s face—and after a moment, he let out another whistle. Two short high calls this time, one longer low sweep. The barks that answered were less controlled, more ecstatic, and within seconds two shaggy Australian shepherds came scrambling over the hills: one white with scattered black cookies and cream flecks, the other black with matching white flecks, their brilliantly deep golden eyes identical. Their tongues lolled in wide grins, fur flying as they raced across the fields toward the farmhouse.

Imre had just enough time to set Luca’s bag down before the dogs pounced him, tumbling into him with their tails wagging furiously. He sank down to one knee and wrapped his arms around them, burying his fingers in their ruffs and surrounding himself with the dusty, warm, living scent of sun-heated fur and happy dog, speckled with pollen and the fragrance of the clover fields.

“These two,” he said as a rough tongue rasped over his cheek, “are Cirikli and Gullo’s pups. Their brothers and sisters live on a few of the neighbouring farms, but Vilagosno and Setitno stayed to keep me company.”

Luca wrinkled his brows, then stretched a hand out toward the dogs carefully. “Vila…Vi…”

“Vila and Seti.” Imre grinned, then clucked his tongue.

The moment they'd been given permission, the dogs swarmed onto Luca. Vila yipped and leaped up on her hind legs, resting her paws on his shoulders and thrusting her nose into his face to sniff him. Luca rocked back with a laugh—a bright and sweet thing like sugar and champagne, a sound Imre could almost breathe in and feel rolling over his tongue; a sound he'd missed deeply. He couldn't help smiling as he watched Luca wrap his arms around Vila and scratch through her ruff, squinting one eye up as she licked his cheek. Seti milled around his legs, watching him, quiet and waiting, until Luca dropped a hand to let her sniff before scratching underneath her jaw until she whined with pleasure.

Luca's eyes lidded, softening. "Hi," he murmured. "Hi, girl." He glanced at Imre. "Hungarian or Romungro?"

"Romungro. Light and dark."

Luca gave him a dry look, a touch of impishness peering past the shroud of misery. "Original, Imre."

"But you haven't asked which is light, and which is dark."

Luca frowned, leaning his cheek against Vila, with her black coat speckled in white. "Light." Then he stroked his hand over Seti's head, fingers smoothing her white, black-speckled coat. "Dark."

"But Vila is black, and Seti is white."

"But Vila's bright and jumping everywhere. She's blinding, like bright white light." Luca laughed again, nuzzling into Vila's cheek, all the while never stopping that scratching that left Seti's hind leg jackrabbiting against the ground until she raised little puffs of dust. "Seti's quieter and more patient, and waits for you to come to her. She's calm as a quiet and peaceful night."

Imre tore his gaze away from watching Luca with the dogs, but it was hard. When Luca smiled like that his thorns vanished to leave a brightness as blinding as Vila's. Interesting how Luca could be so observant about others, even animals in all their simplicity.

But he couldn't quite see himself.

"Very good, angyalka," Imre murmured, then rose and hefted Luca's bag once more. "Come, then. I'll show you to your room."

9

THE LAST THING LUCA WANTED was to let the dogs go, sending them bounding back out to the fields with another of Imre's special whistles—but they had a job to do, just like everything on the farm. He remembered that much, at least. Keeping the dogs from the herds meant leaving the younger goats vulnerable to foxes. Luca didn't know much about wildlife, but he knew this time of year the carnivores would be gorging themselves in preparation for a lean winter, and he wouldn't ask Imre to risk keeping Seti and Vila in just so Luca could play.

But the warm, clean, wonderful scent of dog still clung to him, reminding him of summer days playing with Ciri and Gull, the dogs Imre had had when Luca was little. He'd tumbled in the dirt with them like a puppy himself and come in filthy, leaving his mother and father sighing in despair and Imre chuckling as he loaned him a massive shirt to trail around in while his clothing was in the wash. He couldn't believe Ciri and Gull were gone, but they'd already been adults when Luca was just a tiny thing; he didn't know why he was so surprised.

Maybe it was just another of those sharp reminders that time didn't stop, and neither did the little pains that came with being an adult.

Though at least Imre was smiling again, and no longer looking at Luca like he'd sliced ribbons from his heart.

Luca followed him into the house, stepping into the nearly

overwhelming scent of baking apples that had always pervaded the interior of Lohere. Surrounding himself in that scent was better than wrapping himself in a warm down blanket and burrowing under the covers on a frosty day. He stopped just past the threshold and breathed, taking it deep into his chest.

Yet Imre was moving on, through the narrow foyer, past the anteroom with its half-wood, half-stone walls and round mirrors in ornate antique bronze frames, up the slim staircase of dark, polished oak with its stylized bannisters. Luca followed, trailing his fingers along the stone of the wall, tracing how the texture of the paint wash laid over it changed it. Everything woke more and more memories: that texture under his fingers, the creak of the fifth step, the understated, quiet paintings in black and white ink lined in a diagonal following the stairs, capturing ancient artists' pen renditions of flora complete with hand-scribbled notes in multiple languages. He paused under a sketch of spraying blooms and traced his fingertips over the Latin with a small smile.

"*Alcea rosea,*" he read off softly. "Hollyhocks."

Then took the steps two at a time, catching up with Imre.

Lohere had always been a treasure trove of little wonders and curiosities, but seeing it now was like finding it anew—and Luca had to stop himself from picking up the little silver sculptures on the tiny tables lining the upstairs hallway, or stopping to trace the triangular patterns in the deeply coloured rose, black, and blue runner whose dark shade of cobalt perfectly matched the walls.

Second door from the end. Luca had known before Imre stopped that it would be there, but he couldn't help the little thrill of excitement that shot from the tips of his toes to the base of his spine as Imre pushed the door open, then swept a gently mocking bow and gestured for Luca to precede him.

Luca nearly spun into the room. It was small, but that was what made it perfect; he'd always loved small spaces, places that felt like a secret, somewhere he could huddle like a wee fairy in a wooded hollow and keep all his treasures and mysteries to himself in his own little world. This room had been that place for him, as a child: his special secret hollow, where on weekends he whispered the things no one could know before leaving them safe here when he went back to his ordinary, un-secret, un-special bedroom at the old house in Harrogate.

The bed was a cosy iron-framed sleigh, piled high with quilts and thick, lush pillows. The blue walls had been turned into a deep blue night sky, painted with a glowing moon so detailed it rivalled the real moon, luminous and swollen and surrounded by a thousand wishing stars. A rosewood chest sat at the foot of the bed, polished to a deep shine, its sides carved with ornate vines Luca knew from tracing them over and over. They matched the low carved shelf that sat below the window, piled high with cushions and quilts to turn it into a window seat. An entire wall was taken up by a massive bookshelf full of the strangest, oldest books on the strangest, oldest subjects, and even without touching them Luca knew the feeling of gilt leather spines and the smell of the pages and all the wonders held inside.

And that scarf still over the bed, pinned up in a graceful swoop, those little bells dangling from the fringe.

He laughed, spread his arms, and flopped back onto the bed. He sank in a good foot, nearly swallowed into the thick layers of quilts. Imre chuckled, stepped inside, and set Luca's bag down on the rocking chair in the corner. Then he folded his arms on the footboard of the bed, leaning over the edge to look down at Luca, his hair falling over his shoulder in a tumble of steel and moonlight.

Luca tilted his head back, looking up at Imre with his heart a thing of sweet, giddy prickles. "You didn't change it," he breathed. "My old room."

"Upsized a little. Bigger bed." A small smile lingered on Imre's lips. "Not that you ever slept in here."

The fondness in that smile turned the prickles in Luca's heart into needles, piercing him deep and injecting some strange, aching thing that filled it up too full. He caught his lower lip between his teeth, then dragged his gaze away from Imre, tilting his head back to look up at the painted-on moon. He couldn't remember what he'd said to tell Imre he'd wanted this, years ago—but he remembered the next weekend he'd come to visit, the room had been repainted. He'd tumbled into Imre and hugged him so hard he'd nearly bowled all six-foot-six of Imre to the floor with all three-and-a-half stone of Luca.

And he'd almost, *almost* stayed in the room all night, when it was magic and he didn't want to stop counting the stars. But then the sound of the wind in the trees had crept under his skin, like it always had. And the creak of the barn doors, querulous and moaning, like they were calling out to the owls in the rafters and the hoo-hoo-*hoo*ing owls called back. He'd trembled in the dark, trying too hard to be a big boy, refusing a night light, until he couldn't stand it anymore.

Then he'd bundled up a quilt against his chest, tip-toed down the hall to Imre's room, crawled up onto the foot of his massive bed, and curled up in a ball there, small and unobtrusive as he could be.

And, wrapped in that quilt, tucked into that little corner with the light from Imre's fireplace warming him, he'd slept better than he had his entire life.

"I was afraid of the dark," he murmured.

"You made a very good foot warmer," Imre said dryly. "Are you still afraid of the dark?"

"Not anymore." Luca laughed, then dropped his voice to a deep rasp, scratchy in the back of his throat. "I am the dark. I am the night." When Imre only looked at him blankly, Luca sighed. "Batman? No?"

"No."

"God, Imre, we've got to get you some books from this century. Comic books count."

Luca pushed himself up on his elbows—then froze as a cool kiss brushed his cheeks. Imre's hair, drifting down to curtain both their faces, trailing in caresses as soft as breath against Luca's skin. The cat's-cradle strings of his heart snapped tight. He didn't dare lift his gaze, but he couldn't stop himself, raising his eyes.

They locked with Imre's, hovering mere inches away. So much at Lohere was blue—rich, warm, comforting blue—but it could never match the blue of Imre's eyes, the colour an indescribable shade that Luca could only call the colour of strength. Security. Patience. If a emotions had colours, every emotion Luca had felt as he'd sat in a field for hours and braided stalk after stalk of grass into the perfect ring was in those eyes.

And Luca wondered if Imre remembered that day. That moment. That promise that didn't feel so much like a childish whim when Luca's lips tingled and his heart spun in a crazed tumult like a carnival wheel, his stomach drawing up tight. The slightest tilt of his head and that long, lush beard would brush against his cheeks. A little push, and he could press his mouth to those expressive lips. A little…

A little nothing. Imre pulled back, straightening to his full towering height and looking down at Luca strangely. A subtle shake of his head—at Luca, at himself, Luca didn't know and couldn't figure out what it meant but it cut hard, cut *deep*—before Imre turned away, lifting a hand in a casual farewell flick.

"Take the rest of the day to get settled in," drifted over his shoulder. "I need to go lay down seed, then bring the herds in for the night. If you're hungry, help yourself to the kitchen. I'll be in to make supper once the goats are bedded down."

"Oh," Luca said faintly, voice strangling in his throat. "Okay."

But he didn't even get the *–kay* out before Imre was gone, vanishing into the hallway. Luca stared after him, gut churning, then slumped back onto the bed with a groan, dragging his hands over his face.

"Ah, *fuck*."

10

AS HE WALKED THE ROWS he'd tilled in his farthest two acres the day before, Imre considered the idea that he might just be punishing himself. Hand-seeding was arduous at best, exhaustingly gruelling at worst, manually scattering the mixture of clover and alfalfa seeds that would replenish what the last harvest of sweet corn had drained from the soil. This field would transition into grazing pasture for the goats, until the next seeding rotation.

But he often found the practiced, repetitive motion of casting seeds into the rows soothing and meditative. He could have brought the hopper out and finished in half the time, but sometimes he did things the old-fashioned way just because the physical labour felt good.

And right now, physical labour was *distracting*. Both punishment and meditation, when he needed every last bit of both.

For half a second, as Luca had pushed up close to him, as sweet-smelling breaths had wound through his beard like tugging fingers to infiltrate down to his skin, Imre had almost…

He didn't know. Most of the time he was too worried about planting and harvesting schedules, milking, production, and the million other things that went into running a farm to even wonder about anything else. Very few people tugged his strings that way; it just wasn't how he was wired. He needed…*more*. More than most needed to form a basic attraction, and finding that *more* was difficult enough before looking past issues of compatibility and sexuality.

So he filled his days with seed and feed, his nights with craftwork and planning, and paid little to no mind to thoughts of partners, attraction, sex.

And he needed to keep it that way. Luca wasn't just any pretty young just-legal thing.

He was Marco's *son*.

Imre repeated that to himself each time he flung his arm out to scatter another handful of seed, until the labour and the beating afternoon sun burned the mantra into his skin. By the time he'd seeded both fields and gone over them to track and water the seed, his mind was empty of all save the chores he needed to finish for the day. The goats needed to be brought in, and the two in sick stalls needed to be checked and fed. He'd need to feed the dogs, clean the pumps in the goat barn, muck the horses.

Plenty enough to keep him busy, and his mind occupied.

He headed back into the barn and mopped the sweat from his face with a saddle blanket before saddling up Andras, a sturdy blue roan gelding who seemed built for carrying someone of Imre's bulk. Andras snorted and nudged Imre's shoulder with his velvet nose, lipping his shirt, while Imre fitted a halter and lead to Zsofia, then attached her lead to Andras's saddle. Zsofia stepped out of her stall on high, dainty steps, her show horse breeding in every line of her, her silver dapple coat shining black beneath her blond mane. When she thrust her hand into his palm it was with the air of royalty demanding deference, and Imre couldn't help smiling.

"You, I think, will like Luca," he murmured as he rested his brow to the mare's. "He's just like you. Desperate for simple, kind affection, but only on his own terms—and he would rather bite his own hand off than ask."

He couldn't help but wonder what had happened, as he swung up onto Andras's back and took both horses out into the fields. Marco was a good man. A good, attentive father. Lucia was a kind mother, an intelligent woman, and she and Marco had doted on Luca from birth. Even if they were both busy with their careers—Marco a semiconductor engineer in Sheffield's booming tech sector, Lucia an executive career coach—Imre couldn't imagine either neglecting or mistreating Luca.

So what had happened to leave Luca this mess of thorns, desperate for love but too prickly to let anyone in arm's reach?

The question weighed heavily on Imre's mind as he ran the horses through the fields, letting them stretch their legs, before bringing them about to round up the herds, driving the goats with the horses while Vila and Seti nipped the rebellious beasts' heels to keep them in line. He only kept fifty-odd goats, separated into two herds of twenty-five—as much as seventeen acres would support, when he only used ten acres for grazing pasturage and rotated the rest with seed crops and the apple orchard. But even fifty goats were a fractious, mischievous lot for one man and two dogs to handle, and by the time they'd rounded the little buggers up and into the paddock feeding into the largest barn, the sun was setting in a wild burst of pinks and oranges and blooming, furiously vivid reds.

One thing he'd missed most about North Yorkshire, during his years at uni in Nottingham, had been the sunsets. Every sunset made him think of a song so joyous it couldn't help shouting itself across the sky in a ringing of colours, only for that last poignant note to trail off into the reverent silence of night.

It wasn't until Vila had nudged the last nanny goat into the paddock and bumped the gate shut with her muzzle that Imre realized he had an audience. He whistled for the dogs to go into the house, sending them racing off, the door flap rattling in their wakes. Imre pulled his shirt off and rubbed the sweat from his eyes with it, squinting across the field at the slim figure leaning against the fencewall. Luca rested his elbows atop the uneven upper ledge of the stacked stone wall, chin propped in one hand, pale eyes tracking Imre. When he realized he had Imre's attention, he lifted a hand in a wave.

Imre didn't realize he was hoping for a smile—an impish, sweet smile—until he didn't get one. Just a shallow twitch of Luca's lips, depthless and sad.

What had *happened* to him?

Imre checked Zsofia's tether, then guided both horses toward the wall with a squeeze of his thighs against Andras's flanks. A few goats trailed with curious bleats, but wandered off a few steps later, more interested in their water trough. As Imre cantered closer, Luca leaned forward over the fencewall, stretching his hand out.

"You have horses now," he said, and for all that he wouldn't smile, there was a soft elation in his voice.

"Bought them from a retiring show breeder. A whim, but one I've never regretted."

Imre swung himself down from Andras's back and caressed the roan's neck, until his eyes drooped and he lowered his nose into Luca's palm with a soft, pleased whicker. Luca made a delighted sound as he stroked over Andras's nose, his eyes widening, wonder glimmering in pale green depths. That wonder turned into a quick, spontaneous laugh—that he clamped down on as swiftly as it had been startled out of him—when Zsofia shoved her nose in with a jealous, demanding thrust. Imre snorted and nudged the mare, who stared at Luca imperiously as if challenging his worth, his right to touch her.

Luca stared right back with a bold, fearless curiosity. "You look quite corked off," he said, and lightly rested his hand to Zsofia's forelock. “Are you always like this?”

“You’ll want to watch that one,” Imre said. “It’s not that she’s mean. Just prickly and temperamental.”

Luca hummed a soft sound under his breath and gently stroked his fingertips down Zsofia’s crest to rest his palm to her cheek. He never took his gaze from her dark, intelligent eyes, never noticed Imre watching him, but Imre couldn’t look away.

“They’re never really mean,” Luca murmured. “They’re just scared, is all. They usually have a reason to be.”

What’s your reason, then?

Imre cleared his throat and pushed the thought from his mind. “She’s a good deal like you. Wicked but sweet. Bit of a terror, but she’ll love you as long as it’s on her terms. Do you ride?”

Luca hummed a thoughtful sound under his breath, gaze still fixed on Zsofia. “No. Never.”

“Would you like to learn?”

Luca caught a breath, lifting his head and looking at Imre. “Can I?”

“I’ll teach you. I take the horses out on a daily run to stretch their legs and check the walls. Normally I keep Zsofia on the tether, but you can take her tomorrow.”

Luca looked back up at the mare, still stroking his fingers gently over the delicate bones of her face. She held stock-still for him, submitting to his long, slender hands in a way she never had for Imre, even when she’d demanded Imre’s affection. Luca had a way of moving his hands as though making music with every curl of his finger and flow of his wrist, and he had Zsofia in thrall with each caress of his fingertips.

“Zsofia,” he repeated softly. “It’s a pretty name. Hungarian this time?”

"Aye. You have an ear for the pronunciations."

"I learned from you." Luca worried his lower lip with one tooth. "What if I fall, trying to ride her?"

"Then you get back up and get back on." Imre tore his gaze from watching those soft fingertips graze the regal lines of Zsofia's jaw. "She won't mistreat you." He paused. "…much."

He tugged on both horses' halters and led them toward the gate. Luca trailed on the other side of the fencewall, keeping one hand on Zsofia the entire time, stroking her neck and fingering her mane.

"Can I help with anything?" he asked breathlessly, then ducked his head and cleared his throat. "I mean, if I wouldn't be in the way."

Imre bit back a grin. Heaven forbid Luca look too *eager*. "Do you remember how to rake stalls?"

"Might even be better at it now that I'm taller than the rake."

Imre snubbed Zsofia's lead and Andras's reins to the gate post, then vaulted the gate; he wouldn't risk opening it when one of those canny little horned monsters might rush the gap like it was a game. Righting himself, he dusted his hands off and tossed his head toward the barn just back of the house. "You can clear the horses' stalls before we put them down for the night. I need to check the sick goats."

He strode for the barn with Luca on his heels. Only half-aware he was doing it, Imre shortened his strides so Luca could keep up, though Luca was a leggy thing at just under six feet, his long, free-swinging steps fluid and swift. Together they slipped under the shadow of the barn. Imre flicked the overhead lights on, pointed Luca to the rake on the wall, and left him to muck the two large box stalls Imre had installed after buying the horses.

Imre let himself into the first of the sick stalls—six total, though only two were occupied. In the first one of his best milking nannies, Gia, lay on her bed of sweet hay, breathing shallowly, her square pupils and golden irises glazed. Imre knelt and cradled her head in his lap, soothing her with soft sounds under his breath, stroking the bristly hairs between her horns and down her nose. Her nose was dry, hot, and he leaned over for the towel he'd left resting in a bucket on the stall wall. He dabbed her nose, moistening it, then pulled the feeding bottle from its slot and fitted the nipple between her lips.

Gently he pumped trickles into her mouth, massaging her throat to help her swallow. Mostly water, but mixed with a liquid nutrient concoction and the oral medication the vet had provided to expel toxins while strengthening immune resistance. From the messes in the hay, the last round had worked. Though Gia was feverish and unresponsive, her heartbeat was stronger, her breathing less erratic than this morning. Imre coaxed her to drink the entire mixture, then tugged over her feed bucket, the bin filled with a paste of alfalfa, clover, and dry feed mulched into something that wouldn't require much effort or chewing. He scooped up a thick green gob on two fingers, then slipped his fingers into her mouth.

After a feeble moment her tongue fluttered. Then her lips worked, gumming at his fingers, sucking the paste away.

"Good girl," he whispered, massaging her throat again and reaching for another fingerful of paste. "Come on, girl. Eat for me."

Luca's head appeared over the door of the stall, green eyes liquid. He bit his lip, then whispered, "What's wrong with them?"

"Monkshood," Imre answered. As he fed Gia another fingerful of paste, he watched Luca from the corner of his eye. "I keep my grazing acreage free of weeds, but the goats will stretch their heads over someone else's fence now and then, or get out into the woods and find things they shouldn't. Monkshood is poisonous, and can take hold wild around here."

Luca clutched hard at the rake and peered into the other stall where another nanny, Merta, rested panting in the hay. "Will they be all right?'

"I don't know. Monkshood is potent, but they only nibbled a little or they'd already be dead. All I can do is hope they purge it and manage to recover."

"They look so sad."

"They're in pain." Imre stroked Gia's soft, silky ears, then fed her more, listening to the encouraging sucking sounds as she ate. "If it gets too bad, I'll have to put them down."

Please don't let it get that bad.

"Imre!" Luca gasped, covering his mouth with one hand. "You can't!"

"I don't want to." He closed his eyes, sighing heavily. "But leaving them to slowly suffer to death is far more cruel."

He opened his eyes when the stall door squealed. Luca pulled the stall open and stepped inside, his boots crunching on the hay. He dropped to his knees at Gia's flank, bent over her, and pressed his cheek to her shaggy black and white side, just over her heart. One pale hand stroked down her side, moving gently over her stomach. The goat bleated weakly, then settled, pulling her head away from Imre to lean toward Luca.

"Please get better. Please get better," Luca whispered, closing his eyes. "Please."

Imre stared at him, his heart knotting into the strangest twist. "Luca…"

Luca screwed his eyes tighter shut and turned his face into Gia's shoulder, his own shoulders trembling. "I don't want them to die," he choked, muffled against soft fur.

Ah…Luca.

"Then we'll have to nurse them back to health." Imre couldn't stop himself; he leaned over the warm animal cradled between them and rested his hand to the top of Luca's head. Soft, dark hair slipped over his fingers, catching on the hairs on his knuckles. "Go finish up the horses' stalls while I make these two comfortable, and then I'll show you what to watch for and how to help them if anything changes. All right?"

Luca lifted his head, looking up at Imre with a gut-wrenching mixture of naked hope and vulnerability, pulling Imre into pale eyes that showed a reflection of himself in every pain and fear Luca begged him to soothe.

"Promise?" Luca whispered.

"I promise," Imre answered.

Because he could say nothing else.

When Luca looked at him that way, that pleading gaze pulling on pieces of his heart he hadn't known he possessed…*no* lost all meaning, along with many other things that once meant more than everything to Imre. Honour. Decency. *Willpower*.

He turned his face away from Luca and focused on the sick animal in his lap.

"Go," he said roughly. "The sooner it's done, the sooner we'll get her on her feet."

"Oh—oh, okay."

Imre listened while Luca scrambled to his feet, then closed his eyes and cursed himself roundly under his breath.

No, he told himself, and willed it to mean something. Anything. *No, Imre.*

No.

11

LUCA RAKED OUT THE HORSES' stalls and put down fresh hay, but the soft bleatings from the sick stalls distracted him as Imre massaged the goats' stomachs. He couldn't help it; they'd looked so pathetic, so sad, and he'd almost started crying right then and there like a little sobbing nit. He didn't know what was wrong with him. He hadn't cried over an animal since his cat was hit by a car their first week in Sheffield, and the vet had had to put her down.

Then again he'd not been around animals since then, either. He'd never gotten another pet after losing Purrsia, never wanted to face that loss again. He could chalk the tears up to the fact that he was stressed out and upset, or he could just fob it off to being a big effin' softie for small furry things.

That wasn't so bad, was it? Imre was soft on them, and Imre was…

God, he was amazing. Those hands were just as gentle, just as kind as Luca remembered, whether they were feeding a sick goat or…or…

Or resting on top of Luca's head, just enough pressure and weight to send comforting warmth radiating down through him to pool in the pit of his stomach.

He jerked from his trance to realize he'd just been standing there, staring toward the open barn door and the deepening twilight. His cheeks heated. He glanced over his shoulder at the sick stalls, then propped the rake against the wall and slipped out into the evening coolness. The horses still waited at post near the fence, and Luca leaned in to stretch a hand out for them to sniff.

"Remember me?" he asked softly. "I promise I won't hurt you. I just want to take you inside. Is that okay?"

Zsofia lipped his hand. The other one, a bigger, bulkier horse with a lustrous silvery-blue coat and smoky-dark legs and muzzle, nosed at his fingers. He laughed and scratched their polls. He'd never been around horses except on a school field trip to see horse-drawn carriages, and he'd never gotten to *touch* them. He climbed the fencewall, settled straddling it, and spent a good ten minutes scratching them both around their ears and crests and jaws, until Zsofia's blond eyelashes trembled and the other horse lowered his head to put its full weight into Luca's palm.

Quiet pleasure washed through him, and he lingered a few moments before carefully untying the knots on their leads. He stole a peek at the goats, but most of them had already taken themselves into the big barn. The only ones still milling around weren't anywhere near the gate. He hopped off the fence, pulled the gate open, and gently tugged the horses' leads.

"Come on, now. Imre will kill me if the goats get out."

The horses obliged as if they were used to this, a little hop-skip in their steps as they trotted through the gate, then waited patiently while he closed and latched it before taking their leads again, one to either side, and coaxed them into the smaller barn. Imre was still in with the sick goats, and Luca was as quiet as he could be in urging the horses toward their stalls. He wasn't sure which was which, but they seemed to know their own spaces and split off on their own, each into one stall and then the other. And each waited patiently while he fumbled with removing their tack and hanging it up on the hooks in the stalls, though

Zsofia nipped his shoulder when he pulled her halter a little too tight trying to get at the buckles.

"Sorry, girl." He laughed and pressed his cheek to hers. "Sorry. I'm still figuring this out."

Once he'd hung everything up, he tentatively used the saddle blankets hanging in the stalls to rub both horses down. They seemed to like it, so even if it wasn't quite right, it didn't seem to be bad. Then he filled the water buckets in their stalls from the barn pump and hose, before poking around the feed room until he found a bag that matched the dregs in their feed bags and refilled them.

I'm not so bad at this, he thought with a touch of satisfaction, then peered over the goat's pen again, watching Imre as he leaned over her and murmured under his breath.

"Imre?" Luca risked quietly. "I put the horses in their stalls."

Imre looked up as if pulling from a trance. "You did?"

"And took off their tack and rubbed them down, and fed them." Luca looked away, rubbing the back of his neck and shrugging. "That's what you're supposed to do, right?"

"Aye. Thank you."

A warm rumble, soft and appreciative, and Luca ducked his head and hoped like hell he wasn't blushing as much as it felt like. He didn't know what to say, his tongue thick, but after a few moments Imre spoke again.

"Here. Gia's resting. Come see."

Luca edged into the stall and sank to his knees, looking down at the goat. She seemed to be breathing deeper, and her eyes were closed—but Imre gently pried one open, drawing the lids apart to reveal those strange slit-square pupils goats had. Gia's were so large Luca almost couldn't see the yellow rings of her eyes.

"You can tell how drugged she is on the monkshood by how

dilated her eyes are," Imre murmured. "This is too much, even for low light. Her pupils also don't respond to light. Look." He moved his palm so it cast a shadow over the goat's eye, then moved it again, but the pupil didn't expand or contract. "If she were awake, they wouldn't track moving objects in her field of vision either. That's the best way to tell how conscious she is, by how visually responsive she is. The monkshood causes neurological pain, so she might not be able to get up for a while even if she's recovering."

Luca curled his fists against his thighs. "Is she?"

"Recovering?" Imre looked up at him. Luca felt like that steady blue gaze was measuring him, judging how much he could stand to hear. Then, "She ate more today than she could yesterday. It's an improvement. I don't know if she's truly recovering yet. The important thing is hydration to flush her system, and nutrition to fortify her, so I bottle feed water mixed with a nutrient solution and medication. She'll need another bottle right before bed, then another first thing in the morning. I still need to feed Merta, so I'll show you the proper mix ratio."

Luca nodded, but it took a moment to stand and follow Imre. He lingered with Gia for a few more moments, stroking between her ears. It felt wrong to leave her alone and in pain, but there were other animals that needed help.

Merta was in better shape, and managed to lift her own head while Imre showed Luca how to bottle-feed her and massage her throat. He let Luca hold the bottle, and he couldn't help smiling when the little white goat strained toward the nipple, sucking harder and harder for more.

"She's younger," Imre murmured, as he mixed paste to finger-feed her. "Barely old enough for this year's breeding season. Stronger, more resilient, and she'll recover faster."

"Good," Luca whispered, his heart beating harder as the goat gave a crooning little sound and leaned into him. "I'm glad."

There was something nice about helping Imre settle the goats in and make them comfortable, something that left Luca's chest warm. Watching Imre work with the animals was mesmerizing, the way they seemed to naturally trust him and submit to his touch. Luca wished he had that kind of gift. A way of making small, vulnerable things trust him.

Like you, Luca?

Like you trust him even though he's a stranger you haven't seen for ten years?

He growled at his inner voice. *I'm not vulnerable.*

His inner voice remained smugly silent.

Once they finished, Imre held the door to the stall for Luca, then closed it behind him and offered a towel. "Go wash up. I'll close the herds up and be in to make supper."

"Let me make supper?" Luca scrubbed his hands, then plucked the towel between his fingers and lowered his eyes to trace the red and white plaid terrycloth. "I…I don't want to freeload. I didn't ask to come here, but you didn't ask for me to be here, either. I just want to carry my weight."

"You don't have to do that, Luca. You helped with the horses tonight."

"I need to keep busy." He smiled slightly, though it brought a lump to his throat. "I'll get bored if I don't. When I get bored, I get in trouble."

"I know." Imre chuckled. "Very well. Try not to burn the kitchen down."

"*Hey*. I cooked for myself most of the time during my gap year, you know."

"Curry ramen does not count as cooking."

"How did you kn—"

Luca jerked his head up to find Imre watching him with an arch, knowing look that said he hadn't known a damned thing, but Luca had just given himself away. Luca scowled.

"Oh, you *arse*."

For just a moment, Imre grinned—wide enough to flash fierce teeth and light his eyes with a wolfish gleam, there and gone again, but that grin hit like a punch right to Luca's gut.

"I'll see you for supper then, angyalka."

"Uh. R-right. Yeah. Supper," he stammered.

Then turned and fled to the house, with Imre's deep, rumbling chuckle trailing after him.

12

CLOSING THE HERDS IN, FOR Imre, was just a matter of chasing the last few stragglers into the barn, checking their dry feed and water, and doing spot checks for injuries or illness. Sick or wounded goats were usually easier to spot during herding; they were the ones who fell behind, lamed or dazed and wandering. But it didn't hurt to give them one last look over, and it looked like they'd need their hooves trimmed soon. Might be an easier job with Luca, though he'd have to give him the older goats who were accustomed enough to the process not to kick.

Oy…Luca.

If Imre was honest with himself, he was avoiding going back to the house. Luca had been here less than eight hours, and already the entire atmosphere of the farm had changed. He fit right in as if he'd never left, and reminded Imre too achingly much of what it had been like to have *people.* Friends close enough to be family, people who were in his home as often as not, lighting it with their warmth.

After the Wards had moved away, a certain quiet emptiness had settled over Lohere. Imre's family was sparse and scattered, many Hungarian Romani who had remained in Hungary instead of emigrating elsewhere, and the branch who'd settled in England and taken on the Claybourne name generations ago had been fiercely clannish—so fiercely clannish they rarely married outside of Roma lines, and had few children. Imre had been an only child, his parents passed away years ago. He had cousins he didn't know by name, and little else. He was friendly with the other local farmers, but when they were all busy managing their own homesteads most had little time for anyone save their own.

Lonely, Imre?

He smiled grimly and leaned his elbows against the fence, looking up at the house. The light was on in the upstairs bathroom window, the frosted glass fogged. Luca must still be in the shower. No point in going in anyway, then, unless he wanted to use the downstairs bathroom—but it had only a bathtub, no shower, and he doubted he'd have time for a soak before supper when the antiquated pipes pumped slowly and the bath took forever to fill.

He caught a glimpse of movement against the window, just a silhouette and a hint of paleness, and jerked his gaze away to glare fiercely toward the deep purple line of the evening horizon.

And therein lay the other problem.

A problem that wasn't Luca, but Imre himself.

With a sigh under his breath, he slid his hands into his pockets and pushed away from the fence, heading out toward the field. He told himself he was walking the fences to check for breaches, but he'd walked them just this morning. What he needed right now was the scents of clover and honeysuckle, the sound of crickets, the first soft low call of tiny owls in the far trees, answered by the deeper, more sonorous hoots of the barn owls who kindly kept the mice from his door and his stores of grain. The September night air was crisp as the first bite of a cool red apple, and he closed his eyes, tilting his head back into the breeze and letting it slip over his face and through his hair, washing his thoughts clean until he was blank and empty and quiet.

He'd never minded the loneliness before, when he liked his

silence. Silence was hard to come by, when other people seemed to manufacture noise like a commodity. And Luca seemed to make noise just by *existing*: the bright noise of his repressed emotions, bursting to get out and screaming even when he didn't say a word.

When Imre had been a child, his mother would make stars come out for him. She'd turn down all the lamps in the kitchen, back before the farmhouse had had electricity, then light a single oil lantern in the centre of the table. Then, with one of her darning needles, she'd punch tiny holes scattered across a piece of black cardstock and hold it over the lamp. The lamplight would shine through in beams, bursting through those tiny holes and spreading onto the ceiling of the kitchen in glowing dots of stars against the blue-painted stone.

His father had been the one who'd painted the walls and ceilings of Lohere blue. *It feels alive now*, Robi Claybourne had said, and held his wife and son close. *It feels like a home*.

It did. It had been the Claybourne home for generations, but Imre supposed that legacy would end with him. He was too old for children, and not particularly interested in fathering them by conventional means. Not that forty-six was any age, but…

He exhaled deeply, opening his eyes and looking up at the purpled, star-strewn sky. Not his mother's stars, but familiar ones nonetheless, even if they couldn't hold him tonight. His head was full of as much noise as the house.

This wasn't helping.

He trudged down the hill and back to the house. The bathroom light was dark, so Luca must be out. Imre let himself in through the kitchen door in the rear of the house, then drew up short as savoury scents rolled over him, practically crawling down his throat to curl in his gullet with a hungry, grumbling roar.

Luca stood at the stove, barefoot in a pair of clean jeans and a t-shirt that, for some bizarre reason, seemed to have been designed to fit improperly, clinging tight in the waist but so loose in the neck that it slewed to one side over a pale, curving shoulder, dark blue against white skin. Imre found himself contemplating the sharp protrusion of bone against that fine skin, and promptly redirected his attention to the pot bubbling on the stove. The dogs were nowhere to be found, their food bowls emptied and left in that haphazard scatter that said they'd gorged and run off to play, leaving just Luca and layers upon layers of delectable aromas.

Well. This was new. He wasn't sure what to do with the odd feeling of coming home to a pretty thing in his kitchen, cooking for them both and bustling about with quiet efficiency.

He must have made some kind of sound because Luca started, then glanced over his shoulder and smiled a shy, utterly fetching smile. "Hope you weren't saving that steak for anything. It was already defrosted, so it needed to be cooked soon anyway."

Belatedly, Imre remembered to shut the door behind him, then shook his head. "No, nothing special." He felt an utter dolt, standing awkwardly in his own kitchen like he didn't belong. He cleared his throat. "What are you making?"

"Steak and onions in asparagus bits, and baby potatoes in…um…there's like this really thick cream in an unlabelled container, and it tasted kind of like sour cream so I really hope that's what it is. If it's not, please don't tell me what I just put in my mouth."

Imre chuckled weakly. "Just sour cream. Tastes a bit different when it's made with goat's milk."

"I didn't even know you *could* make sour cream with goat's milk." Luca grinned. "Cool."

"Yeah," Imre said, tongue thick. "Cool."

Luca wrinkled his nose at him playfully. "Don't try to be edgy,

Imre. It doesn't work."

Many things weren't working right now. Imre's brain. His tongue. Thank God Luca didn't seem to notice Imre was just standing there, his hands clenching and unclenching as if looking for something to do to jumpstart his frozen thoughts. The boy moved between skillet and pot, stirring and scrambling, humming under his breath. But after a moment Luca glanced back at him and flashed that sweet grin again, a wild-witch grin, both wicked and innocent and doing entirely disconcerting things to Imre's pulse.

"It'll be done in about ten minutes," Luca said. "I tried to leave hot water in the shower. Don't be a heathen and come to supper smelling like goats, eh?"

"…right."

That cue finally signalled Imre's legs to work again. He ducked out of the kitchen and into the hallway, then dragged himself up the stairs and away from the sound of Luca's voice rising over the kitchen, breaking into lilting, only slightly off-key song the moment Imre was out of the room. Too much noise. Too much *everything*. He shut himself in the bathroom, closed his eyes, and slumped against the wall.

How the hell had he ended up running from a nineteen-year-old slip of a boy in his own bloody *house*?

13

LUCA WAS SURPRISED BY HOW much he enjoyed cooking. He'd spent most of his gap year on mini-holiday, faffing about Sheffield and the surrounding villages. While now and then he'd whipped together something for himself, it was just to fill his belly. He'd never thought much of making something that deliberately tasted good so someone else could enjoy it. But he'd picked up enough watching his parents in the kitchen that it wasn't hard to cube a steak and cut asparagus, and toss them together with onions and a little olive oil and spices.

What was hard, he thought, was realizing that for the first time in a long time he felt happy to *be* somewhere. He'd had a few moments on holiday—moments when he'd had too much beer and was doing something reckless just to feel like he could fly. Those moments had been pure joy, though he'd always had to come down. Come home, when home was never somewhere he wanted to be. Not now. Not ever, though he'd rather have left by his own choice.

But he *wanted* to be at Lohere; he'd realized that the moment the Land Rover had turned onto the familiar curving drive. So much he was afraid he'd embarrass himself, scrambling to do anything he could to earn the right to stay. He didn't think Imre would put him out as his parents had…but if he did, that was the end of things for Luca. That idle daydream of sleeping on park benches in Leeds might well become his reality, and while the concept had sounded glamorously Bohemian when he was ready to cut and run, the reality of cold miserable nights and getting chased about by the police and being treated like human filth when he tried to apply for jobs was neither romantic nor particularly desirable nor in any way funny.

Imre wouldn't let that happen to him, he thought. Not the Imre he remembered.

Would he?

By the time the sound of running water cut off from upstairs, Luca had sunk himself into a brood, mulling over his options once Imre, too, got sick of him and put him out on his arse. He couldn't crash at Xav's; his parents wouldn't let him when Xav was off at uni, but Xav might let him stop up in his dorm for a bit. There were youth hostels, queer youth shelters…

"Concert over, then?" Imre asked at his back.

Luca jerked, heart dropping, breaths halting. He'd not heard Imre come down the stairs; for such a big man he moved with remarkable silence, not even creaking the tattletale fifth step, and Luca nearly dropped the spatula when that quiet voice rumbled at his side.

He looked up. Imre leaned against the counter, sleek as a seal with his damp hair slicked back, water-darkened to iron grey, droplets still speckling his beard. He'd changed into clean, less ragged jeans and another open-throated henley, a soft cream-coloured thing that brought his tawny skin into stark relief, his entire body nearly glowing with lingering heat from the shower.

"Oh," Luca squeaked. "Um."

"Oh?" Imre repeated, and folded his arms over his chest. Corded sinew strained at the shoulder seams of his shirt. "Um."

Luca scowled. "Don't be a prick. You caught me off guard."

"Ever so sorry." Imre glanced at the skillet. "Smells good."

"It's done, I just need to—"

"I've got it."

Imre didn't even wait for him to finish before he reached over Luca's head and opened one of the high cabinets. The deep, pleasantly pungent scent of the bar of dark lava soap from the upstairs shower washed over Luca; the scent clung to him after his shower, too, but it wasn't the same as the heady mix it made when blended with Imre's musk. Luca's gaze fell to the strip of bronzed skin bared when Imre lifted his arms, just a glimpse of ridged sinew and the band of his underwear above the low waist of his jeans, before Luca closed his eyes and let that scent flow into him like a drugging draught of opium.

"You all right?" Imre asked. "You've not come over-faint standing over the stove?"

"A-ah?" Luca snapped his eyes open to find those warm blue eyes locked on him intently. He licked his lips and stared down into the skillet. "N-no. No, I'm fine. I was just thinking."

"Deep thoughts, then?"

"Yeah," Luca said weakly. "Deep thoughts."

He felt the moment Imre stopped looking at him and moved away with an amused sound, leaving room for Luca to breathe. They worked together in silence: Imre setting the table with brightly painted earthenware plates and cups, Luca following up to split portions between them, with the lion's share going to the lion-sized man who probably needed ten times more fuel than Luca. In this moment the rhythm was comfortable, easy. Luca loved the kitchen at Lohere; the dining table right there in the same room, the copper pots and pans and skillets shining on their hooks in stark contrast to the blue walls, the cool stone floors, the old brick hearth, the long banks of windows, the polished wood table centred by a tall glass jar of fresh green apples. Imre poured iced tea, and Luca put out forks and knives.

Then Imre pulled out a chair for Luca and stood over it, waiting.

Luca blinked. It took a moment to click, and when it did he tried to say *what are you doing?* but only got out something resembling "Gnk…?"

"By all means," Imre said with that dry, subtle humour. "Stand to eat, if you're more comfortable that way."

Luca twisted his mouth up, then let it go in an explosive sigh. That sigh, unfortunately, did nothing to dispel the things flitting around inside his chest. He sat gingerly, leaning forward in the seat. As Imre pushed the chair in gently behind him, thick knuckles brushed Luca's shoulder blades. He went stiff, struggling not to jump, but couldn't stop how his breaths hitched in his throat or the tingling prickle on the back of his neck. That prickle was practically a sixth sense tuned to detect Imre, his body heat, his proximity, and it only eased when Imre rounded the table, took his own seat, and murmured something in low Romungro before shaking out his napkin and picking up his fork.

Luca tried not to be obvious about watching him. He'd tasted the food before serving it—the asparagus crisply seasoned and soaked in the flavour of the steak cubes, the baby potatoes boiled to softness and half-mashed in their skins, swimming in a bath of liquid sour cream and chives and basil—and it had seemed fine to him, but if Imre didn't like it then he'd just wasted Imre's good food on a bad meal.

Yet Imre only took one bite of steak and asparagus, then another, before letting out a soft sound of appreciation and spearing a cream-coated bite of potato. But he paused with a fork halfway to his mouth; blue eyes suddenly skewered Luca, and Luca froze.

"Something wrong?" Imre asked.

"Nothing," Luca strangled out, then dropped his gaze to his own plate and picked up his fork. "So, um…tomorrow you'll teach me how to ride?"

Imre swallowed and reached for his glass of iced tea. "In the afternoon. Once I put the goats out to pasture in the morning, we'll need to spend some time on apple picking before the harvest gets overripe." He paused for a sip of tea. "Then I'll teach you to ride, and if you can keep your seat well enough I'll take you out with me to bring the goats back in."

"All right. That sounds good." Luca tried a smile and propped his feet on the rungs of the chair. Last time he'd sat in these chairs the rungs were as far as he could reach, but now his knees bumped the bottom of the table. "That sounds really good."

Imre studied him contemplatively, then mused, "You're not afraid of hard work. So what's this your Da says about being too lazy to go to uni?"

Luca hunched in on himself. That budding spark of warmth at watching Imre enjoy food prepared with Luca's own two hands? Doused as quickly as shutting off the flame on the stove. "It's not laziness," he growled. "There's just nothing I want to do at uni."

"Nothing?"

"No." He glowered at his plate and pushed his food around with the tip of his fork. "I want to do something. I just don't know what. All the usual study courses bore me. And while I figure it out, why waste time getting a degree I don't want and won't need?" He shrugged. "I'll go back to uni when I know what it's for. When it's good for something."

"Sounds practical to me," Imre said nonchalantly, and took another bite of his supper.

Luca blinked. "What?"

Imre blinked right back. "It's sound logic."

"I…oh." Luca uncurled just a little, eyeing Imre warily. "Dad didn't think so. I came back from a weekend in Manchester, and Dad found out I'd not registered for the autumn term this year. He flipped his shite. I got drunk and flipped his bike. He called you, and here we are."

With an amused sound, Imre raised his glass in a mocking toast. "Here we are."

"I don't even know why he sent me out here. 'Go play with goats, that'll make you sorry.'" He snorted and nipped a bite off the tines of his fork. "I think he's just…tired of trying to figure out what to do with me, so he sent me away where he wouldn't have to look at me."

"Do you really think he'd be that cruel?"

"I don't know. I guess I know a different Dad than you do. He's your friend. He can't really be mine."

"I can be, though," Imre pointed out softly. "Your friend, I mean. I'm not your father. I don't want to be. I don't want to be in that position with you. I refuse to treat you that way. So." He set his fork down and offered one broad hand across the table, weathered fingers spread. "Friends?"

That warm, inviting hand tugged at all the empty spaces in Luca as if Imre had snared his fingers in Luca's strings and pulled. He eyed that hand. He wanted…he wanted that, he thought. A friend. And he liked how Imre listened to him, and honestly seemed to *hear* him and give consideration to what he said. Talked back to him, too, but didn't talk down. And Imre's kindness, his strength, the memories of safety and security all wrapped up in that outstretched hand…

Luca bit his lip, then slid his hand into Imre's. Rough calluses rasped against his palm, and a thrill shot up his arm and raised the fine hairs on his skin for a single sweet breath.

"Yeah," he murmured. "Sure. But I tend to get my friends in trouble."

He started to pull his hand back—but Imre's hand tightened for one heart-stopping moment, holding him fast in that massive stone-hewn grip before letting go. Luca pulled his hand back and curled it in his lap, his fingers tingling and light and hot.

"I went to uni with your father," Imre said, one thick brow arching. "I know how to take care of myself."

"Nah. C'mon. Dad's an engineer. I bet he was all pencils and graph paper and studying twenty-four seven."

"Your father," Imre proclaimed gravely, "was nearly expelled for drunken skinny-dipping in the boating lake at Highfields Park."

Luca's eyes widened, and he clapped a hand over his mouth. "No. *No*." He burst into laughter, then tried to choke it back, stuffing it back down inside. "I did not need to picture that. That's my *Dad*. Naked."

Imre let out a long-suffering, weary sigh. "Your father was nude more often than not. One drop of liquor, and suddenly he couldn't stand to be clothed. When we graduated, he burned his textbooks, got drunk on rye, and danced around the bonfire in the raw."

"Imre, *stop!*" Luca snickered, covering his ears with both hands. "That's horrid!"

"I'm simply informing you that I know how to handle the Ward brand of trouble. He acts as though you're the first Ward to crash a motorcycle." Imre's gaze met his, solemn and steady, only a faint glitter of repressed laughter giving him away. "He shot one off the top of the student union building, trying to impress Lucia. Nearly took himself with it. Guess who pulled him back from the edge."

"Mum…?" Luca ventured.

"*Me*," Imre retorted flatly. "Your mother was so disgusted I think she'd have let him fall."

Luca tried to fight a giggle and failed. That giggle turned into a cackle, before he swallowed it down and collapsed back into the chair and let himself *laugh* until his sides hurt, because all he could picture was a tall building and his father, naked and as reed-thin as Luca himself, dangling over the edge by one of Imre's meaty paws while Imre just looked at him with patient, tired disgust.

"Oh," Luca gasped, wiping at his wet eyes. "Oh, you're giving me *so* much ammunition."

"Planning to raise a little more havoc, then? Do some naked swimming?"

Luca choked on his next laugh. The vision in his mind's eye replaced his father with himself. And instead of the edge of the building there was the edge of a lake, Imre's hot hand curled against the back of his neck, swathes of darkly bronzed skin that his imagination refused to define as more than impressions—but impressions were enough to leave Luca struggling to unlock his frozen tongue, on fire from collarbones to hairline, petrified in his seat.

"I…what…naked, I-I…um…"

"I'm teasing, angyalka." Imre said it with that same gravelly, soothing calm as everything else.

Luca was tempted to kick him under the damned table.

But Imre was watching him as though he knew exactly what Luca was thinking, an arch look over the rim of his glass, and when Luca scowled at him Imre's mouth only twitched in a ghost of a curve that spoke volumes for his silent laughter.

"Finish your supper," Imre continued smoothly. "We rise early here."

Luca huffed and stabbed his fork into his potatoes. "Up with the dawn?"

"Not quite that early. And not without enough coffee."

Luca didn't say anything. He didn't know what *to* say, when Imre was still watching him and that image still burned in his mind.

Rough fingers on the back of his neck, that prickle that knew Imre with an uncomfortable familiarity, that scent of lava soap and farm-sweet smells and man. He bit his lip, fixing his gaze on his plate and pressing his tongue against the backs of his teeth. He had to get his head on straight, and just…*stop.*

Before that look of patient, fond amusement turned to disappointment, and Imre dropped him like so much worthless garbage.

14

IF THE REST OF SUPPER was silent, Imre didn't mind—save that Luca was so quiet, so subdued, staring down at his plate. Imre had the sense that prodding, right now, wouldn't be invited or particularly successful. Sometimes even the worst thoughts needed time to stew alone, and if Luca needed his silence then Imre wouldn't pry.

Yet when Imre volunteered to take care of the dishes Luca only mumbled something under his breath and disappeared up the stairs, leaving Imre looking after him, his sudden absence as palpable in the room as if a Luca-shaped cut-out had been left in the world.

Imre lingered on that, as he put away the leftovers for later—the food had been surprisingly good, filling and satisfying, a tantalizing blend of flavours without being overwhelming—and washed up the dishes. Had he said something to upset Luca? Perhaps talking about Marco hadn't been the best idea when the relationship between father and son was so clearly strained, and bringing up Marco's university antics probably made the judgment brought down on Luca seem that much harsher.

And Marco *was* being unfair, Imre thought. Luca had a good head on his shoulders, and his reasons for waiting made sense. Seemed more intelligent and mature than diving in and wasting four years on something that made him miserable.

But it wasn't Imre's place to interfere, or take sides.

So he only finished the washing up and settled in the living room to read, keeping an ear open for a boy who had suddenly gone as quiet as a mouse in the walls.

Yet by the time he'd flicked through a few hundred well-worn, yellowed pages of *Shardik* he'd still heard nothing, and his inner clock told him it was time to check the goats one last time before bed. He tugged his reading glasses off, tucked them away, and took a few quiet steps up the stairs, pausing before the rather vocal fifth step, and called up softly.

"Luca?"

Nothing.

Let him sleep, then. He'd just arrived today, and for all that he'd thrown himself into helping out he was probably emotionally and physically wrung out. A good night's sleep would bring things clear, Imre thought, and maybe tomorrow Luca would let that smile slip free more often rather than hiding it like a guilty confession.

He waited a moment longer, then slipped back down the stairs and out to the barn. Andras and Zsofia dozed with their tails switching—but the goats weren't alone in their stalls. Luca nestled in the corner of Gia's stall with the nanny goat's head in his lap, stroking her face and rocking subtly, his pensive eyes fixed on her and his pale, feline features a portrait of wordless, unguarded sorrow. The empty feeding bottle was propped against his side, and Gia rested quietly across his thighs, her tail now and then flicking.

A strange, throbbing feeling built in Imre's chest, starting somewhere between the top of his stomach and the bottom of his ribs, but with each slow beat swelling larger and flowing into every inner crack and crevice. Something like pain; something like warmth; something like understanding; something like *longing*. Pieces of each and every one and so many other things, until the only thing he could do was hold so very stone-still or he would become a chaos of emotion.

Luca let out a soft, hitching breath and, oblivious to Imre, squeezed his eyes shut. The faint evening light drifting through the open barn doors caught on the wet-glimmering droplets gathered on his lashes in fine, misty beads.

"Please," he whispered, and curled around Gia. "Please be okay."

Those low words pierced Imre's heart. He stepped closer to the open stall door, clearing his throat softly in subtle warning. "Luca."

Luca stiffened, lifting his head, clutching Gia closer protectively and staring up at Imre with wide, tear-dotted eyes, pale green swimming underneath a lake of dewed wetness.

Ah, *God*. Imre stepped into the stall and sank to his knees next to the boy and the goat. "Luca," he repeated. "Come in to bed." He curled his hand against Luca's shoulder. It was hard as stone beneath his palm, yet trembled deeply as fragile paper in a gale. "There's nothing more you can do for them tonight. You need to rest."

Luca's lips parted, before he let out a hurting sound and looked down at the goat. "But Gia looks like she's getting worse."

Imre hesitated, then leaned over the nanny and gently pried her eyes open. They'd dilated more deeply, a worrisome glaze in them, and when he bent and pressed his cheek to her chest her heartbeat was shallow, weaker. Luca was right. Imre bit back a curse under his breath, stomach sinking.

"Sometimes they get worse before they get better," he said. He didn't want to hurt Luca, but he wouldn't lie, either. "And sometimes…they just get worse. But she'll hold until morning, angyalka. Let her rest, while you rest. We'll see how she's doing then." He squeezed that slim shoulder. "Come."

Luca looked up at him again, before that sheen in his eyes burst over into a flood. "Imre…" he choked out, half-whisper, half-sob.

Then Imre's arms were full of lithe limbs and shaking shoulders, as Luca flung himself against Imre's chest. Imre went still, but his body knew what to do even when his mind didn't. His arms enfolded Luca and drew him up close. Even all grown up, he was still so small compared to Imre, and he fit into him in a trembling bundle that Imre could so easily wrap himself around, as if he could use his body to shield Luca from any blow that might come at him.

Yet the wounds that cut deepest, Imre had no defence against.

He could only hold Luca close, and let the boy spend his tears against his shoulder while Gia wheezed and shivered in the hay, and Imre's chest ached with an awful, hollow feeling.

"Luca," he whispered, and stroked his slim back. "Angyalka. Angel. We're doing everything we can for them. I've had the vet in already, but I'll check in on Gia until morning and then call the vet first thing. She'll come right down from Harrogate. All right?" He caught that fine, pointed chin in his fingertips and coaxed Luca to tilt his face up, to let Imre look at him, to meet those red-rimmed eyes. "Will that ease your mind?"

Luca sniffled, then nodded and rubbed the pinkened tip of his nose. "Aye."

"Then consider it done." Imre released Luca's chin and rested his hand atop his head. "Wash up for bed. I'll stay with her a little longer."

"Okay," Luca said, but his lips remained parted as though he might say something else. He braced his hands against Imre's chest, fingerprinting warmth through his clothing; clear green eyes flicked over Imre's face, before Luca ducked his head and pulled back.

It took a moment for Imre to remind his arms to move, to unlock, to fall away. Luca unfolded himself, pulling to his feet, a hay-strewn mess with his lips swollen and his nose and cheeks red. He caught his lower lip between his fingers, twisting it, then asked, "If something changes…you'll come get me? Even if it's bad?"

"You have my word," Imre promised.

"Okay," Luca said again.

He lingered a moment longer, still watching Imre strangely, an inscrutable and fair thing in the moonlight, a mystery in parchment and ink colours, fidgeting at his lip, his shirt. Imre tilted his head, a question on his tongue.

Yet before he could find his voice Luca was gone, fleet-footed in the dark and vanishing into the house.

15

LUCA RINSED OFF THE DIRT and hay of the goats in the bathroom sink, scrubbed furiously at his aching eyes, then changed into a t-shirt and boxers for bed. He curled up in the bedroom he still thought of as *his* even though it never really had been and never really would be, but he couldn't sleep for listening for Imre. Luca should be down there, bedding down in the stall with Gia.

But Gia wasn't his goat, his pet, his anything. It wasn't his place. He couldn't just show up here after less than a day and start tromping around like it was his responsibility to do anything. He wouldn't even know what *to* do if Gia took a turn for the worse at three in the morning and he couldn't wake Imre.

The only thing he could do was leave everything in Imre's hands, and remind himself that Imre had been doing this for longer than Luca had even been alive.

He burrowed himself into the quilts and pillows and willed himself to sleep, but sleep wouldn't come. With a moan, he pressed his face into the cool pillowcase, then rolled over and dragged his bag closer. He'd halfway unpacked, but his laptop was buried under the clothes he'd not yet put away, along with the phone charger he'd spent nearly an hour hunting for earlier and failed to find. He wriggled an arm behind the headboard to plug in both his laptop and his charger, then hooked up his phone and checked the bars.

Three. Not bad. His dad used to complain about the cell service out here all the time, but then again ten years ago people had thought half a megabyte was a fair data plan and brick phones with two-colour screens were just making way for flip phones with tiny, grainy multicolour displays and brushed-chrome finishes. His dad still had one, a pink Razr, and he refused to trade it in for a smartphone.

For an engineer, his dad had some weird ideas about technological progress.

Fuck, he didn't want to think about that prick right now. Not when he was this raw. He flipped his laptop open and checked available Wi-Fi networks. Not one of them said Lohere, though there were about five within range, two with strong signal. Probably the neighbours. He'd peeked in the living room, and Imre still didn't even have a *television*.

Farmers. Bloody hell.

He checked his phone again, but no 3G or 4G data out here. No using his mobile hotspot.

The sound of a door opening and shutting drifted from downstairs. He listened for Imre's footsteps, but he still walked cat-quiet; this time, though, that creaking fifth step snitched on him. Then a shadow passed under Luca's closed door, before another door opened and closed across the hall, at the very end. Luca bit his lip, then rolled out of bed, slipped out into the hall, and knocked tentatively on Imre's bedroom door.

"Imre?"

"Aye?" drifted out, muted through the thick oak slab.

Luca hesitated, then pushed the door open a crack. Imre froze in the middle of lifting his shirt off, arms stretched over his head with the henley snared around his forearms, his hair tangled in the neck of the shirt. Deep burnished light fell from the crackling hearth in a waterfall of flame, turning Imre into forge-lit bronze. His body was a mass of corded muscle with that bulk that only came through years and years of thickening, straining, destroying himself with hard labour and rebuilding over and over again from the stone and earth of the land around him: his shoulders massive, his waist a solid sheet of hard-cut muscle, his chest a broad, defined taper lightly furred with a V-shaped pelt of curling silver and black.

Imre held still one moment longer, one darkened blue eye watching Luca sharply through a gap in his upraised shirt, the only sounds in the silence the crackle of the fireplace and Luca's shallow, swift breaths. He—he couldn't—he hadn't meant—but he couldn't look away, couldn't figure out where to look, and his heart *hurt*, its beating painful and laboured and throbbing inside his chest. Imre was just…too much. Too much everything.

Too much Imre, and Luca stood petrified in the doorway, the question he'd wanted to ask crumbling on his lips.

Imre pulled the shirt the rest of the way off, powerful biceps and forearms flexing and bunching in hard angles. He shook his hair loose, then ran a hand through it, sweeping it to one side and watching Luca from beneath his brows. "What is it, angyalka?"

"Um."

Imre's brows drew together. "Are you all right?"

Luca closed his eyes, pressed his too-hot face into his too-hot palms—then thrust himself out of the doorway and leaned against the wall in the hall, staring across it at—at—nothing. Anything but Imre. *Fuck.*

"I'm fine," he growled, clutching his arms over his chest, trying to keep his heart inside where it belonged. "Just wanted to know if you ever got internet."

Imre leaned out the doorway, silver hair tumbling over his shoulder, one hand gripping the doorway. He studied Luca wryly, practically hanging over his shoulder. “It’s the network ending in oh-seven-four-four. I changed the Wi-Fi password to your birthday this morning.”

Luca flinched back from that warm, silk-smooth baritone right in his ear. His heart gave up on pummelling out through his chest and slammed its way up to the bottom of his throat. “Oh,” he squeaked, staring at Imre from the corner of his eye.

Imre needed to put a shirt on.

And stop remembering things like Luca’s birthday, when Luca was pretty fucking sure he didn’t remember what really mattered.

“What?” Imre blinked at him, then snorted. “Ordering seed is more convenient online. And this Amazon Prime thing is very novel. I could get spoiled.”

Oh. Oh, that fucking *dork*.

Imre really thought Luca was staring at him because the Luddite knew what Wi-Fi was.

Not because he was trying not to see all of…*that*. All those things he shouldn’t be looking at, because Imre was Imre and Luca was Luca and he just…he couldn’t…

Too messy. Too confusing. *Too much*, when all he wanted to do was go to sleep and forget the absolute fuckery his life had become.

“Gotcha,” he muttered, and fixed his eyes on his toes. “Thanks.”

Imre lingered a moment longer, with a searching gaze that pulled at Luca with a quiet magnetism palpable in the space between them. That was the problem with Imre; he was so honest, so rawly and quietly *true*, that his honesty seemed to ask for the same from everyone. That they come to him laid naked and bare as he was to the world, and trust that he wouldn’t find their every point of vulnerability and eviscerate them.

Luca couldn’t trust him that way.

He couldn't trust anyone that way ever again.

But then that rough, massive hand fell to the top of his head, and he closed his eyes, his throat tightening as he tried not to lean into that touch like a cat.

"Goodnight, Luca," Imre murmured.

Luca twisted away as though the sharp stab of *yearning* in the pit of his stomach were a spear-thrust he could dodge, and backed a few steps down the hall. "Um. Goodnight."

He started to turn away, then paused, curling his fingers tight.

"Um…"

"Gia's resting," Imre answered gently. "She's stable. I promise."

"Thank you," Luca said.

Then ducked into his room, and firmly shut the door.

16

LUCA DIDN'T BREATHE UNTIL HE heard the dim sound of hinges creaking, followed by the click of a latch. Then he groaned, slumping against the door and sinking down until his knees folded up against his chest and he could bury his face in his thighs.

"Don't do this to yourself, Luca," he whispered. "Just don't."

He'd dealt with enough rejections lately.

He didn't need to add one more to the pile.

Cursing under his breath, he crawled into bed, sprawled out on his side, and logged onto the Wi-Fi, even if he had a squint-eyed moment wondering if he should use 0112 or 01December.

01December.

This was Imre. He practically spoke in proper nouns.

The Wi-Fi was a little slow, but passable enough to get his email going—nothing but spam, a few Twitter highlights, and a syrupy fake-concerned email from his mum, though he'd have to answer it by morning or deal with an equally syrupy fake-concerned phone call where Lucia Ward waffled between worrying Luca had hurt himself and worrying Luca had burned Lohere down.

But that was a problem for morning. For now, he pulled up Facebook and logged into the web Messenger. His last chat with Xav was at the top of the history, and he tapped out a quick message, typing one-handed with his head pillowed on his other arm.

Luca.Ward: *You up?*

Barely half a second passed before the typing dots popped up on the screen, followed by a new message balloon, that little *bloop* popping out of his speakers.

Xavier.Laghari: *Hey, fuckface. I'm up. Waiting for you. How's the first day on the pig farm?*
Luca.Ward: *Goat farm.*
Xavier.Laghari: *Whatever. Pigs are cuter. You okay out there?*
Luca.Ward: *Yeah. It's not bad. There's horses, and the goats are cute. Cuter than pigs.*
Xavier.Laghari: *What about the guy you're staying with?*

Luca paused. Imre felt like a secret he wanted to keep to himself, and a confession he wanted to scream to the world. He wanted to tell Xavier everything, but he didn't even know what he'd say when one day had left Luca a tangled mess with his insides all knotted up and his heart struggling to shed its weights to float lighter than air. He pressed his lips together, working his tongue against the inside of his cheek, then tapped out two words.

Luca.Ward: *He's okay.*
Xavier.Laghari: *Isn't he gay too?*
Xavier.Laghari: *duelingbanjos.mp3*
Luca.Ward: *Ha. Fucking. Ha.*
Luca.Ward: *It's not like that.*
Xavier.Laghari: *He hot?*

Luca.Ward: *Way too hot.*

Luca.Ward: *My dad would skin me. That kind of hot.*

Xavier.Laghari: *He think you're hot?*

Luca groaned. Who knew what the fuck Imre thought? For someone who was so fucking honest, he was also way too fucking close-mouthed.

Luca.Ward: *I'm pretty sure he still thinks I'm five.*

Xavier.Laghari: *Suckballs.*

Luca.Ward: *No thx. Not my kink.*

Xavier.Laghari: *You dirrrrty. Why you gotta make that gross?*

Luca.Ward: *You make faces. That's my kink.*

Xavier.Laghari: *Put me on vid, you little shite. I want to see you.*

Luca.Ward: *Why?*

Xavier.Laghari: *'cause you're not okay. I can tell. Need to look at you and make sure it's really you.*

Luca.Ward: *It's me. I'm just…*

Luca.Ward: *Sad.*

Xavier.Laghari: *Why?*

Luca.Ward: *Lot of reasons. I mean my parents are fucking knobs who threw me out like a broken toy, and just…I don't know.*

Luca.Ward: *And one of the goats is sick and I'm a tit and getting all attached and I'm scared she'll die.*

Luca.Ward: *And Imre is…*

Imre is. Imre was.

Imre was…

Imre.

How did he explain that to Xav?

> ***Xavier.Laghari:*** *Imre's the hot guy?*
>
> ***Luca.Ward:*** *Imre's the hot *older* guy who's completely out of my league.*
>
> ***Xavier.Laghari:*** *Why?*
>
> ***Luca.Ward:*** *I have all these memories, every time I look at him.*
>
> ***Luca.Ward:*** *All these feelings that…*
>
> ***Luca.Ward:*** *It's like I forgot them. Buried them until I saw him again. Like it's been winter inside me all this time but he's the sun that makes the buried seeds sprout.*
>
> ***Xavier.Laghari:*** *what the fuck*
>
> ***Xavier.Laghari:*** *buried seeds*
>
> ***Xavier.Laghari:*** *You've already been on that fucking farm too long you soppy tit*
>
> ***Xavier.Laghari:*** *jfc have you been watching twilight again*
>
> ***Luca.Ward:*** *Shut it.*
>
> ***Luca.Ward:*** *Point is I thought my annoying baby crush would go away.*
>
> ***Luca.Ward:*** *And I think instead I'm just making it worse.*
>
> ***Luca.Ward:*** *I go weak every time he calls me angel.*

Luca.Ward: *Angyalka*

Luca.Ward: *It's Hungarian*

Luca.Ward: *But he says it with a Romani accent and it just*

Luca.Ward: *It fucks me up so bad.*

Xavier.Laghari: *Awww that's so sweet I'm gonna gag.*

Luca.Ward: *It's killing me. I shouldn't feel like this.*

Xavier.Laghari: *Have you ever told him how you feel?*

Luca.Ward: *When I was five*

Luca.Ward: *I gave him a ring and told him I was going to marry him when I grew up.*

Xavier.Laghari: *AHAHAHAHA YOU SENTIMENTAL FUCKFACE*

Luca.Ward: *SHUT. UP.*

Xavier.Laghari: *:D*

Luca laughed, though he didn't really want to. Not when that laughter just sat atop his heartache, and pressed down on it until it hurt even more compressed into a smaller space.

Xavier.Laghari: *Does he remember that?*

Luca.Ward: *Probably not. He looks at me like he doesn't even know who I am now. Like nothing ever mattered.*

Xavier.Laghari: *So let him get to know you.*

Luca.Ward: *He already knows me. Or the old me.*

Xavier.Laghari: *Bloke doesn't know you the way*

you want him to. Sooo…

So? Luca frowned. So what? So—oh. *Oh.* He sucked in a breath and pressed his knuckles to his mouth, then turned his face into the sheets and groaned. No. Nope. Absolutely not. He couldn't even think that way. He peeked one eye over his knuckles, then pecked out:

> ***Luca.Ward:*** *I can't do that!*
> ***Xavier.Laghari:*** *Why not?*
> ***Luca.Ward:*** *I can't. I don't want to talk about this anymore. I have to go to sleep. We're picking apples tomorrow.*
> ***Xavier.Laghari:*** *Okay, nature boy. Call me if you get in trouble. I got your back.*
> ***Luca.Ward:*** *Thx. 'night.*

Xav answered with a grinning photo that was one third face and two thirds middle finger, tinted blue on brown by the light reflected from his computer screen. Luca snorted and flipped the chat window off right back, but didn't bother taking a photo. He told Xavier to fuck off on a regular basis. He could pull a few out of the bank for this one.

Sighing, Luca plugged his earbuds in and pulled up one of his desktop playlists, then shifted onto his back and stared up at the ceiling while Taylor Swift and ZAYN sighed about not wanting to live forever. He traced the pattern of painted stars that came back to him with a familiarity as deep as muscle memory. Lohere was like that, he thought. Muscle memory.

But the heart was a muscle, too.

And its memory was too long and too deep for him.

It remembered far too much, when all he wanted to do was

forget.

IMRE COULDN'T SEEM TO GET comfortable.

He sprawled against his bed, staring up at the ceiling. He'd flung the duvet back an hour ago; it was too hot with the duvet and the fire going, but too cold with just the fire. But it wasn't the temperature keeping him restless. It wasn't even knowing he'd be up in an hour to check on the goats, just to soothe the boy shut away in his room down the hall.

It was the boy himself, and those wide damned green eyes.

Why was he thinking about Luca? Angry, sullen Luca. Quiet, shyly laughing Luca. Luca entranced by the softness of a horse's muzzle. Luca cradling a goat's head in his lap and crying with pure and utter heartbreak.

Luca pressed against him, clinging to him, trusting Imre to protect and shield him as if Imre was still the same man he'd been ten years ago.

He was starting to think he might not be.

He sighed, dragged a hand over his face, and rolled out of bed. He'd regret this tomorrow, but sleep, right now, was pointless. He pulled on a pair of jeans over his boxer-briefs, dragged on a long-sleeved shirt against the chill, and let himself out into the hall. But he paused as he passed Luca's room; a pale light shone under the door. He leaned in and listened, but couldn't hear movement, typing, any other signs that Luca was awake. Gently, he rapped the backs of his knuckles to the door.

"Luca?" he whispered.

Nothing. With a careful touch, he twisted the doorknob until the latch came free without a sound, then opened the door just a crack. Just enough to peek inside.

Luca curled on his side in the bed: this long thing of pale, slender limbs tangled together in a gangly mess, dark hair spilling across the pillows and leaving his face unguarded. In his sleep, that defensive scowl and pensive withdrawal had relaxed, and he looked almost…

Lost, Imre thought.

Lost without a compass, falling with no idea which way was up.

Luca had fallen asleep with his laptop open in front of him, little black nodules of earbuds in his ears; the laptop was dangerously close to the edge of the bed. The covers were flung back, and goose pimples pricked on those slim, smooth legs. Imre sighed, shaking his head, and eased into the room, moving carefully over the weathered floorboards.

He relocated the laptop to the nightstand, then paused. The crown of woven clover blossoms he had given Luca that morning was draped over the blue fabric lampshade, ringing it in a delicate band. The blooms had wilted, the stems browning, but…he'd kept it.

Imre lightly brushed the fronds of one bloom, then folded the quilts over Luca, pulling them up to his shoulders.

Luca made a sleepy sound, burrowing down into the sheets, then subsided. Imre watched until he was certain he was settled, then caught the earbud cords delicately and tugged them from Luca's ears with a gentle *pop*. His fingers brushed the soft skin of Luca's cheeks, catching the subtlest hint of roughness where a faint prickle of stubble lingered just in front of his ears.

"Imre?" Luca sighed his name in a throaty burr, never opening his eyes. Imre didn't even think he was really awake; just talking to himself, and with another of those sleepy sounds Luca nosed into the pillows, going lax again with a last drowsy murmur. "…Imre."

Don't, Imre thought. His breaths hurt, scouring the inside of his chest. *Don't say my name that way.*

Luca only sighed once more. Imre coiled the earbuds atop the laptop, then smoothed Luca's hair back from his brow. He lingered a moment, letting his fingers slip through hair as dark and shimmering as the gleam of a still black pool on a moonless night.

"Sleep, my angyalka," he whispered.

Then made himself pull away, and slip out into the night and to the barn.

18

LUCA WOKE TO THE SCENTS of frying bacon and eggs and the sound of Imre's voice drifting up the stairs, unintelligible but a familiar, steady part of the quiet music of a Lohere morning.

He squinted against the morning light streaming through the window and wrinkled his nose, pressing sleep-tacky lips together. He didn't remember falling asleep. But he didn't remember putting his laptop away, either, and sometimes he did things in zombie mode that he had no recollection of the following morning.

Yet he remembered dreaming of a great stone statue that spoke, and threaded its rough granite fingers into his hair until he felt the gentle scrape of rock down to his very scalp.

With a yawn, he sat up and woke his laptop up to check the time. Quarter of seven. Fuck his life. Fuck Imre's life. Fuck farm mornings. But his stomach didn't want to go back to bed, not when it was already having a long-distance love affair with what a discerning nose would swear was apple-smoked bacon.

Luca's nose wasn't particularly discerning, but he was quite particularly fucking *hungry*, and that was good enough.

He climbed out of bed, floorboards cool against his bare feet, and padded down the hall. Eager yips met him at the head of the stairs, and Vila tumbled into him; he laughed, draping his arms around her body and hugging the shepherd, then sank to one knee to loop an arm around Seti's neck.

"Good morning," he said, and Seti answered with a ringing bark, then a wet nose pressed against his cheek.

That bark summoned Imre. He leaned around the wall at the foot of the stairs, his sleep-rumpled hair tumbling everywhere and speckled with hay. He held his cell to his ear with one hand; the other clutched a mug of coffee, and he lifted the mug in greeting, offering a brief, distracted hint of a smile before disappearing around the wall again. Luca stood and descended the stairs, Vila and Seti pressed against his legs, then leaned against the kitchen doorframe to listen.

"Aye," Imre said into the phone, setting his mug down on the counter and replacing it with a spatula. He pushed eggs, cheese, and bacon around in the same pan, frying them all together in a massive, dripping heap. "No, they've made it this far, but I think Gia's taken a turn. Could be nothing. Could be something. Couldn't hurt to look." He paused, then, "Stop in for breakfast?" He glanced over his shoulder, caught Luca's eye, and lifted his mug, mouthing *Coffee?* When Luca shook his head, Imre turned his attention back to the phone. "All right. Thanks, Mira."

"Was that the vet?" Luca asked, hope tight in the pit of his stomach and light in the palms of his hands.

"Mira Landers. Best vet in all of York." Imre fit his phone into the back pocket of his jeans. "She's due out on general farm rounds today, so she's already on her way. She'll make us a priority. Twenty minutes or less. Your turn to set the table today."

Luca edged closer to Imre. At least he was wearing a *shirt*, but his trend toward close-clinging, open-throated henleys—this morning's was a dark heathered blue—wasn't much better for Luca's constitution or comfort levels. He told himself not to look, and wedged himself into the space next to Imre, just close enough to reach the overhead cabinets. Where Imre had reached easily, Luca had to stretch on his toes, and his waist pressed against Imre's hip as he leaned over and strained as far as he could.

With an amused sidelong look, Imre reached up, caught up a stack of plates one-handed, and deposited them in Luca's arms. Luca stuck his tongue out at him, and carted the plates to the table.

"You're too big."

"I'm exactly the right size for me." Imre chuckled. "Don't forget to set out for Mira. You might want to fetch a pair of trousers, too. Not that she's a stranger to the scandal of a man's bare legs."

Luca rolled his eyes. "She'll be here before breakfast is over? I thought everything moved slow in the country."

"Not when your animals are sick. Gia's still steady, though. She didn't worsen overnight."

Luca returned to Imre's side to fetch silverware from the drawer—but paused, squinting up at weathered features, the hay in Imre's hair. The lines around his eyes and mouth were a little more tired this morning, the distance in his eyes not quite distraction. Luca reached up, not really thinking, and plucked a stalk of hay from Imre's hair, teasing it free from the waving silver strands.

"Did you sleep in the barn, Imre?"

"Guilty," Imre said, with zero guilt at all. Luca sighed.

"You wouldn't let me."

"I wasn't tired. You were." Imre shrugged, the broad expanse of his back tight. "Figured I could keep watch."

Imre pulled away, then—out of reach, and leaving Luca with nothing but the stalk of hay and the bite of gnawing confusion. Imre's jaw was tight, his head bowed, and he kept his back to Luca as he scraped out three mounded piles of bacon, eggs, and cheese onto the plates.

"Imre…?" Luca asked. That horrible *wanting* ache in his chest longed to press against that broad back, lean into Imre, coax him with his weight and gentle pressure until those taut shoulders relaxed. "What's wrong?"

"Eh?" Imre lifted his head with a blank look, then looked away again. "Nothing. I'm just thinking. Working out my planting schedule. Weather's been strange and unpredictable this last year or two, but I'm trying to plan for contingencies."

Then he was turning away again, just in time to catch the toaster oven as it shrilled. He spilled fresh rolls out into a basket and brought them to the table, while Luca and Vila and Seti watched—and Imre looked anywhere but at them.

Imre Claybourne had just come the closest Luca had ever seen to telling a lie. Not that he thought Imre was capable of lying.

But he hadn't told the right truth, either, and the hitch in Luca's chest said it was very much on purpose.

He just didn't understand why.

19

MIRA'S TWENTY MINUTES WERE MORE like ten. They always were, and the sound of her ratchety pickup came just in time to break the awkward silence that Imre hated all the more because it was entirely his fault. Silence should be a relief. Silence should be calming. Silence should be sweet.

Instead silence was damning, as he tried to pretend he didn't see Luca's many sidelong glances, each one dark with an unspoken question:

What did I do wrong?

Nothing, angyalka. Nothing at all.

The noise of tyres grinding on beaten earth sent Luca racing upstairs to dress, while Imre set out the last of the butter and cream pots at the table.

"Luca?" he called up the stairs. "We'll be in the barn."

A clatter echoed down the stairs. "I'm coming—I'm coming!"

Imre looked down at Seti. Curious golden eyes looked up at him, almost mocking. He sighed, rested his hand atop her head, then headed out to meet Mira in the yard.

She was already climbing out of her truck by the time the house door banged shut: a small woman with spare shoulders and generous hips, her battered canvas utility jacket buttoned snugly around her waist and her tight black micro-braids bound up in a no-nonsense knot swept out of her round, apple-cheeked brown face. She raised a hand, her clear, pleasant voice ringing over the morning.

"Morning, Imre. That apple bacon I smell?"

"Made it because I know you like it." He clasped her outstretched hand and shook it firmly. She had her kit in the other hand, a sturdy steel-bound fishing tackle box. "Still carrying that thing?"

"I'll switch to the old black bag when someone invents one that can survive being crushed under two tonnes of steel and four tractor-grade tyres."

Imre started to respond, but then the side door rattled open and Luca came spilling out into the yard, his boots half-laced, his skin-tight jeans scrunched in odd places on his thighs and calves, his loose long-sleeved shirt inside out and backwards with the tag flipped up to rest in the hollow of his throat. Mira fixed Imre with a knowing look.

"Hired new help, Imre?"

Imre beckoned Luca closer. The boy took a few shuffling steps, then squared his shoulders and closed the distance on brave strides.

"This is Luca," Imre said. "A friend. Taking a gap year from university, and staying over a bit to learn about animal husbandry. Luca, this is Mira Landers."

Luca's eyes widened at the same moment Mira's narrowed: when Imre said *a friend.* The spread of slow-rising pink in Luca's cheeks was fascinating, like watching ink furl in clouds through water, but Imre tore his gaze away as Luca offered Mira his hand. Gone was the surly spark of temper, lost resentment, hurt confusion, replaced by a shy, sweet smile and a tentative spark of hope that caught in Luca's eyes and turned to motes of fire in the morning sun.

"It's nice to meet you," Luca said.

"Luca, hm?" Mira shook his hand with a warm, thoughtful smile. "Worried about the goats, Luca?"

Luca ducked his head and retrieved his hand, only to rake it through his hair, spiking the already sleep-dishevelled strands everywhere. "Yes'm. Gia…I was feeding her and massaging her throat like Imre showed me, and her breathing went funny." His face fell. "I…didn't hurt her, did I?"

"Doubtful. Ugly stuff, monkshood is. Used to call it wolfsbane because they used it to kill wolves back when we still *had* wolves." One reason Imre liked Mira was her calm, factual way of explaining things, simple logic without hyperbole or drama, providing grounded, reassuring reality to counteract panic. And she continued with that grounded calm as she said, "But it kills fast. If both goats survived this long, odds are they'll make it. Just need a bit of babying for a good while. So let's go have a look."

She turned to lead the way into the barn. Luca flashed Imre a nervous, preoccupied smile, then trailed after her. Imre hung back. He didn't think there'd be much room for him, anyway—not with Mira already in Gia's stall, kneeling next to the panting goat, Luca right behind her and peering over her shoulder. Mira checked Gia's eyes, pressed a stethoscope over her heart, then tossed a dry look over her shoulder.

"See anything?"

Luca stammered something, then mumbled, "Sorry" and retreated to lean against the interior wall of the stall. Imre draped his arms over the wall and leaned on it at Luca's shoulder.

"It'll be all right," he said.

But Luca wouldn't look at him, his mouth tight, his gaze fixed on Mira and Gia alone.

Mira pried the goat's mouth open, peered down her throat, sniffed her breaths, then listened to her heart again. She pressed her ear to the nanny's nostrils and mouth, listening with an expression of intent concentration, her brows peaked, before examining the goat's tongue. Gia sat through this with a sort of tired endurance, her eyes rolling slightly and the occasional protesting bleat escaping, only to sigh as Mira set her back down gently in the hay.

"Sore throat," she proclaimed firmly. "Bottle feeding will do that. Not really anything to worry about. But since she's not getting enough air, her heart's labouring a bit. I can give her steroids to boost her cardiac function and relieve the inflammation, but she'll be no good for commercial milking or breeding anymore."

"Do it," Imre said without hesitation.

Luca jerked his head up, staring at Imre. "You mean it?"

"Of course."

Imre could see the moment Luca started to reach for him, arms outstretched—and the moment he remembered Mira, and glanced over his shoulder at her before backing away from Imre, clutching his arms close to himself.

Imre, quite honestly, shouldn't be so very disappointed.

"I'm glad," Luca murmured, fidgeting with his shirtsleeves and watching Mira draw vials from her kit. "I'm so glad she'll be all right."

Mira inserted a needle into a vial and drew a shot of clear fluid up into a syringe. A tap, a squirt, and then she was pinching up a loose bit of skin and fat behind the goat's neck and sliding the injection in deep. Imre had seen it a thousand times, done it himself when necessary, but it still made him wince and look away.

He'd never liked needles, but they came with the territory.

"She'll need a lot of attentive care," Mira said. "They both will. I'll dose them both just to be proactive, but it'll still be a while before they're ready to turn out to pasture again."

"I'll watch them," Luca said quickly. "Both of them. I'll take care of them."

"Well. Imre's lucky he found you, then, isn't he?" Mira finished dosing Merta the same as she had Gia, then slapped her hands to her thighs and pushed herself to her feet. Her smile was arch—kind for Luca, pointed for Imre—as she stepped out of the stall and brushed past Imre toward the house. "Now," she said, while Imre bit back a groan. "I believe someone owes me bacon."

Luca flashed Imre another vivid smile, then dropped to his knees, swept the goat up, and hugged her tight, burying his face in her neck. She bleated softly while Imre tilted his head, eyeing them.

God save him, he thought he might well be jealous of a goat.

As quickly as he'd dropped, Luca was on his feet, an animated bundle of energy already dashing toward the house in Mira's wake. Imre sighed, tilted his head back to the rafters, and stared for a long, centring moment before calling out, "…angyalka."

Luca pinwheeled to a halt, pivoting on his heels breathlessly. "Yeah?"

Imre slid his hands into his pockets and strode closer, nodding toward the tag threatening to tickle the underside of Luca's chin. "Your shirt."

Luca blinked blankly, looked down, then flushed. "Oh. *Fuck.*"

He snagged the hem of his shirt in both hands and lifted, with that sort of guileless thoughtlessness that only Luca could have, standing in the middle of the yard and bloody well stripping.

Imre froze.

Then turned and walked into the house before he saw more than a smooth strip of white skin, and the dip of his navel against the flat lines of his stomach.

Day two.

It was only day two, and that boy was already testing his patience.

20

MIRA'S PRESENCE MADE BREAKFAST BOTH better and worse. With Mira there, Imre had someone to direct his attention to other than the boy sitting across the table from him, shirt now right-side out and front-forward.

But with Mira there, he also saw a wholly new Luca: an eager, intelligent Luca who plied Mira with sharply curious questions about the differences in veterinary practice on a farm, peppered with bashful apologies for the barrage. That burning light in his eyes, when something caught his complete and utter interest…it was both familiar and wholly alien when seen through the lens of age, filters stripped away by the years to let Imre see it for what it was:

Passion, pure and unfettered and raw.

He wondered if Marco had ever seen Luca like this. If Marco even *could* see Luca like this, or if the trouble at home had muddied the waters so much that Marco didn't even realize how much Luca repressed himself, until something brought that passion bursting to the fore.

Not your place, Imre reminded himself, and tore his gaze from Luca to focus on his eggs.

But as he lowered his eyes he caught Mira's sidelong glance, and had to turn away from her long, shrewd stare.

When they finished, Luca volunteered for the dishes since Imre had cooked. Imre walked Mira out to the main barn; since she was doing rounds anyway, he might as well take advantage. He thought she might let him off the hook when the entirety of her attention was devoted to the horses, the goats, even the chickens in their coop out behind the barn. She gave each animal a once-over exam made quick not by carelessness, but by expert experience; if veterinary expertise could be passed down through the generations, then Mira had all the knowledge of her father before her and her grandmother before him crammed into that sharp mind and her capable, efficient hands.

She saw to the dogs last, and snuck them a few treats from her pocket before sending them off to romp with the goats, bouncing as much as the hyperactive, blatting livestock. Imre walked her back to her truck, and quietly passed her a roll of notes that disappeared into her utility jacket with a brief nod. He offered his hand.

"Thanks for switching your schedule to come out first. Luca would have stayed in that stall all night if I'd let him."

"Not a problem. You're not so far out of town, so it wasn't much bother." She shook his hand firmly, then dropped her hand into her pocket and tilted her head. "So what's the real story with the kid?"

Imre forced down a wince, tensing. "I told you already."

"You told me he's a friend with some BS story about a gap year." She frowned. "Feels like I've seen him before."

"Remember the Wards, before they moved out of town?"

Mira sucked in her cheeks, whistling. "Little boy blue's all grown up, then. And apparently your *friend*."

"He is a friend." Imre sighed, raking his hair back out of his face, staring out across the fields. "I'm trying to be his friend."

"Not sure that's something you can try to be. It's just something you are, or you aren't." Mira touched his arm: light, the gentle contact of work-callused fingers that spoke as much for her concern as the softness of her voice. "Be careful, Imre."

He looked down at her, frowning. “Of what?”

She smiled sadly, and let her hand fall. “Of everything.”

21

LUCA FINISHED THE DISHES AND tidying up just in time to step out and watch Mira's truck pull out onto the dirt lane, the early morning sun glinting in sharp winking stars off the roof. He raised his hand in a wave, and thought he caught her smile in her rear view mirror as a slim brown hand slipped out the driver's side window in response.

He liked her, he thought. He liked her a lot. How she was with the animals, how she had *so much* written inside her brain like an encyclopaedia with countless pages, and could answer everything from the number of vertebrae in an Alpine goat's spine to the proper calving time for a Guernsey cow without even stopping to think. He didn't know how anyone could be that smart, but God, he almost envied her.

He lingered on the bouncing, rocking truck, then glanced at Imre. Imre stood with his shoulder propped against the corner of the smaller barn, his mouth set in a grim line—and though his gaze, too, was fixed on the truck, he didn't seem to actually be *seeing* it.

Luca wasn't sure what he saw, but whatever it was, it pulled his brows into a darkly lowering ledge, casting those troubled blue eyes into tumultuous shadow.

Luca drifted a step closer. Imre tensed, turning his head, and looked at Luca for a silent moment in which Luca froze where he stood, trembled, waited for Imre to speak.

But Imre only shook his head—that same shake that had left Luca so confused before, when he didn't know if it meant *not you* or *not me* or *not now*—before turning and walking away, oblivious to the fact that each step ground the heels of his boots into the centre of Luca's aching chest.

Luca swallowed thickly, rubbing at the awful empty feeling just under his breastbone. What had he done *wrong*? Why was Imre upset with him already?

What had Luca fucked up this time?

Imre disappeared into the barn. Luca curled his hands, pressing them hard against his thighs, then squared his shoulders and followed. He stopped just under the shadow of the entryway and watched Imre; the man leaned between the horses' stalls while they hung their heads over the stall doors and pressed into him from either side, his eyes closed and his arms looped around their necks as if drawing comfort from the warmth of horseflesh.

And he didn't look up at all, as Luca drifted past.

Luca took refuge in Gia's stall, settling into a nest in the hay and cradling the goat in his lap. Her eyes seemed clearer, more focused—and when he scooped up a fingerful of her feed paste the way he'd seen Imre do, she stretched her neck toward his hand weakly, her agile lips working needily.

Luca couldn't help smiling, easing the crush of heartache just a few feathers' weights. "Good girl," he whispered, and gave her his fingers to suckle clean, her warm wet mouth tickling over his skin.

He let that distract him from the sounds of Imre just a few feet away, working with the horses until he was just a collection of quiet noises: the faint clop of hooves, the rustle of straw, low whickering snorts, the jingle of tack. As long as Luca rendered Imre down to that, he could be not a confusing, frustrating person who tied Luca up into knots—but just the soothing backdrop noise of a barn, complemented by the morning calls of birds flitting across the sky, the goats making their silly half-laugh, half-cough noises in their paddock, the dogs yipping.

This was nice, Luca thought as he fed Gia another mouthful and stroked behind her ears.

And, he thought, he didn't miss the city at all.

But he glanced up as Imre passed the goats' stalls, face set in stern lines of preoccupation. He fetched a currying brush from a row of them set on the far wall, then turned back. Luca watched him, hoping Imre would at least glance his way.

But he didn't.

Luca pressed his teeth against the inside of his lower lip. It took all his nerve to pull his voice from inside his chest, push it up his throat, force it past his lips.

"…Imre?"

Imre jerked as if he'd been struck, turned his head, blinked at Luca as if he'd forgotten he was there. He said nothing, only stopping, tilting his head, brows canted in silent question. Luca swallowed hard. He almost couldn't speak again and lowered his eyes, fixing his gaze on Gia instead of Imre.

"Was it a lot of money, for Mira to come out?" He barely straggled out a whisper and cleared his throat, trying to boost a bit more confidence into his voice. "I have a little bit in my bank acc—"

"Absolutely not," Imre said firmly, yet there was no censure in the words. Instead, when Luca looked up, the kindness was in those blue eyes again, clearing away the pensive shadows as Imre watched him steadily. "She was coming anyway. I paid for her usual rounds, and breakfast was the tip for seeing us first." His lips quirked. "She says Lohere eggs are worth the trouble, and she'd sell a kidney for my apple-smoked bacon."

Yet somehow, that didn't ease the guilt in the pit of Luca's stomach. Imre was still being strange, and Luca averted his eyes.

Maybe it wasn't *Imre* being strange at all. Maybe he was just being kind to a guest, and that kindness was already wearing thin.

"Oh," Luca mumbled. "Okay."

He'd thought Imre would walk away—but instead his shadow fell over the stall, as he leaned one thick forearm on the door; the morning light falling into the barn caught on the dark hairs on his arm, turning their edges into golden arcs.

"Would you like to stay with her today?" he asked.

Luca perked. "Would that be okay? Didn't you say we had to—"

"I've got the apple orchard. Stay with Gia. You can feed Merta, too." Imre's voice deepened, a warm rumble tinged with approval. "You're good with them."

Pleasure flushed through Luca, lifting him dizzily. "I…I am?"

"Soft touch. Makes all the difference." Imre paused, idly stroking at his beard, toying with the beads tipping the braids, then added, "If she's better after lunch, we'll go riding. Deal?"

"Deal."

Luca nodded quickly, then lingered for a longer look. A faint rim of red ringed Imre's eyes, and those deep lines were still sunken into his face, subtly heightening the shadows and making the lines of his cheekbones into sabre slashes above the trim of his beard, their high ridges starkly pronounced as cliffs. Maybe…maybe nothing was wrong at all, and Luca was reading too much into Imre being exhausted after a long night in the barn.

Luca hesitated, then added, "…if you're okay."

"Why wouldn't I be?"

That calm, curiously neutral response made Luca braver. Imre wouldn't shut him down or dismiss him. He *wouldn't*. "You look tired," he ventured. "Can't you take the day off?"

"That's almost impossible on a farm." Imre chuckled, eyes creasing at the corners, that brief rumble flashing a hint of white teeth. "I'll go to bed early tonight, all right?"

"All right," Luca agreed, and smiled quickly before flushing and looking away again. "I'm sorry for…I don't know. I just…"

"Hm?"

Luca's stomach made one riotous leap, then splashed back down into its place. "…I just want to take care of you," he whispered.

Silence. Luca winced, squeezing his eyes shut and sinking down into his shoulders. Then the stall door creaked, and hay crunched under heavy boots. Imre's warmth drew in on him, leaching the September morning chill from the air.

"I've been taking care of myself for a while, angyalka."

That voice rumbled close, so very close, as real a touch as brimming, comforting body heat. Luca peeked one eye open, holding his breath.

Imre crouched before him, powerful body folded with lithe grace, his hair tumbling over one shoulder in a silvered waterfall that practically fell into Luca's lap. This close Imre smelled of saddle oil and leather and horseflesh, taken in shallowly through Luca's nostrils. His heartbeat tried to stop, but his racing pulse made that impossible, a flooded river breaking its banks and threatening to shatter the levees of his heart.

Intensely blue eyes filled his vision, holding him petrified. "Besides," Imre murmured. "I'm supposed to be the one taking care of you."

Luca's mouth was too dry to speak. He swallowed, took in a shaky breath, made himself meet Imre's eyes. Made himself be brave, when his heart was full and heavy and his stomach was taut with terror and all he could think of was wrapping his arms around Imre's neck and burying his face in his beard and breathing, *I'm always gonna love you, Immie.*

I'm always going to love you, Imre.

There wasn't enough room in his body for the courage to say that. He could only whisper, "It can't go both ways?"

Imre smiled, leaned in. Luca strained toward him.

And Imre pressed two fingers to the centre of Luca's forehead, pushing him playfully back. "Supper's on you tonight, then. Okay?"

Then he stood, leaving Luca frozen, staring, with a lap full of confused goat and his breaths tasting of the salt of Imre's musk.

"Okay," he rasped, as Imre chuckled and walked away.

Luca stared after him. Groaned.

Then slumped forward and buried his face into Gia's warm flank, digging a hand into his hair.

"*Baa-a-a,*" Gia said.

"*Fuck,*" Luca answered.

Just…just…

Fuck.

22

IMRE TOOK ANDRAS OUT WITH the herds, but left Zsofia in her stall; if he had his guess right, she'd be getting a double workout this afternoon with a novice rider.

But that presented its own problems.

He whistled for Vila and Seti. The Australian shepherds came bounding over the grass, then split into familiar formation: Imre bringing up the rear while Vila and Seti took flanking positions, racing up and down the lines of the herd to keep the goats boxed in and moving in the same general direction.

They took the hills at a light trot, moving steadily underneath the rising sun. The sky was that crisp, cloudless blue that came just before a freeze, the air high and hard with a certain loamy tang that promised a deepening autumn soon. He'd get one last burst of clover and alfalfa out of the newly seeded fields, one last harvest of honey from the hives, one last milking before the last of the kids were weaned, and then there'd nothing but snow and fallow earth until March, last frost, and sweet corn planting season. Winter was always quiet, on the farm—a time to repair odds and ends, bottle and can and preserve things, turn milk into cream and cheese and butter, while making sure the animals kept warm and fed inside the heated barns. Winter was the closest he ever took to time off.

But this winter he'd be shut away not with his thoughts, but with a boy who wanted to *take care* of him, and who looked at him as if those ten years apart had left him in drought, and aching to slake some unnamed thirst.

Be careful, Mira had said, and Imre sighed.

He wanted to be careful. With Luca, with that fragile and tender heart.

But he didn't know *how*.

He let his thoughts drift into nothing, familiarity soothing him into quiet as he worked with the dogs to split the herds and drive them toward two separate grazing pastures—both bursting with the latest crop of tall, white-frothing Ladino clover vying for space with purple-blooming alfalfa and the violet droplets of vetch hanging between their fernlike leaves, so prevalent they grew naturally without needing to be seeded. The fields were cut into patches by irrigation ditches turned watering brooks during grazing cycles, and Imre guided Andras slowly between the rows, searching between the plants for any weeds or poisonous invaders. One stray seed pod on the wind could ruin an entire field with lethal invasive species, and decimate an entire herd. Accident had brought down two of his nannies.

He wouldn't let carelessness hurt any more.

The sun was cresting at midmorning and climbing toward noon by the time he left the herds in the dogs' care and made his way back to the farmhouse. He glimpsed Luca as he put the roan gelding down to rest and eat, but Luca had his earbuds in and was so preoccupied feeding Merta from a bottle that he didn't even notice Imre slipping in and out of the barn—or standing in the aisle, watching how gentle Luca was with the nanny, the way he cradled her head and seemed to instinctively know just the right angle to hold both her head and the bottle to ease her drinking without choking or forcing her.

He really was good with them, Imre thought. He hoped like hell the nannies pulled through. It would cut him to the quick if either died—it always did, when he lost an animal to age or illness or predators or fate—but Luca didn't have the experience to know that it was part of farm life. A regrettable part of farm life, but still something to be dealt with and accepted.

If Merta or Gia died, he'd be devastated.

Imre crept from the barn so as not to disturb them, and wheeled a large hand barrow packed with bushel buckets out to the half-acre he'd fenced off behind wooden railings, beyond the farthest storage barn. His apple orchard was a relatively recent addition to Lohere, added only fifteen years ago, but by now he had a relatively strong mix of young and old trees in well-cultivated rows, a blend of Ribston Pippin, Sunset, and Egremont Russet apples that cross-pollinated in different ways each season to produce uniquely blended harvests. This season's yielded sweet apples with subtle notes, with the red-orange Ribston Pippin's sharpness creeping into pleasant counterpoint beneath the dry bite of the Egremont Russet, and the Sunset's sweetness showing up at unexpected moments throughout the crop.

The variations each year fascinated him, and he never tried to control them; he just let them grow as they would and didn't try to hold too fast to any one thing or the other, no matter what the season might bring.

He'd cleared a fair portion of the harvest before Luca had come, but another few good days would get the last of the ripe apples. He set two baskets beneath each fruit-heavy tree, limbs bowed underneath the weight of their bounty, then set to work: losing himself and his troubled thoughts in the focus on picking, inspecting, checking for worms and blight before tossing them into the keep basket or the basket for discards that weren't quite fit for human consumption but that goats and horses would gladly take as part of their winter bulking feed.

A few bees droned around him as he worked, not particularly interested in him when they were mostly keeping to the hive boxes spaced among the trees, building up their honeycombs to guard their queens for the winter. The light backdrop of their looping, buzzing song eased him into a trance as he fell into the rhythm of pick, inspect, drop, move on, now and then shifting position to circle the lowest branches before levering himself up to brace his feet on the trunk and reach the higher branches.

He was just stretching up to catch a ripe, round Sunset apple from an uppermost twig, his feet planted against the thick trunk of an older tree and his other hand gripping tight at the base of a sturdy branch, when Luca's voice rang over the fields.

"Imre?" he cried, then louder: "*Imre!*"

That call sliced through Imre's chest. He lost his grip, lost his footing, crashed to the ground. Gravity and his own weight crushed together in a pounding slam. The apple tumbled out of his hand and rolled across the ground, its thudding bounces matching the erratic, frightened rhythm of his heart. He rolled over, pushing off before he fully found his feet, launching himself across the orchard as fast as his legs would take him.

"Imre!" came again.

His stomach plunged. He vaulted the orchard fence one-handed, ignoring the howl of pulling bruises, and tore around the house just as Luca came skidding out of the barn.

"Luca!"

Imre stumbled to a halt, panting, and gripped Luca's shoulders, dragging him close, searching his face. He wasn't bleeding, bruised, crying, though he stared up at Imre with wide, confused eyes.

"What happened?" Imre growled. "Are you hurt?"

Luca shook his head quickly, dark hair flying. "She's standing up!" He grinned and pointed at the barn. "Gia stood up."

Imre stared at him, then closed his eyes and took a deep, slow breath. "Bloody *hell.*" He let his hands fall away, scrubbing at his shirt just over his heart—which refused to calm down, still convinced that call of his name had been a cry of mortal peril. God *damn* it. "You practically gave me a heart attack. I thought you'd been hurt, or something had happened."

He opened his eyes. Luca peered at him sheepishly through his lashes, scuffing his boots in the dirt and twisting at his lower lip with his fingers.

"Sorry," he mumbled. "I'm sorry. I—I didn't see you, and I don't have your cell number." His eyes lit with hope. "Come see?"

Imre dragged a hand through his hair, then winced when his shoulder pulled. He'd be feeling that in the morning.

This boy was going to kill him.

"Show me," he said, then followed after as Luca grinned and raced into the barn.

Inside, Gia knelt in her stall, her head up and alert, while she nosed at bristles of hay and lipped them without much interest. In the adjacent stall Merta had tucked herself into a corner and was busy grooming herself with fumbling, uncoordinated movements, licking at her foreleg and more often than not missing and burying her nose in the hay.

Luca stood over Gia, his face crestfallen. "I swear she was standing up."

"She's upright. Sitting on her own. That's far better than she was last night." Imre knelt in the hay and pressed his palm, then his ear to Gia's flank, listening to the steady, pumping beat of her heart, then her breaths. When he waved his hand in front of her face, she shook her head, gaze tracking his hand, before fixing on him irritably. He chuckled and scratched between the nubs of her filed horns. "She's weak and likely won't be able to stand on her own for more than a few moments here and there, but it's a start." He shifted his scratching down to under her chin. "Don't you think so, little one? Are you feeling better?"

She promptly clamped her teeth down on the leather band of his wristwatch, and started to chew.

Imre snorted and gently tugged free. "I'll take that as a yes."

Luca watched, leaning against the wall of the stall and fidgeting. "…Mira really helped her," he said.

"That's what Mira does. She's the best vet I've ever known."

"She's really that good?"

"It's a family practice. It's almost in their blood." Imre braced his hands to his thighs and stood. "Like Lohere's in mine."

Luca looked up at him for a pensive moment, pale eyes shadowed, then looked away, plucking at his lower lip. "I wonder what's in my blood."

"Trouble." When those green eyes sparked and darkened, Imre chuckled and rested his hand atop Luca's head, fiercely resisting a *craving* to stroke fully through those black strands. "The best kind of trouble."

Luca offered a wan smile, but little more. Imre extended his hand.

"Give me your phone, angyalka."

With a wrinkle between his brows, Luca fished in his pocket, retrieved his phone, and deposited it in Imre's palm. Imre tapped through to his address book, then entered his own phone number and saved a new entry before handing it back.

"No more shouting across the fields?"

That wan smile turned sheepish. "No more shouting across the fields." Luca's thumbs flew over his phone, and Imre's own buzzed in his back pocket. "There."

Imre tugged his phone out and read the new text on his screen.

Sorry for yelling. Forgive me? <3 <3 <3

He snorted. "Forgiven." He saved Luca's number and stowed his phone again. "Think you feel up for a ride, since Gia's coming out from under the weather?"

Luca brightened as if the sun had just lit up a grey morning. "Really? Now?"

"Wash up and at least have a sandwich, but yes. Now." Imre's nerves were still too frayed to go back to the apples. Better to have Luca where he could see him, until his mind convinced his heart Luca wasn't about to be snatched away by some terrible accident.

"Okay," Luca said, then grinned, bouncing on the balls of his feet. "Okay!"

"Okay," Imre repeated, then exhaled, shaking his head.

Luca was already gone, the house door clattering shut.

Did that boy ever sit *still?*

23

IMRE HAD NEVER SEEN ANYONE fall off a horse as many times as Luca Ward, then get back up and climb right back on.

They'd had a quick lunch, thick sandwiches eaten in bites between explaining how to bridle a horse, how to handle Zsofia's soft mouth with a rope bit, how to soothe her into holding still for the saddle and stop her from puffing out her sides to thwart the girth strap. He let Luca saddle her himself, then made him do it again until he got it right, Luca red-faced and gasping as he lifted a saddle that weighed as much as he did soaking wet, while Imre hid his smile behind his sandwich. He tried so *hard.*

But he didn't quit, and Imre respected that.

Now and then he touched a hand to Luca's shoulder or the small of his back to nudge him in the right direction, then pulled back immediately and put another step of space between them. Each time Luca looked at him oddly, but Imre moved on quickly, pointing Luca to another bit of tack, Zsofia's hooves, the parts of the saddle.

On the fourth try, Luca finally settled the saddle properly. Imre wasn't sure who was more relieved: the boy, or the horse. Zsofia flicked her ears back and let out an irritated snort, but planted her feet and held steady while Luca gripped the saddle fore and aft and tried to lift his leg high enough to get his foot into the stirrup. His boot slipped, and he laughed breathlessly.

"She looks a lot taller this way," he said. "I don't know if I can get my leg up like that."

Imre swallowed the last bite of his sandwich. "You get used to it. Have to get your seat for horseback riding, and that means finding your legs. Here."

Before he could talk himself out of it, he caught Luca around the waist and lifted him. Luca gasped, clutching at Imre's shoulders, staring down at him with the thick fringes of his lashes trembling. He was so *small*, Imre thought dimly, but could hardly hear himself for the roaring of his blood in his ears, strange and hot. For all that lanky height, he was so slim that Imre's hands easily spanned his waist, meeting front and back with that hot skin pressing to his palms through Luca's thin shirt as Imre lifted him up to Zsofia's back and set him down astride.

Luca only clutched at his shoulders harder, as he struggled with spreading his thighs over the mare's broad back. His fingers dug through Imre's shirt and into his flesh, a strangely pleasant feeling—until those soft fingers hit one of the bruises spreading under his shirt. The dull shock of pain snapped Imre from his reverie, and he pulled back, clearing his throat. His head felt strange, and Luca was just *looking* at him, still gripping tight at his shoulders until Imre twisted free and left Luca grasping at Zsofia's mane.

Imre looked away, biting back a snarl at himself.

"Let me saddle Andras," he said. "Just stay there. Get used to it. We'll head out in a minute."

"S-sure," Luca said faintly.

Imre swore under his breath, closed his eyes, and turned away from that stricken look. The blue roan gelding was a shield between himself and Luca, one he took advantage of as he distracted himself bridling and saddling Andras, then swung himself up. "Hold the reins in both hands," he said through his teeth. "Firm grip, but not tight.

Don't pull. Try to always keep some slack, and draw tight only when trying to guide her one way or the other. The reins are for steering and stopping, nothing else. You control speed and forward motion by how you hold your seat, and with your knees against her side. Knees, not heels; heels dig and can hurt her. Sit up straight, squeeze your knees gently, and she'll walk. Sit forward, squeeze more, and she'll trot. She's trained to respond to your seat, so if you sit as if bracing for speed, she'll give you speed."

"O-oh." Luca looked small and pale and terrified, sitting stock-still atop the tall, leggy horse. "How fast can she go?"

"Faster than you can handle right now," Imre said dryly. "Let's try walking. Let go of her mane and take the reins. Stay sitting upright, and very, very gently squeeze her sides."

"Got it." Luca gulped a noisy swallow, then transferred his grip from mane to reins so quickly Imre would think he was a man hanging from a ledge, swinging hand over fist and afraid to let one finger slip. Luca's thighs tensed, and Zsofia took two obedient steps forward, then drifted to a halt when Luca gasped, immediately going stiff, before letting out a whooping laugh. "She moved!"

"So she did. The best language of communication between horse and rider is body language, angyalka. Talk to her with your body, and she'll talk back." Imre used his knees to guide Andras into stepping backward, making room, then turned him about with a light tug of the reins to pace slowly toward the barn exit. "Try to follow me. Take it slow."

"Okay. Okay."

Imre twisted in the saddle, watching Luca. Luca gripped the reins with utter concentration, knuckles white, and squeezed his thighs. He was too far forward in the saddle, his seat stiff, but Zsofia still responded, taking three more steps forward, then stopping when Luca wobbled and went loose, grabbing at the saddle. He took several audibly shaky breaths, flicked Imre a wide-eyed look, then tried again. And again. And again, moving forward in fits and starts while Imre led him a few steps at a time, until he seemed to get the hang of it and Zsofia settled into a steady walk, plodding placidly out of the barn and into the yard.

Where she promptly reared up, tossed her shoulders, and pitched Luca arse over elbows into the dirt.

He went tumbling and landed hard with a yelp. Imre fought the urge to dismount and go to him; this was part of learning. Zsofia came down lightly, then turned and nosed Luca, pushing her muzzle into his cheek. Luca groaned, rolling onto his back and shoving at her face.

"Ow," he muttered. "I don't like you."

Zsofia lipped his fingers. Imre chuckled and guided Andras closer, and leaned down to offer his hand. "Up. Try again. To Zsofia, there's absolutely no reason for you to be on her back unless you *give* her a reason. If you don't know why you're there, she doesn't either."

"I'm there to…go places. Or something."

"Is that your only reason?"

Luca squinted at him sourly, then slid his warm, slender hand into Imre's, before sliding up to grip at his wrist. Imre grasped Luca's fine-boned wrist and hauled him up lightly, lifting him onto his feet. Luca dusted dirt from his hopelessly stained clothing, then scowled at the mare.

"Why do I need a reason at all?"

"You need confidence in what you want. If you don't have it, she'll feel it. You'll make her nervous, and she'll want to get away. Body language, angyalka. Body language."

Luca played his lower lip between his teeth, then said slowly, "…she's beautiful." He stopped, then started again. "When she moves, it's beautiful. And she looks like she can fly." A nervous glance toward Imre. "I want to know what it feels like to fly with her."

Something melted inside Imre, at that look—and he gave Luca his hand once more. "Then get back into the saddle and find out."

Luca flashed a small, fierce, toothy grin, and nodded. He gripped Imre's wrist in one hand and the edge of the saddle in the other, and managed to get his foot into Zsofia's stirrup before Imre heaved him back into the saddle. The boy landed heavily, awkwardly, but Zsofia held patiently still while he found his seat again, took the reins, and nudged her forward with his knees.

And made it half a circuit of the yard before she kicked her hips and hind legs into a sideways twist, and tossed him again.

Then thrust her nose into his hair and blew, puffing him out like a wispy black dandelion.

"Now I *really* don't like you," Luca muttered, and Imre burst into laughter.

"Up," he said again.

Luca glowered at him—but he got up, and let Imre toss him back into the saddle. And let Zsofia toss him back into the dirt. And so it went: again and again, and each time he held his seat a little longer, and took to the saddle a bit more smoothly. By the time the sun reached zenith Zsofia wasn't throwing him on a walk anymore, but the second he tried a trot, leaning forward and pressing with his thighs, she pitched him again, sending him tumbling with his heels over his ears.

Imre circled them at a safe distance, only coming in close to help Luca up until Luca didn't need help anymore and flung himself back in the saddle on his own, brows knit in a thunderously black line of determination and jaw set tight as he followed Imre's murmured instructions with utter silent focus. He was gloriously dirty by the time the glaring sunlight slanted into mid-afternoon, that pale skin streaked in grit, his hair a dusty mess, his shirt and jeans torn and stained—but the ferocious light in his eyes outshone every bit of filth, pale green snapping hot, pretty mouth drawn into a fierce line that now and then stretched into a feral, catlike grin when Zsofia actually did what he wanted.

Imre watched as Luca circled the yard at a slow and careful trot, his body lifting up slightly from the saddle with each of Zsofia's light steps, wild hair flying, lashing in and out of his face and cutting his eyes into blades of tender new grass. That grin was back, triumphant, a grin that was half joy, half war cry, and Imre's heart went slow and heavy as Luca leaned his entire graceful body into a turn, moving with Zsofia's body language and flow with a moment of perfect fluidity.

Luca completed the circuit, then drew the mare to a halt next to Imre with a light tug on the reins, settling his body back in the saddle. Tossing his hair back, he looked up at Imre, panting and breathlessly flushed, eyes alight. "I'm doing it, Imre. I did it."

"Not bad for your first time." That grin was still there, and Imre caught himself leaning toward it, then jerked back enough to make Andras take a little sidestep. "Let's try out in the field. See how you do on the trails."

"Just a sec." Luca fumbled in his pocket, clutching the reins one-handed, and dug out his phone. With a nudge of one knee, he sent Zsofia bumping up against Andras and Luca bumping up against Imre. He stretched his phone out at arm's length. "Take a selfie with me first."

He leaned shoulder to shoulder against Imre, thigh to thigh, his skin so *hot* under cotton and denim, as if he'd absorbed the afternoon sun into himself and gave it back tenfold. Imre's stomach bottomed out, a deep pull of muscle tension tightening in his inner thighs, and he grit his teeth, struggling to hold his seat.

"Why?" he ground out.

"So I can post it to Facebook and make Xav jealous of how much fun I'm having."

Luca angled the phone, his head practically resting to Imre's shoulder, cool hair washing against his neck. Imre caught a glimpse of his own face on the screen: glowering, almost sullen, glaring away from Luca's bright smile, before he fixed his gaze on the fence.

"Fine," he muttered.

Luca laughed. "Oh my god, Imre, you have to smile."

"No."

"Try? Please?"

Imre thinned his lips, and Luca laughed again.

"That's not a smile."

"That is my smile."

Luca snickered, then snapped the shot before turning his head toward Imre. "Why are you like this?"

Imre frowned. "Like what?"

"Nevermind." Luca propped his chin on Imre's shoulder, its delicate point digging in lightly. "Just nevermind, Imre."

Light breaths slipped under his jaw, curled over his ear. Imre turned his head. The tip of his nose brushed against the impertinently kittenish tip of Luca's, skin to skin. The small, strange smile on Luca's lips vanished, and in the shadow of his lashes his eyes were clear and soft, asking a question Imre didn't dare let himself answer. If he spoke a single word, if he moved his lips the slightest bit, that mouth—that pink, overripe raspberry of a mouth—would touch his, and already Imre could *taste* him, a hint of something like berry chapstick and a drugged honeysuckle-wine sweetness that was just *Luca*, kissing the infinitesimal breath of air that separated their lips.

No, he told himself, but the word was faint and small, and the pulse of blood in his aching mouth was so very, very loud.

Luca's lashes lowered, his gaze dropping to Imre's mouth. The flush in his cheeks deepened, a colour prettier than any Imre had seen outside sunset over the Dales. Luca's lips parted further.

And Andras flicked his tail, brushing against Zsofia. The mare started, dancing away and taking Luca with her, gasping and clutching at saddle and reins both, his eyes wide and dazed and utterly lost.

Imre jerked back to reality, heart pounding, throbbing. What the hell had he been thinking?

He *hadn't* been thinking. That was the problem.

And if not for the horses, he'd have damned himself in a moment and a breath, just for the taste of raspberry lips.

Luca was still watching him, still that unspoken question. Imre only shook his head, and guided Andras into turning away.

"Trail," he grunted, set his knees to the gelding's sides—and let him take off, until Luca was only a secondary cadence of hooves at his back, part of the backdrop, pushed to the furthest reaches of his thoughts. As it should be, Imre told himself.

As it damned well had to be.

24

LUCA BARELY HAD TIME TO stare after Imre's back before Zsofia decided to play follow the leader and shot after Imre and Andras, leaving Luca yelping and clutching at the saddle, then her mane, then her reins. The butterflies in his stomach turned into stinging hornets, prickling with a sweet thrill of terror and exhilaration as the mare took off in a canter, following Imre down a narrow beaten trail that led between pastures of budding plants and other fields that were just crushed corn stalks ground into the earth in rows. Luca barely had time to take in more than flashes of green and brown and the occasional reflective blue glimmer of a slow-moving brook, when it took everything in him to keep his seat.

Keep his seat, and not completely lose his head.

He'd only been playing around, resting his chin on Imre's shoulder. But then Imre had turned his head, and that soft, silver-grey beard had flowed against Luca's cheeks, and that kind, firm mouth had hovered over his own. The axis of Luca's world had shifted to rotate around that moment, that whisper of silence, that singular place where their breaths met and mingled while blue eyes looked into him as if Imre saw every bit of the trouble he called Luca.

Then the horses had pulled apart, and Imre had stared at him like he'd been splashed with cold water, only to turn and run.

Because that was what Imre was doing. Running.

Running from Luca.

And Luca was afraid of what he would say, if he caught him.

And so he gave himself to Zsofia: focusing on the strength and fluid power in her body, the way her muscles bunched under him until her movements rolled up through his thighs and his hips, responding when he shifted. The nervous lovely terror in Luca's blood was half Imre, half the rush of wind and the burn of sun and the heave and surge of horseflesh and the pitching earth rushing past, and he leaned into it and let the wind slap the sting of tears from his eyes until he felt nothing but the weightlessness of flight, as Zsofia raced down the dirt path.

Up ahead Imre was a dark lash of the roan's tail and the broad stretch of the man's shoulders, silver hair flowing and tossing in the same rhythm as the gelding's mane. Imre held his seat with a solid power and confidence, his body gliding like an extension of the gelding's, kinetic motion rolling up his hips and arcing through his spine and tossing all the way out to the tips of his hair. Luca let himself watch him for just a single longing moment, but looked away when Imre drew the roan up, easing gently to a prancing halt at the edge of a broad pasture full of yellow grass and lovely purple flowering plants and clover, the air thick with their green, heady scent. Over two dozen goats danced around each other in little leaps, sprawled in sunny patches, nibbled at the clover; on the far end of the field, Vila sat at alert attention, watching over the herd with her head held high and her nose lifted to the wind.

Luca pulled on the reins carefully. Zsofia slowed, but didn't stop, and he tried again, laughing. "Come *on!*"

The horse snorted, then danced backward with a few high, jouncing steps before settling to a stop a few feet away from Imre. Luca leaned down and patted her shoulder, stroking her sleek, burning-hot hide.

"Good girl. See, you do like me."

"You didn't fall off," Imre drawled. "I'm a little surprised."

Luca straightened, glaring at him. "Were you trying to make her throw me?"

"No. I like to let them have their heads where it's safe on the paths. It's good for them to stretch their legs, after staying stabled most of the day. The fact that you didn't end up in the briars is just a pleasant shock."

But Imre wasn't quite looking at him, his gaze on the milling herd of goats, and Luca sighed.

"You like doing that," he murmured.

"Doing what?"

Giving an honest answer, but not a true one.

But "Nothing," was all he said, shaking his head. "Are we bringing the goats in now?"

"Not yet. We're pulling a few out so I can show you how to herd, and how to work with a trained dog."

Why? Luca wondered. *Why are you teaching me how to do these things, when you obviously don't want me here?*

Imre derailed his train of thought with a loud, piercing whistle through his teeth, followed by a series of clicks. Vila perked like a soldier coming to attention, her ears lifting, her gaze trained attentively on Imre—who pointed two fingers to his eyes, then to three grazing goats toward the edge of the field, following each one with a click of his tongue. After the last click, Imre pointed firmly toward the shallow, thread-thin brook that marked one boundary of the field. Vila started forward, tail high, and confirmed with a sharp bark, then shot off to one side, arrowing around on a path that let her cut between the three goats and the main herd. With a nudging nose and soft yips, she worried at them, irritated them into moving, then kept on their heels as they left off grazing and, with annoyed bleats, trotted toward the brook.

"Herd animals are single-minded creatures," Imre said, reciting information almost tonelessly. "Once you get them moving in a certain direction, they'll keep running until they're worn out, or until they hit an obstacle. The trick is keeping them going the way you want. If they see something that frightens them, they'll veer off from the set path. Or, with goats, they'll do it just because they bloody well want to. They're spry and agile and can turn on a coin, so you have to watch them close. Flank them. The only way to change their direction is to cut off their path, until they have no choice but to go where you want. The dogs will always be better at that than you, out in the field. Faster. More responsive. Out here, it's your job to back them up once things get moving—not the other way around. It only takes a few dogs to manage a herd, but if things go south they'll need you. You and a horse are bigger, more effective blockade than a dog."

Luca listened quietly, processing everything as best he could, but with every word the aching familiarity built into a horrible, crushing pressure inside him. "So basically one to either side, like a corridor?"

"It's better with three. Usually with Vila and Seti, they flank while I bring up the rear for effective coverage."

"Is that what you and Dad and Mum are doing to me?" Luca asked, his stomach a hard knot. He stared miserably at the crest between Zsofia's ears. "Flanking and herding me until there's only one way I can go?"

Imre's gaze snapped toward him—then softened. He nudged his horse closer to Luca, until their knees bumped. One large hand slipped into Luca's line of sight, covering both of his, completely eclipsing them in Imre's warmth.

"They might be," Imre said softly. "I'm not."

Then he pulled back and spun the roan about into a trot, taking off across the fields, the dull thud of hooves nearly drowning the words that drifted back.

"Come on. Take the left. Follow my lead."

But Luca stared after him and curled his fingers, rubbing his thumb over his knuckles, where he could still feel the coarseness of that hard and weathered palm.

It took two tries before Luca figured out the right pressure to get Zsofia to go trotting after Imre. They splashed across the brook just in time to meet the goats as they forged through and came out dripping and complaining in high blatting cries on the other side, Vila nosing at their haunches. On the other side of the brook was an empty field, mostly green tangles of roots gone to mulch and mixed in broken bits with loose furrows of dirt. Luca didn't understand what he was supposed to do, until with a whistle Imre began driving the goats in a circle around the field, Vila flanking. Luca hung back and watched, until one of the trio tried to break off and sprint for the farthest hedgerow.

Without thinking, Luca squeezed Zsofia's sides and sent her shooting forward with him clinging to her back, half holding her mane, half holding her reins, instinctively *leaning* the way he wanted her to go, straining toward the goat's trajectory. She obliged, long legs flying, and they shot across the goat's path; it stumbled back, nearly sneering at them with a nasal sound, and veered back toward the other two with Luca on its hooves.

"Like that?" he asked breathlessly, falling in at one side of the mini herd while Vila dropped back to the rear.

"Just like that," Imre said. "Now keep going."

They spent the afternoon that way: chasing goats through the field, while every time Luca thought he had the hang of it Imre brought in a few more until they were herding ten increasingly aggravated nannies in circles, while Luca just tried not to *fall* and shivered every time a gust of cool breeze cut the afternoon heat and sliced right through his sweat-soaked shirt. When two broke off and made a determined sprint for the brook, Luca leaned that way so hard he almost spilled off—but Zsofia was there to catch him, her body flowing under his, stretching into a ground-eating gallop that made his head spin as the wind of their passing tore the breath from his lungs with snatching fingers.

He laughed, standing in the saddle and bowing over her neck, exhilaration belling out his chest and swooping out his throat in a whoop. The mare kicked up clods of dirt as she took a sharp pivot, swerving nearly to the ground, then lunged into the goats' paths; the nannies retreated and rejoined the herd, and Luca clung to the horse's back as she cantered back and fell back into position.

"Too fast!" he gasped, struggling to suck in mouthfuls of cool, sharp-tasting air.

Imre watched him, his body jouncing easily with his roan's steady canter, seeming to have eyes for both Luca and the herd at the same time. "Goats run fast, angyalka. The horse must be fast to keep up."

"This horse likes to dump me on the ground. I'm just waiting for her to try it again."

"So be a nettle, and stick to her back." Imre shoved his hair from his face; sweat darkened pale silver to a deep pewter, shimmering and throwing back the sun in shifting shades. "She'll learn to respect you sooner or later."

"I thought you said she was like me." Luca grinned. "I don't respect anyone."

"Wretch." Imre snorted, then lifted his head sharply. "Straggler."

Luca followed his gaze. A half-grown kid had broken off from the main herd across the brook and wandered too close to the fencing hedgerow, and a gap leading out into dense, untamed forest. Luca gripped Zsofia's reins.

"I'll—"

But Imre was already off: snapping Andras's reins with a sharp, commanding sound, leaning over the massive gelding's neck. The roan leaped across the grass, the thick bulk of its muscles bunching and straining, nearly a hundred stone of horseflesh and man hurtling across the field as if shot from an arrow, the gelding's mane washing against Imre's intently set face, Imre's mane a banner of silver.

He moved like the horse was an extension of his body, hardly seeming to touch the reins, controlling the gelding with twists of his hips and the flexion of straining thighs, every sharp turn drawing his waist into a sinewy curve with his shirt pulled tight in sweat-dappled patches and his broad shoulders cutting the air as they swerved. Left, right, the skittish kid playing chicken trying to get past, darting around the gelding's legs and nearly tangling itself up. But Imre reared the gelding back, both human and equine bodies coiling into near-impossible contortions, sleek power so completely under control down to the last muscle, and as the horse's hooves came down Imre leaned down and scooped up the kid mid-stride, pulling the struggling thing against his chest as the gelding thundered back toward the herd.

A dull, burning pain scraped into Luca's palms, pulling him from staring to realize he'd been rolling and grinding Zsofia's reins in his hands, working and twisting them with his fingers until the raw edges of the leather abraded at his skin. He exhaled slowly, and made himself look away. There was a funny feeling just under his skin, like he had another, second skin made of heat and it fit his body too tight, slithering over every inch of him in a clinging film. And it got worse the more he tried not to look at Imre, when all he wanted to do was watch him *move*. He'd never seen someone with the kind of utter control Imre had over his own body, carrying himself with the complete confidence of someone who expected every last inch of himself to be equal to any demand.

It was that confidence that made Imre so magnetic, because it never bred arrogance. Humble yet not servile, self-effacing yet never cowed. Luca wished…he just…*wished* he knew his place in the world with the kind of certainty Imre had.

Instead Luca felt like a scrap of paper, folded and tucked in someone's pocket, carried around out of habit but not really good for anything.

Imre deposited the kid back with the main herd, then splashed Andras across the brook again to rejoin Luca. Luca grinned at him. "That was really cool."

"It's just part of the job." Imre whistled for Vila, commanding her with a series of short, sharp tones. Vila bounced on her paws, barked, and shot after the practice herd, nipping their hooves and driving them back across the brook to rejoin the main throng. "Let's leave them be and let them graze and calm down until time to go in."

Luca watched Imre from the corner of his eye as he settled the roan next to Zsofia, both horses facing the herd. Beyond, the pastures stretched out into the rolling green and gold carpet of the dales, that red undercurrent starting to give way to rich brown, occasionally splashed with the last brave bloom of a patch of colourful flowers or the thick tufted leaves of stands of trees. From here the Lohere farmhouse was just a glint of sunlight off windowpanes and the slate of the roof rising out of green vines, with the barns spaced behind it like toys and beyond, the reaching orchard branches marching on toward the flat silvery sheen of the small river that bordered Imre's property.

Beautiful, Luca thought. He'd forgotten the Yorkshire Dales were so beautiful.

"What do we do now, then?" he asked softly.

"Watch them," Imre answered. "Breathe. Be."

Luca stole another long look at Imre from beneath his lashes. He was *right there*, his knee almost brushing Luca's, his hands resting casually tangled in the reins and draped between his thighs—yet he seemed so far.

But in his stillness was something of the easiness Luca remembered, the silent warmth he'd wanted since he'd shown up on Imre's doorstep and realized he'd been missing that particular silence for ten noisy, confusing years.

"Breathe," he repeated, then exhaled and settled in the saddle, letting his gaze sweep over the land once more. "Be. Okay."

Breathe. He breathed in the scent of horseflesh and sweat, and the taste of Imre on the wind.

And, lidding his eyes, he tilted his head back toward the sun and just let himself *be*.

25

BY THE TIME SUNSET CAME and Imre gave the signal to start the herd moving, Luca was ready to *just be* a puddle.

He couldn't feel his arse. He *wished* he couldn't feel his thighs; Zsofia looked like a delicate, slender thing, but there was nothing delicate or slender about the rib cage that had kept Luca stretched open all afternoon. Yet he wouldn't have traded those quiet hours for anything, watching the goats and letting the sun bake his shirt dry of sweat and saying not a word to Imre because he didn't need to.

Imre was *there,* and not running away from him.

For now.

But he was tempted to tell Imre to run back to the house and fetch the Land Rover, because Luca didn't think he was going to make it. Not when they had acres to travel, and he was supposed to be on the alert for breakaways or potential stampedes. They covered the slopes at a swift, steady walk, one that let him get used to adjusting his seat when moving at an incline, but by the time they merged the herd with a second group and joined Seti to their guard phalanx, Luca was gritting his teeth as the impact of every step shook up through him and rattled his sore bones.

But he didn't complain. This was Imre's world, and he did this every day. Luca wasn't going to let his city-soft muscles get in the way. He'd survived today. He *had.*

He wanted to be the kind of person who could survive anything.

A blaze of sunset—it made him think of a hibiscus on fire, pink searing and burning at the edges—had doused itself in the cooler purple waters of twilight by the time they rounded the last straggling goat into the paddock, closed the gate, and led the horses into their barn. Luca rode Zsofia right into her stall, then slid down her side and collapsed bonelessly into the hay.

"Ow."

"Tack," Imre said firmly, leaning over the stall door. He propped a broom against the stall. "Then sweep, while I lock up the goats."

"My legs are killing me." Luca thunked his head back against the wall. "My *everything* is killing me. Can't it wait until tomorrow?"

"You can have a soak when we're done." Imre leaned his elbow on the door. "Part of keeping animals is caring for them. Not putting them back on the shelf like a toy and forgetting about them until you want them again. We sweep, we bed them down, and then we clean up and have supper. I'll let you off the hook for cooking so you can soak off the bruises."

Luca groaned, then dragged himself to his feet and draped himself against the door, leaning hard on his arms—shoulder to thick shoulder with Imre. "Please stop reminding me I'm supposed to be a responsible adult."

Imre leaned over and pushed him with his shoulder. "Please stop making me remind you."

Oy. Luca leaned back and answered with his own push. "Stop trying to be fierce when you say that."

"Stop," Imre said with a gleam in his eye and another push, "pointing out that I'm approximately as fierce as a shepherd pup."

Luca grinned, leaning in, drawn by that gleam. "You're a little scary when you're annoyed."

"Name the last time I was annoyed."

“Thinking.” Luca leaned in until their foreheads almost bumped, dropping his voice to a stage whisper. “Thinking *really* hard.”

Imre’s eyes darkened, his subtle not-smile tugging at his lips.

Before vanishing as he thrust back, and disappeared around the side of the stall.

“Sweep while you think,” floated down the aisle, and Luca slumped, dragging a hand over his face.

God *damn* it.

Sighing, he applied himself to taking care of Zsofia, even if he could barely lift his sore, weak arms to grip her saddle and had to drag it off to let gravity do the rest. He rubbed her down as best he could, refilled her feed and water buckets, then stroked her soft nose before kissing right between her eyes.

“Thanks for not being too mean to me today,” he murmured, and scratched under her jaw. “I’ll just have to toughen up until I’m strong enough for you.”

When he stepped out into the aisle, Imre was nowhere in sight. Luca caught up the broom and set about sweeping down the aisle, thought it felt pointless to sweep dirt off…more dirt. He still swished up the loose dust and hay and debris, tamped the packed earth down, and left the aisle as smooth as he could, pausing only to check in on Gia and Merta. Both nannies were resting easily, and had licked their pails of feed paste almost clean.

He smiled and let them lip his fingers, then dragged himself back to work. He was just hanging the broom up when Imre rounded the barn doorway, dusting his hands off.

“Done?”

“As much as I can be. Why don’t you put in concrete?” Luca asked. “Then everything wouldn’t get so dirty.”

“Gets too cold in the winter. Bad for the hooves. Concrete

scrapes at the horses' and goats' hooves. The hard surface doesn't absorb impact shock; it bounces it back. Can hurt their bones."

Luca flushed. "Oh. I hadn't thought of it that way."

"I'm not antiquated, Luca." Imre shrugged, slipping his hands into his pockets. "I'm practical. I'll take the hard way around if it's best for my animals. It's not about me."

Imre leaned against the door of Andras's stall. Luca leaned next to him, folding his arms over his chest and fidgeting with the sleeves of his filthy shirt.

"I get it," he murmured. "I do. You don't want to hurt them. But you sell them to people who might kill them, don't you?"

"Not if I can help it." Full lips set in a thoughtful line as Imre tilted his head back, looking up at the rafters. "Most of my sales are to other milk farms. We'll trade more often than sell. Keeps our stock fresh so we avoid too much inbreeding, and introduces healthy genetic variance. I've some buyers coming up from South Yorkshire this summer to look at the next group of kids."

Luca perked. He had a vague memory of little bundles of fur and bright eyes and tiny hooves, bouncing about on spring-loaded legs. "There'll be kids? Baby goats?"

"In April and May."

"Oh." The spark of excitement snuffed as quickly as it had lit. "I won't be here then."

Imre drew in a deep breath, and seemed to take his time letting it out before rumbling, "Your prison sentence is up in January, angyalka."

Prison sentence.

"…yeah."

Imre said nothing else. Neither did Luca. But after several silent moments, Imre pushed away from the stalls and strode toward the exit.

Luca lifted his head, staring at his broad back.

"Imre…?"

Without looking back, Imre paused. "Ah?"

Luca swallowed back his nerves. "…why are you avoiding me?"

"You've been here for two days, and I've spent nearly every waking moment with you."

Luca's ears burned. He wrapped his arms around himself, forced his thickening tongue to move. "But you look at me, then look away like you're trying not to see me." His lips tasted sour with upset, every time his tongue-tip touched them. "I missed you. But every time I'm too close to you, you find a reason to move away."

Silence. Then, careful and slow and bland: "I'm not avoiding you, angyalka."

Luca couldn't stand it. That *tone,* that empty nothing tone when Imre told untrue truths. He sucked in a hitching breath, glaring down at his feet and scrubbing his shirtsleeve against his face. "Go ahead. Avoid me. I wouldn't blame you."

"Luca…?"

"My parents don't want me around either." He shrugged, pressing his lips together to stop their trembling. "I'm just a problem for them. I need to get my shite together, grow up, and get out of their hair. I'll get out of yours, too."

"They don't think that way." And then that slow-burn warmth as there, and Imre's hand enveloped Luca's shoulder. "And I don't, either. I am sorry, Luca. I'm sorry I made you feel like I was avoiding you."

Luca looked up into grave eyes darkened to near-midnight by…he didn't know. Chagrin. Sorrow. Regret. "Then why do you act like that?"

"It's…complicated." Imre squeezed Luca's shoulder gently, then let go. “Let’s say I’m trying to be a good host.”

“Don’t.” Luca caught that hand before it could go far. Even wrapping it in both his own, he couldn’t completely cover Imre’s thick, massive fingers, but he still tried—pulling Imre’s hand to his chest, holding it over his fast-beating heart, silently begging Imre to *feel* it. “All my good memories, the ones that feel real, are here,” he whispered. “I don’t want to feel like a guest here. Please.”

Imre stared down at him, gaze fixed on their hands, unreadable beneath the gnarled twist of his brows. Slowly he spread his hand underneath Luca’s—until his fingers splayed on his chest, his palm pressed flat, a brand scorching through Luca’s shirt to imprint on his flesh, spanning nearly from shoulder. The heat in that hand burned the breath from his lungs, like trying to breathe near the mouth of an active volcano.

And still…still he leaned into it, because it was Imre’s touch.

“I’ll try,” Imre whispered, then pulled his hand away.

Luca fought himself not to lean after him. The back of his throat drew tight, and he had to look away and take several deep breaths. He didn’t know what he’d expected. *I’ll try* was something, and it was all he could really ask for.

“Luca,” Imre said.

“Yeah?”

“Would you…” Imre faltered, then grunted under his breath before starting again. “Would you like to make a bonfire and cook outside tomorrow night? The first big frost will come soon, and after that it’ll be too cold. Could be our last chance.”

Luca stole a glance at him, but Imre was looking up at the rafters again almost too studiously, and Luca couldn’t help a faint smile. That big fucking oversized dork.

He was *trying*.

"I'd like that," Luca murmured. "Can we roast hot dogs?"

Imre snorted. "Did you see hot dogs in the icebox?"

"Town's only ten minutes out! Can't we go have a shop?"

"No hot dogs," Imre retorted firmly. "I'll show you something better. If you'll be patient, I'll even let you have beer."

"'Let' me." Luca wrinkled his nose. "I'm of legal age to drink, you know."

"It's my brew. I don't let just anyone taste it." Imre paused, then added almost under his breath, "…primarily because I'm not quite certain it's not shite yet."

Rolling his eyes, Luca slumped against the stalls at Imre's side again. "I'm honoured to be your guinea pig."

"I prefer lab rat. Better results from sample groups."

"…you're kind of a dick, Imre."

"I know," Imre answered simply, and Luca laughed.

"You're also kind of ridiculous."

Imre blinked. "Am I?"

"Yeah."

Yeah, you are, Luca thought fondly, and leaned over to rest lightly against Imre's side. And when he laid his head to Imre's shoulder, Imre didn't pull away, and Luca closed his eyes and let himself *wish*, just for this breath and this moment and this now.

"Yeah," he repeated softly, and curled his fingers against the thick curve of Imre's bicep. "And it's kind of a good thing."

26

THIS, IMRE THOUGHT, WAS WHAT Mira had meant by *be careful.*

In the flicker of living room hearthlight, Luca was all ivory, amber, and shadow, the orange flame-glow turning his eyes into the green-gold of evening fireflies. He sprawled on his back on the chevron-patterned rug before the fireplace, sandwiched between the quietly dozing heaps of Vila on one side and Seti on the other. He'd changed into his pyjamas after a soak in the downstairs bath and before the quick pasta Alfredo dinner Imre had thrown together, and now Luca's oversized shirt rucked up above the waist of his loose boxers, baring a pale crescent of his flat stomach, as he held his phone over his head in both hands and scowled up at it.

Imre had tucked himself in one of the deep, plush rockers flanking the leather-upholstered sofa, his thumb holding *Shardik* open at the spot he'd left off, but he'd not read a single line for watching Luca over the tops of the pages and past the rims of his reading glasses.

He'd wanted to set down proper boundaries between them. But his proper boundaries had left Luca hurting and raw, looking up at him with pleading eyes and pressing Imre's hand over the fascinatingly frantic beat of his heart and begging *please, please, don't push me away.*

Yet keeping Luca close posed a problem of an entirely different nature, one that left Imre struggling, caught at a crossroads where every path led to ruin. How was he to protect that sweet, fragile, vulnerable heart when every choice he made could destroy what tattered bits of trust Luca had left in him?

Luca's phone pinged. Luca answered with a disgusted sound and let the phone drop to his chest, then sprawled his arms over his head and glared into the hearth.

"Dad says hullo. Sends his love."

"Ah?" Imre arched a brow and set the book down against his thighs. "Is that all he said?"

"No."

"Want to talk about it?"

"*No,*" Luca retorted firmly, then turned those snapping green eyes on him. "What are you reading?"

Imre lifted the paperback enough to show the cover, with its haunting bear mask framed in a ring of claws. "*Shardik.*"

Luca pushed himself up on one arm, catching his phone as it tumbled down his chest, and squinted at the book. "By that bloke who wrote *Watership Down?*"

"Ah. You remembered."

"…yeah." Luca fidgeted, his toes moving against his athletic socks, before he levered to his feet, wobbling a little before catching himself and peeling from between the drowsing dogs. "Wait here."

Then he was gone, pattering from the living room, out into the foyer. Soft retreating steps on the stairs, the creak of the fifth step, and then that slight weight making the quietest of thumps overhead. Imre arched a brow and tilted his head back to look up at the ceiling with a touch of amusement, following Luca's path to his room by racing footsteps that passed overhead and then back again, before they were back on the stairs and past the creaking, groaning step and slipping back into the living room.

He spilled into the firelight glow breathlessly, then stopped, a book clutched shyly to his chest. Its cover was worn and tattered, thick stock in simple pale brown stamped with a lithograph print of two rabbits among winding foliage. Imre blinked, then chuckled, sinking deeper in the chair with a strange pleasure melting through him.

"You kept it," he said.

"You gave it to me," Luca whispered, as if that was explanation enough, and held the book as tightly as if it were his most prized possession.

"Did you ever read it?"

"Over and over." Luca opened the dog-eared cover with a delicate, reverent touch, his fingers graceful as they turned the pages; his eyes lidded as he traced his fingertips down the lines. "Dandelion's my favourite. I like storytellers."

"Would you like me to tell you a story, angyalka?" Imre closed *Shardik* and set it aside on the glossy oak end table, and stretched out a hand for Luca's book. "Or read you one."

"Ah?" Luca's brows rose, before he broke into a brilliant smile and skittered closer to drop *Watership Down* into Imre's palm. "Yeah. Yeah, I'd like that a lot."

Luca reclaimed his place on the floor with the dogs, dragging a quilt off the sofa with him and nestling himself down into a bundle of pup and bright-patterned yarn and pale skin. Imre cradled the book in his palms and carefully folded the front cover open with his thumb. The pages and cover had that soft feeling, almost like matted felt, the texture of a book that had been handled many, many times; when he'd given it to Luca it had been nearly new, taken from his own shelf and given to the boy as a parting gift on the last miserable day of an otherwise contented, idyllic summer that Imre hadn't known, at the time, would be the last summer his house would be full of Wards, with

Luca always underfoot and Marco turning brown digging irrigation ditches under the sun and Lucia sneezing over combing and trimming the goats' pelts but refusing to give up the task to someone else.

The very last time he'd seen Luca, Imre had given him this book, he realized—a whim, because Luca had read it over and over on nights just like this one, the fireplace warm and crackling and the living room cosy and quiet. Imre traced the lines of his own handwriting on the inside cover, the ink still dark.

With love, my angyalka, the inscription read, and a pang struck his heart and stilled the breaths in his lungs. *Imre.*

Be careful, Mira whispered in counterpoint.

"The primroses were over," Luca prompted, leaning toward him with his eyes bright, that pale, catlike face so open, so eager, and suddenly Imre didn't understand at all.

Didn't understand if he should be careful of Luca's heart or his own, when those clear, guileless green eyes were so tangled up in his thoughts he could hardly lower his gaze to the first chapter.

"Ah," he agreed, took a deep breath, and began. "The primroses were over," he read.

The primroses were over—and it would be a long, long winter with Luca always at hand, but ever out of reach.

27

AND WHEN LUCA FELL ASLEEP by chapter six, tangled among Vila and Seti like a puppy himself, Imre wrestled with himself for over an hour as he watched how golden light played over the soft contour of Luca's cheek and fell lovingly over the long, smooth stretch of his neck, gathering like liquid amber in the hollow of his throat. The fire's flicker glided down slender, coltish legs, gilding their graceful curves and angles, and Imre followed the trickle of light over the slim twist of narrow hips, the arcs of thin shoulders inside the folds of the shirt, the articulation of long, soft fingers half-buried in Seti's pale pelt. Luca had pillowed his head on Vila's flank, and his hair blended in with her dark fur in an iridescent shine.

In his sleep, he breathed through parted raspberry lips, and it was in those lips that the firelight gathered like pools of ambrosia, waiting to be tasted, sipped, taken of in deep and thirsty draughts. Imre tore his gaze away, clenching his jaw.

He'd told himself no, and he'd meant it. Perhaps Luca was a man now, for all that he had his mother's youthful, girlish prettiness paired with his father's lissom build.

But man or not, he wasn't the man for Imre.

Imre was probably, to Luca, still *Unka Immie*, not a man, not a human with aches and that deep lonely twist in the centre of his chest; not a person but an idea, an impression, a sense of *place* and protection and home. Someone Luca trusted to be safe, to be the shelter even his parents couldn't be right now. Even after the shock of years turning their meeting at the railway station into a first time all over again, Imre couldn't let himself forget what his place was, with Luca.

And he couldn't betray his trust that way.

But nor could he leave him as he was, right now. No matter the warm rugs scattered all about, a cold, hard stone floor was nowhere to sleep, especially after the beating Luca had taken today. Imre had given him a tin of ointment to mix with his bathwater to ease the soreness, but Luca would likely wake complaining of bruises in the morning—and a sore back, if Imre didn't get him up to his room.

He set the paperback aside and sank to one knee, gently shaking Luca's shoulder. "Luca," he whispered. "Wake up, angyalka. Just long enough to get to bed."

But Luca only moaned low in his throat, curling up and snuggling deeper into the dogs. Vila lifted her head with a low whine and nudged Luca's shoulder with her nose, then leaned her head against Imre's arm. He made low *shush-shush* sounds under his breath and stroked her flopping, tufted ears before leaning down to kiss the top of her shaggy head.

"Good girl," he whispered, then eased his arms underneath Luca, bundling him up in the quilt, and lifted him against his chest—then closed his eyes, breathing in raggedly as Luca immediately curled up and nestled against him, tucking himself into Imre as if he belonged right there in his arms.

God. Imre's heart had never felt so heavy, and yet his stomach was light enough, strange enough, to lift him to his feet with Luca cradled close. He made such a small bundle, his weight a delicate nothing that nonetheless printed every impression of his body against Imre's flesh.

He smelled like the pups, Imre thought, as he lingered on the firegold-dusted curve of his lashes, the way the impudent tip of his nose tucked into the crook of Imre's neck, warming his skin with his sighing, sleeping breaths. Like the pups, the lilac ointment from the bath, like *Luca*, some indefinable and yet painfully familiar thing subtly reminiscent of warm sweet beeswax—a scent that reached down inside Imre and found old and buried threads of memory and emotion, pulled them all out of shape, tangled and twisted and wove them into something new.

And that new thing hurt, with all the raw edges of something fresh-born and still jagged and sharp and unpolished enough to cut and abrade with every touch.

Imre swallowed back the thick knot of emotion in his throat and carried Luca up the stairs, curling protectively around him on the narrow flight and angling to keep from bumping his head, his feet. Upstairs, he elbowed the door to Luca's room open, and bent to lay him in his bed.

But as Imre moved to let him go, Luca twined one arm around his neck; the fingers of his other hand crept into Imre's beard, burying in deep and clinging with a soft, electrifying touch. Imre sucked in a sharp breath, his heart thudding.

"Imre," Luca murmured.

Still asleep the whole while, and completely unaware of what he was doing.

Imre closed his eyes, prayed for willpower, then gently clasped Luca's delicate wrists and tugged his hands free. Carefully, he laid Luca out on the bed and pulled the covers up over him. Luca tossed restlessly, then curled up on his side, burrowing into the pillow, one arm flung across the bed as if reaching for something, his fingers splayed into a white star against the dark blue sheets.

Imre splayed his own hand and pressed it palm-down to the

sheets, so that his fingertips just fit into the spaces between Luca's without quite touching.

Be careful, he warned himself, then rose, backed from the room, and eased the door closed until it latched without a sound. *Be careful.*

But it was getting harder and harder to listen.

28

LUCA DIDN'T REMEMBER FALLING ASLEEP last night. He only remembered that Vila and Seti had smelled like clover, and Imre's voice had been low and sweet, melding with the crackle of firelight until the hypnotic sound had lulled Luca into a daze. He must have staggered up to bed; he was lucky he hadn't killed himself on the stairs.

Or broken something, considering how much everything *hurt*.

Wincing, he stretched onto his back and let his pummelled, bruised body sink into the mattress. He didn't want to think about what he must look like under his clothing, when hard-throbbing spots of pain pounded over every inch of him. Zsofia had worked him over but good, and he was probably going to walk bowlegged for the next few days.

He didn't remember life at Lohere being so *hard*.

Then again he'd been a little rugrat before, too small to do anything but get in everyone's way, and now and then tote something around to be marginally useful. He'd helped with picking apples, he remembered; Imre had lifted him up as if he'd been lighter than an apple blossom, and Luca had climbed into the highest branches and thrown the apples down into the bushel baskets. When they'd moved from tree to tree, Luca had perched on Imre's shoulder, his heels dangling down over his chest. He couldn't remember if Luca had been so tiny or Imre had been so broad that he could fit on one shoulder with room to spare, but he had a feeling it was a combination of both.

He couldn't help smiling, as he reached over his head to brush his fingers along the tiny bells hanging from the scarf above the headboard, creating a glissando of sound. As his arm fell, he ran his fingertips along the wilted crown of clover blossoms he'd left over the lamp; they were starting to brown, but as they wilted they let loose a thick, heady fragrance that mingled with the breath of cold morning seeping through the window pane. Luca closed his eyes and just let himself breathe that scent, soaking it in down to his bones.

He couldn't remember any time in the last ten years that he'd woken up smiling like this.

But he couldn't hear Imre or the dogs downstairs, and the light through the window was bright enough to tell him it was well past the time Imre normally rose. Luca pushed himself up on one elbow and swiped the touchpad on his laptop, waking the screen. His eyes widened.

8:17 AM?

Fuck.

He started to push up, then caught the blinking message notification in the browser window left open on his taskbar. He clicked over; he had over fifty notifications with comments and likes on his selfie with Imre, and new messages from Xav.

> ***Xavier.Laghari:*** *You tit*
> ***Xavier.Laghari:*** *You post that and disappear?*
> ***Xavier.Laghari:*** *He's so hot *I* might turn gay.*
> ***Xavier.Laghari:*** *I want details*
> ***Xavier.Laghari:*** *Like, now*

Luca closed the Messenger window with a laugh, and rolled out of bed. He'd answer later.

Right now, he just wanted to see Imre.

His laughter became a hiss as his spine twisted, and bruises throbbed up through every inch of his sore, screaming body. He felt like every muscle of his being had been pulled and stretched like taffy, then left to mould into the bed—and now it didn't want to move from the shape it had hardened in. But he dragged himself fully upright, bracing on the wall and uncranking himself until his back popped in a horrible, crunching sound, enough for him to straighten completely and hobble from the room, down the hall, down the stairs.

The kitchen was empty, though he could smell faint after-impressions of baking, something savoury with a touch of spice. A note waited on the kitchen table, written on yellow legal paper, its edges curling and its corner weighed down by the jar of green apples.

Let you sleep in today. Don't get used to it. Stretching and a shower will help the soreness. Breakfast is warming in the oven. Check on Gia and Merta, then meet me in the orchard.

Luca scanned Imre's scrolling, archaic handwriting with its graceful, slanting letters and flowing curl; his signature was just a tall, slashing loop of a calligraphic *I*. The pit of Luca's stomach tightened with a quiet sweetness. Imre might have pushed him hard yesterday, but he'd let him rest. And now…

Now, Imre was waiting for him.

He'd just have to work harder, get stronger, so that one day he'd be up with the dawn, and Imre would never have to wait for him again.

Luca grinned, set the note back on the table, and headed back upstairs to shower.

29

IMRE HAD FILLED OVER HALF a dozen bushel baskets with apples by the time he heard his name, called over the orchard with a laugh and seeming to break the midmorning light into bits of shattered crystal.

"Imre!"

He adjusted his position on the branch he straddled, plucking an Egremont from its twig and looking down through the boughs. Criss-crossed by a latticework of branches, Luca strolled down the rows, lanky and graceful in clinging jeans and a tight-fitting black turtleneck in warm, snug knit with three-quarter-length sleeves. He walked with a subtle limp he no doubt *thought* he was hiding. Imre bit back a grin.

Stubborn.

"Catch," he called, and tossed the apple in his hand downward.

Luca snapped his hands up to catch it, then stood blinking at the apple clutched between both palms as if wondering how it got there. His expression cleared, and he angled an impish look and one-sided smile up at Imre. "Morning." He polished the apple on his shirt, then took a pointed, rather deliberate bite, as fierce as a pup savaging a bone. Still smirking, he kicked a few steps closer to Imre's tree, tilting his head back to look up at him and swallowing. "You're going to break that branch."

"Not if I balance myself correctly."

Luca laughed. "Don't you think someone lighter should be up there?"

"Think you can handle it?" Imre braced a hand against the trunk and leaned over, looking down into those clear, laughing green eyes. "I thought you were afraid of heights."

"I am not! I never said that!"

With a chuckle, Imre swung himself down; the branch gave a threatening creak as it bowed, before snapping back up as Imre touched boots to ground and let go. A shower of leaves drifted down, and he shook them out of his hair. "But Zsofia's so very *tall*."

With a snort, Luca buried his teeth in the apple again, mumbling, "Anything's tall when you're falling off it."

"Best not fall, then."

Luca looked up at the tree. Back to Imre. Up at the tree. Back to Imre. Then tossed the apple, smiling so wide his eyes illuminated like breathless green fire, and stepped closer to Imre, a challenge lighting his face. "Going to lift me up?"

Not the original plan, Imre started to say, but then Luca was swaying closer and instinct brought Imre's hands up to catch him around the waist. Soft knit yielded under his fingertips as if sinking his fingers into equally soft flesh, and this time he couldn't mistake the slim flaring ridges of Luca's hip bones, the way his lower back started to curve outward just below the edges of Imre's palms. Luca tilted his head, his cheeks flushed with the cold. It had to be the cold, Imre told himself. Just as the cold was the reason why his chest felt tight, his breaths like razors.

"Hold on tight," he said, and lifted Luca up.

Luca laughed, clutching at Imre's arms, then letting go and reaching for the branches overhead. Agile as a cat, he pulled himself up, until slim thighs slid against Imre's palms, then Luca's calves, and then he was gone, climbing higher, spry and nimble as a sprite who tucked himself to sleep among the leaves and boughs each night in his moonlit bower, leaving Imre's empty palms tingling. Luca braced himself standing with his feet spread between the uppermost branches, then peered down at Imre through the leaves, hair falling across his face in a tangle.

"Just like we used to?" he called.

"Just so," Imre answered—then ducked as an apple came raining down, shooting toward the half-full basket and narrowly missing clocking him in the shoulder. "*Oy!*"

Luca's merry, delighted laughter answered. "I remember you being faster."

"I remember you being less of a brat."

"Then your memory's broken." Another apple sailed downward and dropped into the basket. "I have never not been a brat."

No, you haven't been, Imre thought fondly, a warmth in his chest that not even the early autumn chill could dispel. *Not once*.

They set to work, then—and for a few sweet minutes, it felt as though Luca had never left. As though the passing years had happened at Lohere, every apple harvest finding Luca a little taller, a little older, a little wiser, a little spryer…and Imre a little less alone. As if he'd not spent the last ten years doing this by himself, now and then hiring hands with time to spare from the nearby farms. As if he'd…

As if he'd not been left behind, time stopping at Lohere while the world moved on without him.

"Heads up," Luca called, just as he came swinging down to a thick, low-hanging branch.

Imre pulled from his thoughts and realized he was standing there, looking down at the rosy red-gold apple in his palm as if reading secrets in its subtly dappled skin. He looked up. The tree was completely denuded of all but leaves and a few shrivelled by-blows that would fall off on their own, soon—and one pretty young man, straddling a branch with his legs swinging, berry lips as ripe as the apples. Luca grinned.

"Which basket do I go in? Discards or keeps?"

Imre snorted, pitched the apple in the keep basket, and reached up for him. "Get down here."

Luca spilled forward without a moment's hesitation, and Imre was struck by the carefreeness of it: how easily Luca trusted that if he fell, Imre would be there to catch him. And catch him he did, snaring him around the waist once more, swinging his momentum about mid-fall and lifting him up to perch Luca on his shoulder. He weighed practically nothing, and Imre clamped one arm across his lap to keep him from flying away, while Luca laughed and leaned into him, Imre's head tucked into the cradle of his waist and hip, one slender hand reaching across to brace on Imre's opposite shoulder, so very warm through Imre's shirt. Luca's weight was a pleasant softness nestled against him, his honeyed scent flooding Imre's nostrils.

"Still too big," Luca teased.

"Big enough to handle you."

Luca let out a choked sound. "You really don't hear yourself when you talk, do you?"

Imre tilted his head enough to eye him sidelong. "There is nothing wrong with my hearing."

"Nevermind. You're hopeless." Luca grinned, then pointed toward the next tree. "Forward!"

Imre had started to step forward—but now he stopped, digging his heels in. "I am *not* Zsofia."

"…you're a lot easier to ride," Luca retorted, blinking with a wide-eyed innocence that did nothing to hide what an utter little *cat* he was. Imre growled.

"*Luca*."

"I didn't say anything!"

Yet that laughter made a liar of him. Laughter that Imre couldn't help but echo, even if it was hard to laugh when every ounce of willpower was caught in burying that brief flash of imagery, that moment's stray thought. The awareness of Luca's thighs pressed against his palm, and that hot, slight, graceful weight propped against him, tangled around him, leaning so very close.

Apples, he reminded himself, and stepped forward to the next tree, positioning himself underneath and giving Luca a boost up into the branches. *Apples*.

"Up you go," he said, holding fast until Luca pulled out of reach.

And told himself he wasn't disappointed, as that warmth escaped his fingertips and left him holding nothing but air and the promise of a very, very long day. Long week. Long months.

And Luca had only been here three days.

30

BY THE TIME THEY BROKE for lunch, Luca had worked most of the soreness out of his body, even if now and then he still felt the saddle bruises as Imre tossed him up onto another branch. His stomach leaped each time, a thrill like riding a roller coaster, and every moment of that thrill was Imre's thick, heavy hands on him and not a bit of it for the rush of gravity trying to pull him down when all he wanted was to fly.

Lunch was leftover steak, asparagus, and potatoes tossed together with lettuce and celery into a salad and served cold, before they were out in the orchard again. Teasing laughter had become easy silence long before, and Luca almost lost track of the time as he settled into the quiet, satisfying rhythm of working with Imre. Only when the sun kissed the edge of the land did they stop, piling bushels of apples into the hand barrow and wheeling them in before mounting up and heading out.

Today, Zsofia didn't throw him. And today, when Imre whistled his signals to the dogs, Luca followed as well, learning to recognize each command without thinking—and a glow of pride took root deep inside his chest when he cut off two straying nanny goats without having to be told, veering Zsofia to round them back up and bring them back in line with the herd. Imre didn't say anything.

But Luca liked to think the long look Imre gave him was tinted with approval, nonetheless.

Once the goats were in, the horses bedded down, the stables

swept, Gia and Merta fed—paste mixed with solid food now, and they stood on their own to crane their necks for their bottles—Luca headed for the shower…only for Imre to beat him inside with one of his low, rumbling chuckles, shutting the door in his face.

Luca laughed, staring at the door. "What in the actual fuck, Imre?"

"You take long showers," floated through the door. "Let me clean up first so I can set up the bonfire while you wash off."

"I don't like it when you're logical."

"I don't like it when I smell like sweat."

I do, Luca thought, and bit his lip on that secret thought. "Just let me know when you're done," he called, and retreated to his room to pick out something to wear.

Something to wear. Like this was a date. Luca plucked at his lower lip, settling on the edge of his bed with a jumper clutched against his chest. This wasn't a date, he reminded himself. Wasn't anything. It never could be. It didn't matter what he wore.

Imre wasn't looking.

Luca sighed and kicked his half-unpacked bag, then rose to start putting the rest of his things away in the chest at the foot of the bed. He was *here*, and he wasn't even unhappy about being here. He might as well settle in, instead of acting like he'd be leaving with the dawn.

Even if that urge to *run* was still there, though he didn't know quite what he was running from.

By the time he'd finished folding things away, the water in the shower had shut off. A light rap shook Luca's doorframe, before Imre's shadow beneath the door moved away and the sound of his bedroom door latching drifted down the hall. Luca lifted his head, staring at the door, then looked down at the pretty wraparound cardigan he'd been about to fold and put away, a translucent black knit with a cowl collar that he'd "borrowed" from his mother's closet years ago and never quite remembered to return.

Fuck it. Maybe Imre wasn't looking, but if Luca wanted to look nice he'd do it for himself.

He could already hear Imre downstairs, by the time Luca picked out a pair of soft-worn, ripped jeans in faded blue and shut himself into the bathroom. The entire room was still filled with steam, the scent of hot damp soap, and a certain after-impression of Imre that Luca breathed in and let curl in the pit of his stomach until his thighs drew taut and he felt strange, his mouth too soft, his throat too tight.

Standing naked beneath the spray, surrounded by clouds of billowing steam and taking that scent into himself, felt somehow sacrilegious. Luca closed his eyes, tilted his head back into the spray, and let the falling droplets strike his lips; trickles slipped past to tease over his tongue, metallic-tasting and hot, and he shivered, drawing the soap and flannel down his body, and told himself this trembling, yearning feeling that pricked all throughout his body wasn't *wrong.*

He stayed until the water ran cold, then dashed out, quivering and chilled, and scrubbed himself off with one of Imre's thick, fluffy cobalt blue towels. He dressed quickly, wrapping himself in the soft, clinging cardigan; its sleeves fell well past his wrists to nearly cover his hands, while its wide, foldover neck fell over his shoulders and bared his collarbones. He wondered if he should bring a thicker jacket. Or just…dress warmer. But as he stared at his reflection—his hair a wild damp mess of black, the cardigan wrapped in tight folds around his waist and hips, his jeans nearly painted on, his cheeks as red-flushed as his lips—his heart tightened oddly.

He looked *pretty.*

He could see his mother in himself, in the pointed tip of his nose and the taper of his chin and the translucence of his skin, and even if he was just fucking torturing himself right now he *wanted* to look pretty, wanted to feel like someone could want him even if it wasn't that big fucking lunk of an oblivious, clueless, blockheaded man.

He rubbed at the tightness in his throat, then shoved his feet into his boots, bunching the hems of his jeans to fit into the boots' high ankles, before heading downstairs.

The kitchen lights were dimmed down to just a few golden lamps, the house silent. Imre was gone, as were the dogs. Another note waited pinned underneath the jar of apples, this time written on a translucent scrap of wax paper.

Follow the light

Just that. Luca frowned, turning the bit of paper over, then tucked it into his pocket and stepped outside.

The night was clear and cool, the breeze just chilly enough to be pleasant against the warmth in his cheeks, the scents of night settling in, green and dark and soft. He understood what Imre meant by *follow the light* as Luca looked up at the tallest hill overlooking the house; atop that hill a beacon of golden firelight shone, flickering and leaping hot, throwing shimmering sprays of orange firefly-sparks up into the sky to dance with the stars amidst a spiral of smoke. Subtle, plucking notes of music wove across the night, the gentle thrum of vibrating guitar strings. That melody lured, melancholy and sweet and beckoning, whispering for him to follow the tugging pull in his heart and let himself be drawn along.

Luca scrubbed his palms against his thighs, then took a deep breath and strode to climb the hill.

With every step up the slope, the tantalizing scents of roasting meat grew stronger, joining with the smoky scent of burning wood.

That soft-strumming music was joined by a familiar voice, deep baritone humming low, weaving in and out of the delicately plucked notes, creating a mesmerizing blend that drew Luca closer, closer, until he crested the hill.

A massive bonfire blazed at the rounded peak, set in a shallow pit in the centre of a wide circle of earth that had been stripped and cleared of all grass. Skewers dug into the dirt at the very edge of the blaze and leaned in just enough to sear and crackle the cubes of meat, mushrooms, and other vegetables speared on their tips. Several large blankets had been layered atop each other to one side of the bonfire, the firelight flickering over patterns of radial zig-zag flowers and mandalas in deep maroons and blues; Vila and Seti sprawled on one side of the blankets, dozing at Imre's side. Just outside the circle of the fire's light, the blue roan gelding cropped idly at the grass, dark against deeper darkness, just another part of the night.

Imre sat on the blanket with his legs folded, his guitar cradled in his lap, the position drawing his battered, tattered jeans taut against tight-flexed thighs; his hair fell over his shoulders in damp waves and left dark spots on a clinging blue-grey henley as he bowed over the instrument and stroked its strings with such delicacy in those large fingers, coaxing haunting, mournful notes forth with an aching sweetness, blending them with the low lilt of his voice in Romani, words Luca couldn't understand but that called out with heartbreak and longing. Firelight cut facets in the darkness of Imre's eyes, making them glimmer against the stark, beautifully chiselled lines of a face transfixed in lost, quiet sorrow. In the stark shadows, the Indian heritage of the Rom shone in deeply burnished skin and softly beautiful lips and the sharp crest of Imre's nose, in the proud peaks of his cheekbones and the thickness of long, curling lashes blacker than the night could ever wish to be.

Luca's breaths hitched, and he stopped just at the crest of the hill; he couldn't seem to move, couldn't seem to do anything but watch Imre. Yet as Luca drifted to a halt, Imre trailed off, lifting his head, those notes silencing as long fingers stilled. Darkened blue eyes flicked over Luca, unreadable, pensive. Luca bit his lip and ventured closer.

"Please don't stop," he whispered. "It's beautiful."

"Lavotta Szerenad," Imre murmured, and fingered a few more soft notes, bowing his head once more. "The Lovotta Serenade. It was better on my father's violin."

"It's…it's lovely, but so heartbreaking."

"Most Roma music is," Imre answered softly.

Luca bit his lip, then settled onto the blanket, sitting on the far edge and drawing his legs up against his side; the fire's heat licked out at him in little tendrils, leaving him caught in the push-and-pull between the flame and the night's cool, brisk teeth. "What do the words mean?"

"I…" Imre hesitated, then smiled faintly, ruefully. "The song itself doesn't actually have proper words, though I've heard a Hungarian folk performer sing to it. I simply say what comes to mind when I play. I don't even remember half of what I say." A gentle, sensitive touch stroked along the neck of the guitar, toying with the frets, raising soft quivers of sound. "But I was thinking of palotáha and prekuidz. 'The day after tomorrow' and 'the day before yesterday.'" Blue eyes once more lifted to Luca, meeting his gaze, stealing his breath. "And how so much changes in the spaces in between."

Luca's heart skipped, a faltering note in the melody of the night. "Yeah?"

"Aye."

Something seemed to hover unspoken between those words, but

then Imre looked away, fixing his gaze on the fire. One hand fell from the guitar to stroke softly between Seti's ears, raising a low whine.

"Would you like to hear a real song, angyalka, rather than me making things up?"

"*Yes,*" Luca answered too quickly, then flushed, pulling himself back just as he'd started to lean forward. "I mean…I would. Yes. I'd like that."

Imre chuckled and transferred his grip back to the guitar, and strummed a few poignant preliminary notes. "This one is called 'Zöld az erdő, zöld a hegy is.' Would you like to hear it in Hungarian, or Romani?"

"Romani." Even if Imre's voice was lovely, entrancing no matter what language he spoke…there was something about the depth and timbre of it when he spoke Romani that cut deep into Luca's heart, and he'd missed it. He remembered, when he was a little boy, that Imre had spoken Romani often, whispering to his animals, murmuring to himself, even exchanging a few words with Luca and his parents when they could understand what they'd picked up from him, but…he'd hardly spoken more than a few phrases here and there, since Luca had arrived.

What had changed?

"Ah," was all Imre said, before trailing off. His fingers stilled on the strings, and he gazed into the fire silently for long moments.

Yet before Luca could ask what was wrong, Imre's hand struck the belly of the guitar lightly, fingertips tapping out a rhythm, setting time. He nodded his head in time, gaze focusing, and after a few more steady beats those clever, swift fingers twined deftly in the strings, calling forth notes in sweet, aching tangles, at once lively and lonely, melodious and melancholy, a fast-moving river of mourning pouring through swift twists and turns of song. And Imre's voice joined that song: baritone whispers that wrapped themselves around Luca's heart and pulled so hard he felt that rough-beating organ must leap out of his chest, so desperately did it want…*something*.

As if it would live inside Imre, flow past his lips on those lyrical notes in fluid Romani to take up inside his chest, paired side by side with the heart that gave rise to song so lovely and so strange that it made beautiful dark magic of the night.

That spell held Luca so intently, his breaths gathering in his chest and never letting loose, his blood following the tumbling spill of notes that painted a portrait of loss so deep it left him hollow. As if whatever Imre called out for was missing from inside Luca, and the only way to ease that emptiness was to share it, lessened somehow between them. And while Luca knew Imre didn't sing for him, never for him…

Still, he felt the quiet loneliness in that lilting baritone voice with every heavy, painful beat of his heart.

He was beginning to recognize at least the words of the refrain by the time those deft fingers slowed on the guitar strings, even if he couldn't understand the meaning. Imre's voice trailed off, dying into a breathless silence, as the last ringing note faded into the firelight. There was nothing but the silence, the sound of their breaths, and the wet glimmers lining Imre's eyes, clinging to his lashes in precious droplets. Luca caught a breath, pressing a hand to his chest, gripping tight to his shirt or he would reach out.

Reach out for Imre, and never let go.

"Imre…?" he whispered, and Imre came to life, the statue he'd become once more moving, breathing, a man of flesh and blood instead of ancient and sorrowing stone.

"It's nothing," Imre whispered, voice thick. Distant eyes focused on Luca, tearing into him with the raw pain reflected in those depths, before Imre looked away, dragging the backs of his knuckles against his eyes and taking a deep breath that heaved his shoulders. "My family settled in England many generations ago, but there is a long story of roving in our history. People make magic of the roaming ways of the Rom, but many times we left because we were chased away, driven out in our bare feet onto roads lined with nails." Imre curled his fingers against the guitar again, raising an echo of sound. "That is what the song is about. 'Na de mila pe romende.' *Don't let suffer more the feeble*." He pressed his lips together, head bowing, moonlit hair falling to shroud his face. "Some things carry with them ancestral pain, angyalka."

No—no, Luca couldn't sit here with this distance between them and that roughness in Imre's voice and this pain scouring the inner walls of his heart. He shifted across the blanket, slipping over to settle next to Imre—hip to hip, knee to knee, and he leaned over, resting his shoulder against Imre's. He didn't know what to do. How to ease that ache. And so he only tried to *be* there, to tell Imre…to tell him…

"I'm sorry," he choked out thickly.

"It is not your fault," Imre said—but after a moment he leaned back, subtle but *there*, that massive weight seeming to push Luca steady. "We hold. And we stay. As we say among the Rom, we are many stars scattered in the sight of God."

Luca didn't know what to say.

And so they held, and they stayed—together, as the fire burned and the sparks reached up for the stars.

31

NOT UNTIL THE ROASTING MEAT began to smell of char did they pull apart; Imre laid his guitar to one side and leaned forward to turn the skewers, while Luca rubbed at his arms and tried not to feel the chill in the wake of Imre's warmth. He still ached inside, but something about sitting in the quiet together had eased it, somewhat. He'd thought Imre would pull away from him, put distance between them.

It almost hurt more that he hadn't.

Imre finished with the skewers, then sat back, leaning on one brawny arm; with the other he tugged a covered basket closer. "The food is almost ready. Would you like a drink?"

Luca hesitated, then nodded. "Sure."

Imre flipped the basket open. The interior was lined with ice, and inside sat a covered pitcher of frothy amber liquid. He retrieved two mason jar mugs from another basket, scooped a few cubes of ice into each, then carefully poured each full, stopping just short of the building, frothy head foaming over. With an arched eyebrow, he offered a mug to Luca.

"Take it slow on an empty stomach."

Luca tilted his head curiously, then curled both hands around the mug; cold condensation chilled his palms. He took a careful sip; the loamy, bitter taste of beer flowed over his tongue, countered by a tart sweetness and popping into a lovely fizz. He blinked, then took another, deeper sip, savouring it and letting it roll around his mouth before swallowing. “What kind of beer is this?”

“Apple beer.”

“Like cider?”

Imre chuckled and took a sip from his own mug, speckling his beard with foam in light little spatters along his upper lip. “Not quite. It’s just…beer. With apples.”

“It’s sweet. Fizzy. I like it.”

“Perhaps I am not such a terrible brewer as I thought.”

“Nah.” Luca couldn’t resist: he reached over and wiped the foam from above Imre’s upper lip, the prickles of his beard scratching against Luca’s thumb. “Not that bad at all.”

Luca’s thumb grazed Imre’s upper lip, its delineation so stark that it cut like a crease of paper against his skin, heated pressure and an almost velvety texture that clenched him up in so many delicious knots. Imre stilled, his lips parting. Storms clouded his eyes, crackling with a dark-lit, intense charge as he watched Luca in silence. Luca froze. He couldn’t breathe; not when Imre’s mouth was so hot under his touch, his breaths washing over Luca’s skin, the silence between them sparking. If he dared, he could just…oh, *God…*

Imre pulled back sharply, tossing his head to clear his hair from his face, turning away before Luca could catch more than a glimpse of an unreadable expression. Hurt shattered that breathless moment into pieces and scattered them across the dirt, until Imre spoke.

“Dinner’s burning.”

He was already rolling forward onto his knees, beer wedged in the dirt, and catching the skewers to pull them back out of the fire. Luca stared at him dully. Right…dinner. Imre had pulled away because…dinner.

And because Luca shouldn’t be touching him that way.

He swallowed back his disappointment, marshalled a smile,

nestled his mug in the blankets, and shifted to his knees to dig in the basket. Plates and utensils were stacked inside, separated and cushioned by cloth napkins. “Here,” he said, setting the plates out on the blanket in easy reach. Imre reached for a fork, and Luca intercepted, putting it in his hand before sinking back on his heels to watch as Imre quickly raked the sizzling meat and vegetables off the sticks, arranging them on the plates. When he was done, he tossed the skewers in the fire, then dropped back into his seat and nudged one of the plates toward Luca.

“Shouldn’t be too burnt. Char just adds flavour. Give it a try.”

Luca reclaimed his place at Imre’s side, but with the plates and their drinks between them like a boundary line reminding him not to cross. He bit his lip, then picked up a cube of brown-seared, dripping meat with his fingertips; the heat soaked into his skin, threatening to burn, before he popped it into his mouth and let that warmth melt over his tongue as he bit down into meat seared succulent enough to practically dissolve. Sweet-savoury flavour burst in his mouth, rich and almost luscious, and he let out a low moan as he chewed and swallowed, closing his eyes and taking his time to absorb every bit before it went down.

“What is this?”

“Venison steak tips marinated in sweetened Worcestershire sauce and berry ale.”

Luca started to lick the sauce and flecks of char from his fingertips—then froze. “I’m eating Bambi?”

Imre let out a short, rough laugh and picked up a bite of his own. “You’re eating a buck the foxes brought down but couldn’t finish off. He’d have starved to death slowly if I’d not put him down.”

Eyeing him, Luca snorted and reached for another bite, picking up a glistening, toasted mushroom cap. “You don’t like killing anything, do you?"

"Not unless it's the most merciful solution. If not for grocery stores, I'd likely be a vegetarian."

"You're so odd, Imre."

Imre tilted his head, watching Luca through the curtain of his hair. "How so?"

"You're this big hulking sulking brute, but you've got sensitive hands and sensitive eyes and you're really this gentle giant who won't kill meat animals and nurses sick goats."

With a dry look, Imre shifted to stretch out, lying back with his bulk propped on his elbows, long legs stretched out; his body twisted in a powerful pull of sinew as he reached over himself to snag another bite from his plate. "I can't tell if that was a compliment or not."

"It was." Luca looked down at his hands, plucking at the mushroom. Just as quickly as the rich scents and flavours had roused his appetite…it soured, curdling in his stomach. "You make me feel safe." He swallowed. "Not many things do that anymore."

An odd stillness settled over Imre. "Has someone been making you feel unsafe at home?"

"Not unsafe that way, just…" Luca shook his head. "Not on steady footing."

"Luca…? What's the matter?"

Fuck. Luca bit back a frustrated sound, closing his eyes. He hadn't wanted to put this on Imre, not when he was already enough of a burden. He'd be upset. Luca's parents were his *friends*, and he was dealing with Luca as a favour. The rest of this…it wasn't Imre's problem. And maybe it was the beer, but Luca suddenly wanted to cry—just burst out crying, burrow against Imre and beg him to be safe always when nothing else was. Everything else changed, fell apart, turned sour and awful, but Imre…Imre never changed.

Imre was Imre, solid and faithful and immovable as the foundations of the earth.

"They're…" Luca choked, then breathed in and tried again. "They're getting divorced. Mum and Dad."

Imre's inhaled breath said everything, followed by a measured silence. Then, "I'm sorry," he said gently. "I didn't know."

"They've wanted to for a long time. The only reason they didn't is me." Luca opened his eyes, staring at the fire until it burned its image into his retinas, and smiled bitterly. "So that feels fucking great. I've been making my parents miserable way longer than I actually intended to."

"I don't think it's like that, angyalka."

"*Isn't* it, though?" He dropped the unappetizing bit of food back on his plate, then just let himself fall back, sprawling on the blanket, staring up at the sky. "They were going to get divorced as soon as I turned eighteen. I'd known since maybe…I don't know, I think I was eight or nine when I overheard them fighting, then talking things out like they were already negotiating with barristers at the table. We hadn't even moved to Sheffield yet and they were planning ten years in the future, counting down every day until they were free of me and free of each other. And I…" The stars overhead, a wheeling galaxy so bright it turned the sky purple and crimson, blurred into a mess of colours and lights. "I got scared. I got so scared, even more the closer I got to eighteen, and I guess…I started doing daft stuff and it made them scared, too. Scared enough to stay together to try to solve the problem of Luca."

He sniffled, dashed at his eyes. He was struggling not to break down in front of Imre when Imre was so *strong*, but he'd been holding this inside himself for so long, an ugly truth he'd never even told Xav, refused to even look at head-on because that just made it even more real and even more terrifying.

"If they solve me," he said, "if I do everything I'm supposed to do and live the way they want me to live, my family will fall apart. And I know I'm not supposed to care, because I'm an adult now and it's off to uni and then a life of my own, and their life isn't my life anymore, but…" He smiled, but it was just this stretching grimace that made his lips tremble. "I care. They're my mum and dad. My whole life they've been my mum and dad, but being my mum and dad has been making them miserable, and I'm selfish because I still don't want them to stop."

"I'm sorry, Luca. I…I never imagined. They kept up a very convincing act."

There came the sound of plates hissing against the blankets, then clanking—and then Imre's silhouette blocked the firelight, leaning over Luca, his warmth falling around him in a cloak, hotter than the radiant waves from the bonfire. Imre propped himself up with one arm reaching over Luca, hand braced to the blanket, caging him with Imre hovering over him. Silvered hair tumbled down in waves, brushing against Luca's cheek, throat, and shoulder like spidersilk and starlight, little lifelines drawing him up and up and into those warm, sorrowful blue eyes, the creases around them speaking a wealth of silent emotion.

"But you're no one's problem," Imre murmured. "You don't need to be solved, angyalka."

"Don't I?" Swallowing thickly, he looked up into Imre's eyes. "It was easier when we moved away, and you didn't see us anymore. They don't hate each other, or anything. I think they're even friends. They just…want different things. And I guess they realized after me how incompatible they are. They live in the house but have wholly separate lives, and still think I don't notice."

"That happens that way, sometimes. It's regrettable, but some relationships just don't work. It's not that one person or the other was wrong; just that they were wrong for each other."

Luca's lips trembled. His eyes welled again, no matter how he tried to stop them. "But why did it have to be my parents?"

"Because even parents make bad decisions, sometimes." Imre's fingertips softly grazed just beneath one of Luca's eyes, brushing away tears, calluses so gentle despite their roughness. "But I think they would agree you were the best decision they ever made together, no matter their other mistakes."

Don't do this, Luca thought, staring up at Imre with those large hands on his skin and the bulk of Imre taking up his world, blurred through the prisms of his tears and yet so familiar Luca would know every aching shape of him in the darkest of nights. *Don't be so gentle with me, don't make me love you like this, don't do this at all…*

"Then they can't really yell at me for mine," he straggled out weakly. "I…I guess growing up is making bad decisions and owning it, instead of ducking it."

"Something like that." Imre smiled slightly, knuckles tracing tingling lines against Luca's skin as he brushed his hair back from his brow. "But it will be all right, Luca."

He couldn't stand it. That touch, that warmth, so close yet so far away when everything Luca wanted to ease this awful pain eating away inside him was completely out of reach.

With a hitching breath, he twisted away, ducking out from underneath Imre and sitting up, reaching desperately for his beer and cradling it in both hands. He pressed his mouth against the rim of the mug, staring into the fire, holding his entire body tense to the point of pain because if he didn't, he would tremble. Imre was slow motion in his peripheral vision, silently rolling back onto his back, then shifting to sit up. Those blue eyes touched him, questioning him with their heavy weight, but he wouldn't look. He took a gulp of his beer, the liquid sloshing against the glass and against his lips, and closed his eyes, swallowing it down and letting the slow, pleasant burn work down his throat and through his flesh until it eased the awfulness inside him into something he could live with.

"You know what really bothers me?" he whispered.

"Hm?"

"There's this silly part of me, this completely daft and childish part of me, that wants to believe in fairy tale love. In that kind of love that just...*consumes* everything, and becomes such a part of your life that you can't live without it. You make them better and they make you better, and you lift each other up until you can do anything together. And even when you fight, you never stop loving each other, and you always find a way." He muffled a miserable sound against the rim of the mug and closed his eyes. As long as his eyes were closed he wasn't crying, wasn't fucking streaming fat wet tears down to plop and splash into his beer, wasn't breaking inside, struggling to speak. "I...I used to think marriage fixed everything and made you love each other forever. Like those wedding rings were some kind of fucking magic talisman. But it's hard to believe in that when the two people I need to love each other most are falling apart right in front of my eyes."

"Their love doesn't have to make you stop believing, angyalka," Imre rumbled. A light touch brushed Luca's shoulder, then firmed, curling, stroking, soothing and rhythmic. "Nor does love have to be about marriage, or even about anything romantic. Lasting love of any kind needs neither a priest nor a ring to endure."

Luca lifted his head, once more meeting Imre's eyes. God, for such a granite slab of a man he had so much trouble masking his emotions, and he watched Luca with such concern that for a moment Luca could almost believe Imre could ever love him.

"No?" Luca whispered, and Imre smiled gently.

"No."

Somehow, it didn't make him feel any better. He was such a fucking mess, and trying so hard not to fall apart all over Imre, trying to get his head on straight and stop being a nit when Imre had made dinner and built this bonfire and it was supposed to be a nice night. Luca braced himself with another sip of his beer, breathing in deeply, squaring his shoulders.

"I…I should tell them I know."

"Why?"

"So they can stop this," Luca answered; the words were more bitter than the aftertaste of beer on his tongue. "Maybe out there is a life that'll make them happy. I should stop making them hold on to this life. Go have my own life, let them find theirs. They'll still be my parents." He sighed, shrugging. "Just…parents on different paths. I want them to be happy, so…that's the right thing to do, isn't it?'

"If it feels right to you, then it is." Imre's hand fell away, and he once more leaned back on his elbows, staring into the fire. "Another part of growing up is letting go of those codependent familial bonds…but part of being family is never letting those bonds completely die." Imre trailed off with a thoughtful sound, then continued, "As we grow, relationships change. We become more of one thing, less of another to the people we love—and they become more of one thing, less of another to us. With parents, with siblings…it's easy to think of them as extensions of yourself. But then suddenly you grow up and you're at odds with them and they're at odds with you, and you have to see each other as separate people for the first time." He chuckled softly. "It feels like cutting a piece of yourself out, a chunk of your body and soul, and looking at this alien organ, trying to imagine it had once been inside you." He shifted his leg enough to bump his thigh against Luca's in a little nudge. "That's terrifying, angyalka. It's all right to be afraid of that. It's part of what's most frightening about adulthood."

"I feel like if I were really an adult, I'd already have moved out on my own. I wouldn't be so dependent on them that I have no choice but to let them push me back and forth between them."

"It's possible to be an adult in some things from a very young age, and never grow up about others for the rest of your life. Everyone takes a different path."

"But I can't make my path forging down the middle between them, can I?" He bit his lip. "If they're two halves of a beating heart, I'm the thread that stitched them together. There's something poetic in that, but…" He shook his head, shifting to lean on one hand. "Thread's just thread. It's not a thing on its own. It's just a tool to make other things."

Then it came: warmth, covering his hand. The roughness of a callused palm over his knuckles. He lifted his head sharply, chest tight. Imre still looked into the fire, that beautiful face serene and thoughtful, but his hand rested over Luca's, linking them in a moment of quiet comfort.

"There is that, as well," Imre murmured.

Luca flushed, averting his eyes, or he would fall apart. He lifted the hand holding his beer so he could scrub his sleeve against his eyes, then laughed shakily. "This is some really, *really* strong beer."

"It rather is." Imre chuckled, but didn't move that hand. That hand that held Luca to earth, that seemed to whisper an unspoken reminder that even if it wasn't the kind of love he craved, he was still…still *loved*, and that love mattered, too. "I'm still working out a few kinks in the brewing process."

"I like it. Should bottle it and call it Two Sips."

"Two Sips?"

"Because that's how much it takes to get you drunk."

Imre laughed—one of those rare rough, roaring laughs, brief yet so wholehearted that he threw his head back with it in a shower of steel and silver and iron hair, white teeth flashing. Then he retrieved his own mug, lifting it and extending it to Luca.

"To Two Sips apple beer."

Luca clinked his mug to Imre's, beer sloshing. "To Two Sips," he said, and tossed back the rest of his drink.

To us, he thought as he swallowed the fizzy, sweet-sour brew. *To wishes and wantings that can never come true.*

But never in a lifetime would he dare to say that aloud.

32

IMRE ALMOST HADN'T RECOGNIZED LUCA, when he'd come up the hill to the bonfire. Even though he was always a pretty thing, there was something different about him tonight; he wore a black cardigan that wrapped in elegant layers around his slim frame, his bare shoulders peeking impudently past the cardigan's wide collar, whitecaps frothing a dark sea. With his hair still damp and messy, his eyes wide and uncertain, the bonfire's blazing light falling over him in a sheet of gold, he looked so delicate the wind might well blow him away, send him flying like a dandelion clock, dancing on the wind.

For a moment, Imre had wondered how it might feel to dance with Luca, spinning him about until he laughed.

Then he'd bowed over his guitar, and told himself as long as he kept his hands on the instrument, he'd keep them off the boy.

Yet it was hard. So fucking hard, when Luca was so fucking hurt, and when Imre didn't know the words sometimes the only way he knew how to comfort was with touch, with closeness. Everything made sense, now. The abrupt move to Sheffield. The shroud of hurt Luca wore around him, dulling that brightness. The strangeness of Marco just banishing him to the fields. Imre still didn't know what to do with the information; in uni Marco and Lucia had been inseparable. He'd never seen two people more in love, and in those younger days he'd secretly been envious of them. He'd never had anyone look at him the way Marco and Lucia looked at each other: as if the world had fallen away, and there was nothing left but galaxies swirling around them as they lost themselves in each other.

He'd thought their relationship was fine. That everything was all right.

Maybe he'd been as much of a naïve idealist as Luca.

He lingered over that, as they ate in companionable silence. Wondering. He'd long accepted he would likely spend his life alone, but he'd at least had the comfort of knowing his friends had…something. Someone. Yet when all they had to bind each other was Luca, and the weight of that was wearing Luca thin and tearing him to pieces…

Imre didn't know what to do with that. How to fix it, when he couldn't.

And so he only let Luca have a silence he seemed to need, and kept that soft, slim hand clasped under his own, a reminder that if Luca needed to talk more, Imre would listen.

But even when their plates were clean, Luca remained silent. Imre watched him sidelong; the boy looked so *lost*, pensive, as though he'd come apart at the seams and some vital part of him, some *weight* of him, had slipped out and away and left him empty and searching for it. Imre bit the inside of his cheek, but told himself to hold his tongue. Wait him out.

Nothing would come of pushing Luca before he was ready, no matter how desperately Imre wanted to ease that look on his face.

And so he watched the fire, shifting only to accommodate Vila when she laid her head across his lap. There was a peace in this that he hadn't felt for some time—and he settled into the silence, no longer counting the minutes until a sensible farm owner would be in bed and not riding high on the sweet drifting buzz of apple beer, watching a bonfire crackle with the most beautiful boy he'd ever seen resting at his side.

"Imre?" Luca murmured.

Imre pulled from his reverie, glancing at him. Luca was still watching the fire, his eyes half-lidded, their green slightly glassy; he toyed and plucked at his lower lip, plumping it to fullness.

"Hm?"

"Why didn't you ever…?"

"Ever…?"

"You know. Meet someone. Settle down." Luca shrugged one shoulder. "You can't be the only gay British Hungarian Romani goat farmer in the world. There's someone like you out there, isn't there? Someone right for you."

Imre arched a brow; his heart laboured roughly, pulsing into a sharp pang. "You assume I'd only be attracted to someone just like me."

"No, I…" Luca bowed his head, cheeks flushing. "I don't know. I don't know what I'm asking."

"Mm. To answer what you did ask…" Imre exhaled heavily, lowering his gaze, watching Vila and tangling his fingers into her ruff. She let out a soft, pleased whine and leaned into him. "It's not so easy, for me. I can't…separate sex from love. It's not how I'm wired." He paused, struggling for the words to explain. "I've heard it called demisexual lately, but I suppose before we had those definitions some would just call it being an old romantic. I only know it means that I can't be with someone, can't touch them or anything more, unless I at least believe I could truly love them."

And yet here he was with his hand curled over Luca's, and the memory of that long, lithe body pressed against him, until even now his body remembered the print of Luca's flesh and lean frame.

No.

He took a deep breath, continuing, "Most of the men I meet base initial attraction on physical interest, and want physical chemistry before emotional intimacy. My…particular ways…often don't suit them very well; nor do their needs suit me. It's a certain incompatibility of being, I suppose. Sometimes I envy them the freedom to simply follow their desires."

"That sounds lonely," Luca said softly.

"It has the potential to be." More than potential, if Imre were honest with himself. If he really wanted to look, there were ways to find other men like him. Websites, apps, simply dating about. But he'd never wanted that; he didn't know *what* he wanted, but something was settling inside him, a quiet ache that said he'd find it if he just looked at it head on. "But I have many other loves in my life. I am alone, but not lonely."

Luca's warmth shifted closer. "You're not alone right now, either."

Imre lifted his head, and found wide eyes watching him. Watching him as though there was no world but Imre; watching him as though there was nothing between them but the stars above and the slow sweet air of their breaths. Imre thought he'd known loneliness before, but that *pain* struck hard, struck deep, as he stared into eyes the clear green of a translucent spring brook and lingered on parted berry lips that seemed to offer everything he could never have.

He could hardly breathe, each inhalation a rough thing inside his chest. He tore his gaze away, fixing on the fire, the heat, the night, anything but Luca.

"It's good to have company on the farm again," he forced out, trying to keep his voice level.

Luca's hand curled beneath his—slowly, forming a fist.

Then slipped away, leaving only cloth warmed by their joined body heat and nothing else.

“Yeah,” Luca said listlessly, into a silence Imre was afraid to fill. “I guess it would be.”

33

HE DIDN'T HAVE TO WORRY about the silence for long. Luca had drained his second mug of beer in minutes, almost desperately. Imre had pondered stopping him, but right now the last thing Luca seemed to need was someone questioning his decisions, his autonomy.

So he only let Luca do as he wished, then gently pried the empty mug from his lax fingers as Luca's eyelids began to droop, his body slouching forward. When he fell onto his back, one arm stretched over his head and his slender fingers curled, Imre caught himself lingering on the sleek flow of his body, the perfect carelessness of his sprawl, the way his hair spilled over his fingers like ink splashed over white paper.

Then Imre looked away, and made himself think of anything but how Luca had looked during those few moments he'd stretched beneath Imre and looked up at him with those pale eyes so vulnerable, so sweet.

When he glanced back, Luca was asleep.

And while Luca slept, Imre let himself look: let himself linger on the pale delicate lines of his face, on the way his lips parted on slow sighing breaths, on the graceful taper of his body and the narrow lines of his hips and the subtle parting of his bent thighs. He was in so many ways a stranger to Imre now; the boy he had been, that child who'd followed Imre everywhere, wasn't in this young man who moved as though his body were made of music and laughter, who carried his hurts inside as if they were jewels to be hoarded, small and shining things that belonged to him and only him. Only now was Imre beginning to understand just how much Luca had closed off, walled away inside himself, now that he understood what had happened at home.

No matter that Marco and Lucia had sent him off like a recalcitrant child, Luca was more a man than Imre thought anyone realized, and had been carrying a responsibility no one should have to bear for far too long, struggling to support it with those slim shoulders while no one held him up at all.

And yet when he looked at Imre, it was as though something was struggling to break past, something that begged for someone, anyone to just…

Let him be small, for a few moments. Let him stop pretending that he could handle everything, when those tears that even now left his lashes dried into curling, pretty spikes had said he very much couldn't.

That urge, that ache, that *need* to protect him, to shelter him, rose strong in Imre once more, so overpowering he almost couldn't breathe with it. He caught himself reaching for Luca, his body moving of its own volition—and stopped, with his fingers hovering just above those parted lips. It would be so easy to touch them, to feel their softness and their warmth, in this one stolen moment where there was no one to see, to judge.

God. No. No. If he did, he wouldn't be able to live with himself. Luca was asleep. *Defenceless*. It wouldn't be right.

As if it could ever be right were he awake, either.

Imre pulled back, clenching his fist and pressing it to his chest, over his pounding heart. He would keep Luca safe, he told himself. If he stood alone at home, if no one would hold him up…Imre would, for as long as he was here. There was no rite of adulthood, no ceremonial passage that said in order to be a man, Luca had to face everything alone. Alone, and unloved.

Do you love him, then, Imre?

Of course he did. He had always loved the Ward family, had always…always…

Are you lying to yourself, Imre?

That soft voice taunting him was Luca's, with that throaty burr that turned every word into a husky beguilement. And when he thought of slim arms around his neck, of a soft voice in his ear whispering *I'll always love you, Imre*, it wasn't the boy in that memory.

It was the man who lay before him now, resting peacefully and oblivious to the tempest raging through Imre's heart.

He made himself pull back. Distance. He needed distance, needed to busy himself. He kicked dirt over the bonfire and stood, breathing roughly, watching it smoulder out, before beginning to pack everything up. By the time he'd packed both baskets—separating dishes and leftovers into one, trash into the other—and secured them to Andras's saddle, Vila and Seti had wriggled over to flank Luca, snuggling against him for warmth in the chill that had descended with the fire doused. Imre shooed them to their feet, then knelt and gently shook Luca's shoulder.

"Luca."

Dark lashes fluttered, then closed again. "Mm."

Imre smiled faintly. This was turning into a pattern. "You can't sleep here. Think you can make it back without falling out of the saddle?"

"Mmmnh."

"*Luca.*"

"Mmmnnnnh."

With a sigh, Imre watched the stubbornly sleeping boy for a few moments longer, then slipped his arms underneath him and lifted him up, slight and slim and gangly against Imre's chest. "Come on. I've got you."

Luca remained limp, as Imre carried him to Andras and lifted him carefully astride. He managed to prop him draped over the gelding's neck, and hurried to fold up the blankets and stack them behind the saddle, glancing over his shoulder every few moments to make sure Luca hadn't fallen off. Once he was done, he swung up behind Luca, catching him between his arms and pulling him back to keep him safely cradled against Imre's chest, caught between his flanking thighs.

And even if he shouldn't, as he nudged Andras forward and set the roan on a gentle trot toward home…Imre leaned in and nuzzled into Luca's soft, dark thatch of black hair, breathing in his honeysuckle scent and letting himself feel the warmth of him, wrapped up safe in Imre's arms where he belonged.

But he doesn't, he told himself. *He can't. Marco would kill you both.*

Even that one moment, that breath, felt like a betrayal of his friend's trust, a violation of his own honour.

Sitting straighter in the saddle, Imre made himself focus on keeping the trail in the dark, and guiding Andras home.

Even if, once Luca left again in January, it wouldn't feel like home again for a very long time.

34

THE LAST THING LUCA REMEMBERED was the taste of apple beer, and the sky wheeling overhead into a streaking mosaic; the scents of woodsmoke and Imre, and how soft the blankets were underneath him. Then nothing.

But he came to with his head fuzzy, his vision blurred, and the world rocking back and forth.

It took him a moment to realize only two of those were because he was tipsy.

He was wrapped in the most glorious warmth: as if he'd pressed up against the radiator in the coldest winter, all steel and comforting heat soaking into his bones. Only that steel had flex and flow, the stretch of taut skin over hard-corded muscle, rocking and rolling against him gracefully.

He was in Imre's arms.

He tilted his head back, looking up at Imre from below. His vision tried to clear, focus, but there were still two too many of Imre, shadow-creatures wavering atop the more solid Imre who looked out over Luca's head, gaze distant, brows a tight line. That movement was the horse, he realized. He was on the horse with Imre, and Imre's powerful thighs were wrapped around him, hips pressed to his hips, undulating forward with each of the roan's slow strides. It roused the most delicious slow feeling in his blood, and he leaned back harder into Imre, letting himself sink into it.

Imre blinked as Luca moved, then looked down. "You're awake."

"Tiny bit." Luca's mouth felt thick and soft, his tongue not quite obeying, but he managed to smile and tack on a small, "Hi."

"Hello." Imre's silky voice flowed against Luca's ear, breaths curling against his neck, and he sighed with pleasure.

"Sorry," he mumbled, and let his head roll against Imre's shoulder. "I guess I can't hold my beer."

"It was rather strong beer." Imre chuckled, and ah God, the sound was a roll of thunder and the tremor of a stampede, shivering into Luca's back. "And you did work hard today. I'm not surprised you're tired."

"You're not tired."

"I'm just more used to not showing it, angyalka. And I'm accustomed to this. This is my life. It's not yours." Imre's arms tightened against his sides. "You're doing a good job. I'm proud of you."

Luca's stomach tightened, and he clutched his fingers against the saddle. A hot flush ran through him from head to toe. "You…are?"

"Of course," Imre answered simply. "Why wouldn't I be?"

"No reason." Luca shook his head—and immediately found that to be a mistake, when everything *swam* dizzily. He winced, closing his eyes and laying his head to Imre's shoulder again. "Thank you."

"There's no need to thank me. You're the one doing the work. It's nice to have help around here again."

"Maybe…"

"Maybe…?"

Maybe I could come back, Luca wanted to say. *In the summers, on breaks…come back to help. To be with you.*

But his tired lips didn't want to say the words. His tired heart didn't want to risk another crack. And so he only said "Nothing" and let himself drift again, falling into a half-doze and fighting himself, with every step of the horse's lolling gait, not to tell Imre that he felt so very, very *good*.

35

HE DIDN'T WAKE AGAIN UNTIL they were in the barn, and the change in the roan's stride shifted him to awareness just as Imre swung down. Thick hands encircled Luca's waist, holding him in the saddle; he lifted his head, blinking muzzily down at Imre.

"If I lift you down," Imre rumbled, "do you think you can make it into the house on your own?"

"M'not drunk," Luca slurred. "Just sleepy."

"Either way, you're drifting."

"I can make it."

"All right."

Imre swung him down, then, swirling him as though lifting him in a twirling dance, while Luca gasped and clutched hard at his arms. When his feet touched ground he swayed forward, falling into Imre's chest, stumbling into the solid rock of him. He winced, hunching into his shoulders, and peeled his face from Imre's chest long enough to peek up at him.

"…sorry."

"Now you see why I was worried." With a chuckle, Imre set him to rights, easing him upright gently and then letting go. "Go up and get changed for bed. I'll be in in a few to make sure you didn't pass out in the middle of the foyer."

"M'not *drunk!*"

"Inside, angyalka."

Luca stuck his tongue out at Imre, then turned and marched toward the house.

And promptly tripped over the toes of his own boots.

It was only a little stumble, rocking forward and then catching himself again, but he scowled and glared over his shoulder, pointing at Imre. “Not. Drunk.”

Imre held both hands up. “I didn’t say a word.” And he remained silent as Luca stalked through the barn and toward the house, until soft words drifted after: “…I hear hydrating helps with the hangover.”

Luca snapped a middle finger in the air, then stomped into the house with the dogs milling around his ankles.

He really *wasn’t* drunk; just a little bit tilted, and he made it up the stairs without killing himself, then into his room. Kicking his boots off was the easy part. Wiggling out of his jeans was harder, and he sprawled on the bed, wrestling and wriggling when his hands didn’t quite want to obey his commands and his fingers were a little numb and floaty. He’d just flung his jeans across the room, swearing, and stumbled into clean boxers by the time he heard the door open downstairs, and then the creak of the fifth step. He glanced up from rummaging for a t-shirt as Imre passed his open door, just a glimpse of bronzed flesh moving in and out of his vision as Imre stripped out of his shirt on his way to his room.

But that glimpse nagged at Luca; had that been…? He bit his lip, then peeked out after Imre—but he was already gone, vanishing into his bedroom. Luca crept down the hall and peered around the door, watching as Imre tossed his shirt onto his bed. His shoulders, chest, and back were dark with broad, spreading bruises, more on the right side than the left; underneath his tawny skin the marks had turned the dark, livid, painful-looking purple of a second-day bruise. Luca curled his hand against the doorframe, worrying at his lip.

"When did that happen…?"

Imre started, shoulders jerking slightly, then glanced over his shoulder. Both brows rose, before he looked down at himself. "Yesterday." He shrugged. "I fell out of a tree in the orchard."

Luca frowned. "Oh. When I…?" He winced. He'd been so excited he'd not even been thinking. "I'm sorry."

"I was careless. Don't worry about it."

"Does it hurt very much?"

"No more than I'm used to." Imre turned to face him, raking a hand back through his hair. "Being a farmer is rather like letting nature use you as a punching bag, then coming back for more."

"Still…it looks painful." Luca twined his fingers together, scuffing his socks against the floor. "Do…you have any salve or anything?"

"There's the ointment from the bath," Imre answered. "Works just as well directly applied to skin."

"Could I…? I mean…do you want me to?"

Imre fixed him with a long, measuring look. Some odd shadow passed over his face, before he exhaled. "Will it make you feel better?"

Luca nodded quickly. "Yes."

"Then yes."

"Okay." Luca tumbled back and tried not to think too hard about what he was doing, what he'd asked for, what he *wanted*. "Okay. Be right back," he said, then fled with his heart thumping erratically in his ears.

36

IMRE WAS BEGINNING TO THINK he might be a masochist.

He should have told Luca no, and sent him to bed. Instead he'd laid the fire in the bedroom hearth and now was sat here on the edge of his bed, waiting for those soft pattering footsteps to return. He wasn't accustomed to letting anyone touch him or anyone wanting to care for him, to look after the various bruises and injuries he accumulated daily when managing a farm by himself. And he wasn't sure what to do with the twisting in his chest as Luca ducked back into the room, still in that pretty cardigan that wrapped so close to his body and left those lovely shoulders bared, the tin of lavender salve clutched in one hand.

Luca fidgeted in the doorway for a moment, then drifted closer, unscrewing the tin. The faint scents of lavender, eucalyptus, and clover permeated the air, and Luca bit that plush, soft lower lip, drawing it into his mouth and playing at it as he sank down to sit next to Imre with a good foot of space between them.

"Is this okay…?" he asked shyly.

No, Imre thought. No, because Luca was looking at him with such trusting innocence and all Imre could focus on was that pink glistening lower lip and the fact that Luca was in his bed, both half-dressed, and God every moment of disinterest he'd felt when other men had tried to entice him with pretty lips and sly glances and roving hands was coming back to bite him when he could hardly breathe for the scent of Luca on the air, overwhelming even under the ointment.

But that was Imre's problem. It shouldn't have to be Luca's. He could keep his wayward thoughts under control, and so he took in a deep, slow breath, then smiled.

"Of course."

Luca answered that smile with a hesitant one of his own, washes of pink spreading over his cheeks, then shifted to climb further onto the bed, moving onto his knees behind Imre.

"Try to hold still, okay?"

"All right."

Imre closed his eyes, braced himself, and told himself he could handle this. It would make Luca feel better, ease that hangdog look of guilt in his eyes, so he would stop blaming himself for minor injuries Imre was accustomed to.

But the moment those heated, salve-slicked hands pressed against his back, he had to bite back a groan, tension rolling through him as soft skin slid against his flesh.

Luca froze. "…did that hurt?"

"No." Imre swallowed, shaking his head. "No, it's all right."

But it wasn't all right. It was far from all right as that hesitant touch swept over his back, then firmed, stroking the slick ointment into his skin. He hardly felt the dull pain of pressure against his bruises; he only felt the faint warming burn of the ointment as it absorbed his body heat and gave it back to him, and the delicate touch of slender fingers that grew more confident by the moment. Each brush of those fingertips shot through him and tightened in his thighs; he clenched his hands against his jeans, struggling to breathe slowly and evenly as he let his head roll forward. Every touch both melted him and coiled his tension tighter, sinking into his flesh in trails that lingered with a pleasant, deep simmer.

Was…Luca slowing down? Those soft fingers slipped lightly

between Imre's shoulder blades, then spread against his skin, a five-pointed star branding into his flesh.

"Is that better…?" Luca whispered, husky and quiet; he swayed closer, body heat almost touching Imre's back. Imre held himself perfectly still, his mouth dry.

"Mm. Does ease things a bit, aye."

"I…" Luca's voice trembled…and then that splayed hand slipped upwards, stroking, lingering, building a dark and dangerous fire in Imre's gut as long, slender fingers teased under his hair and curled against the back of his neck. "Does it feel good, Imre…?"

Imre lifted his head sharply. He could have sworn aloud, but his mouth wouldn't move, frozen, his entire body captured as Luca slid his arms around his neck, leaning into him from behind and pressing the entirety of that lithe body against him, moulded close and making his flesh tingle and prickle everywhere Luca touched. Imre took a shaky breath and curled his hand against the boy's forearm. This…he wasn't…he couldn't be understanding this, he had to be misreading…

"Imre," Luca whispered—then slid around his body, slinking against him, all sweet angles and slender grace until Imre's lap was full of smooth limbs, pale thighs spread to either side of his hips and straddling him, lissom frame pressed against him chest to chest, stomach to stomach, hip to hip. "*Imre…*"

Fuck. *Fuck.* Imre couldn't breathe; somehow his hands had found their way to Luca's hips, and as he lifted his head to look up at Luca their noses touched. Those sweet berry lips were so close, parted, Luca's breaths shallow and loud, soft fingers tangled in Imre's hair. Imre shuddered with a low groan. *No*, he told himself.

Until Luca kissed him.

That lush, overripe mouth pressed sweetly to his, slack with a needy, delicious *wanting* that drew Imre in, overwhelmed him, drowned him in the taste of honey and apples and fever-flushed warmth on Luca's lips. God, he'd never imagined that plump, taunting mouth would be so *soft*, yielding so utterly to his, pressure only making those pretty lips mesh and meld with his all the more. And then the hot barb of Luca's tongue stung him with a darting lick, only to return for another taste, slipping shyly deeper, and *fuck*…fuck, Imre melted as weakness rolled through him, a warmth that burned in his spread thighs and tightened in his stomach and tingled in his palms. He couldn't stop himself. He stole a sip of the ambrosia that had tempted him for days, drinking of those lips as though they were wine, intoxicating and…

Intoxicat*ed*.

And even as Luca moaned and swayed into him, Imre swore, breaking back, pulling free of those hypnotic lips. "Luca," he rasped. "Luca, don't."

"Why?" Luca's lips—those perfect lips, now wet and swollen, and Imre couldn't look or he would *break*—trembled. "You don't like me? Imre…" Luca rested his brow to Imre's, fingers stroking through his hair in luxuriant, coaxing touches that felt far too good, shivering down to Imre's toes. "I missed you. I missed you so, so *much*…"

"You're not thinking straight." Imre gently grasped Luca's wrists, stilling his touch. "You're drunk, Luca. I won't take advantage of you."

"It's not taking advantage. I know what I'm doing…I know what I want, Imre, I *do*…"

"This is not the time to decide that," Imre said firmly. "What would your father say?"

"Fuck my father!" Luca exploded, eyes welling with a burst of tears; he jerked at his wrists with a sobbing breath. "Fuck him. He's an arsehole, and I shouldn't have to ask for his permission. He wants me to be an adult, so he doesn't get a say."

Imre sighed, carefully tightening his grip on Luca's wrists, then relaxing. "He would still be upset. And disappointed in us both."

Luca pouted. "My dad knows you're gay. He knows I'm gay. He still sent me here."

"Exactly." Imre let his hands fall away, and forced himself not to settle them on Luca's hips again, instead bracing them on the bed to either side of his own body. "Because he knows that just because I'm gay doesn't mean I'm some predator, and he can trust me with his son."

"But can he trust his son with you?" A subtle rock brought Luca's hips against Imre's own, and Imre hissed through his teeth as pressure and friction tore through him, rousing things he'd thought he'd buried, leaving him trembling as he dug his fingers into the duvet. Those pretty bare shoulders enticed him, begging to be kissed, licked, nibbled, bitten all the way up to the rapid flicker of Luca's pulse against his long, slim throat.

"Luca," he rasped, tensing his entire body to keep himself still, to keep from rocking up to meet those slender hips, that hard pressure. "Y-you…you shouldn't…"

"*You* shouldn't," Luca whispered, and teased his lips in an open-mouthed brush against Imre's, sparking through him fiercely. "I should."

Imre caught that beautiful face in his palms, burying his fingers in wild black hair, stilling Luca. It was all he had the willpower to do, when he couldn't bring himself to pull away from those lips hovering so close, straining toward his. And yet for all that Luca was pushing, almost *begging*…he was also shaking, his fingers curled against Imre's shoulders, digging in sharply. Imre swallowed thickly.

"You're terrified right now," he rasped. "Do you even know what you're doing?"

"I know enough. That's not what I'm afraid of. Imre, please…"

"What are you afraid of, then?"

"You not wanting me."

Imre looked up into those wide, wet eyes, shimmering behind the haze of tears, and cursed himself once more. "Angyalka." He brushed his thumb against the first trickling spill, shaking his head. "It's not a matter of desire. It's a matter of what's appropriate."

Luca stiffened. "You still see me as a little boy. Like *family*."

"No." God, this would be easier if he could. "You are a young man. A beautiful, entirely maddening young man. Not a child. And I do not see you in a familial light."

"So it's just that I'm too young."

"Or I am too old."

"You're not that old."

"Old enough to hurt you, Luca." Sighing, Imre leaned into Luca. "I can't bear the thought."

But Luca jerked back, pulling his head from between Imre's palms, glaring at him. "I'm not fragile," he hissed. When Imre only looked at him helplessly, those budding tears burst over in fast-racing wet streaks, pouring down Luca's cheeks like a sudden thundershower against window glass. "I'm *not!* You just…you just…why don't you just…just say…"

He tumbled out of Imre's lap. Imre reached for him, but Luca twisted away, stepping back, stabbing Imre with a look of bitter recrimination.

"Just leave me alone," Luca bit off.

Then, with a harsh hitching sound rising past his lips, he turned and fled the room. The door slammed closed in his wake, leaving Imre alone.

Alone with the scents of lavender and honeysuckle, the taste of Luca's kiss burned into his lips and guilt a terrible and heavy thing doubling the weight of his soul.

37

SIX STEPS. ONLY SIX STEPS to his bedroom, yet by the time he crossed those six steps Luca was blind: with tears, with frustration, with mortification, with harsh and ugly realization.

He flung himself into the bed and curled around a pillow, burying his face into it to muffle his sobs—as if, as long as they didn't carry down the hall, he could pretend Imre wasn't there to hear them. Pretend Imre wasn't there at all, and hadn't proven to him what Luca had always known, deep down, even if he hadn't been able to admit it:

Imre was only attracted to men he could love. Men he could see himself falling in love with, the kind of love that for Luca was just a childish dream. And Luca had thrown himself at him like a desperate, drunken prat, and Imre had rejected him. Pushed him aside like the pathetic little shite he was. Imre didn't want him. Would never want him.

Because Luca would never be someone Imre could love.

38

IMRE DIDN'T SLEEP THAT NIGHT.

Everything in him wanted to follow Luca, dry his tears, pull him close and soothe him until the aching, bitter sobs that Imre could hear even from down the hall quieted. But he couldn't. He *couldn't.* He had to do what was right.

And what was right was sending a quite drunk young man to bed on his own, even if it meant shattering his heart.

What if he hadn't been drunk, Imre?

What if he'd been sober, tumbled soft and pale into your lap and begging for you?

He couldn't answer that. Every path his thoughts turned down only ran up against that confusing roadblock of *can't, shouldn't, won't.*

He wasn't accustomed to this kind of confusion. He liked to render problems down to simple decisions, but there was nothing simple about this. Not when he'd told Luca exactly how Imre worked, how he was wired, and yet Luca pushed all his buttons and made him question everything he knew about himself. About what he felt for the boy. About what he *wanted,* when his body still tingled with the touch of those soft, warm hands.

Groaning, he dragged his fingers into his hair, burying his palms against his eyes, and listened to those hitching, sniffling sobs until they quieted, and told him the agony of this ache was exactly the punishment he deserved.

Luca was *too young*. He was Marco's *son*. He was…he was…

He was so fucking tangled up inside Imre, and Imre swore under his breath as he touched his fingers to his lips, and tasted Luca on the tip of his tongue.

39

LUCA CRIED UNTIL HIS THROAT was raw and his eyes were tired and he couldn't keep them open any longer. He never felt like he fully fell asleep; every time he started to sink deep, the horrible thing clutching in the centre of his chest dug its claws in and punctured another hole in his heart. And he woke completely close to dawn, his head throbbing, his vision bisected in white slashes.

But the hangover headache didn't hurt nearly as much as the memory of Imre pushing him away, and looking at him with something too close to pity for Luca's liking.

With a muffled whimper, he buried his face in the pillow. He didn't know how he was supposed to go down there and look at Imre over breakfast, talk to him, work alongside him as though nothing had happened.

If Imre hadn't already called his father, and told him it was time to take his wayward son back.

Luca had been a prat. A drunken, immature prat, throwing himself at a man who didn't want him.

It was better to be mostly certain of rejection than to know for fucking sure.

He lay there for over an hour; if he moved, he'd throw up—or just throw all his things into his bag and bolt before Imre woke. Make the four-mile walk into town on his own, and take the nearest train to anywhere he could afford with what little was in his bank account.

Maybe he could just…disappear. Become someone else. Someone who could forget he'd ever been such a little nit, and start over completely new.

God, he was full of the most bullshite fantasies.

Groaning, he rolled over and swiped a hand over his laptop keyboard, then dragged it off the nightstand and onto his chest. Facebook Messenger said Xavier had been active less than a minute ago; Luca sure as hell hoped so. He opened their chat window, then snapped out several rapid-fire messages.

Luca.Ward: *Xav*
Luca.Ward: *Help*
Luca.Ward: *FML*
Luca.Ward: *No seriously, just fck it.*

A new message popped up almost immediately.

Xavier.Laghari: *Uh-oh*
Xavier.Laghari: *Trouble in paradise?*
Luca.Ward: *I got drunk last night on Imre's weird apple beer*
Luca.Ward: *and threw myself at him*
Xavier.Laghari: *Bow-chicka*
Luca.Ward: *No bow-chica!*
Luca.Ward: *fuck you*
Luca.Ward: *He didn't want me.*
Xavier.Laghari: *What did he say?*

Luca hesitated, eyes welling again as he replayed the scene again. Imre fending him off with those rough hands, that *look*, almost haunted, heavy and rueful. He scrubbed at his face, then rattled out:

> ***Luca.Ward:*** *A bunch of shite about me being drunk, and not taking advantage. And stuff about my dad. It's really hard to kiss a guy who's talking about your dad.*
> ***Xavier.Laghari:*** *But did he actually say 'I don't want your narrow white arse, Luca Ward?'*
> ***Luca.Ward:*** *I hate you*
> ***Luca.Ward:*** *And he didn't say it like that, no. He didn't have to.*
> ***Xavier.Laghari:*** *I dunno*
> ***Xavier.Laghari:*** *You were drunk*
> ***Xavier.Laghari:*** *He was probably doing the right thing*
> ***Xavier.Laghari:*** *Being a gentleman.*
> ***Xavier.Laghari:*** *I wouldn't want to fuck a drunk girl. Like she might not even remember it in the morning and it's just not cool and all kinds of messy and I might hurt her, and shite?*
> ***Xavier.Laghari:*** *Remember that whole special day class back in A-levels about drunk consent not being or something like that?*
> ***Xavier.Laghari:*** *So maybe he was doing that*
> ***Xavier.Laghari:*** *Trying to be good to you and all.*

Maybe. Luca considered it, for a few moments. Imre was just that kind of noble. Daft fucking loyal sheepdog of a man. But Luca couldn't and wouldn't hang his star on that; it was just asking for more heartbreak, more unrealistic expectations, feeding the notion that if he just…tried again sober, this time it would be all right and Imre might…

Might actually see him as a man, and not a boy.

He thunked his head against the pillows miserably and dragged his hand over the keyboard. God, he *wished* he'd been drunk enough to forget the whole thing ever happened.

Luca.Ward: *bfrhdjfvhkbjlkn;m*
Luca.Ward: *Or maybe he just didn't want me.*
Xavier.Laghari: *Debbie Downer.*
Luca.Ward: *Realistic*
Luca.Ward: *Rick*
Luca.Ward: *Ok that was bad*
Luca.Ward: *But you just gave me an idea*
Luca.Ward: *One that might save me from death by endless mortification*
Xavier.Laghari: *Yeah?*
Luca.Ward: *Yeah.*
Xavier.Laghari: *Text me later and tell me. Gotta go. Class.*
Xavier.Laghari: *Love you, you skinny ignorant prick.*
Luca.Ward: *You and that silver tongue.*
Luca.Ward: *Later, bb.*

He closed the IM window, then pushed himself up against the headboard, plucking bitterly at the pretty cardigan he'd passed out in, now stretched out from sleeping in it. He'd probably ruined it, unless he could shrink-wash it back into shape. He seemed to be good at ruining things.

His gaze drifted to the clover wreath on the lamp. Its petals were almost completely brown now, the stems limp and dark and an odd watery, rotting shade, its smell cloying. It was dying; nothing he could do could save it.

And even if his little gambit worked, with Imre…nothing would ever be the same.

IMRE LAY MOTIONLESS IN HIS bed until morning, staring at the ceiling and asking himself questions he had no answer to, chasing himself in tormenting circles. By dawn the hearth fire had burned down to embers, and Vila and Seti had come bounding into the room, crowding up onto the foot of the bed and huddling there for warmth. Seti laid her head over his knee, looking up at him with a mournful whine; she'd always been the one more sensitive to his moods, and she leaned hard into him now, watching him with sorrowful eyes until he stroked over her head and caressed her silky, tufted ears.

"C'mon, girls," he said, and rolled out of bed. "Let's go do something about breakfast."

Mundane things. Ordinary things.

As if he hadn't just ruined his relationship with one of the most cherished people in his life.

He threw himself into cooking—rolling dough and first cutting it into pie crust, before flattening the rest into squares. He washed over a dozen apples, cored and sliced them, tossed them in sugar and cinnamon, and first filled the pie crust before folding the dough squares around apple chunks to make triangular fritters. With a sprinkle of extra cinnamon and sugar, he put the pastries in the oven to bake, then unwrapped sausage and set it to sizzling along with hashed potatoes.

The food was close to done, the smells just hitting that peak blend of rightness, when soft, tentative steps on the stairs warned him Luca was coming. Even without looking he could sense the boy creeping, as if trying to move without being heard, but that fifth step gave him away every time. Imre steeled himself, fighting to suppress the quaking in his stomach and the crackling, brittle edges cutting away inside his heart, and breathed in deep before making himself look up with a smile, watching Luca through the kitchen doorway.

"Good morning."

Luca froze on the stairs, a faun poised before flight, looking at Imre with wide, hurt eyes that tore at Imre's gut and laced him up in bindings of regret and sorrow; Luca stood so forlorn, hunched in as if making himself small, one hand digging into the opposite arm and stretching the knit sleeve of the cardigan he still wore. He wet his lips, then whispered,

"Morning."

Imre turned the heat down on the stove, then turned to fully face Luca, folding his arms over his chest. He didn't know what to say, but there was no beating around it, and he wasn't fond of waffling. "Are you all right?" he asked.

Luca parted his lips, then closed them again, expression stricken, before he dropped his gaze to his stocking toes. "Hangover from hell," he mumbled. "But I'll live. I've had worse after a bit of raw hundred proof."

"City life," Imre said dryly. "But that's not what I meant, Luca." He sighed. "About last night…"

Luca's shoulders tightened. His voice rose to a pitch peak, cracked, then settled again as he said, "Oh…sorry I passed out on you. Did you have to carry me back? I don't remember."

"Andras did most of the heavy lifting. What do you remember?"

Luca shrugged. "Sparks. Watching the stars. Things are a bit fuzzy after that."

Imre studied him, a frown pinching between his brows, deepening the pressure headache of a sleepless night. Luca looked anywhere but at him, and the longer Imre watched him, the smaller he shrank.

So. That was how he wanted it, then.

Imre would respect that, if that was what made Luca feel safe.

"Okay, Luca," he said softly. "Okay."

"Okay?" Luca repeated, his voice tiny.

"Okay." And Imre told himself his chest wasn't aching with the pangs of loss, when anything lost had never been his to start with. Told himself he wasn't burning with the need to take Luca into his arms and kiss that hurt away, as he picked up the spatula and pushed the crackling, popping sausage in the pan. "Breakfast is almost done, and will take the edge off the hangover. Then we can take out the herds."

"Okay. I'll…I'll go wash up and get ready." Luca turned away, but then paused, one hand on the stair rail. "Imre…?"

"Yes?"

"Are we still friends…?" Soft, pleading, vulnerable, heart-rending, and Imre fought against his closing throat, fought against his frozen tongue to speak. To say the only words he could, if they could ease even the smallest amount of fear in that throaty voice.

"Of course, Luca. Always."

Luca said nothing.

There was only a pregnant silence, and then the creak of the fifth step as he retreated up the stairs.

41

IMRE DIDN'T KNOW WHY HE was surprised, when Luca began avoiding him.

Luca came back down dressed for breakfast with his phone out and his earbuds in, and whenever Imre looked up he always got the sense that Luca had been looking at him just the moment before, yet every time his gaze was locked on his phone, tapping away, the cord of his earbuds creeping between his lips and catching between his teeth. Imre let it go, and simply set out a plate in front of the boy.

He didn't know what to say to Luca, anyway. Didn't know what to think. He wanted to blame last night on the apple beer, on…anything else but that Imre himself was a terrible man, but he was no more fond of lying to himself than he was to anyone else.

And if he was honest with himself, Luca had been distracting him from the moment he'd stepped off the train. That distraction became *torture*, with the tacit knowledge that Luca…

Luca desired him.

Or had that been the apple beer talking? Apple beer, and the lonely ache of just wanting someone to understand him? If it had been a moment of intoxicated desperation, no wonder Luca wanted to forget. Pretend it had never happened.

For Luca's own sake, Imre should probably send him home. Talk to Marco, help them sort things out. But as he studied that bowed head of crow-black hair, he couldn't even think about making that call.

Right now the last thing Luca needed was to be rejected again, and flung back into that tense role as the last standing beam keeping the walls of his home from collapsing in. He needed safety. Security.

So Imre would have to get himself under control, and provide that.

And until he could, maybe Luca's distance was for the best.

Yet it ached when, the moment he'd cleared his plate in record time, Luca slipped from the table and vanished out the back door without looking back. Imre dragged his palms over his face, thudding his elbows onto the table with a sigh.

Fuck.

That morning was only the beginning. After Imre finished his breakfast and washed up, he headed out to find Luca in with Gia and Merta, feeding them and listening to their heartbeats. Imre left him with the goats and saddled both horses, a silent invitation that Luca was welcome to join him in taking the goats out. And a few moments later, Luca emerged from the nannies' stalls to swing up onto Zsofia's back, moving much more smoothly than he had just two days ago.

But he didn't say a word to Imre, as they rode out. He spoke to the dogs, calling to Vila and Seti, laughing and scratching behind their ears. He murmured to Zsofia, stroking through her mane. He called out to the goats as they trotted up the hill, spurring them on as he chased Zsofia on their heels.

Yet not a single word for Imre.

Not even on the ride back; Luca's earbuds appeared out of nowhere, and they were back in his ears, the cord back in his mouth, before they even found the trail. He nudged his knees into Zsofia's side and took off, standing slightly in the saddle and leaning forward; Imre caught only a glimpse of his face, fierce and stone-set, hard with a quiet determination Imre had never seen before.

Imre let him run, until he was nothing but sun-dapples over pale skin, the flow of dark hair, the shimmering blond lash of Zsofia's tail.

Back at the farmhouse, he set Luca to finishing out the last of the orchard. There were only a dozen trees left to be picked; Luca could handle that himself, and it would give them both the space they needed. When Imre asked "Would you mind?" Luca only nodded, looking somewhere past Imre's shoulder, eyes glassy and distant. Imre closed his eyes, taking a deep breath, ignoring the twist in his chest.

When he opened his eyes again, Luca was already walking away. Imre watched him while he stacked the hand cart with empty bushel barrels, then headed out. Imre should follow him; he needed to check the beehives and see if they'd produced enough surplus honey for one last harvest before closing up the hives for winter. But it could wait another day.

Right now, it was easier not to see that detached, emotionless look on Luca's face.

Luca stayed out in the orchard through lunch. And this time, Imre brought the goats in alone; when he returned, there was only the silhouette of Luca in the bathroom window and, when he went inside and upstairs, a closed bedroom door.

He ate dinner alone, and left a tray outside of Luca's room.

And so it went. Luca would stay close long enough to learn what he needed to do—whether it was trimming the goats' hooves and horns, checking the growing new fields of alfalfa and clover, or walking the pastures to recognize and pull deadly weeds that could harm the goats. Then he'd be off, working until he sweated, throwing himself into every moment of it with a diligence that would be admirable if Imre wasn't so *worried*. The boy was skittish as a cat, and if ever they brushed close enough to almost touch, he jerked away, expression glassing over in a way that shot daggers into Imre's chest.

Imre had done this. He'd done this, by shoving Luca away when he was vulnerable.

How was he supposed to do the right thing when every right thing to do was completely wrong?

He didn't want to push. He *couldn't* push, couldn't do anything but wait for Luca to come to him, even if Luca never did. And there was always enough work to keep busy, and those earbuds standing solid as a wall between them in the quiet moments. Always enough work to never look directly at each other; to turn every conversation into a dry, emotionless exchange of information; to let them go their separate ways to the tasks that made the farm run smoothly, and all the smoother for a second pair of hands sharing the labour.

But there was never enough work to fill the empty ache in Imre's heart, where Luca's laughter had lived for those few short days.

42

THIS WASN'T WORKING.

Luca had thought he could make himself believe the lie, if he just held on to it long enough. If he just acted like nothing had ever happened, until the rawness of that night faded and everything could return to normal: silent warmth, easy laughter, teasing conversation, the comfort of home.

But Lohere didn't feel like home anymore. Not when, with every moment that Luca didn't fill with work and more work, he flashed back to that night: Imre cursing under his breath, pulling away from him, *Luca, don't.*

Luca, don't.

He'd been such an arsehole. Writhing all over Imre, drunk and off his fucking rocker, then throwing a tantrum. He just wanted to *forget*, but his brain was as much of an arsehole as he was; good memories were fleeting things, their warmth easily dulled with time and faded into nothing, while every bad thing that had ever happened remained sharp and fresh and clear.

Listening to his parents fight, curled small in his bed with his knees hugged to his chest, staring at his toes and humming music under his breath as if that could drown it out. Kids in second form pulling his hair, shoving him into walls, calling him *queerbait* and *pansy* and *fucking fairy fag*. Stuttering in front of the class in the middle of a fifth form speech assignment, and the snickers that followed. Coming home with perfect marks anyway, and his parents smiling thinly and looking right through him because they were trying so hard not to see each other that they didn't see him, either. His first cigarette, and puking on Xav's shoes. His first beer, and puking in Xav's lap. Sneaking off from home and slinking in the corners of dark, dank, smoky gay bars, hoping someone would *see* him but even more hoping no one would recognize him and tell his parents he was out skulking around places like this.

Going home alone when everyone looked through him just the way his parents did, mortified and sick that he'd thought anyone would ever notice him.

There'd been Will, but…

He'd never been under any illusions that he was anything more than the path of least resistance, for Will. But at least Will had made him feel wanted.

At least Will didn't pull away from him and growl *Luca, don't.*

He closed his eyes, gripping the ladder leading up to the hayloft in the storage barn near the orchard. He needed to *stop*. Stop reliving every moment of it. Stop digging the wound deeper. Stop being weird around Imre, and running away every time the man came within arm's reach. Imre probably already hated him. Luca just needed to stop making things *worse*.

But he didn't know how, when every time he caught those dark, thoughtful blue eyes, every time he glimpsed Imre moving with that effortless ease, every time Imre looked as though he might reach for him only to pull back…

His heart tore in two, fragile as wet tissue paper, and he ran not from Imre, but from the ache of longing and the sting of rejection.

This was normal, he told himself. People were rejected all the time. They swung, they missed, they moved on. Even if they were in love. Even if…

Stop.

He had work to do. Over the past week they'd cleared the fields of weeds, brambles, poisonous plants, anything that could hurt the voraciously omnivorous and not particularly discerning goats. Imre was in the barn milking nannies who were already starting to run dry as their kids weaned, but he'd asked Luca to bring down some old hay bales from the loft that had gone bad with damp and mildew, but could still be used to insulate the orchards and the apple trees' roots. If he focused on that and nothing else, he'd get through today.

And then curl up in bed and hold his pillow close, as if he could ease the ache in his chest if he just applied enough pressure, a tourniquet on a broken heart.

He pulled himself up the first rung of the ladder—then hissed, stepping back down. Fuck. The soles of his feet were starting to blister; his socks were too thin for days of hard labour in these boots, and even though he'd tried double-layering he'd still managed to rub swollen bubbles against his heels, the knuckles of his toes, the balls of his feet. As long as he was standing on even footing the pain was just a dull bit of background noise, but the second he pressed his full weight down on the rung it shot upward into his gut with nauseating intensity, a sickening and heavy burn. He took a deep, shaking breath and braced himself to try again.

"Luca?" The barn door creaked open at his back, and Imre's voice drifted through. "While you're up there, would you mind checking for the spare feed buckets for the stanchion? One of the girls is bucking, and she kicked one loose and cracked it."

Luca stiffened, gut dropping into a leaden knot. "Sure," he ground out without looking back, and gripped onto the ladder rungs again, pulling himself up as quickly as possible—away from Imre, away from the gaze he could feel watching him with a sort of mournful question that seemed constant lately, unspoken and yet hovering in the air between them.

Pain stabbed through the soles of his feet. He ignored it, ignored the rasping burn, even as it made his toes curl and brought tears to the corners of his eyes, stinging. But as his foot came down, one of the blisters on his heel burst. Agony shot through him as raw flesh dragged against fabric and boot leather. His foot slipped. His grip slackened.

And the world tilted back, the barn rafters skewing crazily as he fell.

There was one dreamlike moment when he didn't understand what was happening. A moment in which the barn roof seemed to recede in slow motion, and he saw his own hand in crystal clarity, reaching for the ladder rungs that were already too far away, the toes of his boots kicking up just beyond his fingertips. Then time accelerated in a terrifying flash that tore through him in a frigid rush and trembled every organ in his body and locked up his muscles as gravity wrapped him in a hard fist and slammed him down. He had one second to curl up, brace for impact.

Before he crashed into the warmth of Imre's body, captured in steel bands of arms, his fall halted abruptly as Imre caught him, lifted him against his chest, turned into the force of impact in a rapid swinging spin before stumbling to a halt. Breathing hard, Imre stared down at him, eyes wide, naked fear stark in the sharp scintillating edges of his deep blue gaze.

"Bloody Christ," Imre gasped, his grip hard on Luca, grasping him too tight, fingers digging in. "What happened? Are you all right?"

Heart thumping, Luca stared up at Imre. He'd rather have crashed into the ground and broken every bone in his body than this: wrapped in Imre's arms, carried by that easy strength, sheltered by that protective nature that made Imre *Imre*. He hadn't even heard Imre moving, but he'd been *there*, ready to catch Luca when he fell, without hesitation. Luca's hands had fallen against Imre's chest, and underneath his palms he could feel the rushed, powerful beat of Imre's heart, racing as swiftly as his heaving breaths, as sharp-edged as the raw emotion in Imre's eyes.

Luca couldn't stand that. That emotion, that concern over *him*, the fact that even after Luca had made such an arse of himself Imre was taking care of him, worrying over him, saving him like the little nit he was.

He shoved at Imre's chest as hard as he could, kicking, twisting until Imre had no choice but to let go, arms dropping away but rough hands grasping Luca, steadying him as Imre set him down. Luca bit back a cry of pain that came up his throat like vomit as his feet touched ground, sucking it in like a withheld scream as he twisted away from Imre's touch.

"Fine," he forced out through his teeth. "I'm fine."

Imre only stared at him, that penetrating question in his gaze once more, aching and haunted by melancholy, by something almost like grief. That gaze pulled at Luca, tearing at the bleeding wounds inside him, the humiliation that Imre could never understand when Imre was quiet and patient and wouldn't be ripping himself to awful pieces over something so simple as *Luca, don't*. Imre would be able to take a rejection in stride. Imre would be calm and understanding and kind, and move on with his life. But Luca wasn't Imre. Luca didn't know how to *be* Imre. And Luca couldn't stand to be near Imre.

So he ran.

He ran from the barn, the pain in the soles of his feet spurring him on as he thrust out into the midmorning light and ran without looking back.

43

IMRE CLAYBOURNE WAS NOT A violent man.

But he was very close to ripping the earbuds out of Luca's ears and dropping them into the bloody damned roto-tiller.

He sat across the breakfast table from the boy, watching him just to see if Luca would look up, make eye contact, even acknowledge that he was in the room. He'd tried to grow accustomed to Luca's silences, tried to give him the space he needed, but for the past week all he could see every time he looked at Luca was his foot slipping on the ladder and just how easily he could have ended up a mangled and bloody wreck, torn and broken, if Imre hadn't moved fast enough.

That was what kept haunting him. If he'd been a second slower, if he'd started to leave after asking Luca to fetch the spare feed bucket, *if* so many things. So many things that would have meant he'd failed Luca. Failed to protect him.

And even if he'd been there, even if he'd caught him at the last moment and taken the force of the impact with his own body, even if he could still taste the rank, bitter terror in the back of his throat while his mind caught up with what his body already knew, that Luca was safe…

Luca had run from him.

And somehow, Imre still felt as though he'd failed him.

They needed to talk. This couldn't go on. Stabbing at each other with silences, ignoring the bloody gorilla rampaging about the room and tearing everything apart while they pretended nothing was wrong. Imre didn't like deceptions, didn't like lies. But every day was a lie of pretending that nothing had happened, that he didn't know the feel of Luca's hands on his skin and the taste of his lips, and even though he understood why Luca needed that lie he didn't understand how they were going to survive three more months like *this*.

"Luca."

Nothing. Luca was tapping at his phone again, and even with the earbuds wedged tightly in his ears, Imre could hear the music he was playing, something with a blasting, swift rhythm. He had the cord between his teeth again, working it with his lips, chewing little dents in the rubber coating until, if he wasn't careful, he'd chew right down to the wire. He hadn't touched his pancakes, and it worried Imre; he was skipping lunch every day, barely picking at breakfast, and even if the trays Imre left outside Luca's room each night came back empty, the dark shadows under Luca's eyes made Imre wonder how much of it Luca was eating and how much he was tossing out the window or feeding to the dogs.

"*Luca*," he tried again, but Luca didn't even look up.

Imre bit back a snarl, bubbling up inside him with a surge of frustrated annoyance that caught him off guard, when he normally…didn't. Ever. His father had been a calm, gentle, slow-speaking man, and he had raised Imre to follow in his footsteps, to choose consideration above anger, to manage his emotions with deliberation and intent.

But his father had never dealt with a maddening little *cat* of a man who would rather drive them both completely up the wall than talk about what happened and clear the air.

He ground his teeth, fingers twitching as he fought the urge to snag the earbud cords and *pull*. "Lu—"

His phone rang in his back pocket. Imre sighed, lifting up just enough to pull it free, then sank back in his chair and eyed the caller ID. Luca stopped his tapping and shot him a sidelong look, gaze unreadable, before looking down at his plate, setting his phone on the table, and picking up his fork. Imre swiped the call and lifted his phone to his ear.

"Good morning, Marco."

The fact that Luca didn't immediately tense and bolt said his music actually was that loud, and he hadn't even heard Imre calling his name. Imre exhaled, shifting in his chair to settle sideways so he could lean his head and shoulders against the wall, turning his attention to the phone.

"Hey, Imre," Marco said. He sounded strange: tentative, strained, his voice tight. "How're things going?"

"Everything's fine. You?"

"Life is life. I just…wanted to…I…you know."

Imre glanced at Luca from the corner of his eye, watching as he stabbed at his pancakes, turning them into mush. "You wanted to know how Luca's doing."

"…yeah."

Imre didn't have to hesitate a moment before answering, "He's settled in quite well." Hell would freeze and the sky would fall before he would betray Luca's trust by telling Marco a word of the tension between them, the strangeness, that heated and desperate kiss. "I've gotten quite a bit more done with his help."

"Good. That's good," Marco rattled out, a little too quickly. "I'm glad to hear it. He hasn't caused any trouble?"

"None at all. It's been nice having him around."

Even if he was savaging those pancakes more than eating them. Imre held back a smile, fondness blooming in a warm patch in the centre of his chest and making his heart beat a little harder, no matter his frustration, his…his…

He might as well admit it. He was *hurt*.

But he'd hurt Luca, too.

"I don't know how you handle him, Imre," Marco said.

By recognizing him as an adult instead of commanding him like a child, Imre thought.

But that, too, he kept to himself.

"As I said, I think he just needed a change of scenery and time to cool off," he diverted smoothly, then pressed forward. "Listen. Marco."

"Hm?"

Imre pressed his lips together. Maybe it wasn't his place to ask, but they were his *friends*. "…are things all right with you and Lucia?"

"Eh?" Marco's quick, nervous laugh made a lie of every word he said. "Sure. We're both busy with work, but things are fine. We're both just worried about Luca."

"Ah." Imre sagged against the wall, closing his eyes. These bloody Wards and their deflections and evasion were going to kill him. At least he knew where Luca got it from. "All right, Marco. All right. Just a moment, would you? Luca's right here."

"Wait, no, I don't think—"

But Imre was already pulling the phone away from his ear, Marco's voice retreating into a distant panicked murmur. Imre tapped the button to mute the sound from his end, then waved his hand in Luca's line of sight.

"Luca."

This time, Luca looked up. He eyed Imre warily, then pulled his earbuds out of his ears, letting them fall to coil atop his phone. Imre waited, but when he said nothing, continued:

"It's your father. Did you want to talk to him?"

Luca immediately stiffened, eyes widening, before slitting into a scowl. "What? *No.*" He jerked his face away, glaring across the kitchen. "He knows my mobile. He could have used it any time."

Imre watched Luca, internally sighing, wishing he could reach across the table, rest his hand to that stiff shoulder, tell him with the warmth of touch that it would be all right. But he didn't doubt Luca would pull away from him, so he only tried with his clumsy words.

"I didn't tell him anything," he murmured.

Luca hunched into himself, red washing brilliantly across his face. The legs of the chair scraped roughly; he thrust it back, shoving to his feet.

"What the fuck is there to tell?" he snapped, then turned and stalked off.

Imre tilted his head. There was something…*off* about Luca's stride, a subtle hitch; he wasn't sure if it was tension or something else. He might have turned his ankle in the saddle, or—

"Imre?" Marco's voice rose from the phone speaker. "Are you still there?"

Imre dropped his head into his palm, resting his elbow on the table, and unmuted the phone. "Here."

"He doesn't want to talk to me, does he?"

"Have you tried to call him?"

"I've texted a few times." Marco made a rueful sound. "I think the only reason he answers is so I don't drive out there to make sure he's alive."

"Do you think I'd let anything happen to him?"

"That's not what I—" Marco made a frustrated sound. "No. I'm sorry. I'm trying to act like… Nevermind."

"Marco…?"

"Nothing. I'm just not very good at this parenting thing. Especially the part about being right and infallible, when right now I'm not really sure I am."

Imre rubbed his temples. "Do you think it was a mistake, sending Luca here?"

"Do you?"

"No. Even if your reasons might leave something to be desired."

"Imre?" Marco asked wistfully. "Is he happy, at Lohere?"

Not right now, but then neither of us are.

"I'm trying to make sure he is," Imre deflected carefully. Apparently he was learning a thing or two from the Wards after all.

"That's all I really want." Marco sighed. "He just seemed so lost. Unhappy and directionless. I just wanted him to be happy. To *do* something instead of wasting his potential. When you have an adult son who's so bloody smart but never seems to want to apply himself to anything, you feel like you failed as a parent."

"That's not something you can force on him by taking his choices away from him. He's at an age where he can decide for himself, good or bad, and deal with the consequences—good or bad." And Imre was the pot calling the kettle black, when he'd flat out told Luca that night that Luca wasn't capable of deciding for himself…but he'd been *drunk*. That guilt would get its hooks in Imre's heart one way or another, whether it was guilt over desiring Luca or guilt over hurting him by refusing to give in to his advances. He stared at Luca's half-finished, abandoned plate, forcing his attention back to the conversation at hand. "What's done is done. We're making the best of things. I'm sure he'll talk to you when he's ready."

"Will he?" Marco asked, and the aching, lost note in his voice nearly broke Imre's heart. He closed his eyes.

I don't know.

Not his place, he reminded himself. He couldn't get between father and son, couldn't fix their problems when he couldn't even fix the problems between Luca and himself. "I hope so," was all he said. It was the best he could offer. "Marco, I'm sorry, but—"

"No—I know. I remember the schedule at Lohere. Go take care of your goats, Imre."

"Will you be all right?"

"Yes. And Imre?" A dry, faint laugh. "You know I love you, right? You giant grump."

Imre chuckled. "I love you too, you feckless arse. Later."

He ended the call and dropped his phone on the table, then rubbed his fingers to his eyes with a groan.

Too many complications.

He set himself to finishing his breakfast; he didn't have much time to spare, when he needed to get the animals out in the fields and then spend the day pasteurizing and bottling the last of the milk, marking the labels with expiration dates, putting it in cold storage until market day. But as he stood to clear away his empty plate and put Luca's away in case he wanted it later, the table rattled. No—the phone Luca had left on the table rattled, vibrating with a buzzing chime. Imre glanced down without thinking, automatically scanning over the screen, and immediately wished he hadn't.

A new text window had popped up over the lock screen, bold letters he couldn't help but absorb before he could shut them out.

> ***hey sweetlips heard you got banished to the arsecrack of nowhere***
> ***harrogate eh***
> ***want some company***
> ***gonna be out near there on holiday this wknd***

could take your mind off it all baby
i got time, hotness

The contact name was only *W. K.* Imre felt dirty just reading it—like he'd violated Luca's privacy, not to mention the sheer crassness of it all. But that was how people Luca's age spoke, he supposed.

People Luca's age.

Imre closed his eyes and turned away. People Luca's age. People Luca might be intimately involved with. People who were none of Imre's business. He shouldn't care. He *didn't* care. Luca's life was Luca's life.

And Imre needed to remember exactly where he belonged in that life, before he made any more disastrous mistakes.

THE BLISTERS, LUCA THOUGHT, WERE his punishment for fucking everything up.

He couldn't stand this. The careful distance, the way it hurt to even be in the *room* with Imre, until he didn't know what to do but run even though it was the last thing he wanted to do. He didn't know how to *stop*. Not when he was too mortified to look Imre in the eye. Not when his chest ached and his stomach bottomed out every time he drew close enough to catch Imre's scent. Not when he couldn't stand the pity in Imre's eyes, now that he knew—he *knew*—how Luca felt, this sad little boy pining after a man who could never want him.

Not when the only way he could even sleep at night was to wear himself to the bone.

If he was working, he could at least be useful and not this miserable shade haunting around the house. It was the only way he could think of to apologize to Imre for his dreadful behaviour: throwing himself into taking care of the animals, taking care of the farm. If they were working, he could be with Imre without having to *talk* to him. So he wore gloves to cover the first reddened blisters, and walked with his back stiff to hide his limp. When the blisters burst and soaked his gloves and socks, he washed them in the bathroom sink and poured stinging alcohol over his skin, wrapped his palms and soles in gauze, then hid them away again, threw himself back into work, and avoided those quiet moments with Imre where he might notice that

Luca never took his gloves off.

If he was focusing on the pain, he wasn't thinking about Imre. About the silence. About those long, searching looks he could *feel* even when he wouldn't look, expectant and patient.

About the taste of his lips, and how for just a moment they'd crushed together in a breathless, heated lock.

He sat on the foot of his bed, dabbing his feet with cotton swabs by the quiet light of the rising sun. After nearly a month of this he'd have thought they would heal by now, but each swipe brought the alcohol-soaked swabs away pink; he hissed at the stinging pain, sucking back a whimper. He should have toughened up by now. Healed and hardened into calluses, so he would be strong enough to *handle* this.

He couldn't do that right, either.

His laptop sat open at the bed on his side. Over the weeks that had passed, it had become his lifeline, his connection to Xavier and a friendship he hadn't managed to ruin. He had a few other friends back in Sheffield, but they were the kind of friends he'd only connected with because they happened to be in proximity to each other and bored at the same times. Once they'd drifted off to university, there'd been no reason to stay in touch, leaving Luca a fucking Billy No Mates—and though Will still texted him now and then, it was only when he wanted to hook up.

Luca *still* hadn't answered his last few texts.

Xav was the only one who still really spoke to him. Still cared. Luca couldn't even remember how they'd met, though there was a vague recollection of bumping into each other, books scattering, and nearly starting a fight. How they'd met didn't matter.

All that mattered was that Xavier was *there*, even when things got rough.

And Xav was there now, a bloop from Facebook Messenger pulling Luca from his grit-toothed work over his feet to look at the message window.

Xavier.Laghari: *Good morning, sunshine*
Xavier.Laghari: *How are we on day 27 of your maudlin exile*

Luca grimaced, set the first aid supplies on the chest at the foot of the bed, and dragged his laptop across his lap, settling cross-legged with his damp soles carefully turned upward to let the wounds air out.

Luca.Ward: *It hasn't been 27 days yet*
Luca.Ward: *has it*
Xavier.Laghari: *24 actually*
Xavier.Laghari: *and the fact that you had to ask says you believed it could be 27*
Xavier.Laghari: *plus not like 24 is any better*
Xavier.Laghari: *its almost October for fuck's sake Luca*
Luca.Ward: *Why the fuck are you counting?*
Xavier.Laghari: *Club's got a betting pool going*
Xavier.Laghari: *how many days until you break*
Xavier.Laghari: *and start begging for hot sexy goat man's dick*
Luca.Ward: *why are you like this*
Luca.Ward: *no seriously why*
Luca.Ward: *I hate you*
Xavier.Laghari: *You only wish you could.*
Xavier.Laghari: *Seriously bb you okay?*

Xavier.Laghari: *like you barely talk anymore*

No, Luca wanted to say. *I'm not okay and I haven't been okay for weeks.* But he only said what he'd said every time Xavier had asked:

Luca.Ward: *I'm fine*
Xavier.Laghari: *Really?*
Luca.Ward: *yeah*
Xavier.Laghari: *ok look I'm having a sensitive moment*
Xavier.Laghari: *so like don't waste it*
Xavier.Laghari: *talk to me*
Xavier.Laghari: *tell me all your deepest innermost feelings*
Xavier.Laghari: *let me cradle your tender little emo heart*
Luca.Ward: *fuck*
Luca.Ward: *you*
Luca.Ward: *in*
Luca.Ward: *your*
Luca.Ward: *salty*
Luca.Ward: *arse*
Xavier.Laghari: *why my arse gotta be salty*
Luca.Ward: *it'll hurt more that way*
Xavier.Laghari: *baby why your love gotta hurt so bad?*

Then a pause, the little animated dots that said Xavier was typing, going on for so long that Luca expected an entire paragraph. But instead all that popped up was two words:

Xavier.Laghari: *vid chat?*

Luca stilled, biting his lip, then tapped out:

Luca.Ward: *why?*
Xavier.Laghari: *because i want to*
Xavier.Laghari: *maybe i miss your pretty face*
Luca.Ward: *liar.*
Luca.Ward: *fine.*
Luca.Ward: *sec*

He clicked the video chat button on the Messenger window, gave the browser permission to access his laptop webcam, then waited for Xavier to accept. A few moments later the window expanded onto a black screen, then resolved into a grainy video: a close-up of Xavier's neck and jaw, bristles of stubble against dark brown skin the colour of deep-burnished oak, the white of his t-shirt collar, a glimpse of his dorm room past the curling thatch of hair at his nape. Then he pulled back, settling in full view and dragging a hand back through damp hair with a cheesy, broad grin that bunched his round cheeks up into arcs underneath his eyes.

Luca eyed him sourly. Xav was much, *much* too cheerful for this early in the morning. "What."

"Well you look like shite," Xav chirped.

"Please wait while I strip naked and jump into your lap. I'm overwhelmed by your flattery and must have you."

"Gonna have to pass. You look like ten-day-old arse, and I'm not really into the whole 'fuck a corpse' gig, eh? Save the pigs and stiffs for Hameron. The fuck are you doing to yourself?"

"I'm just tired. Farm work is hard work."

"Luca." Xavier sighed, fixing him with a long look, arching a sceptical brow.

Luca looked away, wrapping his arms around himself. "Hn."

"*Luca*." Dark brown eyes softened. "I'm being serious here for once in my life. C'mon, baby boy. Talk to me."

"Xav…" Luca groaned, then sagged back against the wall behind the bed, rubbing his hand over his chest. "I don't even know where to start. I don't think you understand. What I did…it was so, so much worse than just embarrassing myself throwing myself at him."

He sighed, scrubbing a hand through his hair, darting his eyes away from Xavier's curiously interested gaze. This wasn't like Xav, this quiet, supportive silence—but it was every bit like Xav, to have his back when he needed it.

Luca had just never *needed* it this much before.

He plucked at his lower lip, tugging, then continued, "He's demisexual. He's not a one and done guy, prick first. Like, sex is this…emotional thing for him. Special, eh? And maybe it is for me too, when he's the only one I've ever really wanted and I love him so much it's killing me and I can't really tell the two apart, but it's *different* for him. He told me what it's like and then I just…I ignored that and stomped all over his boundaries." He rubbed at his throat, at the ache there. "It was so shitty, Xav. It was so shitty of me, and I don't know how to say I'm sorry when I'm pretending the whole thing didn't happen and he's *letting* me. He's letting me be this complete fucking prat and act like a shitty dick to him because he's…he's…" Luca blew out roughly. "He's just like that. He'd let me walk on him in cleats if it would make me happy. Feels like that's what I'm doing, and I don't know how to stop."

"Stop pretending, for a start," Xav pointed out.

"It's kind of gotten to be a habit."

"Habits are made to be broken, my wee baby bird." Xav shook his head with a rueful smirk. "Look, you talk about this Imre guy like he hung the moon. So if he's so great, then he's probably open to talking this shite out without yelling and going all spare. Just you two. Sit. Talk."

"I don't know. I just—"

A light rap rattled against his door. He froze, heart thumping.

"Luca?" drifted through the door in Imre's quiet rumble, and Luca swore.

"*Fuck!*" he hissed under his breath, scrambling for his socks.

"Luca?" Xav asked. "What is it?"

"Shh!" Then, louder, "Just a second!"

Luca slammed the laptop closed, yanked his socks on over his aching feet, then grabbed the mess of ruined cotton swabs, bottle of alcohol, and roll of gauze, and stuffed them under his pillow. His gloves were on the nightstand, but if he put them on it would look weird; he tucked his arms against his chest, wrapping them around himself and stuffing his hands into his armpits like he was just cold or—or—it didn't matter, he just didn't want Imre to see his lacerated palms.

He took a shaky breath, then called, "Come in?"

After a long hesitation, the door eased open just enough for Imre to lean in; his gaze flicked over Luca, brows knitting, dark blue eyes careful, almost wary. "Am I interrupting anything?"

"Just on vid chat with my friend back home." Luca cleared his throat, fixing his gaze on the doorframe just over Imre's head. He still…still couldn't look directly *at* him, not without his heart trying to rip itself to pieces. "Nothing important."

"Ah," Imre said. He held an awkward moment, then said, "I'm

going into town for the day. To market. There's not much to do if you want to stay home. I'm keeping the goats in while I'm out."

Let him go, he told himself. *Easier to avoid each other if one of you isn't here.*

Sit. Talk, Xavier said in his head.

He sighed, closing his eyes, squaring his shoulders. "Do you need help?"

Imre took so long to answer that Luca thought he must have left the moment his eyes had closed, until: "I could use a hand loading and unloading the truck."

"Okay." Luca's voice cracked; he cleared his throat again. "I'll be dressed and ready in a minute."

Luca opened his eyes. Imre was watching him strangely, a furrow in his brows, but then he just…nodded. Nothing else.

Nodded and ducked back out without a word, closing the door behind him.

Cursing, Luca fell backward onto the bed, then dragged the laptop's lid up again.

"He has a nice voice," Xavier said.

Luca scrubbed his hands over his face. "Kill me."

"Talk to him."

"About what?"

"All the shite stewing inside you? What the fuck good does bottling it up do?"

Sighing, Luca flopped his hands away from his face and turned his head to glare at the screen. "You wouldn't understand."

"You'd be surprised." Xavier scrunched his nose. "How long are you there? January?"

"Yeah."

"Can you really stand staying like this until January?"

Luca winced. "…no."

"Then why wait?"

He didn't have an answer for that.

He did, however, have a ticking clock and Imre waiting for him, and he still needed to wrap his hands and feet.

At least the weather—colder by the day, the windows dewed every morning with frigid condensation that never quite formed into frost—meant Imre would be even less likely to question the gloves.

"I need to go get dressed," he said, and pushed himself up. "Later."

"Later. Love you, skinny prick."

Luca couldn't help laughing; it felt like the first time he'd smiled in weeks. "Love you too, arsehole," he murmured, then disconnected the chat and stared at the computer with a sigh.

Cooped up in the Land Rover with Imre.

This, likely, had not been his smartest idea, but it still didn't rank quite up there with his hall of fame high of getting drunk and sloppy all over the man he'd loved since he was knee high to a bloody damned cricket.

"Fuck my life," he said again, and knelt to lace up his boots.

45

LOADING BUSHELS AND BUSHELS OF apples into the back of the Land Rover was the easy part—even if, through Luca's gloves and the gauze underneath, the edges of the bushel baskets' grips cut into his palms, leaving him grinding his teeth to keep from hissing in pain where Imre could hear. Luca was getting used to ignoring the pain.

He didn't think he'd ever get used to ignoring Imre.

Luca kept his eyes on his feet as Imre counted over the baskets, several heavy sealed boxes, rattling coolers that exuded smoky chill breaths, and a crate of covered jars, before helping him secure the camper over the Land Rover's bed and snap the clamps into place, turning the flatbed into a covered compartment. But when Imre let himself into the driver's seat, Luca hesitated, staring at the handle of the passenger's side. It wasn't a long drive into town, it…wouldn't be so bad, and then Imre would be busy and maybe he wouldn't need Luca there at all, so maybe he should just stay here and—

"Coming?" Imre asked mildly.

"…sure," Luca mumbled, and pulled the door open to climb into the passenger's seat.

He fumbled with the seatbelt; it took six tries to actually buckle himself in while Imre waited patiently, not starting the engine until Luca was settled and huddled against the door, staring out the window. He told himself he couldn't smell Imre. Couldn't *feel* him. Couldn't hear his every movement. Not one bit.

Fuck.

Fuck.

He closed his eyes as the Land Rover pulled out of the drive and onto the road. The shivers of the engine rumbling up through him were making him queasy, turning the terrified unease in the pit of his stomach into a quivering slurry sloshing miserably about.

He dug in his pocket for his phone and his earbuds, then stared down at them. He couldn't keep doing this. Shutting Imre out; avoiding it. Imre wasn't the one who'd fucked up, and acting like this was just punishing him for something he didn't even do. But Luca didn't know what to say, how to start, and he closed his eyes, balling up his earbud cord in his fingers, fighting for words. But all he could find was a whisper of his voice, barely managing to force out:

"I hate this."

"Hm?" Imre asked. "Hate what?"

"The silence." Luca bit his lip, then tugged and fretted at his earbud cords. "You never talk to me anymore."

Imre remained quiet; Luca risked a glance from the corner of his eye, but Imre's gaze was on the road, distant and contemplative, his fingers lightly tapping on the steering wheel.

Finally, "You haven't seemed to want to talk," Imre said, slow and measured, then nodded toward Luca's fretting, cord-entangled hands without taking his eyes from the road. "And it's hard to talk through those."

"Yeah, I…" He pressed his lips together, forcing his hands to still, the earbud cord wrapped so tight it cut into his fingers: first a sharp burst of pain, then numbness as the circulation slowed. "I guess I've been tired. And thinking about a lot of things."

"Anything you want to talk about with me?"

"Nothing you need to hear. It wouldn't help." Luca lifted his head, making himself look at Imre fully, forcing himself to be brave. "I've been kind of an arsehole. Ignoring you." He darted his tongue over his lips, then, before he could lose his nerve: "I'm sorry."

Imre's lips curled at the corners; even if he kept his gaze turned forward, something softened and gentled around his eyes. "You don't need to apologize."

"Maybe not, but I should. I…I messed some things up. I didn't…listen right. I wasn't fair to you."

"About what?"

Luca couldn't answer that. Not when his pulse was roaring fit to drown out his voice, not when he could hardly breathe in more than shallow scared gasps. He pressed his hand to his chest, then looked away, out the window. He hadn't realized how much time had passed, but he could see the rooftops of Harrogate over the next hill, and at some point the road underneath them had turned from dirt to pavement.

"Nevermind," he said softly, rubbing at his chest. He'd…at least he'd apologized. "You meant it when you said we're still friends?"

"Of course," Imre answered without hesitation. "Why wouldn't we be?"

Luca smiled faintly. That queasiness in his stomach settled, even if it left behind an acid, melancholy taste of bitter longing.

Of course it was that simple. Because of course that was Imre.

"No reason," he murmured. "So what's this market thing?"

"You don't remember the weekly farmer's market?" Imre frowned. "I was supposed to go last week, but we were busy."

Luca shook his head; he tried to remember a farmer's market, but Harrogate was nothing but a memory of tea at some very fancy place where his parents made him wear nice clothing, all overwhelmed by memories of Lohere Farm and the bitter feeling that if they'd never left

Harrogate, his parents wouldn't have stopped loving each other. "I don't remember much about town, honestly. I think maybe I blocked it." He shrugged. "When I got off the train, it felt like I'd never been here before. Nothing felt familiar until Lohere, except that ugly-arse rail station."

"You were young when you moved away," Imre pointed out gently. "I called ahead to reserve a stall. We'll be selling off the extra apples while they're still fresh, and some raw honey I bottled before you came. I'll be meeting with buyers who'll come out for the manure from the goat barn. I might be able to negotiate a trade. Usually I trade with the Caldwells a few kilometres down the road for fresh hay, since I don't grow my own, but they lost half their crop to damp rot this season and they've none to spare. The market is a good place to meet other farmers from farther out and make a trade here and there."

"So…you sell shite?" Luca wrinkled his nose. "Ew."

Imre laughed, quiet and brief. "Not 'ew.' Goat manure is better fertilizer than cow or horse manure. It's higher in nutrient value for the soil, with a lower pH."

"…science-ing it doesn't make it less gross."

"It's nature."

"Nature is gross," Luca said firmly, earning another laugh.

"If you say so, angyalka."

Angyalka. Luca's breaths caught. He hadn't heard that nickname for *weeks*. Hadn't heard anything but brief murmurs of *Luca* to get his attention, followed by terse instructions that he barely stayed long enough to absorb before running away to throw himself into work. He couldn't endure that word, that nickname, because it made him want to be Imre's angel, want to be…

Stop.

"I say it's gross," he forced out, and managed a smile, even if his lips trembled. "And I say you *still* sell shite."

"Yes, Luca," Imre responded with wearily amused patience. "I sell shite."

Luca snorted out a laugh before he could stop himself, so sudden it scraped his throat—but it released the tightness in his chest, letting him breathe in great gulping giggles. And then Imre was laughing too, and they were laughing together, and god everything was all *wrong* still but at least there was this.

At least they could laugh, easing days and days of silent tension. At least they were talking again. At least Imre had accepted his apology.

At least Luca hadn't lost his friend.

46

Luca might not remember Harrogate, but the tall, classical buildings felt familiar nonetheless, their architecture evoking that sense of *home*. And as Imre pulled the Land Rover into the parking lot off the market, Luca leaned over to peer down Cambridge Street—a busy riot, with dozens of shopkeepers setting up their stalls, several customers already wandering around even though most of the stalls were only half-ready. The zig-zag brickwork of the street was familiar, clean and pale, and a vague memory teased at him of the fluttering green canopies of pop-up pavilions, the taste of scones, the snap and billow of banners flickering in the breeze. Sun through the canopies, he remembered. Being small, and looking up to see the sun turning canopies translucent, shining through the tiny holes in the canvas weave.

"I've been here," he murmured, pressing his fingers against the window.

"You'd come up to market with me and help out." Imre killed the engine and unsnapped his seatbelt. "You'd sit on the table and count people's change for them, swinging your legs."

Luca laughed. "I don't remember *that*."

"It happened. You were my good luck cat. I always had more buyers when you were there."

"I'm not a cat!"

"You aren't?"

"Make up your mind. Am I an angel, or a cat?"

But Imre just gave him an amused look, shaking his head and slipping out of the Land Rover. Luca huffed, then shook his head as well and climbed out. A rush of scents washed over him, riding the sharp bite of chill morning air: baking pastries, fresh-cut flowers, leather, tart citrus fruit, hay, the smell of livestock, fabric dye, sizzling spiced meat, so many other things it almost made him dizzy, thick and almost as overwhelming as the sheer *noise* of it, people chatting and calling out to each other, heavy boxes and items slung about and thudded to the street, clanging tent poles.

Imre popped the camper top with a squeal of hinges. Luca pulled himself from staring at the flurry of activity, and slipped back to Imre's side.

"Where's our stall?"

"Not far." Imre hauled out a bushel basket and passed it to Luca, then stacked two more into his own arms, thick biceps bulging and straining against his shirt fit to split the seams. He tossed his head, a few silvered strands drifting across his face. "This way."

Luca tried to lift the basket of apples enough to brace it a bit more against his chest—then winced when pressure cut into his palms. He caught a hiss under his breath as the gauze under his gloves *scraped,* leaving behind a worrisomely wet feeling and shocking pain through his hands.

Imre paused, glancing back. "Are you all right? Is it too heavy?"

"No." Luca shook his head quickly and forced a smile, then used his thigh to push the basket up so he could wrap his arms around it instead of holding by the handles. "I'm fine. Lead the way."

Imre lingered, watching him oddly, but then turned and led him through the busy crowds. Several people called out Imre's name in greeting as they passed; Imre always acknowledged with a nod and a rough sound, but didn't slow until they reached an empty stall with a little folded paper placard reading *Reserved: Imre Claybourne Lohere Farm*. Imre and Luca offloaded the bushel baskets, then snagged a rolling, folding hand cart that had been left under one of the stall's tables and dragged it back to the Land Rover. Unloading was a matter of minutes with the cart, and in two trips they'd brought every bushel, basket, box, crate, and cooler and piled them in a haphazard stack behind the stall's front. Imre shook out a rolled canvas banner printed with *Lohere* and a stylized, silhouetted blooming clover flower in white on cobalt blue, and draped it over the stall's front.

Luca watched him, biting his lip and fidgeting, then glanced over his shoulder. The bright colours drew him like silver to a racoon, and the smell of baking pastries gnawed at his stomach and made his mouth water. He toyed with his sleeve.

"Could I go look around a bit, or do you need me to stay?"

Imre glanced up from checking a portable refrigerator that had been built into the stall's side, raking Luca over with an amused look. "Hungry?"

"I wouldn't even know where to start." He bounced on the balls of his feet. "They have *pie!*"

Luca pointed toward a booth a few down, where a tall woman with sun-streaked blond hair was just setting out fresh, steaming pies along a wooden counter. Imre turned his head, then chuckled.

"*They* are one of my largest buyers of Lohere apples for their pies. Would you like to stop by?"

"Yes!"

Luca didn't mind the patient indulgence in Imre's glance. Nor did he mind working through the building crowds toward the pie stall, when Imre's bulk forged a path that made it easy to follow. He didn't even mind the line that was already forming at the stall, with its sign reading *Shaunnessy Bakery* in scrolling, cheerful script.

But he minded very much when the woman behind the counter caught sight of Imre, lit up with her eyes bright and breaths coming swift, and flung herself from behind the stall and into his arms.

“Imre!” the woman crowed, hugging him tightly. “What a delight; we missed you last week.”

Imre went subtly stiff; Luca didn’t think the woman even noticed, but Luca did. His jaw hurt, and he didn’t quite understand why until he realized he was grinding his teeth. He was being irrational, being a prat, but it was hard not to notice how the woman looked up at Imre with her cheeks flushed and her lashes fluttering.

When it was the same way Luca looked at Imre, too.

Imre loosely gripped the woman’s waist and gently pried her away. “Morning, Sally,” he drawled. “Had some things to handle at Lohere last week. You open yet?”

“Not quite, but you know you’re always welcome to anything you want.” She dimpled—then glanced past Imre at Luca. Her voice immediately turned sugary, like he was five fucking years old, as she said, “And who is this? Did you bring your nephew, Imre?”

Luca bristled, simmering, mouth opening to snap something back—but Imre intercepted smoothly.

“Family friend,” he rumbled. “You don’t remember the Wards from in town? This is their son.”

“Oh, you’re *Lucia’s* boy!” She laughed. She had a pretty laugh; *she* was pretty, an older woman in her late thirties or early forties with that certain refinement that turned the advancing lines on her face into marks of grace, yet a casual, friendly openness that Luca was trying hard to focus on rather than the sudden urge to *bite her face off*. At least, on recognizing him, that syrupiness had left her voice to leave warm familiarity. “You’re pretty as your mother. I’m *so* jealous of those eyelashes."

He forced a smile, even if it felt more like a baring of teeth. "You can get the same thing in a tube of Maybelline."

Sally had started to offer her hand, but then faltered, blinking, and looked back and forth between Imre and Luca as if looking to one of them for guidance. Luca mentally kicked himself. Fucking *arsehole*. He took a deep breath, made his teeth unclench, and offered his hand in apology, trying that smile again.

"Sorry. I'm Luca."

She hesitated, but then shook his hand, her smile returning, albeit wary. "Nice to meet you, Luca…"

Imre fixed Luca with a long look, arching a brow, and Luca fought not to shrink back. But Imre only sighed, and diverted Sally's attention with, "Luca was hoping to try one of your pies. We could smell them the moment we stepped out."

Sally brightened. "Oh, of course! This way, please."

Luca hung back, plucking at his lower lip, the pit of his stomach heavy. But then Imre caught his eye and tossed his head, a subtle, beckoning gesture, and even if Luca was embarrassed as all bloody hell…there was no way he could say no, when Imre called.

Sally's wariness evaporated as she proudly displayed an array of fresh pies just out of the oven, talking about her process, ingredients, experimental flavours with clear pleasure in her work and an excitement that made it hard to dislike her. And she nearly beamed when she segmented out little sampler slices for both Luca and Imre, and Luca tried the blueberry crumble and nearly melted as sweet-tangy blueberry and sugar and pastry burst on his tongue in a delectable wash—while Imre rumbled his appreciation of a slice of walnut strudel pie. Imre and Luca swapped samplers, pushing bites of one thing or another on each other, until they were laughing and Sally glowed with pride, and suddenly it wasn't so hard to like her at all.

Especially when, after Imre finished discussing supply with her and Luca trailed him back to the Lohere stall…Luca realized within an hour of opening for business that Sally's reaction to Imre wasn't exactly uncommon.

He'd barely had time to help Imre set out the most attractive bushels of apples interspersed with cloth-wrapped wheels of goat cheese and clear, golden jars of honey before a line started to form. He'd proposed setting out a sample platter, and when Imre had agreed Luca had busied himself picking out one of the smaller personally-sized cheese wheels from each type and cubing them with Imre's pocket knife. So he didn't notice, at first, just *how* long the line at the Lohere stall was, when people blended in and out of the crowd. But a particular high, falsetto giggle pierced his concentration, and he glanced up, watching as a blushing woman with a thin, delicate nose and a cute brown pixie cut blushed and giggled over picking out apples, watching Imre from under her lashes. Luca quirked a brow, biting a back a smile.

Because Imre didn't even *notice*.

That fucking lunk. The entirety of his attention was on the apples, on picking out the nicest ones to bag up an even dozen for her, while she was throwing out hint after hint. And she wasn't the first, or the last; Luca couldn't help watching, trying not to be obvious, as a litany of coy smiles and fishing commentary and "accidental" brushes of hand to hand over exchanged pound notes passed through in a parade. He just kept his mouth shut, hung back, kept the sampler platters refreshed, and fetched anything Imre asked him to get—from plastic bags to zip ties to sample cups for milk to a fresh receipt pad, while the stock dwindled minute by minute, hour by hour.

Things slowed down around the lunch hour, when people

wandered off to buy ready-made food from the kebab stalls and Sally's pies and wherever that delicious scent of baking bread was coming from. Luca finally had a chance to sit down, when he'd been constantly replacing the shelf displays as they were bought out over and over again, leaving Imre free to handle transactions and deal with ogling customers. But now Luca sank down atop a crate, trying not to wince when, now that he was no longer standing, his sore, aching feet burned; his hands weren't doing much better, but at least the gloves and bandages had insulated them from too much more damage and kept a clean buffering layer between him and the food he'd been handling.

Imre eyed him thoughtfully, then levered himself down to sit on the edge of one of the tables. "You all right?"

"Wasn't expecting it to be this busy." Luca laughed, scrubbing his hair out of his face. "I'm good."

"Want something to eat?"

"Not sure I could afford anything here."

"I'll bring you something." Imre lingered on him, watching him until Luca had to avert his eyes from that intense gaze. "You look tired. Take a rest. I'll be back."

"Okay," Luca said, unable to help smiling as he watched Imre push to his feet, then stride away with those long, lazily powerful steps that made him stand out in any crowd.

This was better, he thought. They'd been working alongside each other for weeks, but not *together*. Even if there'd not been time for much with the deluge of customers, they'd spoken to each other easily and freely, and it was easier and easier to look at Imre without feeling like he wanted to curl up in a ball and cry.

He should have apologized ages ago, he thought.

Maybe his dad was right, and he really did need to grow up.

He relaxed, watching a stall a bit across the way—more of a pen, really, where fuzzy brown and white baby donkeys cavorted and kicked about, while parents brought their children by to stretch their hands out and try to pet the fractious little balls of fluff. Luca smiled to himself, stretching out in the sun and letting his bones go loose as he watched and thought he could happily spend the rest of the afternoon like this, soaking up the warmth and listening to the donkeys snort and whicker.

But before long Imre returned with a stack of Styrofoam cartons piled in one arm, and two glass bottles of lemonade dangling from his fingertips. He sank down atop a crate and dragged another one over to use as a table, then divvied the cartons between them. Luca pried one open to find a steaming lamb gyro with thick sour cream and chives, with salted chips—and in the other, an enormous wedge of Sally's blueberry crumble pie. He swallowed back the rush of saliva, and hefted the overflowing gyro in both hands to take a massive bite.

And nearly choked on it as Imre asked mildly, "So…did Sally do something to offend you?"

Luca coughed, swallowed, then wiped his mouth against the back of his mouth, flushing as he stared at Imre, then looked away. So much for *that* being dropped. "She called me your nephew," he muttered.

"And I corrected her."

"She was *drooling* over you."

Imre quirked his brows together, looking at Luca oddly as he picked up a thick, crispy chip. "She was not. Her mouth was quite dry." When Luca only stared at him, Imre cocked his head quizzically. "What?"

"Oh my God." Luca couldn't help laughing. "You're a fucking rock. You have rocks in your fucking head. Your brain is leaking out your beard." How could Imre not—how could he be so— Luca dragged a hand over his face, groaning. Lunk. Complete and utter lunk. "The cheese isn't the only reason you've got long lines, Imre."

"…it's not?"

"How did you survive to adulthood?" Luca sighed, watching Imre fondly. He had the damnedest look on his face, like a giant clunky iron robot frozen struggling to parse data that just wasn't compatible with his system. "They're flirting with you. They've *all* been flirting with you. And you're completely oblivious."

Imre coloured, flushing deeply underneath tawny skin, and muttered gruffly under his breath. "That is the most *ridiculous* thing I have ever heard."

"Don't believe me if you don't want to." Luca grinned and popped a bite of lamb into his mouth. "I'm just going to sit back, watch, and laugh."

With a sour grumble, Imre looked away—but after a moment, without ever meeting Luca's eyes, he reached for something hidden under one of the Styrofoam cartons that Luca hadn't noticed: a delicate purple crocus blossom, pale at its heart and blending into darker, more vibrant violet along the crinkled edges of its petals. Luca watched curiously, then stilled, chest seizing, as Imre leaned over and tucked the flower into his hair—nestling it just above his ear, the cool kiss of its petals brushing his temples, dewed with moisture, the stem weaving into his hair. Those rough fingers grazed his temple, the upper curve of his ear, came a breath away from brushing his cheek before Imre withdrew, leaving Luca staring, frozen, a flutter of warmth starting in the centre of his chest and trembling its way up to burst across his face until not even the noonday sun could rival the heat under his skin.

Imre…? he wanted to ask, but he was too afraid to open his mouth, to let himself think too hard, to wonder what it meant when knowing Imre, it might mean nothing at all but an innocent and kindly whim—and Luca couldn't want, couldn't wish, couldn't bear to destroy his own heart again.

And so he said nothing, while Imre lowered his gaze, looking almost as though he might be *avoiding* looking at Luca as he said, "Eat your lunch before the customers start coming back." He picked up his gyro, then added in a low, irritable growl, "And there will be *nothing* to laugh at."

THERE WAS PLENTY TO LAUGH at.

Luca didn't know how he kept a straight face when, for the rest of the afternoon, Imre was an absolute fucking *mess*.

And it was the most adorable thing Luca had ever seen.

He almost felt guilty for pointing out how many of the customers had been flirting with Imre, trying to get his attention—because as people began drifting back to their stall after lunch, Imre turned from calm, graven stone, unshakeable and collected, into a clumsy, fumbling wreck. He dropped things. He stammered. He avoided eye contact. He blushed. He ruined receipts, until Luca had to step in and gently take the receipt pad from him and finish ringing a customer up while Imre glowered sullenly at his feet and stuffed apples in a bag. He was like a boy who didn't know what to do with a love note passed in grade school, all elbows and flustered grouchiness, and Luca had never wanted more than to curl his fingers in that thick, lush beard, tug him down, and kiss him.

The ache nestled between his ribs, a quiet thing that was somehow more bearable than before, settling inside him like a precious secret rather than a pernicious infestation with vicious and biting teeth. He kept his laughter to himself when he didn't want to fluster Imre any further, but he couldn't stop smiling—and the more Imre sulked, the broader Luca's grin grew. Though now and then he stopped and touched the flower tucked above his ear, and told his heart to hold itself still.

Hold itself still, and not take Imre's gentleness and softness for anything more than what they were.

He was just finishing with a soft-lipped man who looked *quite* disappointed when Luca took over for Imre—who was currently skulking in the back of their stall, pretending to look busy checking the near-empty crates—when a familiar voice rang over the street, calling his name with friendly warmth.

"Luca!"

Luca ripped off the receipt copy and passed it to the customer along with his carefully wrapped jars of honey, then glanced up. Mira wove her way through the thinning afternoon crowds, sunlight shining off her bare shoulders in gleams of gold against brown, her violet and yellow sundress patterned with irises and standing out bright against the pale backdrop of the pavement. She wore her hair down today, and her braids swung against her back and drifted across her face as she drew closer, a wicker shopping basket dangling from one arm and covered by a draped cardigan, the other hand lifting in a wave.

"Ms. Landers!" Luca waved back, grinning. "Hey."

"Hey, you. And call me Mira." She drifted to a halt before the stall, flicking Luca a knowingly amused once-over. "You haven't broken anything yet. I'm impressed."

"Oy! I'm not *that* much of a helpless city boy."

"He's been somewhat helpless," Imre tossed out from behind him.

"Shut it, Imre," Luca growled. "He works me like a fucking draft ox. I'm not helpless."

Mira laughed. "Little hard work is good for anyone. How're the goats?"

"Better," Luca answered. "They're still weak, but they're eating solid food and Merta stands on her own all the time now. Gia has to lie down more, but she's still okay."

Her eyes warmed. "I'm sure they're doing that much better for your care."

"I like it," he admitted shyly, then ducked his head. "I like working with them."

"Aye? Maybe you've got a vet in you, under that pretty face. Let me know if you're ever looking for an apprenticeship."

"Really?" Excitement prickled through him, and he couldn't stop his grin. "I mean I've not declared for uni yet, but…okay. Okay!"

Mira chuckled, then transferred her gaze from Luca to Imre. "…you look like you've had a rough day."

Imre prowled to Luca's side, glowering down at Mira. He was still red in the face, his hair a tumbled mess from raking his fingers through it, his beard out of shape from dragging his hand over his face repeatedly. "I don't want to talk about it."

Luca smirked. "He just figured out half the reason his shite sells so well is because he's gorgeous."

"Well you've just ruined the charm of it, now." Mira grinned wickedly. "Half the fun is that he doesn't even *know*."

Imre made a strangled sound; fire-red darkened the tips of his ears, and he scowled thunderously. "I would thank both of you to *stop that* entirely."

"Oh do stop sulking." Mira chuckled, shaking her head, hand on her hip. "Look at it this way. Now you've twice the pretty men. Twice the business. There's a gaggle of grade school girls who've been giggling and watching Luca for the past half hour, and pooling their pennies to see if they can afford an excuse to come over."

Luca stiffened. "…*what*."

Mira cut her eyes to the side with a subtle toss of her head. Luca darted a glance sidelong—and sure enough, there was a group of girls in their school uniforms, toying with the straws in their colas and watching him, leaning over and whispering to each other with smiles that ranged from sly to sweet to shy to embarrassed; the one boy in the group wasn't any better, hanging back and ducking his head but now and then darting a nervous, curious glance at Luca.

"Smile, pretty thing," Mira teased, and he spluttered, looking away quickly and scowling, hating how *hot* he immediately bloomed, face boiling.

"I just—I don't—!"

She leaned in conspiratorially. "Don't worry. I won't tell them they aren't your flavour of choice. Wouldn't want to cut into your sales."

Luca choked on a sound. He suddenly didn't know what to do with his hands, where to look, and he darted a glance at her, at Imre, then down at his fussing fingers, twining them together, before looking back up at her shyly. "I…I never told you…"

The quiet sympathy in Mira's gaze almost undid him. She looked at him with a frank honesty that spoke far louder than any words, and for a moment her eyes flicked to the crocus in his hair before returning to his with a small, understanding smile.

"You didn't have to, pretty thing," she said. "You didn't have to."

48

BY THE TIME SUNSET CAME, Imre was ready for home.

Market days always wore him out. Even if he enjoyed reconnecting with the people he knew in town and from the outlying farms, in the end he was more of a solitary creature than a herd animal, and the energy of social interaction was draining. Home, right now, was a welcome beacon calling him through the descending night, a promise that kept him moving as he and Luca packed the empty crates and baskets back into the Land Rover, bade their farewells, and buckled in for the drive back to Lohere. Luca was quiet in the passenger's seat, but gone was the tense, hostile, repressed silence of before; this was a silence Imre could live with, comfortable and calm and tinged with both mutual exhaustion and the mutual satisfaction of a day's hard work.

He'd missed that while they'd been busy ignoring each other, dancing around each other, looking anywhere but *at* each other. And even if they'd still not truly talked through what happened, Luca's soft *I'm sorry* had done much to ease the tension and soothe the raw edges of Imre's hurt.

He watched the boy sidelong as he dozed against the window, unfazed by the Land Rover jouncing onto the dirt road just off town. Luca's eyes were almost fully closed, just glints of green in the shadows; he still wore the crocus Imre had impulsively bought from one of the florist' stalls, even though the petals had gone limp and begun to curl hours before.

Luca shifted with a drowsy sound, turning his head enough to fix a sleep-soft gaze on Imre. "Mmnh…? Everything okay?"

Imre smiled slightly, turning his gaze back to the road and turning off onto his drive. "Everything's fine, angyalka. We're home."

Yawning, Luca pushed himself up, scrubbing at his eyes with gloved fingers. The back of his wrist brushed the crocus loose and he jerked, catching it, his breaths hitching as he tucked it back into place. Imre caught himself lingering on the flush in his cheeks, soft spots of pink, and looked away quickly, just as Luca looked up with wide eyes to catch his gaze.

He parked the Land Rover, and together they slipped out; Luca rounded the truck toward the rear, but Imre shook his head and beckoned toward the house. "It'll keep. You're tired. We'll unload in the morning."

It said everything for how tired Luca was that he didn't argue with Imre in that way he had, like he was so desperate to prove his worth through hard labour. Imre couldn't help keeping a close eye on him as they stepped into the house; he had that odd hitch to his stride again. Imre didn't know if he should ask, if pricking at Luca's pride would just open that rift that had only begun to heal.

But as the lights of the foyer fell over them, he stilled as Luca lifted a hand to tuck his hair back and Imre glimpsed red on his wrist, seeping from beneath the edge of his glove. A single trickling streak, dried and crusted to his wrist, segmented in cracks that matched the seams in his skin.

Blood.

Imre frowned, stopping and catching Luca's forearm lightly, looking down at the smear of crimson. "Luca. You're bleeding."

"Eh?" Luca looked down, then coloured and looked away, face

setting oddly, at once guilty and deliberately expressionless. "Oh."

"Did you cut yourself?"

"…no."

Imre frowned, then guided Luca to the kitchen with a light tug and gently nudged him toward the table, before switching the lamps on in a wash of gold. "Sit. Show me."

Luca sank into a chair and scrunched down into his shoulders, slit-eyed gaze fixed glassily to the side; he set his mouth in a tight line, made several wordless sounds under his breath, then slowly peeled one glove off, then the other. Underneath his hands were wrapped from palm to fingertips in gauze—and that gauze was soaked in watery patches of dried blood, pink in some places, rusty in others. A sharp concussive shock thudded through Imre's chest, and he dropped to one knee, swearing.

"Bloody *hell*," he growled, reaching for Luca's hands. Luca started to jerk them back, but Imre caught his wrists, grasping firmly, something fierce brewing inside him, something that made it hard to breathe. "Don't you *dare*. Be still."

Luca sucked in a hitching sound, biting his lip, but bowed his head with a nod. And he held still while Imre peeled away the gauze, working carefully, trying to keep gentle but still wincing when Luca flinched and hissed as his reddened, blistered palms were revealed. They were *lacerated*, the skin split over and over, half-healed, split once more, blood seeping from thin wounds and several puffy blisters just waiting to pop. Imre stared, cradling those slim hands in his, his heart aching and his throat tight.

"God *damn* it, Luca."

Swallowing audibly, Luca said in a small voice, "It's normal. They'll callus and then it won't happen anymore."

"It's not normal." And suddenly that hitching stride made sense, and Imre cursed himself for not realizing sooner just how long Luca had been forcing himself to work through the pain. "Let me see your feet."

Luca didn't move, kept his eyes averted—but didn't stop Imre from pulling the laces on his boots and easing his shoes off, setting them aside. He was afraid of what he'd find, under the double layers of socks. He stripped away one pair, then the other, to find more bloodied gauze and beneath that, Luca's soles a raw mess of shredded skin and exposed flesh.

"*Luca.*" Imre cradled slim ankles carefully, turning Luca's feet to look at the full extent of the damage. "Why didn't you tell me?"

"I…I didn't want to bother you. I wanted to be able to work."

Luca's lips trembled, and he scrunched himself small. Imre couldn't stand it. He couldn't *stand* it, and he released Luca's ankles to lay his head in the boy's lap, wrapping his arms around his waist and fighting against the burn in his eyes, fighting not to fucking *break* when his angyalka had been *hurting* himself, and hadn't trusted Imre enough to take care of him.

"You stubborn little *cat*," he rasped, pressing his face into Luca's thighs. "You never bother me. Especially not with this. What if you'd gotten infected?"

Luca leaned against him after a long moment, and then the back of one soft hand rested against Imre's hair. "I cleaned them with alcohol…"

"I should have noticed it was disappearing." Imre closed his eyes, struggling to get himself under control. "You're off your feet. For the next two weeks."

"What?" He felt more than saw Luca stiffen. "But…I can still help…"

Imre pushed himself up, looking up at the boy. "Not like this," he said firmly. "I won't have you hurt yourself further. Calluses happen when blisters have time to heal. Instead of giving them time to heal, you've just added injury on top of injury. It stops now."

Luca's face fell, his eyes brimming. Imre sighed, reaching up to brush his knuckles under the beads welling on the lower curls of dark lashes.

"All I'm doing is insulating for the winter and moving the chickens to their indoor coop, Luca. I can handle that alone. Stay inside. Rest."

"I…I don't want to be useless to you…"

"You aren't." Imre offered a smile. "Even if you never lifted a finger, you couldn't be."

Luca pressed his lips together, then whispered, "Can I at least do the housecleaning and cooking?"

"Luca."

"Please."

"*Luca.*"

"I will start rattling off the walls, sitting in this house doing nothing for two straight weeks." Luca smiled shakily. "*Please*, Imre."

"Very well. But—" He held a hand up. "Only light work. Nothing that aggravates your hands. If you can do it sitting down, do so. I've a few tall stools in the attic that will reach stove height; I'll bring them down tonight." He could *see* Luca gearing up for another stubborn assertion in the tightening of his jaw and the spark in his eyes, and cut him off with, "Promise me. Only light work. And not for a few days, after you've started to improve."

Luca sighed. "I promise."

"Good." Imre rocked back on his heels, then pushed to his feet. "I'll run you a bath with Epsom salts. Should help the wounds drain and dry out, and then we'll clean you up fresh."

“But—”

“I wouldn’t argue right now, Luca.” Imre looked down into those damp green eyes, his heart twisting. He didn’t know if he was furious with Luca, furious with himself, or just falling apart inside at the idea of Luca in pain…but his temper was burning under the surface, anger and concern warring in a chaos of emotion he wasn’t accustomed to, didn’t know how to channel, and didn’t want to tempt with the slightest push when it might explode into something he wasn’t ready to deal with. “Just don’t.”

Luca said nothing, watching him with wide eyes, but after a moment he nodded, lashes lowering.

Imre brushed his hair back, tucking it so that the soft black strands flowed over the petals of the crocus, then turned and left the room before he gave in to the tempest inside him, and did something he shouldn’t.

49

HE'D MANAGED TO CALM HIMSELF by the time he finished running Luca's bath in the downstairs bathroom, staying close to continuously test the temperature of the water so it would be warm enough to soothe but not hot enough to burn, slowly sifting in a box of Epsom salts and dissolving them in with his fingers until the box was empty. He rummaged in the cabinet, then, digging through his rather large array of various bath salts and oils. He didn't often have time for long, hot soaks, but sometimes he liked them after a hard, sore day or on a frigid winter evening—and the various blends of aromas and textures from the salts and oils helped him relax, drift.

He thought, now, they might help Luca's hands and feet, and he squinted at labels until he found the bottle of pure aloe extract, sea salts, and a bottle of thick tea tree oil. He dumped them into the bath, then swirled it together into an aromatic, steaming mix, little clear pools of oil making iridescent dots on the surface, then dried his hands on a towel and returned to the kitchen. Luca was still huddled miserably in the chair, legs tucked against his side and his hands curled in his lap. Imre sighed, shaking his head fondly as he drew closer and took a knee next to the chair, holding out his arms.

"Come on, now."

Luca lifted his head, blinking. "Wh-what? You don't have to carry me…"

"You're not walking on those feet until at least tomorrow.

Bandages or socks, right now, will just make things worse until those blisters have dried out overnight. And since I'll not have you barefoot and stepping into an infection…" Imre cocked a brow. "Looks like I'm your legs, tonight."

Plucking at his lower lip, Luca lingered on Imre with a heart-rending look of wide-eyed uncertainty, searching his face, before his lashes lowered in a sweep and he leaned in, slipping his arms around Imre's neck. Imre slid his arms underneath Luca's back and knees and, hands full of soft, sweet-smelling young man, lifted up to his feet. An immediate surge of warmth shot through him to the deepest depths of his stomach, and he inhaled his breath and held it, trying not to drug himself on Luca's scent. He'd thought with the distance he was *over* this…but the second he had Luca in his arms, head nestled against his shoulder and breaths fingering through his beard and lashes brushing his throat, that hard hot feeling pierced his heart once more and he fought not to think of the taste of raspberry lips or the feeling of slender fingers in his hair, husky voice whispering *Imre, Imre please.*

He swallowed roughly and thought, instead, of Marco saying *Imre, you fucking arsehole, how could you* as he turned to carry Luca into the bathroom. Sinking down, he set him lightly atop the toilet lid, kneeling once more to look at him at eye level.

"Do you need help undressing? Will it hurt your hands?"

Luca shook his head quickly, clearing his throat. "I can handle it." He stared at the bath. "You…that smells nice…you did that for me?"

"Of course I did that for you."

"But…you're upset with me."

"Not with you, no." Imre sighed, propping his forearm on his knee. "I'm upset with myself for not noticing before. I'm upset that I was so intent on giving you your space to work things out that I let you work yourself raw like this."

Bowing his head, Luca fidgeted at the hem of his t-shirt. "I should have said something sooner."

"You should have. But this was on both of us." Imre brushed his fingers beneath Luca's chin, coaxing those green eyes up to meet his. "We live together. We work together. Which means we can't do this again. If something happens, we talk to each other. Instead of dancing around each other. All right?"

"All right."

Yet still, those words waited unsaid between them. Those questions. Still as they looked at each other, there lingered the memory of a kiss, a quiet, desperate plea, and whispered emotions that Imre needed to believe had been the liquor talking and nothing else. He knew he should say something. Follow his own advice. Clear the air.

But some secret part of him—some terrible, dishonourable part of him—couldn't stand it if Luca said *oh, aye, sorry, I didn't mean it. I was just pissed out of my mind*.

And so he only smiled, and leaned in to press his lips to Luca's forehead. Chaste, always chaste, even if he breathed him in for a moment before pulling back.

"I'll be just in the kitchen making dinner. Call me if you need help with anything."

"Okay," was all Luca said, even if those soft syllables seemed to promise something more in the hitch of his voice, in the sigh of his breaths. "Okay."

Leave, Imre told himself.

But still it was long moments before he stood, and let himself out into the kitchen.

50

LUCA LISTENED TO THE SOUNDS of Imre moving away for long moments before he started to peel out of his clothing gingerly, awkward with only his fingertips. It probably would have been easier to let Imre do it, but right now he was too raw to handle the idea of those rough hands stripping him naked, after those rough words had already left him bare.

Imre's head in his lap. That choke in his voice. He almost wanted to hate Imre for caring so fucking much, because it made it that much harder to stop loving him.

Luca left his clothing in a pile on the floor, then lowered himself carefully into the bath. The warm water *stung* at first, and he hissed as he settled against the side, submerging his hands and feet and waiting for the ache to stop. He sank down until the water rose up over his chin and stopped just below his nostrils, letting him breathe in the warm, tingling scents rising on curls of steam to envelop him and ease his rattled nerves.

He *had* to stop letting Imre get under his skin.

There was something wrong with him, he thought. He couldn't ever be satisfied with things that would make most people content. He had a solid path to university and a career of his choosing, if he'd just *choose*—and he'd rather throw it all away to drift between pillar and post, not even sure where the days and nights went in a haze of circling thoughts and clouds of smoke and the buzz of beer or gin or whatever the fly-by-night friends he'd had in Sheffield pressed into his hand that day. He had Imre's friendship, something he'd thought he'd ruined…

And still, *still* he wanted more.

"Fucking knob," he muttered, only it came out in bubbles that rose to the surface and popped—and with a groan, he sank down in the water until it closed over his head, and let himself *drift*.

He remained like that until he couldn't breathe anymore, then surfaced and reached for a flannel to slough the water off his face. As he rose from the water, the wilted crocus came loose from his hair, floating along the surface. He caught it, and set it gingerly aside on the toilet lid.

He felt better, at least, soaking in the soothing water and letting it ease away the burn of his shredded flesh. He could've ruined his hands if he'd kept going like this. He was a knob *and* a wanker. He stared down at his reddened palms, the broken skin puckered and white above pink flesh. Mira had said he was good with the animals; so had Imre. These hands had helped piece sick animals back together. Maybe…maybe that was what he wanted. What he wanted to *do*.

And if he'd cocked up his hands, he could've ruined that before he'd ever had a chance to try.

"Knob, wanker, and a *shite*," he hissed, then growled and settled to scrubbing himself off.

When he was done, he pulled the stopper from the tub and watched the water swirl down the drain, leaving him damp and shivering and curled in the bath. He wasn't supposed to stand up, but he was bloody naked and…oh fuck. He reached over to snag the massive, thick bath towel Imre had left atop the toilet and draped it around himself like a cloak, pulling his knees up to his chest. He felt fucking pathetic, but…

"Imre…?" he called tentatively.

A few moments later, Imre's shadow appeared under the bathroom door. "Everything all right?"

"Aye, I just…" Luca cleared his throat. "I'm done…and you told me not to walk."

A particularly lengthy silence followed. Then: "Are you decent?"

He hunched into the towel. "…got a towel over me."

The door creaked open, almost warily. Imre peered inside, then relaxed and stepped in further and crossed to sit on the edge of the tub. "I'll take you up to your room and leave you to dress, then bring you dinner in bed. Does that sound fair?"

Luca wrinkled his nose. "I know I sound a right prat, but…I don't want to eat alone in my room like it's punishment at boarding school."

"You don't sound a prat," Imre said with a chuckle. "All right. I'll bring you back down after you've dressed, and we can eat in the living room. We can even watch a film. Better?"

"…you don't have a telly."

"You aren't the only one with a laptop, *prat*."

"That's still a lot of toting me around."

"You weigh less than a feather." And then Imre's fingertip was pressed lightly to the tip of Luca's nose, leaving him crossing his eyes, staring at the coarse ridge of his knuckle. "Those are the only options. I *want* to fetch and carry for you, even if what I'm fetching and carrying is *you*. So. Bed, or let me tote you about. You can pick one, but no more excuses for either."

Luca scowled and snapped his teeth at that finger. "I told you you're not my father."

"Not even close. What I am, however, is a friend who knows your shite for what it is, and won't let you hurt yourself any further."

"You know my shite, eh?" Luca eyed him sidelong, then snorted. "All right. Living room. I pick option B."

"Then let's get you out of that tub so you can stop shivering like a wet kitten, and get you into some clothing."

Before Luca could protest, heated arms slid around him, muscle straining against the seams of today's henley—pale grey, this time—and enveloping him in molten stone with nothing between him and Imre but the towel that barely wrapped around him enough to be decent, his bare arse an inch away from touching open air, his legs completely exposed and draped over Imre's arm. Luca froze, heart constricting and palpitating in erratic shudders, and clutched at the towel, arranging it over himself and drawing it tighter and trying so very hard not to…

Not to *anything*.

He risked a glance up at Imre, as Imre carried him from the bathroom with hardly a moment to snag the crocus before he was out of reach—but Imre was looking over his head, gaze focused ahead on their path. Calm, always so calm, but there was something about the taut line of his throat and the set of his shoulders and the way his fingers bit *just* a little into Luca's naked thigh that built a whispering, quiet tension Luca didn't understand. Whatever it was, it made his gut quiver and his breaths shallow. He'd never felt so small and vulnerable as he did near-naked in Imre's arms.

And yet he'd never felt so *safe*, either.

He bit his lip, taking these moments—these moments when some silent intuition told him Imre wouldn't, couldn't look at him—to drink Imre in again, re-imprint the subtle elegance and rough, wild beauty of his face, his body, the way he carried himself when Luca had refused to let himself look for *weeks*. His heart slowed. His breaths stilled.

And when Imre looked down at him as they crested the stairs, time stopped in a single sweet moment when Imre offered a faint, distracted smile, and Luca smiled back, tucking his head underneath Imre's jaw and letting himself *lean*.

He clung to that comfortable moment for a few seconds longer, until Imre elbowed his bedroom door open and set him down carefully on the bed. Neither said a word, while Imre checked the drawers of the bureau and fished out a clean pair of boxers and one of the large, oversized t-shirts Luca liked to sleep in. He set them on the bed at Luca's hip, then straightened, searching him discerningly.

"No socks, no gloves, no gauze," he said. "I was serious. You need to let the wounds air and dry. Try not to come into contact with anything that will stick to the raw areas. Call for me when you're ready to come down." He arched a brow. "Unless you'd like me to dress you, too."

"*No!*"

"Thought not. Independent little cat." Imre smirked. "I'll be finishing dinner."

He turned away, but paused when Luca called after him.

"Imre…?"

"Hm?"

Luca hesitated, meeting that one blue eye turned over Imre's shoulder. "Why am I a cat now, and not your angel anymore?"

"You're still my angel. You will always be angyalka." Imre's gaze softened. "But that doesn't change that you're stubborn and independent, fickle and ferocious, playful and petulant as a cat. You move like a cat. You've grown into yourself, and you stretch and slink into long limbs like a feline thing. Leggy and delicate."

Whatever answer he'd been expecting, it wasn't that. Luca made an odd sound in the back of his throat; he wasn't even sure what it was trying to be, when words weren't quite working and it felt like the flutter in his stomach was trying to climb up onto his tongue. He ducked his burning face away from Imre, scowling. Damn that man and his bluntness, his honesty, his…his…his *complete and utter oblivion* to what things like that could do to Luca. The way he just casually tossed something like that out.

With no idea that his every word had the power to bind Luca up in its coils, and make him feel at once beautiful and wretched.

"Oh, just get out," he growled, scowling at his knees.

Imre chuckled. "His Majesty's wish is my command," he said, and disappeared out into the hall.

"Fucking *arse*," Luca muttered, staring down at the crocus still caught in his fingertips, then snagged his clean t-shirt and buried his face into it.

And *screamed*, muffling the sound to a muted groan.

God *damn* it, Imre.

51

BY THE TIME LUCA CALLED for him again, Imre had laid out plates and drinks on the coffee table, stoked the fireplace, and dug his laptop out from under the desk in his ill-used office. He didn't use it for much other than tracking breeding lines, yields, harvest and planting dates, breeding and kidding dates, and supply orders, but he had a Netflix subscription. Not that he could remember the password, but he'd figure it out in a minute.

"Imre…?" drifted down the stairs, with that subtle plaintive note that Imre couldn't help but smile at. Prideful little monster; it wasn't hard to see he couldn't stand imposing on Imre like this, but he wasn't quite seeming to grasp how little Imre *minded*.

Even if, when he could still feel the warmth of Luca's naked, damp body enveloped in a towel, he was trying very hard not to suspect his own motives.

"Coming," he called, and took the steps two at a time to Luca's room.

Luca curled on the bed, dressed in his pyjamas with his knees drawn up, carefully not clasping his hands and just as carefully letting his feet dangle over the edge by his heels. Clean and dry, they didn't look nearly so terrifying, and Imre let go of a little of the worry that had been curdling and stewing inside him.

"How're you feeling?"

"Better," Luca mumbled against his knees. "The bath was nice."

"Good. I'll fetch the aspirin so you can have a few with dinner; should help. Ready to go down?"

"Eh, ah."

"Informative." Imre bent over Luca and gathered up the bundle of boy into his arms. "Up you go, then."

As Imre straightened, Luca let out a little yelp, before those slender arms came around his neck. Luca's wrist pressed against Imre's throat, and through that thin, fine skin the soft flutter of the boy's pulse moved against Imre's neck in time with his own heartbeat, a shudder and throb of blood pounding through his veins. Imre could feel Luca watching him as he carried him out into the hall and down the stairs; it was almost strange, how he always *knew*. Even during those silent weeks, he'd known the moment his back was turned that those pale green eyes were on him, connecting them in ways that tugged and tore at him and made it impossible for him to ever stray too far away.

What are you doing, Imre?

He dragged his thoughts back on track and glanced down at Luca, meeting those wide eyes with a smile before veering into the living room and settling him down in the corner of the deep, yielding sofa, right in the nest of quilts Imre had layered against the leather. He wrapped the blankets around Luca's shoulders, then pulled back and headed back up the stairs, taking the steps quickly to duck into the bathroom and fetch the aspirin from the cabinet. He swung back through the kitchen and picked up two trays with steaming, deep bowls of lamb stew and fresh-baked bread with a buttery, crisp crust balanced next to hot mugs of tea.

When he returned to the living room, Luca had tucked himself up in a ball again, hiding his hands and feet underneath the blankets. The click of claws on stone warned before Vila and Seti came swarming in, tumbling over each other and then spilling themselves onto the rug before the fire, sprawling out in a tangle of black and white with their tongues lolling and tails swishing.

Imre set his tray down on the coffee table, then unfolded the legs of the other and placed it carefully over Luca's lap. Luca shifted enough to fit his legs underneath it, and flashed him a brief, rather pensive smile.

Imre settled down next to him, twisted the cap off the aspirin bottle, and set it down on Luca's tray. "Comfortable?"

"Mm," Luca answered with that same distracted smile, and reached for the bottle. He tilted his head back, shook a few pills into his mouth, then reached for the tea mug. Imre had deliberately made the tea cooler than normal so the mug wouldn't burn Luca's palms, but still when the boy winced, eyes twitching at the corners as he lifted the mug to his lips and swallowed a gulp, it took everything in Imre not to snatch the mug from his raw fingers and cradle it to Luca's lips for him.

"Can you handle a spoon?" he asked, as Luca set the mug down.

With a nod, Luca picked up the carved wooden soup spoon. "Hold it between my fingers like this, see?" He positioned it so the handle of the spoon was clasped between his index and middle fingers, resting primarily against the unblistered sides, and supported by the edge of his thumb. "Been doing it for weeks."

Imre set his jaw, glowering at him, fighting back the growl building in his chest. *Weeks*. Luca had been in pain for *weeks*, hadn't said a word, and Imre hadn't even *noticed*.

Luca winced, hunching into his shoulders and flashing a sheepish smile. "Sorry."

"If I have to watch you like a hawk to keep this from happening again, I will."

"It won't happen again," Luca promised, and Imre arched a brow. Luca laughed. "It *won't*. I'll be good."

"I'm not even convinced you're capable."

"Am I really so terrible to put up with?" Luca's lower lip thrust out.

"No." Imre sighed, and rested his hand to the top of that silky head of messy hair. "And I am never just putting up with you, angyalka."

Luca beamed, then scooped a bite of stew into his mouth. Imre chuckled and settled his tray at his hip, keeping it in easy reach but leaving his lap free for his laptop. In between stealing bites and listening to the faint clink of Luca's dishware, Imre woke the laptop up and pulled up the desktop Netflix app, typed in his email, then took a stab at his password.

User name or password incorrect. Please retry. Forgot your password?

He frowned. He'd set up this account some five years ago on a different computer that had saved the password for him, and he'd promptly forgotten it. He usually wrote his passwords in Romani, if only because they were less likely to be in common language lexicons used to test accounts for vulnerabilities and crack them, but everything he could think of—clover, apples, goats, family, all words that represented something *important* to him, something he'd remember—didn't work.

Luca leaned over, peering at the screen, a one-sided grin tugging at his mouth. "Sure you know how that thing works?"

Imre stared at him flatly. "You finished?"

"Nope."

"…I forgot my password."

"Use the password retrieval link."

"Hn." Imre scowled and picked up a bite of his stew instead, and Luca laughed, sweet and bright.

"Imre, are you being stubborn?"

"*Hn.*"

"I thought goats were stubborn, not giant oxen."

"I am not an *ox*. Don't you start." Imre eyed him sourly, but at least he was laughing. That laughter seemed a balm on everything, and Imre was beginning to realize he'd do anything to hear it. With a grumble, he clicked the *Forgot your password?*, then typed in his email address before tabbing over to his mail client to watch for the reset link. "What do you want to watch?"

"Dunno." Luca wriggled over, edging closer and pushing his tray with his thighs and elbows. "I kind of like those historical things. Like, I think there's a new one on Netflix with Jason Momoa?"

"Who?"

"Big guy. Aquaman."

"…who."

Luca let out a long, slow sigh. "…he's tall and tan and has a beard and long hair, and he's really fucking hot. One look and it's like, *phwoar*."

Imre cocked his head, idly toying with his beard. "I could be convinced to watch this."

"Thought you said you don't like men like you."

"I have varied and nuanced tastes." Imre eyed the little wretch. "And he sounds nothing like me."

"Uh-huh." Luca just smirked in that maddening way of his. "Got your password yet?"

Brat.

But the email was there in Imre's inbox, and he clicked the link. A few taps and he'd reset his password to *@ngya1k4*; at least that, he wouldn't forget. The Netflix browsing window welcomed him far too cheerfully, before blooming into an array of tiled title cards in bright colours.

"There."

"Oh my God, Imre." Luca made a choked, amused sound, staring at the screen. "The last thing in your watched queue is *Frasier*?"

Imre scowled. "I like Niles."

"You're so *old*, and I love it." Laughing, Luca reached for the laptop. "Give."

Sceptical, Imre handed the laptop over; he couldn't help but marvel at how Luca handled it with the edges of his hands, keeping his fingers spread away, before manoeuvring the touchpad and keyboard with his curled knuckles. Luca was nothing if not ingenuity in the face of sheer, prideful stubbornness.

...brat.

He watched while Luca found the series he wanted, then pulled up the page. "Ready?"

"Aye, if that's what you want to watch."

"It is," Luca said firmly, setting the laptop on the coffee table at the midpoint between them.

And then promptly tucking himself against Imre's side, snuggling against him in a mess of blankets and lanky limbs.

Imre froze, looking down at Luca. Luca tipped his head back, eyes wide and a little too innocent, a little smile playing about his lips.

"So we can both see," he said. "You don't mind, do you, Imre?"

Imre groaned. He didn't know what the hell had gotten into Luca tonight, but that little imp was going to be the death of him.

"No, angyalka," he said. "I don't mind."

With a happy sound, Luca burrowed against him and dragged his tray over to balance on one tucked-up thigh; sighing, Imre stretched his arm along the back of the couch and turned his gaze to the laptop screen as the opening credits began to roll. He wasn't quite sure he understood the show; something about the colonial fur trade and the big bloke—Momoa, Luca had called him—fighting for a place and livelihood among settlers who wanted to crowd him out? Maybe. But it passed the time, and by the time the first episode had ended they'd both finished eating and set their trays aside. Imre sank down to relax a bit deeper into the couch—and in response, Luca shifted down to rest his head in Imre's lap, pillowing his cheek against his thigh, this light warmth that drew Imre's attention no matter how he tried to ignore it.

And it seemed only natural, to let his hand drift from the back of the couch to rest on Luca's waist. Beneath the blankets Luca's body dipped into a smooth curve, a cradle that seemed made for the curl of Imre's fingers to fit *just so*, to find their way into the dips and hollows of his hip bones and stomach and settle there, with Luca's soft, shallow breaths lifting and lowering his fingertips. Those breaths seemed too loud, as if the laptop's noise had faded to just a whisper and the crackle of the hearth was nothing more than a sigh. The only sound in the room was Luca's breathing, and the dull dreaming thud of Imre's heart.

Luca shifted onto his back, his warm weight moving against Imre's thigh; his shirt caught on Imre's fingers with the movement, until the fabric rumpled upward and suddenly it was bare skin under Imre's palm, his spreading fingers. Bare skin and pure radiant heat, a smoothness like wet silk moulded over lean sinew, a sweetness that soaked up into his palm and held him as though he were melded, flesh to flesh, with Luca. He stared dazedly down where his hand pressed, skin to skin, to Luca's body, a hazed and drugged slowness entering his thoughts, holding them back until his mind ran apace with a sluggish heart that would linger and mew over these moments for ever and always, holding a few seconds fast for a lifetime.

So pale, he thought. Luca was so pale, his skin sweet crescents between the dark splay of Imre's fingers. As though Imre's touch were fine gleaming wood stain, painted against glistening white ash branches.

"Imre?" Luca whispered, voice trembling, coming to him through that dream-soft haze as though speaking through water.

Imre dragged his gaze to Luca's face. To those wide, confused green eyes. To those flushed cheeks. To parted raspberry lips, moving and sighing with every swift breath. His mouth ached, as he lingered on those lips; as he parted his own to speak, but nothing came forth. If he spoke, reason would assert itself; if he spoke, reality would pull him back from a trembling edge that seized the breaths in his lungs and held him teetering on the verge of giving in to something hungering and wicked and terrible.

Luca swallowed, his throat working, his lips closing and then parting again on a delicate dart of his tongue. That pink, pink tongue, and Imre followed its every movement, the wet sheen glistening behind.

"Luca," he breathed, his name a sweetling caught in Imre's throat.

With a soft, almost frightened sound, Luca sat up—until they sat shoulder pressed to shoulder, Luca's arm caught against Imre's chest, his stomach still burning under Imre's palm. Too close, something in Imre's mind warned. Too close, when those raspberry lips were just inches away, tempting him from over the curve of Luca's shoulder. The boy's gaze dipped to Imre's mouth as though he could follow this wanton and wretched train of thought, and that honeysuckle scent dizzied Imre like wine as Luca leaned closer.

"What's wrong?" Luca asked softly. "Why are you looking at me that way?"

Because, Imre thought distantly, and answered that question not with his words, but with his lips.

Were his thoughts not so slow they might have caught up to the moment, and seen it for what it was. Were they not so slow, they might have halted him in his tracks, taken firm rein of his body and his impulses to stop him before he could even move. Were they not so slow, they would have reminded him of those gentle words of caution, *be careful*—Mira both his conscience and his voice of reason where both seemed to have deserted him.

But his thoughts were left far behind, as he leaned in and caught that soft, overripe mouth and tasted it the way it begged to be tasted, teasing its curves in savouring nibbles just to feel its plushness and how it gave and parted and let him sink into each pillow-soft, yielding caress.

And when Luca leaned into him with a low, breathy moan…Imre was completely and utterly lost.

Every ounce of desire he'd bottled for weeks built into a bursting swell and flooded him, breath and body and bone, until he was caught on its racing tide and swept along, swept under, plunged into a drowning, submersive heat that immersed him head to toe in every sense of *Luca*. The warmth of that slim body pressed against his own. The lissom grace of long arms slipping around his neck. The rush of Luca's pulse against Imre's palm, as he curled his hand against his throat, stroking his fingers back into the soft tangles of hair at the nape of his neck. And the taste of his mouth—the taste, the scent, the warmth and wetness of his lips, his tongue, as Imre groaned and sought deep, so deep, as if within the heat of Luca's mouth he could find the secret that left his heart so completely at the mercy of such a slight, fragile wisp of a boy.

This was too raw, too real, cutting him open and leaving him tender inside, every sensation too intense to endure. As though he were an open wound of sheer emotion, and every shy, darting taste of Luca's tongue, every soft sound the boy made, touched that wound and left Imre vibrating with the sharp, searing shocks of pure, perfect, overwhelming *pain*. Never had the pleasure of a kiss—a consuming, breathless, tight-locked kiss of such lusciously slow sweetness—been such pain, tearing him open and bleeding him out.

And he would bleed every drop out for Luca. For this feeling. He would rip himself to shreds, let himself be torn apart by the silent hurricane inside him, this soundless tempest, this whirlwind whisper of delicate touches that struck with a hammer's blow. He would destroy himself for this kiss.

But he would not destroy Luca.

And in the race between his common sense and his impulse, his common sense finally caught up, then overtook him and blocked his way, a stolid wall of disapproval warning him against going any further. His gut wrenched at the thought of parting; Luca tasted of every honeyed intoxication Imre could ever imagine, and he wondered if his fascination was because that kiss was forbidden…or because he desperately wanted it not to be.

"Luca," he whispered, then stopped and filled his mouth with one last taste, one last savouring moment to draw that delectable lower lip into his mouth and capture it in his teeth and suckle it as though he could glean every last hint of flavour from it and keep it for himself. No. *No*. He had to stop, had to think reason, think sense. He was not a man given to rash behaviour, and he was stepping outside of everything he had ever known of himself, watching himself from afar as he did things and desired things that belonged to an Imre Claybourne other than the one he recognized in the mirror each morning.

He made himself part from Luca's mouth, from Luca's gasping, pliant eagerness. That succulent mouth was swollen to reddened fullness, glistening, Luca's dark lashes lowered, his pale skin blooming all the way down to his throat, and *God* he was so lovely Imre just wanted to keep him this way—but he couldn't. Regret and shame soured the heat in his gut, turned it into a curdled mess churning in the pit of his stomach. Luca was so vulnerable right now.

And Imre had forgotten himself, taken advantage, and violated not just Luca's trust…but Marco's.

"I can't," he forced out, the words like thorns gouging inside his throat. He stroked his thumb along Luca's jaw, taking him in while he could. "Luca, I'm sorry. I…I shouldn't have done that."

Luca's eyes drifted open—for a moment dazed, a hazed and beautiful shade darkened as though a thousand clouds reflected off the surface of a clear green pool. Then they sharpened, clarified, as Luca's brows knit together, the lax soft line of his mouth tightening.

"Then why did you?" he bit off.

"Because I…" Imre swallowed. "I…cannot explain it. Please…please tell me you understand, angyalka. Tell me you understand why I can't."

Every drop of emotion drained from Luca's face. That flush melted away to leave pale skin as white as ice. Luca just stared at him. It would almost have been preferable had that gaze been accusatory, angry, condemning Imre for the louse he was—but more than anything, Luca just looked *tired*.

"I understand," Luca said quietly, then looked away, gaze fixing on the laptop screen, the TV show that was churning on without a care for the tension stretched on a thin cord between them.

Nothing else. Just that, and something curled up small in Imre's chest and *hurt*, this shrivelled and tangled little knot.

"Marco is my dearest and oldest friend," he continued, and even to him it sounded weak. "You are his *son*."

"I said I understand." Luca pulled away from him, that warmth leaving him as Luca settled at his side once more, wrapping himself up in the blanket. Still his voice was too quiet, too calm, too even, even as he said, "You don't need to grind it in."

"I'm not trying to." Imre spread his hands. Helplessness hovered over him like a guillotine that would never fall, leaving him perpetually trapped, afraid to move one way or the other. "I'm sorry. I don't…know how to deal with this. This is outside the realm of my experience."

"Yeah. Mine too." Luca's lashes swept down. He took a deep breath. His mouth trembled for a moment, then firmed. "You kissed me first this time, Imre. And we're both sober."

"I know. And again, I apologize."

Silence. Silence that broke Imre's heart, that made him afraid he'd ruined their friendship once more, that made him afraid he'd destroyed Luca's trust. Luca remained motionless for so very long, until he took another deep breath, visibly gathered himself, and looked up at Imre, his gaze so very weary but his wry, self-deprecating smile genuine, no matter how small.

"It's all right," Luca murmured. "Let's just be friends and it'll be okay." He shrugged, shoulders a touch stiff, then looked away again with a low, sheepish laugh. "Promise I won't sulk for another month if you don't."

"I don't *sulk*," Imre shot back without thinking, and Luca's laughter strengthened.

"Keep telling yourself that, Imre." He sighed, tilting his head back against the couch. "I have no idea what's going on. Want to start the episode over?"

Imre met Luca's eyes, searching, asking a question even he wasn't wholly sure of. Part of him couldn't believe it was this easy. Part of him didn't *want* it to be this easy, when he was raging inside, tearing at himself with claws of guilt and longing, leaving nothing of his heart but shredded ribbons.

But if he was to bleed, he would rather bleed alone. And if Luca was all right, good. At least they'd talked, somewhat. At least it was out in the open. Luca had said he'd understood. Imre only needed to let it go, and move on.

If he even knew how.

52

IT WAS A POINT OF pride, Luca thought, that he didn't break down sobbing and beg Imre to kiss him that way again. And again and again and again, until this unquenchable thirst was finally slaked, until he was drunk and sated on Imre, on his kiss, on the way it felt when Imre looked at him *just that way* and took him into his arms and rested those hot, broad hands against Luca's naked skin.

But he didn't.

Because Imre couldn't.

Because Luca was *too young*. Because Luca was *Marco's son* and not a real person with an identity, needs, longings of his own. Because Luca was…Luca was…

Luca was what Luca wasn't, and what Luca wasn't was *enough* for Imre.

He was tired of sobbing and wailing over that. Tired of hating himself for it. It just was what it was, and one day, he'd get over it. He'd rather be Imre's friend than have nothing at all, and maybe one day…one day, they'd look back on this and laugh.

But on this day, as he stared at the laptop screen and tried to make himself focus on the story and not the man at his side…

All he could do was hurt. Hurt, and bottle it all up inside like he was hoarding it for himself because it was too precious to give to anyone else. He'd thought it had burned, to humiliate himself by throwing himself at Imre only to be rebuffed as unwanted, undesirable.

But the truth was even worse, and scored that much deeper, branding and scarring his aching heart.

Because the truth was that Imre *did* want him.

Yet refused to even see him as more than every reason why he shouldn't.

53

"DIARY OF A HOUSEBOUND PRAT, day twelve," Luca muttered into his phone as he scrubbed around the burners on the stove with a toothbrush. "The massive oaf I live with is growing entirely too spoiled. He doesn't wipe his feet proper on the mat. He leaves his dirty laundry on the bathroom rack like I'm supposed to just pick it up. This morning, he had the nerve to ask if I knew where his blue argyle socks were. Does the shite fancy me a bloody housewife?"

"Oh, like you'd complain," Xavier piped from the phone, laughing. "You practically *are* the doting little husband. Just need to consummate, eh?"

Luca snorted, propping the phone against his ear and turning to rinse the toothbrush in the sink, scrubbing it free of black grime with his thumb. This stove looked like it hadn't had a proper deep cleaning in all its cracks and crevices in years. Then again, most of Imre's house was like that: clean on the surface, but missing all those little touches like wiping down the upper edges of the baseboards or dusting the topsides of the living room ceiling fan blades. Imre had kept it plenty *tidy*, but he'd never gotten it the kind of clean that happened when you cooped a nineteen-year-old boy up in the house and told him he couldn't do anything more strenuous than cooking and cleaning.

And by the time Luca was done, he'd be able to see his *reflection* in the wrought iron of the stove burner covers.

"No consummating happening here," he sighed. "Don't even put that thought into my head."

"Aw, still no luck?"

"Can't have luck for something I'm not even trying for."

Xavier let out a dry laugh. "Giving up so easily?"

"I just…" Luca wrinkled his nose, checked the toothbrush, then set to scrubbing at the next burner—pausing only to shift his grip when the toothbrush handle pressed into one of the still-tender spots on his mostly healed fingers. "I'm not sticking my hand in that fire again, y'know? Things are better when we're friends. We talk. We're there for each other, instead of being awkward and weird. We're honest with each other, and overall just try to be good to each other."

Or that's what Luca had told himself, over the last two weeks. Imre…Imre was always Imre. Kind to him. Gentle. He spoke when Luca wanted to speak, didn't when Luca wanted quiet or solitude. It had mostly been up to Luca how normal he wanted things to be, and so he'd decided right then and there, sitting on that couch with Imre looking at him like he'd just desecrated a shrine, that he'd rather hold on to the good things than keep reaching for what was impossible when wanting the impossible could ruin what made their friendship *work.*

And it *had* worked, for the most part. He teased Imre, and Imre teased him back. They laughed over the dogs' antics together, and Imre mock-chided him for sneaking Seti and Vila tidbits from whatever Luca was making for dinner. And after dinner every night, they stood side by side over the sink, Imre washing, Luca drying, their arms brushing while Imre quietly caught him up on how the animals were doing, what needed to be done next, as if Luca was a part of the farm and needed to know every plan and everything Lohere needed.

He liked that. He liked feeling like he was an integral part of Lohere, and he didn't want to lose that for the short time he had it.

So it was only in the dark of night, curled in his bed alone, that he touched his lips and remembered that moment of heated pressure, and how Imre had pulled him close and stolen his breath and set his world on fire.

"So…" Xav mused. "That sounds a hell of a lot like what you'd want in a relationship, eh? That kind of thing's good between boyfriends, innit?"

"You can have those things in a friendship without it being about sex or love or any some such."

"Look at you, sounding all mature. Baby boy grew up when I wasn't looking."

"I did no such thing." Luca propped his hip against the counter, exhaling and wiping the back of his wrist across his brow; a few strands of his hair had escaped the handkerchief he'd tied over it, and tickled annoyingly in the film of sweat forming on his skin. "Look, I'm just…trying to be sensible about things. People fall in love all the time with people who don't love them back. You'd have to be a fucking arse to throw away a good friendship over something like that." He shrugged, idly tapping the toothbrush against his elbow. "So I'm trying not to be an arse. Even if it hurts sometimes."

"*Love hurts,*" Xav sang, merrily and entirely off-key, his voice cracking on every change in note. "*Love scars, love wounds and marks…*"

Luca winced. "So does your singing voice."

"Aren't you Mr. Chuckles today. Cheeky fucker." Xav huffed. "Speaking of wounds and marks, how're you healing up?"

"Better. Mostly healed over, just a couple of tender spots. Imre's not letting me off the hook a single day early, though."

"Someone's got to put a curb on your self-destructive rampage, eh?"

Luca turned back to the stove. "I'm not self-destru—"

He froze as he caught a glimpse of motion through the kitchen window, then leaned forward, rising up on his stocking toes to peer out through the curtains. Little wispy, feathery flakes fell down out of a clouded, heavy sky, catching on the wind and swirling briskly side to side before cartwheeling downward again and leaving white speckles across the dirt of the barnyard, the grass of the fields beyond, the roof of the barn. Luca caught a breath, grinning.

"It's snowing!"

"No way. Not *fair*. It's bare and spare here."

"No, it's—ah, I didn't think first snow would be this soon!" Even if he'd caught hints of it, in the past few days. The darkening skies, a certain whiff on the air, like breathing in pure metallic ice. Luca bounced on the balls of his toes, then dropped the toothbrush and padded for the door to stuff his feet into his boots. "I'll talk to you later."

"Going to run out and make snow angels?" Xav asked.

"Maybe. Maybe!" Luca laughed, wiggling his boots up over his ankles and tugging the laces just tight enough to make them stay. "I need to go. The animals are outside and Imre might need help and I—I—I just need to go!"

Xavier laughed indulgently. "Bye, fuckface."

"Bye!" Luca said, then shoved his phone into his pocket and spilled outside.

Tiny flakes struck him immediately, peppering all over his body like little ice kisses, and he laughed, stopping just past the door and tilting his face up to the sky. Cold wind cut razors through his t-shirt and jeans and turned his entire body into a rash of goose pimples, but he ignored it with a pleased sigh as he closed his eyes and just let those delicate, fragile little kisses pepper over his cheeks and melt against his skin. He'd always loved first snow, and Sheffield had had some right blizzards, but it wasn't quite the same when they fell over blocky buildings and cars and streets and the tiny, useless patch of yard at the house, while the buildings funnelled the wind until the snow fell in clumps and channels and bars. He'd missed this kind of snow: just an endless swirl across endless fields, quiet and peaceful and bringing with it a silence that fell, one flake at a time, to blanket the world.

He opened his eyes, licking melted snowflakes from his lips and breathing out frosted smoke. The momentary question of *where would Imre be* was answered by the distant figure he made atop the closest hill, standing with his close-fit wool-lined leather jacket buttoned snug around him, feet planted, hands in his pockets while he looked out over the rolling dales. Luca wrapped his arms around himself, rubbing cold arms with even colder fingers, and skipped across the yard to vault the fence and climb the hill.

He stopped at Imre's side, gazing out over the fields; from this high he could see the goats in their far-off pasture, prancing and kicking and snorting at the flakes landing on them as if they were either utterly offensive or the most delightful toys they'd ever seen.

"It's snowing," he murmured, and immediately felt an utter tit for stating the obvious.

Imre's lips twitched at the corners. "So I see." His shoulders were dusted with snow against the dark leather of his jacket, dotted snowflakes mingling into the silver and white and deep steely grey of his hair and beard, making them seem all the paler until the blue beads braided in stood out bright. He turned his head toward Luca. "You're not wearing a jacket."

"I'm not cold." He laughed, holding a hand out to catch snowflakes in his palm. They wouldn't *stick*; they melted on contact with his skin, until he held a palmful of snow-dew. "It's so pretty. I wanted to come see. Country snow isn't like city snow."

Imre inclined his head with an amused sound. "It is lovely."

"Are you going to bring the goats in?"

"If it holds through the end of the hour, yes. And I think it will." Imre squinted up at the sky. "It's looking like we'll have fairly heavy snow for the next week. Those clouds are full enough to drop a litter, and I don't trust the look of them. We should insulate the barns and be prepared to be snowed in within the next few days."

Luca groaned, slumping. "…don't tell me we'll be trapped inside the house. This is the first time I've tasted fresh air in weeks."

"Not completely. We'll put up covered walkways to the barns. Should only take a day or two to get it done, but it's best to do it before we truly need it. The animals will still need our care, even in a blizzard, though we should lay in extra wood and kerosene at the house, put out extra feed and water in the event we're trapped inside, and check the backup generator in case the power cuts to the barns' heating systems." It wasn't hard to tell that Imre was talking more to himself than to Luca, making his to-do list out loud, his eyes distant with rapid-ticking thoughts. But then he focused, glancing at Luca with a distracted smile. "You don't have to worry about it. I'll take care of the animals until the worst of the weather passes. If the winds are too strong and the drifts are too high, it won't be safe for you out there."

Luca bit his lip. "I don't like letting you go out there alone, Imre."

"I've been doing it for years."

"But you don't have to now."

Imre shook his head slightly. "Your hands, angyalka."

"They're fine."

Luca let himself follow impulse, then—even if his heart beat in a twisting strange lurch that told him he shouldn't, when his impulses were terrible, full of wanting and needful things, and yet if they were friends it shouldn't matter, it should be all right, and he wasn't going to hold himself back from that closeness with Imre when distance hurt Imre—while the only one that intimacy hurt was Luca.

And so he slipped his hand into Imre's, pressing their chilled fingers together, letting them warm each other as they touched palm to palm.

"See?" he said softly, and tried not to breathe in the heartache of that coarse, beloved touch.

Imre had ways about him, and one of those ways was a certain stillness when something startled him, arrested his attention. That stillness settled now, as he looked down at their clasped hands. He shifted his grip to stroke his thumb over Luca's palm, raising a sharp shudder-shock of sensitivity that tingled in his knees and tightened in his stomach, tracing the pinkness of new skin and the slightly rougher areas of fresh-forming calluses.

"I see," Imre murmured, and didn't let go of Luca's hand. "Tomorrow, then."

Luca swallowed back his heart, and tore his gaze away from Imre to look out over the fields, as the wind blew harder and the snow came down in thicker gusts, a curtain of lace and frost. "And today?"

Imre's grip shifted once more. His fingers splayed, then laced with Luca's, clasping them tight and holding them tangled together.

"Today," he said, and his rough-accented voice spoke in the language of Luca's longing, "we'll just watch the snow fall."

IMRE WASN'T SURE WHAT WOKE him. Maybe it was the creak of a floorboard, or the querulous groan of an opening door. Maybe it was a soft whispered curse, or the curious whine of the dogs stretched by his bedroom fireplace. Maybe it was a rattle of the shutters, the boom of the wind as the building snowstorm outside gained strength and howled itself through the night. Maybe it was the pressure at the foot of the bed.

Or maybe it was just that way he always somehow *knew*, when Luca was near.

As if every time they touched created a polar charge, a building energy making static on the air between them, crackling and sharp.

He opened his eyes. Outside the night was a wall of white, turning the darkness into light as the moon caught on the edges of snowflakes high, high in the heavens and shattered into a billion pieces on their sharp edges to rain downward in a blizzard of shimmer and shadow. They'd just finished staking out the walkways that afternoon, and none too soon; the storm had held off for two days after that first snow, but by dinner tonight the cold crisp twilight had disappeared into a whiteout. The snow, piled high against the walls of the house, made it feel frozen and silent, insulated in a timeless place full of secrets.

And so it seemed only fitting that a little cat of a man was curled at the foot of his bed, making himself small as if he could hide and keep his presence secret from Imre if only he didn't take up too much space.

Imre pushed himself up on one arm, watching the forlorn bundle Luca made, tucked up in the very corner as if trying to fit into the same space he'd occupied when he was just a wee boy, wrapped up in a quilt the way he always had and coaxing a sigh from Imre's lips, from Imre's heart.

"Luca."

Luca's shoulders stiffened, and he peered back, one eye visible past his hair, green-gold and gleaming in the firelight. "I'm sorry," he whispered. "I think the furnace is out, and there's a draft in my room."

"I'll take a look and fix it up in the morning." Imre shifted across his king-sized bed, to the side farthest from the hearth, and pulled one of the pillows out from his stack of two to settle it in the empty space left behind. "…you don't have to sleep at the foot of the bed, angyalka."

Luca turned to face him, his heart in those firelit eyes, a siren calling its song to Imre in alluring notes. "Are…you sure it would be all right? I can…I can sleep by the downstairs fireplace…"

This was unwise, rash—yet Imre would not, could not allow his own troubled thoughts to deny Luca even the smallest comfort or kindness. "There's no point in wasting wood on a second fire, and the room would take hours to properly warm. This one already is." He pulled the covers back over where he'd lain, offering Luca the spot already heated by his body. "Come."

Still Luca hesitated, but then untangled himself from the quilt and crawled up to the head of the bed, kittenish in his oversized boxers and shirt. He curled himself up against the pillow, curling on his side facing Imre, watching him quietly with one cheek pressed into the pillow and his body drawn up in a ball. Imre pulled the covers back up over him, gently tucking him in, then settled back against his own pillow, folding his arm underneath his head.

“Thank you,” Luca whispered.

Imre smiled faintly, and closed his eyes against the loveliness of his angyalka nestled into such a sweet, soft bundle so very close, those slender bare limbs in Imre’s bed. “Go to sleep, little cat,” he murmured. “Goodnight.”

55

ONLY BECAUSE LUCA WAS EXHAUSTED from working all day did he manage to fall asleep with Imre so near, yet utterly untouchable. Yet he didn't sleep for long; even if the rush and sigh of the wind outside calmed him with its rhythmic lullaby, his dreams were restless things without shape or form. Only sounds, musical notes that each seemed to quiver inside him in vibrating strings of lonely, resonating pain. He was accustomed to tossing in his sleep when his dreams wouldn't let him be.

He wasn't accustomed to a warm body there to stop it.

He came to blearily, aware only of a sense of heaviness, of pressure. And a scent, familiar earth and hay and musk and man, wrapped up in body heat and entangled around him. He opened one eye; a taut plain of bronzed muscle filled his vision, tawny naked skin and the sharp contrast of deep, steel-grey curls of finely scattered chest hairs, a few scratching against his cheek. Hard sinew bunched under his palms; Imre's shoulders. His legs were caught and tangled in fabric over powerfully corded sinew; Imre's legs. And his waist was encircled by bands of heated iron, locking him in place.

Imre's arms.

His next breath caught and wouldn't let back out, stuck like a swallowed stone. He opened his eyes more fully, looking up at Imre. So close; so close his beard flowed in a soft wash against Luca's cheek and mingled with his hair, one cool blue bead warming itself against

Luca's jaw. Iron and silver locks drifted into Imre's relaxed, sleeping face and spread in a fanning tangle over the pillow. It was like waking up in a lion's embrace, the great beast turned docile and peaceful and beautiful in dormant sleep, and Luca tried so very hard to talk himself into pulling out of Imre's hold before Luca began to *want*, but couldn't.

He was a traitor to their friendship, because he wanted nothing more than to stay here forever and always, wrapped up in Imre's arms, in Imre's bed.

And he couldn't.

He couldn't, so he held on to this moment while he had it, while Imre wasn't awake to push him away and remind him who he was, why he shouldn't, why *they* shouldn't. He wrapped his arms around Imre's neck, tangling his fingers in that tumble of hair he loved even more for its silvered sheen, running his fingers slowly along the braids scattered throughout.

"I love you, Imre," he whispered, barely more than a breath.

Then he pressed his cheek over Imre's chest and listened to his heart and willed himself to sleep once more, no matter what dreams may come.

56

IMRE WAITED UNTIL LUCA'S BREATHS evened into sleep to open his eyes. He'd thought he would give himself away, when Luca woke. He'd barely managed to control his breathing, harder still to control his wayward heart. He'd not slept an hour, not a minute, not a wink. Not since the moment Luca had rolled over against him in his sleep, and Imre had wrapped his arms around him without thinking and not yet talked himself into letting go.

Were he a decent man, he'd have let Luca know he was awake, let go, retreated to their respective sides of the bed.

But how could he be a decent man with such sweetness tucked against him, clinging to him so trustingly?

How could he make himself let go, when Luca's soft words were the thread binding Imre to Luca and Luca to Imre? If Luca saw himself as the thread stitching his parents into a single broken heart…then that quiet whisper had laced Imre to the boy through and through, until his heart was no longer whole without Luca sewn into it.

I love you, Imre.

Imre closed his eyes, pressed his lips into Luca's hair, and held on tight 'til morning.

57

SOMEHOW IMRE WASN'T SURPRISED THAT, when he woke on the morning of December first, Luca was nowhere to be found.

Since that first snow, sleeping in had become a habit. The farm had gone into hibernation, and short days and long nights meant late mornings where they drifted into each other sooner or later in the kitchen, and whomever woke up first made breakfast before they trudged together down walkways walled by corridors of packed snow to feed and water the animals, check on the beehives and the fences, check the barn insulation and heating, and watch the nanny goats for signs of heat.

Imre normally found the winters too idle, when he was more wedded to hard work than he had ever been to another person, but there was a certain quiet pleasure in the downtime now. He showed Luca how to make candles from beeswax, and set the dinner table with Luca's first lumpy, misshapen efforts. He showed him, too, the many things that could be crafted from goat horns, how to purify and jar honey, how to can and preserve apples, how to properly cure cheese for aging—all the little things that passed the hours on a farm in winter.

All the little things that let them pretend everything was normal, no matter how many times the conversation died for endless seconds each time their hands brushed, lingered, then pulled back as they avoided each other's eyes.

One more month, Imre reminded himself. One more month before he sent Luca back home to Marco, and life would return to normal. The farmhouse would be empty, desolate. Things would be rough back in Sheffield, with Luca's absence likely changing nothing. Luca would find his way, Imre thought. Luca always found his way, with that stubborn strength he hid behind impish smiles.

It was Imre who'd be lost, once Luca was away and likely never coming back, moving on to a life that had no need of Imre and a farm that was just a fond childhood memory best left in the past.

He sighed, staring across the kitchen of the empty house. He had an idea why Luca was starkly absent this morning, but he couldn't help thinking maybe he should start trying to get used to this now.

Before he was already gone.

Imre fished a small parcel from its hiding place atop the fridge, tucked it into the inner pocket of his jacket, and stepped outside into the snow.

The morning was dim and silvery and chill, the cold biting and nipping at Imre's cheeks, the sun playing peekaboo between the clouds and throwing wan, pale radiance down to make the snow glitter with winterlight; every breath cut with edges of ice, frost riming his breaths and kissing his lips and crackling in tiny crisp-scented icicles inside his nose. The drifts had piled so thick in the overnight winds that it was hard to tell the actual dales from mounded snow. A pair of fresh footsteps led across the field in front of the house, winding down toward the trail leading between low hills and out toward the broader pastures.

He followed that path of footsteps as if led on a tether, to where they ended at the crest of a low rise. Luca sat atop the low stone wall there, his legs dangling over the edge, his body wrapped up in a heavy black wool coat with the high collar pulled up around his jaw. His skin was white with the cold save for the pink-flushed, wind-kissed points of his nose, cheekbones, and ears. His gloved hand draped over his knee, a lit cigarette dangling from between two fingers, the thin coil of smoke and the cherry ember burning away untouched.

Luca looked out over the fields and the bare spindly trees, his eyes half-closed, remote, his lips parted as though he'd started to say something and then forgotten what it could be. His earbuds rested in his ears, trailing into his pocket. His shoulders shook in a subtle shiver; a few dustings of fresh snow dotted his hair, though the sky was clear now. Imre wondered how long he'd been out here, but didn't ask. He said nothing, as he moved to stand at the fence close by and, hands in his pockets, watched the land and sky with Luca in silence.

Luca didn't seem aware that he was there; he didn't move, didn't look at Imre, though his lips closed into a bitter line. But after long, silent minutes he replaced the smoke-cloud of his breaths with the smoke of the cigarette, taking a long drag before blowing out a steady, bitter-scented stream, tapping the thick curl of ash from the tip to pepper down onto the snow, and tugging the earbuds free from his ears. He coiled the gnawed, frayed cord around his fingers, then stuffed them into his pocket before flicking the cigarette with his thumb.

"Sorry," he murmured. "Figured with the snow it couldn't hurt much."

"You're fine," Imre answered, but said nothing else. Luca looked like he'd bolt, if Imre pushed too hard. And so he did what he was best at:

He waited.

And finally, "Am I?" Luca asked, his voice cracking. "Don't feel all that fine."

"First day of December."

"I try not to think about it." Another slow drag off the cigarette, then twin streams of smoke through his nostrils. "I'm twenty now. That's some kind of bloody milestone, isn't it? No longer a teenager."

Imre stepped closer, until he could lightly bump Luca's arm with his elbow without crowding him. "It's just another day, if you want it to be."

"I don't know what I want." Luca stared down at the cigarette, then stubbed it out against the fence, grinding it into the stone at his hip. "I guess that's half my problem."

"We could go into town. Catch a film."

"That sounds like it would be torture for you." Luca's soft, brittle laugh made Imre want to reach for him, take his hand, but he reined himself in firmly. Luca tilted his head back, staring up at the sky, throat working in a swallow. "Let's just…let it be another day, Imre."

"If that's what you want."

Imre debated, pressing his lips together, fingering the brown paper and string wrapping the parcel in his pocket. The gift had been an impulse, and if Luca didn't want to do anything for his birthday, perhaps he'd not want even that little reminder. But if not for his birthday, Imre likely would have bought it just because it needed to be done anyway…so after a few moments of struggling with himself, he slipped the long, slim rectangular parcel from his pocket and offered it to Luca.

"Package came for you yesterday, though."

Luca blinked down at the parcel. "Eh…?"

"Open it."

With a knit to his brows, Luca plucked at the twine, then unfolded the paper. Inside, in a carved wooden case, rested a new pair of earbuds, soft black rubber tips affixed to polished wooden casings. The website Imre had ordered them from said the wooden casings provided better sound quality and acoustics; he'd never really looked into anything like that, so he'd just picked the prettiest ones in gleaming walnut, and hoped Luca would like them.

Luca stilled, his eyes widening, his breaths catching. "Imre." He gently plucked the earbuds from their fitted velvet beds, turning them over, before smiling slowly, eyes lighting. "You didn't have to."

"You've nearly chewed through your old ones. They seem important to you."

Luca's smile faltered, and Imre wished he hadn't said anything. But still that curl lingered around the boy's lips, and he stroked his fingers lightly down the woven nylon cords of the wooden earbuds. "I guess…they're how I block things out. If I shut off what I can hear, I don't have to see or feel, either. All I feel is the song." He snorted softly. "Even if it's part of why I'm so useless."

A certain sharp edge to his voice caught Imre, and he turned to look at Luca fully, rather than watching him from the corner of his eye. "Useless…?"

"Other people have all these fascinating hobbies. Papercraft, or they weld furniture from metal recyclables on weekends, or they make candles from beeswax from *their own* bees, or they're just really, *really* into something." He clenched his fist around the cord, jaw setting in a tight line. "I'm not really into anything but reading and my music. I don't *do* anything. I don't make things. Not like other people. Not like you."

Imre frowned. Had Luca been comparing himself to Imre all this time?

"You don't have to be like me, angyalka."

"I…" Luca stared down at his hands. "I always wanted to be. I always looked up to you so much. Admired you. I still do."

"I find that amusing, considering how I admire you."

Luca made a strangled, confused sound. “What? Why? I’m a complete and utter prat. What is there to admire about me?”

“Everything.”

Imre took a moment to gather himself, sort through his thoughts and string them into words that would make sense; while he considered, he pulled himself up onto the wall next to Luca, settling at his side and leaning forward to brace his elbows on his thighs.

“Not many twenty-year-olds know themselves the way you do, Luca,” he continued. “You’re smart. And you know what you want, even if it’s not yet taken a concrete shape. You know you’re seeking something to feel passionate about. Something you can commit yourself to. That doesn’t mean you have to find what that something is exactly right at this moment.” Imre laced his fingers together, studying his hands, the scars—legacy of a lifetime on the farm, of throwing himself into it to let it break and burn his body and rebuild him into the man he needed to be to hold Lohere together on his own. He supposed that was his passion, cut into his skin. “Some people try to find that something for their entire lives, and might be old and grey before they figure it out—and there’s nothing wasted in the things they learned along the way, no matter where their lives might take them. Twenty isn’t so old to still be unsure. But the time you spend finding your way isn’t useless. *You* aren’t useless.”

Quiet, Luca wound the cords of the earbuds around his fingers; Imre watched while he made a cat’s cradle, then tumbled it apart. He seemed so much older in this moment—older, stranger, already weary and bowed with the weight of a decision he didn’t know how to make.

Imre only wished he could carry some of that weight for him, but Luca’s choice was Luca’s own and no other’s.

“I’m just afraid I’ll settle on something and then end up miserable,” Luca finally said, as quiet as the silent blankets of snow.

"And I'll have wasted that, too."

"You'll have learned what you don't want, and that's not a waste. Nor will it be too late to change, if you want to." Imre chuckled. "When I was twenty, I thought I wanted to run away and join a traveling Roma music troupe. Wander the world with my guitar."

"Why didn't you?"

"That's not really a way of life anymore. Dancing in town squares for pennies. Most of the professional Roma music troupes play concert halls and fine events now, and…frankly, I'm not that good." He laughed again, shaking his head. His younger self had been such a mess, up in the hayloft at all hours of the day and night, banging away at that guitar until his mother shouted at him to leave off, he was bothering the chickens. "And I really do love Lohere. I was just…kicking at my traces, bucking at the idea of following in my father's footsteps because I needed time to figure out who I was and that I wanted Lohere for *me*, not because it was what he expected."

Luca blew out a cloud of frost-rimed breath, thicker than cigarette smoke. "That's the heart of it, eh?"

"Hm?"

"Dad wants me to be like him. An engineer. I'm not interested, but I keep pushing aside any thought of what I want because it's not what he expects. And I'm tired of the fallout every time I lean off the path he thinks I should follow. His way is straight forward. Mine's…I don't even know. Tangled off sideways. But I can't go sideways and won't go straight, so I end up going nowhere at all."

"Where does your path lead, then, if not engineering?"

"Fucked if I know, mate." Luca snorted.

Imre smiled slightly. "All right, what do you want?"

"Fucked if I know that, either."

Luca set the earbuds delicately in their case and propped it on his thigh, then braced his hands against the stone of the fence and leaned back on them, tilting his head back to look up at the clear, cloudless sky. He looked as though he might smile or cry at any moment, and in him Imre saw that fragile, bright crystal creature he'd known so very long ago, full of a million beautiful emotions he couldn't contain.

"The way I felt when you were teaching me to ride," Luca murmured. "Teaching me how to care for Gia and Merta. Is…is that passion?"

"Only you can really know that. Was it something you loved?"

"It fascinated me." Luca's mouth twitched pensively. "I felt…like I could do that forever. Especially caring for the goats. Feeling like there was something in my hands that made them feel better. Knowing my work helped them be healthy again. Like it was something only *I* could do."

"Sounds like passion to me."

"Hm." Luca sighed heavily, then glanced at Imre. "Mira, then?"

"I'll get you her number, if you want it."

"I think I do."

They remained that way for some time: silent, side by side, watching the sky together. And Imre wondered that he was questioning himself, now. Luca had perhaps found a path, but Imre was suddenly wondering if, now, Lohere was enough for him. If Lohere could ever be enough for him, when come January it would be empty once more and he wasn't certain the work would fill that quiet absence ever again.

"Imre?" Luca murmured.

He pulled from his thoughts, looking at Luca sidelong. "Hm?"

"Thanks. For the earbuds." Luca bumped Imre's elbow with his own, jostling him lightly. "And for being my friend."

"Always, angyalka."

"Always?" Luca repeated, and his voice cracked on a strange note.

It was that strange note that prompted Imre to shift over, lean closer, settle with Luca shoulder to shoulder, warmth given and warmth shared, as he answered, "Indeed."

Even when you leave and, just like your father, never look back.

58

AFTER DINNER, LUCA'S PHONE BUZZED. He glanced up from his laptop; he'd been researching local veterinary schools, curled in a corner of the couch while Imre sprawled in the opposite corner with a book, reading by firelight. He caught the arch of Imre's brow over the top of the pages, then sighed and dug in the pocket of his jeans for his phone.

A new text notification popped up, from his mother's number.

Happy birthday, dearest ❤❤❤ she wrote. ***Your father sends his love, too.***

Luca groaned. He'd done his best, throughout the day, to just…forget. Not think about it. He had better things to think about, even if he wasn't looking forward to hearing his father's opinion on Luca's notions about working with animals. Marco Ward would probably call him a child hoping to spend his life playing with puppies and kittens. And if he didn't answer the bloody text, Lucia Ward would probably call him ten times until he either picked up or she got annoyed enough to call out the bloody cops to haul him up on charges for ignoring his mum.

He didn't know what to say to her. Maybe his dad had been the most vocal in pushing him every way but the one he wanted to go, but his mother was just as passively complicit, and infantilized him even more than his father.

He twisted his lips up, tugging at the lower, then settled on a simple ***Thx.*** There. He was minding his manners without having to say more than necessary.

He'd hoped she would leave it alone at that, but a few moments later his phone buzzed again and a new text popped up. ***Are you doing all right there? Are you working hard?***

Luca thinned his lips, eyeing his phone, then shoved it back into his pocket without answering.

Imre set his book down in his lap, watching him. "Everything all right?"

"Just fine," Luca answered, and dragged his laptop across his thighs once more. "Never fucking better."

He was grateful when Imre, unlike his mother, held his silence and let it go.

59

"I NEVER THOUGHT I'D SAY this," Luca announced, "but I'm really fucking starting to hate snow."

He sprawled on his back in front of the fireplace, Vila and Seti's heads draped over his stomach. The dogs watched him with mournful eyes, and he imagined they felt just as penned up as he did: wild animals who needed to be outside *running*, but the outside was a wall of snow piled almost to the second floor of the farmhouse.

The walkways had blown over the night of Luca's birthday in blizzard winds, and they'd been out there pushing them back up in the dark, wrapped up from the tops of their heads to the tips of their toes, finding their way by lanterns and roped together with lengths of cord to keep from wandering off into the fields and never finding their way back. They'd barely made it into the barns to make sure the animals were mewed up tight and the heaters were venting properly to prevent carbon monoxide poisoning before the wind had kicked up to shrieking levels, chasing them back into the farmhouse and locking them in.

And this time, Imre had refused to listen to Luca's arguments the following mornings when he'd ventured out into the blowing cold and walls of snow to feed and water the animals every day. Imre had gone alone, leaving Luca inside by himself, worrying himself sick until Imre appeared in the doorway again, stomping snow from his boots and his beard crusted with ice and his gloved hands shaking as he took the hot mug of tea Luca had waiting each time.

Imre glanced up from his laptop, eyes thoughtful behind the reflective gleam of thick, black-framed reading glasses. He'd been working at something all day, and when Luca peered over it was just an incomprehensible mess of spreadsheets and numbers and dates, though he'd recognized the names of several of the goats, picked out Gia's and Merta's names blocked out in red highlight. Imre had been so absorbed in his work that he'd only mumbled something unintelligible when Luca asked what the red meant, so Luca had tactfully let him be.

Now, though, Imre chuckled, closing the laptop lid and setting it aside on the end table. "I think it's quite lovely. There's something soothing about settling warm and quiet before the fire, while the rush of wind and snow sucks the sound out of the world."

"It was soothing the first day. Now I'm just bloody bored."

"Nothing on Netflix, then?"

"Balls to Netflix." Groaning, Luca sat up. The dogs tumbled with little yips, then rearranged themselves at his hip, Vila's head stacked atop Seti's. "I got two days outside, what with you mewing me up like I'm at convent just over some blisters. *Two.* And then the snow's all down and I'm stuck up in here and going bloody sideways. We've not even gone to effin' market."

Imre propped his fist against his temple with an indulgent laugh, blue eyes glittering with a touch of taunting humour. "Surely there's winter in Sheffield. Or has the city done away with such archaic inconveniences?"

"Don't you start with the sass," Luca growled, jabbing a finger at him. "You could go *outside* in winter in Sheffield."

"Because you have street sweepers and people who salt the roads in Sheffield," Imre pointed out. "On the farm we make do, angyalka.

Is it truly so terrible?"

"No." Luca deflated, sighing. "I just don't feel like reading, or watching the telly, or just *sitting* here. I want to get up and *move*."

"I suppose if I tell you to go take the stairs up and down a few times, you'll say I'm sassing off again."

"You *are*."

"Duly noted, old man. I shall keep my whippersnapper's impudent tongue to myself."

"Oh, you're a fucking riot, Imre." Luca sprawled back against the rug and idly scratched behind Vila's tufted ear, burying his fingers into warm fur until he found soft, pliant skin. "Is this what it's like for you every winter? Just…sitting? Making shite and then lounging around like a great bloody bear in hibernation?"

"Sometimes." Imre shrugged and tugged his glasses off, then folded them neatly and set them atop the laptop. "I never really noticed. Always seems something to do. House repairs, things to make. Took half the time with you here, though. Reminds me of when my parents were alive, and we'd all work together and be finished and out of things to do in rather short order." His chuckle made his eyes gleam in the firelight, the corners crinkling. "You sound like my mum when she'd get tired of weaving blankets or stitching quilts. She was a restless woman."

"What did she do, then?"

"Well…" Imre trailed off, gaze growing distant, thoughtful, his voice soft with something almost like reverence, for these memories. "Da would fetch his violin, and I'd fetch my guitar. My mum played pipes, and tambourine. She'd wrap herself in bells. That scarf over your bed was hers. She'd tie it round her waist, over her skirts, so that it chimed every time she moved. And we'd play and sing and dance together, until we were breathless and tired and happy with it and suddenly not so bored at all."

Something about listening to Imre like this was almost breathtaking, when Luca could see it: Imre as a boy, younger than Luca's age, though Luca thought he'd be strong and wiry even then—and in Luca's imagination his mum and dad were shadowy figures with his same dark skin and tumbles of dark hair and thoughtful, intelligent eyes, all earthy clothing accented with bright colours and that subtle inflected accent to their voices, singing and laughing and *happy*.

"That's why you always told me to be careful with the scarf," Luca murmured. "Because it was hers."

"Ah," Imre answered softly. "I've many of her things in the attic, but that one was her favourite."

"I…I think I'm jealous. That you had that. A close family, two parents who loved each other."

"There's no such thing as the perfect family, angyalka. They fought, too. But yes…I was lucky, I think. That they loved each other, and me. And that they gave me enough slack in my lead to find my own way."

A subtle note of longing in Imre's voice made Luca wonder how much he missed them. How much he missed those winters, laughing together and singing. And he wondered, too, if it hurt more to have never had that kind of family at all, or if it hurt more to have had them…

And then lost them, to time and the endless march and movement of life.

God, winter thoughts were *depressing*.

Luca pushed himself up again, untangling himself fully from the dogs and digging his phone out of his pocket as he stood. "Look, I can't play a musical instrument for shite. But I've got iTunes and pretty much any kind of music you could imagine, so nothing saying we can't dance now."

Imre's brows rose. "I suppose I wouldn't mind reviving an old tradition."

"Good." Luca grinned and scrolled through his playlist, then settled on a track. "I love this song."

He tapped play, and a slow R&B beat with a perky reggae influence came piping out of the phone. He dialled the volume up to max, then set the phone down on the coffee table—then promptly shoved the coffee table to the side, clearing space in front of the hearth and kicking the rug aside until he stood in his bare feet on the fire-warmed stone floor; Vila and Seti skittered out of the way, chasing the rug and then tumbling down into a puppy pile on top of it.

Imre stood slowly, his movements contemplative, his head cocking to one side curiously. "'Walking side to side…' Does she mean…" His brows drew together, and he shot Luca a *look*. "*Luca*."

Luca burst out laughing and held both hands up. "What? I didn't write the song!" Imre's incensed look only set him off into fresh snickers. "Oh, come *on*. You can't be that scandalised."

Imre sniffed haughtily. "I've heard worse."

"Uh-huh." Luca let himself sway a little with the beat, rolling his shoulders. "C'mon. Let's dance."

"I don't know how to dance to this." Imre cocked his head in the other direction, frowning deeply as he shifted his feet. "The beat is too slow."

"It's not the kind of music where you move around fast, stomping and clapping and twirling to the beat." Luca bit the inside of his lip, just *listening*, feeling the slow, rolling beat; the sound had a different kind of energy, bright but not fast-moving. "It's more like…the kind of music you feel in your hips and the pit of your stomach and the column of your spine. Like this."

He tried to show Imre—lifting his arms over his head, letting his hips roll side to side, following both the beat and the vocals. He slid his arms together, the roll starting in his fingertips, flowing down his arms, into his shoulders, until his back arched as if his spine slipped and rolled in molten oil dripping down each vertebrae, letting himself *feel* it in the drawing pull in the pit of his stomach and the way each beat seemed to hit right in time with his pulse, little faster moments of swift wordplay prompting a quick-sharp snap of his hips. As the song blended into another verse and the rolling movement played out in a bend of his knees, he straightened—to find Imre watching him oddly, gaze intent, expression unreadable.

"I see," Imre said neutrally.

Luca flushed, clearing his throat, looking away—suddenly feeling awkward, silly. "You try."

"Mm."

He risked a glance back, but Imre was still watching him oddly, not moving. Luca bit his lip again. "…not even once?"

Silence—until Imre shook himself, blinking and shaking his head. "I'm sorry. I was distracted trying to understand what they're saying." He stroked his beard, then repeated, grave and slow, "'I give zero fucks and I got zero chill in me.'" He trailed off into a thoughtful rumble. "I could see that being a viable life philosophy."

Luca's awkward tension dissolved as laughter hit him sharp enough to gutpunch his breath out in a whoosh; he doubled over, digging his fingers against his chest as he struggled to drag in enough breath to even get it under control, when the more he tried to shove it down the more it just squeaked out in wheezing, chirping giggles.

Imre stared at him, utterly deadpan. "What?"

"Nothing—nothing, I—" Luca wheezed, scrubbing at wet eyes

and choking on a snicker. “Oh, *God.* Imre, you’re the best.” With a few more broken chuckles, he managed to rein himself in, and took several more deep breaths before straightening and reaching for his phone. “One sec. Lemme start the song over.”

Imre looked confused, but just shrugged. Luca stopped the music, then set the track to repeat on loop before setting the phone down as the opening bars began again.

“Okay. Can you get the beat?”

“I…think so.” Imre lifted his arms stiffly over his head like he was about to do pull-ups. “Like this?”

Luca choked out another snicker, then cleared his throat and swallowed it back. “You don’t have to raise your arms if you don’t want to. Focus on moving your body first.”

Imre frowned, but lowered his arms; his head began to bob slowly, tracking the rhythm, before he started to sway back and forth, his shoulders moving with a touch of grace but the rest of his body stiff as a bloody plank. “This feels rather bizarre, to stand and dance without moving my feet.”

“Come on—you have to move your hips like this.” Luca rolled his again, a movement that made him feel like he was belly-dancing with the figure-eight his hips traced in sharp side-to-side motion, pulling first on one side of his waist with a pleasant stretch of sinew, then the other. “Try it. Just your hips.”

With a scowl, Imre managed a kind of jerky left-right hip pop before stopping. “My hips do not move like that.”

“Everyone’s hips move like that.” Luca moved to stand behind Imre and gripped his hips. “You’re too stiff. Follow my hands.”

He tried to guide him—tried to nudge him in at the waist to urge his hips one way, then the other, catching those stiff movements and shaping them as best he could as powerful muscle flexed under his hands, pulling in a rough bunching and stretching of corded blocks that rippled all the way up Imre's back, making his shoulder blades writhe under the tight henley. Imre endured it a few moments longer, then stopped, not budging another inch, and tossed a glower over his shoulder.

"I was not meant to dance this way."

"Try. C'mon—*oh!*"

Growling, Imre turned in Luca's grip and hooked a powerful arm around his waist, jerking him close against Imre's body. Gasping, Luca froze, grip shifting to clasp onto the hard iron flex and flow of Imre's biceps as he stared up at him, a thunder and riot churning through his chest.

"Enough, brat," Imre rumbled, glowering. "No amount of poking and prodding will make me understand what you are trying to make me understand."

His grasp eased around Luca's waist, then fell away. Luca stumbled back quickly, struggling to catch his breath. For a moment he'd thought—it didn't matter what he'd thought. But there was something odd about Imre right now, something almost dangerous, a certain quiet, vibrant tension about him, and Luca didn't know what to do with it or with himself.

And so he only turned away, swiping up the phone and turning off the song.

"Fine," he mumbled. "You have a better idea?"

"I will show you how I dance. Give me that."

Imre swiped the phone from Luca, leaving him blinking and staring while Imre thumbed through the listing of tracks. He tapped one, listened to less than half a bar of snare-drum trap music, then frowned and moved on to the next, a poppy little Ed Sheeran tune. Imre made the most adorably disgusted face, then moved on to the next and hardly listened to ten seconds of Jason Derulo before he was on to the next and the next and the next, skipping through KPop and R&B and JRock and rock and even a couple of Disney tunes before he settled on opening bars of delicate strumming Spanish guitar that fell quickly into Spanish-influenced pop, enticing some unnamed listener to *come in the singer's direction, blessings, heaven*.

Imre listened thoughtfully for several long moments, then nodded solemnly. "This will do."

Luca blinked. "…that's Justin Bieber."

"Who?"

"Oh, *God*." Luca dragged a hand over his face, laughing helplessly. "All right. I'm game. Show me. What do I have to do?"

Imre said nothing, just listening as the song rolled into nearly purring Spanish, lyrical and blood-stirring, the beat sensuous and bright; Luca could only recognized a few words from old A-levels classes, *acercando* and *armando* and *pulso*, but he could sing the chart-topping lyrics by heart.

Imre nodded as if he'd confirmed something for himself, then stopped the song, started it again from the beginning, and set the phone down on the coffee table.

Then he hooked his arm around Luca's waist again, dragging him close so swiftly and so roughly that Luca's stomach turned cartwheels, breath tumbling out of him as Imre spun him into his grasp.

One rough hand clasped Luca's, holding it to one side as if for a waltz, while the other guided Luca's other hand to Imre's shoulder before his arm once more wrapped around Luca's waist, scorching him through his clothing. Fuck. *Fuck.* He was a mess inside, worked up into electric knots, and he'd been telling himself for weeks and weeks not to *want* but it was so fucking hard when Imre was so close, brilliant cobalt eyes burning into him, steel strength holding him tight against that fiercely, powerfully hard, overwhelmingly large body. And Luca's mouth went dry as Imre growled and he *felt* it, every word vibrating between them in a rumble that shivered through him and lit up his every nerve ending with fire-spark shimmer.

"Follow my lead," Imre rumbled—and then spun them both into motion.

If Luca followed, it was only because Imre's body led. Pressed chest to chest, hip to hip, thigh to thigh, it was impossible *not* to move with Imre when every luxuriant movement of corded sinew pushed and pulled, flowed and swayed, moulding to Luca's body and showing him where to go. It wasn't quite rumba, wasn't quite salsa, wasn't quite samba, but it was fast and spinning—and Imre's swift, deft steps guided Luca until he was swirling across the living room, clutching at Imre, heart racing and blood roaring and his body feeling lighter than feathers and ash and fast-rising sparks with how easily Imre handled him, strength and grace and wildness all in one. His head swam, intoxicated on nothing more than this, when Imre never looked away from him, held him captured with every step until each movement centred on bright-burning blue eyes and the heat of their bodies crushed together.

The room flashed by in a whorl of colour as Imre spun him, nearly flinging Luca out to the length of their stretched arms, then tumbled him back in, spinning him close and clasping him tight as a little front-back step rolled Imre's hips into Luca's, then drew back to pull Luca's into Imre's, fluid and sinuous and making his spine slip until a pleasant little knot of sensation built in the very hollow of his back. Luca's knees went weak and soft, and he dug his fingers into Imre's shoulders to stay upright.

"So your hips do move that way," he gasped.

"When given good reason," Imre purred—then dipped Luca

back, tearing a soft sound from him as Imre bent him nearly down to the floor, the sudden rush and the stretch of his body making something molten coil inside him.

Molten and melting deeper, as the angle forced him to bend a leg to maintain balance, his thigh nearly wrapping around Imre's hips, spreading him open until Imre fit *between* his legs and something far harder than the ridge of Imre's zipper pressed into Luca. For a moment they held that way, Imre's face nearly buried into Luca's throat, lips hovering above his collarbone, beard scratching and nestling gently against his thundering pulse.

"I find this good reason," Imre whispered, then swung them both upright, pulling Luca back into his arms.

Imre clutched him tight. Luca clutched just as tight, holding fast, not a breath of space between them, leaning closer and closer while his stomach wrung into aching knots and every inch of his body flushed hot, too hot. He didn't know how they'd come to be like this, resting brow to brow, noses almost brushing, and he was so afraid, so afraid any moment now Imre would break it, would shatter Luca like he'd shattered him again and again instead of just holding him close and looking at him with those darkening eyes that seemed to fill Luca's world, stormy and burning into him as if he actually *saw* him.

Saw *him*, and not just a problem to be ignored until it went away.

And when Imre twirled him into another dizzying spin and back again, Luca's chest seized as he pressed harder into him, taking in every breath Imre exhaled, burning inside from the hovering closeness of Imre's parted lips, from the roughness of his panting breaths making his thickly muscled chest swell against Luca's.

"*...Imre.*"

He curled his fingers against the nape of Imre's neck, buried in the lustrous softness of his hair—but that whisper of his name, that touch against his skin seemed to pull Imre back to himself. He sucked in a sharp breath, his gaze clearing somewhat…but he didn't pull away, didn't stop the sinuous back-and-forth of their steps.

"Luca," he breathed raggedly. "Luca, I cannot…"

Yet he was hard against Luca, and even as he said *I cannot* his fingers clenched against Luca's back, fingertips hot brands pressing in, shirt bunching against Luca's skin and searing through him with the pressure, the friction, the possession in the touch. Luca clung to him and silently prayed that grip would only hold tighter, that Imre wouldn't thrust him away.

"Why not?" he begged. "Why can't you?"

A low, tortured groan escaped Imre's lips. "I…am trying to remember…"

"Let me remind you why you can." Luca pulled his hand free from Imre's and captured that rugged, sensuously beautiful face in both his palms, leaning into him. They were still moving together, but it was almost an afterthought, an aching rhythm of motion that suggested and promised and begged for more. He leaned hard into Imre, into the heat of him, melting into his flesh and whispering desperately. "You don't have to say no. Not if you don't want to."

"Angyalka…"

Imre drifted to a halt, but if anything his grasp on Luca only tightened, both arms around him now. Against Luca's body Imre *trembled*, drawn so taut his muscles were slabs of stone that shivered in a quiet earthquake of tremors. Haunted blue eyes consumed Luca, watching him with something so raw and hot in their depths it could only be desire.

Luca wet his lips, struggling not to give in to the terror and longing and need raking his heart to fluttering shreds. "Is it so wrong that I want you to look at me the way you are now?" he breathed.

"That I want you to look at me and only me." He stroked his fingers through Imre's beard, trailing back to bury into his hair; he could hardly breathe, his heart blocking his airways, but he still managed to force out, "I don't want to beg, Imre."

Then he risked it: risked the most terrifying thing he'd ever done sober, only wishing for a sip of that sweet apple beer to give him courage as he leaned in and pressed his mouth to Imre's. Only for a moment, but it was enough to taste the hot cider they'd had with dinner on his breath; enough for the firmness and fullness of Imre's lips to imprint on Luca in perfect caresses of smooth, heated skin; enough for the scratch of Imre's beard to flow over Luca's cheeks, teasing friction against his mouth that made his flesh burn and sensitized him to every tiny taste of Imre.

He pulled away, struggling with himself, struggling not to break down, to cry, to…to…he didn't know. But his heart was breaking, when he'd tried to stop loving Imre, tried to be his friend, but every day of silence had built inside him into an awful fullness, a thing he couldn't hold in any longer or it would overflow his banks and shatter him, sweep him away until he was nothing in the face of the enormity of it.

"…but I will," he finished.

He would beg. He would plead. He would do *anything*, if only Imre would *see* him.

But Imre only closed his eyes, swearing softly under his breath, leaning harder into Luca until their noses brushed. "Bloody *hell*, Luca."

"I know…I know you can only be with someone if you can love them. But isn't there anything about me that you could love?" Luca pleaded. "Even one thing?"

Imre's eyes slipped open. He stared at Luca intently, something fierce burning hot enough to turn cobalt stones into brilliant blue fire. "Don't ask me that," he growled, but rather than push Luca away, he only grasped him tighter until Luca could hardly breathe for the pressure of powerful arms, of possessive hands.

"If you won't tell me, then…then…" His lips trembled. He could barely force his voice past his lips, small, not even a whisper. "Then…will you kiss me?"

He steeled himself for the *no.* Steeled himself for something about his father, about his age, the million other reasons Imre had when Luca could feel that desire, that arousal that said Imre must feel *something*, for his body to stir for Luca. And from the haggard, tormented way Imre looked at him, any moment now Imre would pluck Luca's heart from its frightened, dizzy, foolishly hopeful high and dash it down low to shatter it once more against his implacable logic and honour. Silently he pleaded with him not to, because Luca's heart couldn't handle breaking one more time.

But maybe it should.

Maybe Imre should break his heart this one last time, so Luca would remember his place, forget how to feel this destructively painful love, and be able to accept that Imre couldn't, wouldn't, and didn't *want* to love Luca the way he craved to be loved.

Imre's lips parted. Luca closed his eyes, tensing all over, biting his lip hard to give himself a focal point, pain to distract him, something to centre his world on so when those words came, he wouldn't cry. Not where Imre could see him.

But Imre said nothing. Luca felt him moving—and then sucked in a breath, pulse jumping, as Imre's beard brushed against his throat, softly scratchy bristles teasing against his skin until prickles stood up all over him and he couldn't *breathe*. Then heated lips brushing over his neck, and his mind spun as a little sharp-shocking thrill rushed through him.

"Im—*ah!*"

The hard edges of Imre's teeth bit down. Luca cried out softly, rising up on his toes, fingers digging into Imre's hair. Gently, so gently, Imre drew Luca's flesh into the heat of his mouth, capturing his skin against warm lips and the fiery well of dampness that was Imre's mouth, his teeth, a teasing and circling tongue that traced burning-rough circles against Luca's throat. He whimpered, curling forward, raking at Imre's hair as the man bit down just hard enough for a subtle spark of pain, just enough of a sting to whip the pleasure of that sucking, teasing mouth into a sweet-sharp lash, a bolt that struck deep in the pit of Luca's stomach.

"O-oh my God," he gasped. "Imre…"

Imre slowly released that captured bit of flesh, leaving Luca's neck throbbing. His breaths curled in hot washes over Luca's throat as he rumbled softly, "I have wanted to do that for some time." He lifted his head, then, looking down at Luca, watching him with a strange mixture of that quiet, graven calm that was so *Imre*…and a kindling, smouldering hunger that made him seem someone wholly new, an Imre that Luca had never known. "*Now* I will kiss you."

Barely a moment for the flood of emotion to rock Luca with an earthquake's force—shock, disbelief, elation, hope, joy—before that firm, hot mouth crashed down on his. He'd never thought Imre could kiss like this: consuming, deep, as if Luca were an ocean and Imre would submerge himself utterly in his depths. He *felt* like the sea, a thing of ebbing and flowing tides, of power and strange wild mystery and silent secrets, as Imre's kiss throbbed him from head to toe, filled him with a rushing and crashing desire.

Nothing had ever made him feel at once weak and powerful, small and strong, desiring and desirable as the way Imre kissed him:

like a man willingly surrendering to something all-consuming, lips locked and caressing against Luca's as if Imre were drugged and craving, teeth nipping and teasing, tongue tracing and delving in delicious sweeps. As overwhelming as Imre could be…more overwhelming was the knowledge that Imre *wanted* him, and the power of that left Luca nearly drunk with it. *He* had driven Imre to this—to the rough desperate clutch of his hands, to the low groan in Imre's throat, to the hard fierce bruising pressure of his kiss, to the burning, shuddering tension in Imre's body.

And there were few things more powerful, more sensual, Luca realized, than feeling desired by someone you loved.

He moulded himself against the towering bulk of Imre's body, whimpering in the back of his throat as Imre's teeth toyed with his lower lip, sinking in and teasing it to sensitivity, tingling his mouth and sending ripples of heat radiating out to the tips of his fingers and toes. Luca retaliated by capturing Imre's upper lip, tracing it with his tongue, tasting Imre—and was rewarded by a broken, gasping snarl, a crushing grasp, the rush of a heady high that he could make Imre react that way.

Then solid ground tumbled away and they were falling; Imre dropped back onto the sofa and dragged Luca with him, pulling him down until Luca sat across Imre's lap with his legs stretched to one side and that hard ridge in Imre's jeans pressing up against his bottom. Deliberately, Luca shifted his hips, moving against him; Imre tore back from his lips with a rough, gasping groan, eyes half-closing, hips lifting as his head fell back against the edge of the couch. Luca's own cock throbbed in response, and he slid his fingers over Imre's chest, following the hard contours underneath his shirt, revelling in the way taut shudders seemed to follow his fingertips. He hadn't known how desperately he needed to feel wanted until Imre was hard against him, holding him tight, dragging rough palms and long spread fingers over Luca's back and breathing like a beast out of control.

"Imre," he whispered, kissing the corners of Imre's mouth, then daring to kiss him fully again, sinking himself into the depths of Imre's lips and burning all throughout as that hot mouth claimed him again, as Imre tangled his fingers in Luca's hair and cupped the back of his head and dragged him down until firm lips dominated and possessed and *destroyed* him. Utterly wrecked, trembling, his limbs liquid, he shifted to straddle Imre's lap, heat to heat, moving against him with wonderful surging jolts of pleasure and friction that pushed up inside him, hollowed him out, left him empty and aching and *wanting*, a needy dark pleasure that begged to be filled.

He arched his back to the heavy hand that stroked slowly up his spine, grinding his hips harder to Imre's, and Imre jerked with a low growl; his cock pulsed *hard* against his jeans, hard enough to thrust roughly between Luca's legs, and a trembling luscious terrified heat started in the pit of Luca's stomach, running liquid and swift. His lips went slack and soft against Imre's, unresisting as that wild mouth tormented him. His fingers twitched with the sudden want to *touch*, to slip his fingers inside Imre's jeans and trace his fingers over his cock, to find out if his skin was soft or slick, to see if that hardness was as hot against skin as it felt through denim, if it was as thick and heavy as it felt, and he flushed with a rush of embarrassment and need that he could be so *wanton*…yet he still craved.

It was hard not to when Imre's touch, his kiss, made Luca feel more sensual, more beautiful, than he ever had in his life.

But Imre broke back gently, shifting his grip to catch Luca's arms loosely just below his biceps, stilling him. Imre looked up at him, head resting against the back of the sofa with that glorious corona of silvered hair spread and tumbling around him, his mouth wet and red, eyes so dark they were nearly black.

"Shh," he said huskily, around swift, panting breaths. "Shh. Slow down. It doesn't have to be more than a kiss. Not now."

Luca closed his eyes, slumping forward with a groan, resting his brow to Imre's shoulder. His entire body felt like a livid heartbeat, pumping too much blood to every point of contact, until he felt swollen and sensitive *everywhere*. "Sorry. Sorry, I…" He swallowed, wrapping his arms around Imre's neck. "I want everything, and I'm…I'm afraid of it at the same time." But the little scared knot inside him loosened its grip as Imre settled his arms firmly around him, holding him close. He breathed out shakily, trying to calm himself. "I…I don't know what it means, that you're kissing me right now. That you aren't telling me *no*, just *slow down*."

Imre's voice thrummed against his ear, a quiet, sighing hum of breaths. "What do you want it to mean?"

"I…" Luca held him tighter, fingers curling in the back of his shirt. "I want to just…be *with* you, Imre. It doesn't matter what we call it, boyfriends or whatever or nothing at all, I just…want to be together." He swallowed the lump of fear in his throat. "Couldn't you ever see yourself being with me?"

"Ah, Luca…" Imre's hands slid in warm, soothing strokes up his back, kneading into his body. "Easily. But you know it's more complicated than that. If your father ever finds out—"

"Screw my father!" Luca flared, then scrunched his nose. "Well not literally, but—"

Imre let out a short, startled bark of laughter, his body shaking under Luca's. "The idea never crossed my mind."

"Ohthankgod. That's just naff." Worrying at his sore, aching lower lip—which tasted metallic-sweet in a way it never had before—Luca pushed himself up, bracing his hands on Imre's chest to look at him eye to eye. "Look, I'm only here for a few more weeks. A month at most." He ducked his head, looking away from those curious, gentle cobalt eyes. "I…like kissing you. I like touching you. And you seem to like kissing and touching me."

"I do."

"Then can we just…stop pretending we don't want to, until I leave? You can't pretend we haven't been circling around it like bloody berks for weeks."

A tired smile flitted across Imre's lips. "Closer to months."

"And all it's done is make things tense and upset both of us." Luca sighed. "He never has to know. We don't have to have sex, we just don't…but I just want to be with you and like you this way, and not have it be wrong."

Imre regarded him frankly, shaking his head slightly. "Do you know what you're asking me, Luca? Do you know how hard it is for me to be casual about things like that?"

"Believe me, there's nothing casual about this. About how I feel." Just those words struck roughly as a slap, as if this…this *thing* that had been eating him alive with every waking moment, every waking thought, was something that he could easily brush aside. His eyes stung. "I'm just…I'm just being realistic. If all it can be is the next few weeks, then just…just…let it be *this* instead of nothing at all." He smiled, but his mouth quivered no matter how he tried to hold it straight, his vision starting to blur wetly; this shouldn't *hurt* so much. He was getting what he wanted, sort of, so shouldn't he be happy? Shouldn't he—he— "I mean…how could it be more, right? I'm just some useless barely-legal prat, right?"

"No. No, angyalka. You're not that. You're not that at all. Come here."

Imre's hands were as gentle as his voice, as he drew Luca

down—and shifted him in his lap until they were no longer wrapped around each other with their bodies crying rough and heated counterpoint to this quiet, aching pain. Luca curled up against Imre's chest, and let Imre guide his head to his shoulder; he drew in a hiccupping breath, fighting this bittersweet wanting, this trembling need, while Imre stroked through his hair and pressed kiss after kiss to his temples, the corners of his eyes, his cheeks, the bridge of his nose, his beard a comforting roughness and his lips a soothing warmth.

With a sigh, Imre leaned his brow to Luca's temple. "Is this really what you want?"

"No," Luca admitted, closing his eyes. "But it's all I can have."

"All right."

Luca's next breath lodged in his chest, sticking in his ribs. "…you…you mean it?"

"Yes," Imre answered in that simple way that was so very Imre, that honesty that could never be anything but what it was. "I care for you, Luca. A great deal. And even if I know we are treading lines we should not cross…I cannot bring myself to deny you any longer." Rough fingers caught Luca's chin, tipping his face up, and he opened his eyes just in time to meet Imre's before firm lips touched his, plied gently, melted through him with a warmth that was as much pleasure as frustrated, keening pain. That kiss lasted only moments before Imre exhaled and let go, leaning into Luca again and holding him so very close. "Or myself. It only hurts us both to no good end. "

Luca searched Imre's eyes, looking for the lie, the deception, the condescending indulgence one would spare a child. But there was only the man he loved, looking at him with warmth and weariness, sweetness and sorrow, honesty and a hurt as quiet and enduring as Luca's own.

"Until January, then," Luca whispered, and Imre let out a low rumble of agreement.

"Until January," Imre repeated—then drew Luca up into a kiss that set his world on fire.

60

IMRE HAD NO FUCKING CLUE what he was doing.

And that was not a feeling he was accustomed to.

Even when he had been Luca's age, he had been accustomed to deciding what he wanted and maintaining a path until he arrived at his destination or, on further consideration of the situation, chose a new path. Even when he was inexperienced, he was certain of his decisions; it was how his parents had raised him, to own what he chose and uphold what he did, accept when he made mistakes, and move forward from that.

We are not people who flinch, his mother had told him when he was very young. He remembered Emanaia Claybourne leaning over him with her long, dark hair rippling down her chest, playing over his shoulders as she cut apples into slices with a pocket knife and deft hands. *Not from the difficult things. Not from the pain. We are Claybournes—born of the clay and earth, and we will stand as firm. If you choose something, you do not waver, do not flinch. If you make a mistake, you face it, and you have the honour to admit it. If you do something, you do it with everything in you, because we don't fucking half-arse.*

He'd rarely heard his mother curse, and his eyes had rounded while he'd frozen in his chair, unsure if he should laugh or accept the situation with the gravity it seemed to deserve. But then his mother had laughed herself, her eyes warm and bright and as blue as his, and ruffled his hair before offering an apple slice.

You don't need to be told this, I think. You're a good boy. A kind boy. Sometimes too kind, I think. But stay kind, my love. There are not enough kind people in this world, and I would rather raise a son to be kind than to be the sort of strong that most men seek. True strength comes from kindness, Imre. Not cruelty. Remember that.

Yet Imre had trouble remembering anything—his resolution, his strength, his focus—when Luca was in his lap, his lips melting like candy underneath Imre's, and his heartbeat fast and frightened as a bird's underneath Imre's palm.

The sort of man his parents had raised him to be wouldn't be in this situation. The sort of man his parents had raised him to be would remember that Luca was only twenty, and that Luca's parents were Imre's trusted and dearest friends. The sort of man his parents had raised him to be would never betray that trust, no matter the ache of desire, of longing, that drew him to be impulsive, to be reckless, to give in to things he never should have wanted.

But his heart seemed to belong to a different man, and that man cradled Luca close and kissed him as though he might well lose him tomorrow.

He very well could, if the slightest whisper of this reached Marco.

But then Luca let out a tiny moan, sweet as a drop of sugar on the tongue, and Imre forgot Marco. Forgot Lucia. Forgot everything except Luca's slender fingers buried in his hair, and the rough soft heat of Luca's tongue twined with his, lingering in strokes as luxuriant and slow as a cat's purring stretch.

There was something addicting about how Luca tested and feinted, one moment bold and arching into Imre with little teeth teasing at his mouth and plying lips demanding every caress and slick-locked taste, the next going limp with a shudder the moment Imre stroked his fingers down his fluttering throat, or teased the tip of his tongue with scraping teeth. He tasted so bloody *perfect,* all wet berry lips and bruises—and Imre was a very, very bad man, because all he wanted to do was pin Luca back against the couch and drink and drink of those lips for hours, until Luca was boneless beneath him and that slim, lovely body turned so very supple and hot.

Only Luca. Where a hundred hot-eyed glances and invitingly curled lips had done nothing for him, where the coy looks and flirtatious sallies at the market had left him cold…only Luca could do this to him, no matter how many reasons Imre conjured for why he *shouldn't.*

His breaths burned as though he'd run a hundred miles, aching inside his chest. He tore back, stopping himself before he crossed his own boundaries, those invisible lines that said *slow, slow, no need to rush.* Luca set his blood on fire until he couldn't think straight, couldn't make choices with the slow, careful consideration he preferred.

Bloody hell, this boy was going to ruin him.

He opened his eyes, looking into a hazed, too-bright green gaze. Against Luca's pale skin his mouth was a bright, lush red, almost obscenely soft and wet, and Imre shuddered at the hot, possessive bolt of rough and hungry desire that shot through him. He'd never thought of himself as the sort of man with such urges, such tendencies, but then he'd never had a pretty sylph sitting flushed and breathless in his lap, either, watching him with an adoring gaze and awakening long-dormant things Imre thought he'd buried ages ago.

Luca's gaze flicked back and forth over Imre's face, before his flush deepened and he ducked his head with a shy smile. In the silence—the phone had fallen still long minutes ago to leave only the rush of their breaths and the whispered wet sounds of lips mating and parting—Imre touched his fingertips to that swollen mouth, tracing its tenderness, and groaned as flesh as soft as cotton candy gave underneath his fingertips, nearly wrapping his fingers in yielding, inviting warmth caressed by the heat of Luca's breaths.

Delicately, Luca touched his tongue to Imre's fingertips, wet and taunting, then kissed his fingers, watching him through his lashes; Imre's gut tightened into a burning knot, his inner thighs turning hot and taut and pulling hard at that sensitive centre of arousal that built at the very base of his cock. His mouth ached, his tongue tingling in a sensitized echo of contact, wanting to claim and taste and delve deep all over again—but if he did, he might well forget himself entirely, with those glimmering green eyes watching him so sweetly and enticing the most deviant things.

He needed a diversion. Anything to clear his head and cool his blood.

And so he let his hand fall away from Luca's mouth, swept the boy up against his chest, stood, and headed for the stairs.

Luca let out a startled yelp and wrapped his arms around Imre's neck. By the time he'd stopped reflexively kicking his legs and relaxed his slight weight against Imre's chest, Imre had crested the stairs and strode down the hall to the bedroom. He elbowed the door open, then tumbled Luca down onto the bed, spilling him against the handmade patchwork quilt in varying squares of deep, rich blues. The room was dark save for the fire Imre had kindled after his evening shower, leaving it to warm the room until bedtime; the firelight cast edges of gold against the splayed tendrils of Luca's hair, turning it to smoke-black cinders and flame. Against the dark colour of the quilt Luca's pale skin nearly glowed, wide cat's eyes looking up at Imre, smoky, pupils dilated.

“Imre…?” he whispered, licking his swollen lips.

“Only to sleep,” Imre murmured, reminding himself as much as Luca. He leaned over him, caging that slender, fragile body between his arms as he braced his hands on the bed, the mattress sinking under his weight. “But I want you in my bed, Luca.”

Maybe *that* would silence the possessive thing snarling and twisting under his skin, when he refused to allow it anything else tonight.

“O-oh.” Luca’s eyes widened further, and he mumbled in a small voice, “…I’m wearing my clothes.”

“You should do something about that.”

Luca bit his lip—that damned *lip,* that overripe raspberry lip that was going to drive Imre beyond reason with its slickness and softness—then dropped his hands to pull his t-shirt up, baring the waist of his jeans. Imre watched, riveted, blood slowing to a volcanic flow of liquid fire, as Luca flicked the button of his jeans open, every movement pushing his shirt to expose little bite-sized glimpses of pale skin as he drew his zipper down. A lithe twist of his hips and his jeans slid down over short, loose pale blue boxers, slim svelte thighs, graceful calves. He kicked the jeans off when they hit his ankles, knocking them off the foot of the bed, then sprawled out beneath Imre once more, lifting his chin almost defiantly to bare his vulnerable throat and the faint red mark left behind where Imre had bitten him.

Mine, that possessive animal seemed to snarl, and *Shut up,* Imre snarled back. He was not a fucking animal. He’d wanted to be safe for Luca before traded kisses and whispered, temporary promises, and he damned well meant to be safe for him now.

But he wasn’t sure Luca was safe for *him*, especially when the boy reached up to catch one of the braids in Imre’s hair and twine it around his fingers, throaty voice nearly purring. “Better?”

"Better," Imre agreed, and pulled out of reach before he *did* something. He caught the edge of his own shirt, pulling it up over his head—only for Luca to make a strangled sound.

"Oh!"

Imre pulled his shirt off, peeling it down his arms, then glanced at Luca—who stared at him with his eyes rounded, cheeks a deep, burning red. Imre grinned, tossed his shirt over the high-backed chair in the corner, and unbuttoned his jeans.

"Close your eyes, if a naked man is so very *scandalous*."

Luca's eyes narrowed, before he hissed and jerked his gaze away, fixing it on the headboard. "Oh, you *arsehole*."

"Guilty as charged."

But Imre made short work of stripping down to his boxer-briefs, then fetching a clean pair of cotton pyjama pants from the trunk at the foot of the bed, pulling them up around his hips, and cinching the drawstring. When he sank onto the bed on one knee, Luca peeked back at him from under the wild tumble of his hair. Imre settled down against the headboard, leaning back—then caught Luca's chin lightly, tilting his face up. He wanted to *see* those pretty green eyes, wanted to…

To what?

Luca was his, but only for the rest of the month. But he'd been refusing to let himself see the desire in Luca's eyes for weeks, refusing to let himself feel the things that desire roused, burning as much in his heart as in his flesh, and if he was going to do this he was going to be a Claybourne and not damned well half-arse it for the little time he had.

He leaned in and stole another taste of those lips, just enough to remind himself why he should keep his hands to himself and why he very much didn't want to, then murmured, "If I'm an arsehole, what does that say for your taste in men?"

Luca drew up to settle against the headboard next to him, leaning against his arm, swaying into his kiss, his eyes lidded and smoky. "That it's absolutely fucking terrible."

"I'll have to agree with you there." Imre traced his thumb against the corner of Luca's mouth, absorbing the sensation of soft skin, then released his chin to slip his arm around slim shoulders, drawing that lanky frame into the crook of his arm and sighing. "I am terrible, Luca. In ways you cannot begin to fathom."

"I have trouble believing that." Luca nestled against him, resting his head to his shoulder; wisps of dark hair tickled against Imre's collarbone. "You're the kindest, most honourable man I've ever met. You're practically a saint."

"Saints do not have the thoughts I have."

A teasing smile split Luca's lips, and he rested his hand to Imre's chest, skin to skin, the slight hints of new calluses on Luca's fingertips raising sparks of sensation. "I thought you were pure and chaste and romantic."

"Romantic," Imre growled. "Not pure. Most definitely not chaste. I'm demisexual, not a bloody monk."

Luca laughed, snuggling against him and closing his eyes—and repositioned himself as Imre slid down the headboard to settle against the pillows, stretching out on his back with Luca melded against his side, one slender leg shifting to tangle with Imre's brazenly. Imre sighed, watching him with fond exasperation. *Little cat,* he thought, but closed his eyes and settled back against the pillows. Perhaps sleeping skin to skin with Luca wasn't the best way to rein himself in, but right now—after the haunted, hurt way Luca had looked at him, that fragile whisper of *until January,* he couldn't bear to let Luca sleep alone.

And maybe, just maybe, Imre didn't want to be alone himself.

He'd thought Luca would just drift off, but after long minutes he shifted against Imre, venturing softly, "Imre?"

"Hm?"

"Have…have you ever been in love before?"

Imre opened his eyes, turning his head. Luca watched him over the curve of Imre's shoulder, one pale hand curled in front of his face. Imre studied him, then answered, "A couple of times."

Something darkened in Luca's eyes, his brows knitting. "Why didn't it work out?"

"We just wanted different things."

Imre could think of two men he could say he loved, perhaps. Juarez, a young gamin Japanese-Peruvian man with a lost and haggard look and a secret he would never say to Imre, who'd stayed a season to help with the harvests and then taken his secrets and his pain away on the same wind that had blown him into Harrogate—because whatever he'd needed, Imre hadn't been it. And Thomas, thin bookish Thomas, who'd hated goats and farm life as much as Imre had hated the idea of living in close concrete walls and walking paved streets away from the pastures of Lohere. He could remember the taste of each of them, the way they'd smelled in those soft warm moments just out of the shower, yet it was as much of an echo as the impression of them in his bed.

And he wondered, now, if he'd loved them…or if he'd just told himself he did, to keep himself from shutting them out and refusing to let them invade him with their lips, their bodies, their touch.

"Sometimes," he murmured, "you can love someone with all your heart, but you're just not meant to be together."

"What were their names?" Luca asked faintly.

"Is that really something you want to know?"

Luca parted his lips, then stopped, lowering his eyes.

"No…maybe not." He uncurled his hand enough to pluck and pull at his red-sheened lower lip. "Do you still love them?"

"In a way."

"What…kind of way?"

Imre thought for a moment, searching for the words to explain, then said, "The way you love a memory. Something that isn't real anymore and can never be real again. It's a fondness that belongs not to the person or thing, but the place they occupy in your history and the fingerprints they left on the glass walls of your heart." That was how he thought of hearts, so often. As glass-walled lanterns with soft firelight flickering inside, burning in many colours. Fingers reaching for that light could leave smudges on the glass that dimmed it, or only filtered it into delicate new shapes. But he pulled himself from the past into the present, meeting Luca's shy, watchful gaze once more. "But if you're wondering if I'm still pining for the one that got away…" He smiled slightly, and tucked a lock of Luca's hair behind the delicate curve of his ear. "No. There is no one that got away. There were just lives moving on divergent paths."

"Is that what I'll be, when I leave?" Luca's voice was thick and low. "Fingerprints on your heart."

"Angyalka." Imre shifted onto his side, propping himself up on one elbow and facing Luca; he curled his hand against the back of Luca's neck, drawing him in to kiss his brow, cool fine skin against his lips. "Don't you know you've been part of my heart for the past twenty years? There is no one whose memories are deeper engraved into me."

But Luca pulled back, staring down at the deep midnight sheets, clenching his fingers against the cloth. "Except Dad's. Except Mum's."

"They aren't here right now." Imre wanted to coax those pretty green eyes up to his again, but Luca had drawn in on himself, and Imre wouldn't force it. So he only kissed the top of Luca's head, then rested his hand atop that inky crown. "You are."

"Yeah. I guess I am." Luca offered a wan, faltering smile. "Will you hold me until I fall asleep, Imre?"

"Of course." It wasn't hard to tell what Luca was thinking, asking about Imre's past lovers, thinking of when he would leave—and if Imre couldn't quite ease his fears and insecurities when Luca didn't speak of them directly, he could at least offer him physical comfort. He stretched his arm along the pillows, once more making room for him. "Come here, little cat."

Luca grumbled, but scooted over and tucked against him again. "I'm not that little."

"I would wager I'm approximately four times your body weight. Possibly five."

"Because you're an *ox*."

Why that little— Imre narrowed his eyes, then rolled over, pushing Luca down to the bed underneath him and pinning him there with his body. He stretched out fully atop that slight frame, struggling not to shudder at how Luca's lithe angles and slender lines moulded against him, finding space in every crevice and hollow until they locked together as if they'd been carved to fit. Moving carefully, he settled his full weight against Luca, while Luca gasped and squirmed, bursting into breathless laughter.

"*Oof*. Get *off!* Imre!" His laughter peaked in a high shriek, almost a giggle, and he thudded his fists ineffectually against Imre's shoulders, the impacts barely registering. "I—I can't breathe—!"

"Well that just won't do." Chuckling, Imre braced his elbows to either side of Luca's shoulders, lifting himself up enough so that he wasn't crushing his little cat. "So missionary's right out, then."

"Imre!" Luca made a spluttering sound, flushing up to the tips of his ears; his gaze flew to the side, fixing on the fireplace. "I—I wouldn't mind—um—" He darted another glance at Imre, then scowled, poking his tongue out. "Oh, you're just fucking with me."

"Am I?" Imre leaned down and nuzzled his nose to Luca's. "I just wanted to hear you laugh, angyalka."

Luca's scowl relented, easing into a pout. "Did I seem so sour?"

"Miserable as a stormy day."

Imre shifted to slip an arm around Luca's waist, lifting him off the bed a little—then held him close as he rolled over, twisting onto his back and pulling Luca atop him. Luca made a startled sound, but settled quickly, stretching out over Imre's body with his arms folded on his chest and his chin propped on his crossed wrists.

"Better?" Imre asked.

"Mm."

"Then go to sleep, Luca."

Luca sighed in assent, eyes lidding, but then asked, "Imre?"

"Yes?"

"How do you say 'goodnight,' in Romungro?"

Imre paused, searching his memory, then frowned. "You know, I don't know." And it was strange, for him, not to have a word on the tip of his tongue, natural and ready, but that one just wasn't there. "Romungro is a very specific Carpathian dialect of Romani, and not even my parents spoke it completely, after generations in England with English as our primary language. But in general Romani, you might say 'lachhi tijir rat.'" He stopped as a memory struck him, then shook his head. "No…'loki rat' might work better."

"Loki…loki rat," Luca tried, attempting to mimic Imre's accent, then again, slower. "Loki…rat."

Warmth bloomed in Imre's chest, and he smiled. "It eases my

heart to hear that language spoken in this house again, angyalka."

"It does?" Luca's answering smile lit his eyes. "Will you teach me more? I think I still remember some things you taught me when I was little. Hungarian, too."

"As you wish." Imre chuckled and pulled the covers up over them both, settling the duvet snugly over their bodies. "In the morning. Loki rat, Luca. Loko sojbe."

"Loki rat, Imre," Luca answered, looking far too pleased with himself, then burrowed down against Imre.

And within five minutes he was asleep, this feather's weight laid atop Imre's body and moving in slow, soft breaths, his warmth trapped between Imre and the duvet and building higher and higher, sinking deeper and deeper. Imre sighed, and closed his eyes.

Until there was nothing but the dark, the heat and softness of Luca's body, and the lonely snow-scoured wind, its mournful howl asking Imre again and again if he could ever be ready for the day when Luca left Imre behind for the life he was meant to have.

61

THE VERY NEXT MORNING, THE first of the goats went into heat.

Luca wasn't sure what he'd been expecting. They'd already moved the bucks into a separate pen in the big barn a few days ago, anticipating what Imre had called the usual annual heat cycle, but mostly the goats had been normal when they'd been checked each morning. But this morning, he heard them bleating and crying all the way from the back door of the house, echoing over even the blizzard winds. He glanced at Imre worriedly.

"Are they okay? Do you think something got in with them?"

"No," Imre said grimly, pulling his coat on. "I know that sound. At least one of the does is starting estrus, and the billies can smell her."

"Let me come with this time?"

Imre gave him a sceptical look. "It's still coming down pretty bad out there."

"So hold on to me."

Luca grinned and hooked his arm in Imre's, leaning into him—still high on the fact that he *could*. High on waking up tangled up in Imre, when the last time he'd been in Imre's bed he'd woken to the sheets already cold and Imre gone. Not this morning. This morning Imre had looked up at him with sleep-warmed, darkened eyes, this great lazy lion of silver and sand stretched out in his bed and so breathtakingly gorgeous, a smile on his lips as he'd rumbled *good morning, angyalka* and drawn him in for a lingering, drowsy kiss that left Luca's mouth tasting of Imre and the sweet heady wine of slow-burn longing.

He leaned up and stole another kiss now, pushing himself up on his toes and still barely able to reach enough to brush his mouth across Imre's. "I trust you," he murmured against Imre's lips. "You won't let me get lost. And you might need help, if the goats are being weird."

"I've never needed help before, brat." Imre chuckled his deep, thunder-rumble chuckle, resting a massive hand on Luca's waist and nipping his upper lip. "Put on a proper jumper under your coat. Layer up under your jeans. I won't let you get lost, but I can't do much against frostbite."

"You mean it?" Luca laughed, bouncing on the balls of his feet. "Okay!"

He turned and sprinted from the kitchen, up the stairs, before Imre could change his mind. In his room he stripped in record time, then wiggled into a pair of knit leggings and a thermal undershirt, before dragging his jeans and shirt on again. His hoodie, his winter jacket, two pairs of socks, gloves, and his boots later, and he was tumbling down the stairs to meet Imre at the door, answering Imre's patient amusement with a grin.

"Ready!"

"You're rather excited about goats mating, angyalka."

"I'm curious," he said and caught Imre's hand, tugging him to the door. "And I want to go *outside*."

"You may regret that in a moment."

"I won't!"

…he did.

The moment he stepped past the threshold, frigid wind slapped him in the face hard enough to dash his head to the side. Icy granules drove into his cheek, focused into a shooting funnel by the half-open sides that kept the force of the wind from blowing the walkways over more often. He gasped, but the air hurt like swallowing razor blades. He'd thought it was bad when they'd had to come out in the storm to push the walkways back into place, but he hadn't known what *bad* was until he was struggling to even breathe the painfully cold air that felt like it would freeze him into permafrost from the inside out.

Imre had already pulled the collar of his coat up over the lower half of his face, but he gestured to Luca, pantomiming pulling something over his head. Luca fumbled for the hood of his hoodie, pulling it from under his coat, and dragged it up over his head, then zipped his coat up higher until the collar closed over his mouth and nose, insulating them and trapping the air until it warmed before he breathed it in. Imre reached for his hand. Luca slipped his into it, and Imre's strong fingers grasped him tight, a solid reassurance that it would be all right.

Then, together, they trudged toward the barn, the blatting goat calls leading them forward, following the wooden barriers of the walkway, the snow piled so high it nearly spilled over the four-foot walls and through the gap into their narrow pathway. Even with the shielding walls and roof, the wind still buffeted them, and it was slow going to the barn; Luca held Imre's hand so tight he thought he would break it, though after the first few minutes he couldn't even feel it when the wind bit through his gloves and chilled his fingers. He couldn't believe Imre had been going out in this *alone* every day.

Like fuck Luca would let him do it anymore.

Stepping into the heated barn was like stepping into a furnace, heat blasting him even as the wind eased off. Luca gasped, dragging his collar down and hoodie back, scrubbing at the snowflakes crusted and iced to his eyelashes before rubbing his hands together, trying to rub the feeling back into them. “Bloody *fuck!* Is it always like that?”

“Never,” Imre answered grimly. “Weather’s been shifting strange the past few years, getting worse every year. Seasons are off. Lucky it’s not affecting the crops yet, but it will.”

Luca bit his lip. “What will you do then?”

“Find a way.” Imre unzipped his outer coat and shrugged out of it, his lips setting in a hard line. “I always find a way.”

I wish I could help, Luca thought, but bit his tongue and followed Imre deeper into the barn.

The pen where they’d isolated the five billies of the herd was a mess of pawed-up straw, feed troughs kicked over, even the water trough knocked on its side. The bucks themselves were fractious and milling about, occasionally butting at each other half-heartedly but mostly gathered in the corner of the pen closest to the larger pen for the does, bleating and flapping their tongues and rolling their eyes, stomping about. The smell from the pen was *foul,* bitter urine everywhere. They’d rather clearly rammed the wall of their pen; it bulged outward in several spots, the chicken wire stretching between the boards warped and almost torn.

“So that’s why you use the chicken wire,” Luca said, eyeing the bucks.

“They’d jump the fence otherwise, or tear it down. The chicken wire snares their horns and they don’t like it, so they leave it alone after a few butts.” Imre moved past to the does’ pen, and levered himself over the fence to drop down in the dirt and hay among the milling nanny goats. “Come on. I’ll show you how to tell if a doe’s in heat.”

Luca arched a brow. “Well that’s something they never covered in A-levels.”

But he climbed the fence, swinging himself over and dropping down at Imre's side. Imre wasted little time in corralling a young-looking doe who was barely more than a kid herself, but she was standing oddly and panting with her head low, her tail wagging sharply, soft bleats spilling constantly past her open mouth, while the underside of her tail looked wet and red and swollen. With a gentle, capable touch, Imre held her still, soothing her with gentle pats while showing Luca the physical symptoms—the swelling and discharge, sticky tail, frequent urination, while explaining the behavioural signs, from personality changes to noisy vocalization.

"This'll be little Darrow's first heat," Imre said. "Looks like about nine of our other girls are gearing up, too. Can you tell which ones?"

"Um." Luca felt a bit naff wandering among the goats and peering at their hindquarters, but when he caught a hint of red and a wet, wagging tail, he pointed. "Her."

"Cara? Spot on." Imre stroked between Darrow's ears, then moved to check Cara. "I wasn't sure if she would go into heat this season, as old as she is, but girl's still ticking."

"So, um…how does…the whole thing work?"

"Basically," Imre said, leaning over to check Cara's tail, "we put them in a separate pen with the bucks, and let nature do its work. If they don't rut this estrus cycle, they will again in a few weeks when the girls come to again."

"Lovely."

"Part of the work." Imre caught a rope lead hanging on the wall, and deftly looped it around Cara's neck. "Let's get them moved into the breeding pen."

"Right, then."

Luca had no idea what he was doing—but he'd never let that stop him before. And there was some part of him, too, that wanted to prove that no matter the season, he could *help* Imre. Be useful. He didn't want to give full voice to the thought forming in the back of his mind, not when he was already tempting fate and pushing his luck by begging for these short few weeks. He couldn't let himself think about longer. Imre wouldn't have it, anyway.

Imre wouldn't have *him*.

So he threw himself into working, so he wouldn't have to think about it. Together he and Imre roped the nine does, and led and herded them to an empty, high-walled pen in the back corner of the barn. They made them comfortable with feed and water, then left them shut in the pen and went back for the bucks. The bucks were harder to handle than the does, leaping and twisting and rolling their eyes and bleating, and one even tried to ram Luca only to trip over its own feet and stumble to the side.

"God, I hope I'm not like this when I've got a bloody hard-on," he muttered, tugging at a buck's lead while the billy goat dug its hooves into the barn floor and pulled back, then turned its head and chewed on the rope.

"Only— " Imre swore and shouldered a kicking buck over, deftly catching it by the hooves and lifting it up in both hands, dangling like it was trussed from a spit. "Only a little."

"A little?!"

"Would you rather I say a lot?"

"Arsehole," Luca muttered and gave the rope another tug, ignoring Imre's gently taunting laughter when he was more focused on getting the buck to the pen without *touching* it, when it smelled absolutely wretched.

For goats that had been charging the fence to get at the does before, the bucks were hell to herd across the barn, fighting just for the sake of fighting—but after nearly half an hour of shoving and tugging and chasing and hauling, they managed to get the five bucks into the pen, pushing them through a gated chute one at a time and immediately slamming the chute behind them before manoeuvring the next into place. By the time they were done Luca was out of breath, sticky, sweating, and more than happy to pull himself up onto the fence of the pen to rest and watch. Imre leaned next to him, folding his arms on the fence and propping his chin on them, waiting in companionable silence.

Within less than five minutes that companionable silence was broken as a good deal of ritual sniffing and posturing and bleating turned into—oh, *God*. Luca tilted his head; he didn't want to look, but he couldn't look *away*. "…that is the most fascinating and disgusting thing I have ever seen in my life."

"The miracle of nature," Imre murmured blandly.

"It's so *loud*." Then one of the bucks—oh, oh *gross*. "Oh. Oh God. And *sticky*."

Imre's almost bored expression never wavered. "That just means he's done," he said, and if Luca didn't know better, he'd think Imre was mocking him with that flippantly neutral tone.

"…how many times do I have to watch this?"

"As many times as it takes. Probably have to mate them a good hundred times for the whole group to make sure it takes." Imre shrugged. "It's quite beautiful, really."

"The hell it is. Imre?"

Imre arched a brow. "Yes?"

"You *nasty*."

A brief laugh shook Imre's shoulders. "Wait until you're apprenticing with Mira." He paused, then added pointedly, "And collecting semen samples from breeding bulls."

"*No*. No way."

"Being a veterinarian isn't just about keeping watch over sick animals and splinting broken bones." Imre turned his head, resting his cheek against his forearm, lazy eyes watching Luca over the jacket bunched against the hard rise of his bicep. "It's about making sure every animal in your care is as safe as they can be during every process of their life, whether it's breeding or birthing or nursing the ill."

Luca blew his cheeks out, kicking his feet lightly against the fence and leaning back, looking up at the rafters and the flickering banks of fluorescents. "I know that, logically. Just…thinking about the reality of it. It's scary."

"Bull semen is scary?"

"*Yes*. But that's not what I meant and you know it." Luca bit his lip. "Apprenticing with Mira. I…I still haven't called her."

"I know."

"That'd be making a decision, wouldn't it?"

"It would," Imre agreed softly.

"That's the scary part."

"Whatever you decide, angyalka, I will support you."

Luca couldn't look at Imre as he said, voice strangling a bit too much to pull off the light note he was going for, "What if I decide to stay here and just be a farmhand for the rest of my life?"

Say it, he begged. *Say you want me to stay*.

"Then," Imre said dryly, "I will provide you with earplugs, to mute your father's screaming."

Luca choked on a dry, brittle laugh. It wasn't a *get the fuck out*, at least. "Thanks."

They fell silent, even if the goats more than made up for it—bleating, squealing, even outright screaming. Luca watched them for a time, then looked away; he was trying to make himself get used to it, but he'd have to take it in stages and enough was enough for one day.

"I'd like to say they're giving me ideas," he muttered, "but after seeing that I think I'm like to remain a virgin for life."

Imre's brows rows. "You've not…?"

Heat crawled up Luca's throat. "Oh…ah…no." He ducked his head, curling his hands in his lap and fidgeting them with a rough laugh. "I know. Twenty-year-old virgin when everyone else is fucking around by the time they're fifteen, eh?"

"Nothing wrong with that. I was thirty-one my first time."

Bloody hell, Luca thought. And a man who looked like Imre, who was as good and kind and considerate as Imre, as passionate and dedicated…he could have anyone he wanted, wrapped around his little finger and begging for more—even if the fact that he'd never do that to anyone was part of his appeal. And secretly, Luca thought he liked that; that a man anyone would expect to be the kind of person who could easily use others for his own gratification without consideration just…didn't.

Because he was noble like that, Luca thought. Because he was gentle. And he thought even if Imre wasn't demisexual, even if he was into just being casual, he'd be the kind of person who'd make even a one-night stand feel cared for and safe.

Or maybe that was Luca's wishful thinking, wanting to know how even one night with Imre would be.

"Was…was he one of the ones you loved?" Luca ventured. "Your first."

"One of the ones I tried to love." Imre's eyes lidded, darkening with a shadow. "That was how I learned trying wasn't enough for me."

"I guess…no matter how old we are, sooner or later we've got to fumble around to figure out what works for us, eh?"

"Indeed. Sometimes you just *know*, but now and then you've got to hack about a bit to figure out how to put it into practice." Imre smiled slightly. "So you've done a bit of fumbling?"

"Sort of? My friend Xav let me kiss him when I was trying to figure out if I'm really gay." Luca grinned sheepishly. "Then he said I taste like penny candy and asparagus, and told me to brush my teeth if I'm going to kiss him again."

Imre snorted an amused sound. "Were you together?"

"Xavier? Nah. He's straight, and we're just…not like that. He was just trying to help me. He's pretty chill and not the type to flip out about catching the gay or some shite." Luca looked down again, fidgeting with the zipper of his coat. Should he tell Imre…? But…Imre had told him about the men he'd loved. Luca took a deep breath, then blurted, "There was this one guy." He stopped, then. How did he explain it? "We fooled around a little when I was faffing about with my gap year. We were at school together during A-levels, but I never noticed him until after, when I was trying to figure out why I recognized him at the coffee shoppe. He'd give me free cappuccinos, and we'd hang out in the park after his shift and kiss a little, maybe fumble around under our clothes. Nothing else. We weren't really boyfriends or anything like that."

"Why not?"

"I just…" Luca shrugged. "We felt like each other's holding periods. Like we were both waiting for something else, but at least we were waiting together." He twirled the tongue of the zipper in his fingers; it felt more loose and nimble than *his* tongue, when his words came out thick and awkward. Some part of him wanted to tell Imre that it wasn't anything, that it had never been anything, but…why would Imre care? "He was nice, though. Will. His name was Will. We were kind to each other," he fumbled. "I think he's why I didn't want to go to uni just yet. Not that I was skipping to be with him, but… He made me realize I was waiting for something, and I needed to figure out what before I decided what direction I want to go."

"Hm," Imre rumbled. "So that's who was texting you last month."

Luca stiffened. "You *read my texts?*"

"Not on purpose," Imre answered quickly, then cleared his throat. "You left your phone on the table when we weren't speaking. I saw something about 'I got time, hotness,' and tried not to read the rest. My apologies."

The very precise, formal distaste with which Imre said *I got time, hotness,* articulating every syllable with slow and exacting pronunciation, wrung a laugh from Luca. "…don't ever say that again." He trailed off, exhaling. "Yeah…yeah. I guess that's how it was. I never texted him back, though."

"Not my business." Imre fell quiet, and Luca thought he was done with it, until he added almost under his breath, "…but I'm glad."

"Aye?"

"Eh."

Luca grinned, and kicked his heels idly against the wall of the pen. "Okay, then."

Imre pushed himself upright, gaze sharpening as he watched the goats. "Looks like they're going to need help."

"*Help?*" Luca gulped, staring from him to the goats—where one of the billies was struggling to mount a patiently standing doe, clumsy and wiggling his hips without doing anything at all.

"Happens." Imre pulled the gate open, then paused and glanced back. "Coming?"

"Oh, *God,*" Luca groaned—but pushed himself forward and dutifully slipped off the wall.

Breeding goats wasn't supposed to be so *literal.*

Thankfully, it wasn't quite as disgusting as he'd been expecting. He held the doe steady while Imre helped the buck position himself, and once the deed was done they retreated to the fence once more. They leaned against it together, before Imre glanced at Luca and bumped him with his elbow gently.

"We can likely leave them overnight," Imre said. "I'd wanted to watch just to be sure they were getting on, but now that they've had a go once they'll keep at it for a few days. By then the next few should be in cycle, and we can change them out." He tossed his head toward the gate. "Let's muck and feed the rest, then head back up to the house."

"Oh, ah."

This, at least, was familiar: cleaning out the pens, putting down fresh hay, putting out food and water with the nannies butting around him and leaning in close. A few nosed at him a bit too hard, biting at his shirt and jacket, eyes wide, and he laughed, prying free.

"What's gotten into them?"

"They smell the billies on you. The ones having a go at you will probably go into heat in the next day or two." Across the aisle where he was cleaning the empty bucks' pen, Imre hauled a massive bale of hay down from his shoulder and ripped it open with his pocket knife to send the hay bursting free. "Hoping this season will go easy and none will take heat out of cycle."

Luca watched him, idly scratching behind one of the nannies' ears—only to realize it was Merta, thrusting her hand under his palm like she recognized him. He liked to think that she did, after how long they'd spent together in the sick stall. "What about Gia and Merta…?"

"I can't breed them. Not after giving them steroids. It passes into the offspring, and into the milk."

Luca looked down into her rectangular pupils, and scratched

under her jaw; she responded by catching a mouthful of his sleeve and gnawing. “So they’re just…here, not doing anything, for the rest of their lives?”

“They’re alive. That matters.” Imre kicked a tipped feed trough upright, setting it back into place, then dragged the hose over and turned it on, gripping the spray nozzle and showering it over the entire reeking pen. “They’ll be cared for. And they’re still part of the herd. They still help with the kids, and with keeping the others safe. Goats tend to rear communally, so they’ll have as many kids as they want come spring.”

“Oh.” Luca smiled, and leaned down to nuzzle between the stubby lumps of Merta’s filed horns, breathing in her furry, warm scent. “I like that. Do you like that, girl? I do.”

“Baa,” Merta said, and Luca laughed.

“Yeah,” he said. “Me too.

I like that, he’d said. When what he’d really meant was *I like you.*

I like that you didn’t care about losing a product.

You cared about saving their lives.

And he couldn’t tear himself from watching Imre, as he worked with that quiet confidence that bled into the smallest of gestures, the most insignificant of actions. It was strange how everything was exactly the same, even though everything had changed with a gasping, needy kiss freely given, freely shared.

I like you. I love you, Luca thought, and hugged Merta close. *And I don’t know how I’m going to let you go.*

62

EVEN IMRE WAS FROZEN DOWN to the bone by the time they detoured by the smaller barn to take care of the horses, then made the last short dash from the rear barn door to the side door of the house. Vila and Seti crowded around them, yipping and nosing, as they stomped snow off their boots and shed their coats.

"Here," Imre said, reaching for Luca's coat before he could hang it from the wall pegs. "I'll toss that in the wash. In fact, everything we're wearing should go in."

Luca grimaced, peeling out of his gloves, then staring at his splayed hands. "I think I have goat semen frozen between my fingers, and I am not happy about that fact." He brought his hands in close and sniffed, then gagged, squeezing his eyes shut and turning his face away. "Oh God, it smells so *rank*."

Imre chuckled and took the gloves, too. "I confess I take an increasing number of scented baths during breeding season."

With a horrified look, Luca wriggled out of his hoodie, then ripped his shirt off over a clinging black thermal that hugged every line of his body. "Scented with *what?* Bleach?"

"You may have the bath first, if the smell is so very offensive to your senses."

Luca paused, hands curled in the hem of his thermal. "…we…don't really have to take turns, do we?" he asked, with a pink tint to his cheeks that Imre doubted was wholly the cold. "I mean…we could probably both fit?"

"But that would—"

Imre stopped himself before the naturally logical response came to its completion: *but that would make actually getting clean very difficult.*

From the shy, hopeful way Luca watched him, Imre doubted he was thinking very clean things at all.

Imre considered, tilting his head. "I suppose it would be more efficient to bathe together."

Luca rolled his eyes, laughing. "Efficiency. That's what you care about? You—"

He broke off as Imre caught his chin lightly in his fingertips—and rewarded Imre with widened eyes, trembling lashes, a softly enticing hitch of breath and the silent part of cold-pinkened lips below warmly flushed cheeks. Those little moments of innocent surprise and uncertainty beneath Luca's biting sarcasm made Imre feel like a very bad man indeed, for it roused something growling and hungry inside him to reduce Luca to such a state of trembling vulnerability all because of his touch, his words.

He had no damned clue how he'd fought this as long as he had.

"I told you," he murmured. "Slow. I prefer to take my time, angyalka." He stroked his thumb down the delicate line of his jaw, letting its sharp, defined angle crease into his flesh, feeling as though he was defiling and leaving his mark on that pale skin just with the coarseness of his touch. "Do you honestly think I am so entirely immune to the temptation of a beautiful young man naked in the bath with me?"

"I—I—"

Luca's throat worked in a swallow, drawing Imre's gaze down. His mouth ached, lips tingling, itching to leave another mark on pale skin; he made himself pull away, giving both Luca and himself room to breathe, lingering only long enough to brush his knuckles down Luca's cheek before turning away.

"Remember to blink," he tossed over his shoulder, chuckling. "I'll start the bath."

"Arse," floated after him weakly, but he only laughed and ducked into the downstairs bathroom.

He dropped their coats atop the hamper and set the water to running as hot as he thought either of them could stand it, then dug in the cabinet, reading through the labels on the various salts and oils for something that would help ease the smell of goats in rut without overpowering. Just something to make them both feel *clean*. He settled on one of his favourite blends from an herbalist who often set up a stall at market, a deep smoky mix of amber, leather, cinnamon, and teak wood with a delicate floral undertone of roses and hollyhocks. He poured a judicious amount of the bath oil into the water, swirled it in, then followed up with a hefty handful of faintly aromatic bath salts.

Anything to distract himself from the fact that he'd just agreed to bathe with a little cat who had his claws sunk in deep under Imre's skin, and digging deeper.

Deep enough to draw heart's blood.

That's Marco's son, his inner voice reminded him, and

That's not all he is, he shot back. *I'm not going to reduce him to that instead of letting him be his own person.*

For fuck's sake.

He was really down to arguing with himself.

With a sigh, he pulled his shirt and undershirt over his head and draped them over the hamper, then kicked his boots off and stepped out of his jeans. He was just hooking his thumbs in the waist of his boxer-briefs when Luca slipped in—then froze in the doorway, eyes wide, staring at Imre with a stricken expression on his face.

"Uh."

Imre arched a brow, but tactfully kept his underwear in place. "Did you forget what I just said?"

Vivid colour returned to Luca's skin, and he looked away, dragging his fingers through his hair. "No, I didn't…I…it's okay."

Was it, Imre wondered? But he stepped out of his boxer-briefs, peeling them down his legs and adding them to the pile atop the hamper. When he stepped closer, Luca went still, looking down at his feet, his tongue caught between his teeth, the pink tip just barely showing.

Imre brushed his fingers to Luca's cheek. "Is this too much, angyalka?"

"No—no, I…" Luca shook his head, then caught Imre's hand and pressed his cheek into his palm. "I've just…never seen you completely before." The shy look Luca fixed on him from under his lashes nearly destroyed Imre, sweet and warm with a sort of trembling longing that pulled on him deeply, drawing him through some irresistible force to step closer. And to step into Luca's touch, as he reached out to rest one pale hand to Imre's ribs, fingers splayed hot against his skin. "May I?"

It took a moment for Imre to realize what Luca was asking—but when he did, he almost said *no*. Not when he wasn't certain he could resist those soft hands on his body, exploring him, touching him. But nor could he resist that quiet, earnest gaze, and against his better judgment he nodded, swallowing hard.

"If you wish."

Luca said nothing. He ducked his head again, then lifted his gaze once more, pale eyes traveling over Imre's body as intimately as a touch, drifting from head to toe, darting away as they dipped low, then flicking back shyly in a sidelong glance before skittering away as Luca blushed, his lower lip creeping between his teeth so enticingly that Imre was forced to curl his fingers into slow and tightening fists to keep from dragging him up and claiming that mouth in a kiss. Especially when Luca's fingers followed the path of every look—fingertips touching at the hollow of Imre's throat, skating down in feather-light touches over his chest, each one tracing sensitive lines like arrows pointing straight down to the coiling tightness in the pit of Imre's stomach, heightened by a touch of damp coolness that said Luca must have washed his hands in the kitchen sink, for he trailed droplets that kissed soft, cold bites against Imre's skin.

He fought himself to hold still as stone, to let Luca explore as he pleased, but each touch—as the splay of Luca's palm turned feather-light brushes into caresses, as every stroke ventured lower over Imre's ribs, his abdomen, his waist, his hips—stole another gasp of air until he was barely breathing in shallow draughts, while heat pooled lower and lower until he couldn't stop the throb of his cock, swelling against his thigh and rousing no matter how he tried to ignore it.

And when Luca's fingertips brushed against his length, sweetfire pleasure dug deep, burning hooks into him. He clenched a groan behind gritted teeth, closing his eyes, tilting his head back. For three short, agonizingly wondrous breaths he let himself savour it: the way that smooth, warm palm cupped his cock, fingers curling over him, enveloping him in delicious heat that travelled over hardening flesh in silky drags of sensation, tentative and slow.

Then he caught Luca's wrist, gently prying his hand away, breathing roughly, every inhalation straining against the bars of his ribs as though they were his rapidly shredding self-control struggling to escape its self-imposed prison.

"Ah—be careful, curious little cat," he whispered, opening his eyes.

Luca looked up at him guiltily, his eyes wide and dilated, his tongue darting over his lips. He curled his fingers against his palm. "Sorry." His breaths shook audibly. "I…is it weird to say you're beautiful?"

"No." Imre released Luca's wrist and cupped his face in both hands, drawing him up so he could kiss that abused, tender red mouth, tracing the outline of Luca's lips before leaning into him with a sigh, nuzzling his temple. "Nor is it strange that I find you lovely, Luca. But we only made peace with this last night. Let's not rush."

"O-okay." Luca leaned into him, fingers curling against his chest, his body electric and lithe against Imre's. "Bath, then?"

"Bath."

Imre caught the hem of Luca's undershirt and tugged it upward, baring the sleek lines of his waist, his stomach. Luca lifted his arms, letting Imre strip the shirt from him—and if Imre lingered, letting his fingertips graze the outlines of Luca's body and absorb the sensation of smooth skin, God, he was only fucking human. And Luca was beyond lovely; he was gorgeous in a strange, fey way. Where his clothing tended to slim him down to a frail willow lathe, beneath he was smooth-flowing angles, budding yet delicate masculinity, square shoulders blending into a graceful V and a toned, narrow waist, stomach, hips. Even if his skin was flawlessly smooth, beneath was the trim, building muscle of a young man rather than the softness of a boy, pulling into a tightly sinuous flex as Luca slid his arms free from the shirt and then let them drop, shaking his hair out of his face.

Luca ran his hand down one arm, then offered Imre a rather shaky-looking smile and tugged his shirt out of his grip. "Maybe let me undress myself, or I might forget what 'slowly' means."

Imre realized he was just *looking* at Luca, lingering on the faint sheen of sweat beginning to mist on his skin as the steam from the bath made the bathroom into a sauna, turning pale skin into shimmering frost and highlighting the contour of smooth pectorals. Clearing his throat, Imre tore his gaze away with a nod and made himself think of practical things. Checking the temperature of the water. Shutting it off so they wouldn't overflow it together. Stacking flannels on the shelf alongside the tub. The unseasonal storm, and whether or not the barn generators' fuel would last until he could get into town again. The bees, too, still preying on his mind, and giving him something to fixate on other than the sound of Luca's zipper slipping downward and denim rasping and crumpling.

"So, um…how do we both fit?" Luca murmured at Imre's back.

Imre risked a glance over his shoulder. A quick glimpse of long, coltish legs and the maddening V of dipping sinew framing Luca's navel and tapering downward, and Imre looked away, breathing out roughly. Bees. Bees.

Bees.

The bloody hell was wrong with him? He was the one who didn't like to rush into anything, but a minute alone with Luca, clothing shedding and soft fingers on his skin, and he was ready to break all his own rules.

He seemed to be breaking quite a few rules, where Luca was concerned.

Dragging himself back on track, he stepped into the bathtub, then sank down into the steaming, aromatic water. It rose up around his hips and to just above his waist, enveloping him in heat; he settled with his back against the side of the bath and spread his bent legs, then stretched a hand out to Luca. "Come here."

Luca bit his lip, fidgeting, then slipped his hand into Imre's and stepped over the rim of the tub. Imre tugged him down, pulling him into his arms and permitting himself the luxury of *touch* as he guided

Luca to sit between his legs, wet skin slipping like damp silk under Imre's palms and reigniting that heat in the pit of his stomach. Luca settled between the cradle of his thighs, leaning back against his chest; the heat seemed to melt them together, and Imre exhaled a soft, pleased sigh as Luca's body fit against his, contact of skin to naked skin a quiet-burning pleasure.

He slid one arm around Luca's waist, crossed the other across his chest to curl over one smooth shoulder, and leaned them both back to sink down deeper into the water. "Is this all right?" he murmured against the delicate curve of Luca's ear.

"Yeah," Luca breathed huskily, tilting his head back against Imre's shoulder. "I like it."

"Good." Imre pressed his lips to Luca's shoulder, and relished in his soft intake of breath. "So do I."

Silence, then. And yet as so many of their silences were, this one was right and simple, calm and relaxing, and even if Imre ached with the smoothness of Luca's body pressed tight between his thighs, he could ignore it to be content with this: with the taste of water droplets kissed away from Luca's skin, the soft sighing sound of his breaths, the scents of rosewater and teakwood and a lovely, melted young man growing more and more pliant in Imre's arms.

Luca curled his hands against Imre's knees and turned his head, rubbing his cheek to Imre's chest. "It's nice, like this," he murmured. "Intimate."

Imre chuckled. "I am very fond of small intimacies, angyalka."

"I think I like them, too." Luca paused, then added, "But…you're tense. You're worrying about things."

"Am I so easy to read, then?"

"I pay attention to everything about you, Imre. I…I notice things."

“Ah, Luca.”

Imre nosed at Luca’s throat, then kissed his pulse, which leaped against his lips. He couldn’t tell him—that his tension was more the struggle against his own rousing body. He didn’t know if he was afraid Luca would be hurt at how Imre restrained himself, or afraid he just wouldn’t understand. But this was *new*, for Imre—as new as if he were twenty and fresh himself, and just figuring his body out when it wasn’t something he was accustomed to, these rough and uncontrollable surges of pounding desire. It left him unsettled, and until he had a handle on it so he didn’t feel like a bloody animal in heat, he’d rather not misstep and say the wrong thing.

And so he deflected with, “The bees, mostly.” He sighed, resting his chin on Luca’s shoulder. “I can’t remember a winter this bad in my lifetime. I’m going to have to go out to check the hutches. They’re probably buried in snow, which is insulation enough, but I need to be sure. If the bees die, the orchards die. The clover fields die, and with them the bulk of my grazing feed.” He snorted softly. “That, and I just don’t want my bees to die.”

“But there’s no walkway to the orchard.”

“I know.”

Luca sat up against him, twisting to look over his shoulder with a deep frown. “Imre, you could get lost, or stuck in the snow—”

Imre stopped him with a kiss, just enough gentle pressure to make those delectable lips turn soft against his, Luca sighing with a soft sound as Imre tasted him, lost himself in tracing the shape of Luca’s mouth with the tip of his tongue. When he drew back, he smiled.

“I know every inch of Lohere as well as I know my own body, Luca,” he said. “I won’t get lost.”

Luca’s jaw set, his eyes snapping. “You’re right. You won’t.

Because I'm going with you."

"No," Imre growled, tightening his grip on Luca as if he could shield him from something that hadn't even happened. "Absolutely not."

"So you're the boss of me now?" Luca twisted more to face him, tucked up sideways between Imre's legs and glowering with a firm ferocity that belied his years. "We'll take it in stages. First to the storage barn together, but we're going to run a rope from the big barn out to the storage barn as we go. That's halfway. Then we run another rope out to the orchard. Tie it to the fence. Hold on to the slack end and stay together while we check the bees. Then we follow the rope back, and we stay safe. *Together*."

Everything in Imre wanted to argue. Luca would blow away on the slightest wind—yet with the way Luca glared at him now, he seemed as though his will would withstand a typhoon. Imre had always known Luca was stubborn, but he'd never seen this kind of steel beneath his mulishness, a quiet and firm determination that made his eyes snap, that made Imre question why he was actually so against this. He'd wanted to treat Luca as an equal. If he meant to do that, that meant accepting his input, considering it fairly.

And accepting that Luca wanted to protect him as much as he wanted to protect Luca.

"That is actually a workable plan," he admitted grudgingly.

"You still don't like it."

"I don't like the idea of losing you in the snow."

"And I don't like the idea of losing *you* in the snow." Luca poked Imre's chest firmly, blunt fingernail stinging a little against his skin. "So we make like it's the Antarctic, we work together, and we keep each other safe." There came that stubborn, proud tilt to his chin. "Got it?"

"Yes, sir." Imre relented with a chuckle and a sigh. He didn't wholly like it, but didn't wholly dislike it, either. "Tomorrow, then?"

"Tomorrow," Luca repeated, then frowned, eyeing Imre. "What's wrong?"

Imre considered for a moment. As resilient and stubborn as Luca was, there was still that fragile crystal brightness, so easily dimmed, so easily hurt, and Imre didn't want to dull that glimmer with clumsy words. "You always say you want to take care of me," he finally said. "It's not something I'm accustomed to, or know what to do with. Yet it seems you're quite serious about it."

"Well, fucking yeah." Luca's gaze sparked. "That doesn't mean just helping with meals or doing the wash—you need to put your shite in the hamper and not just leave it around, by the way." When Imre barked a startled laugh, Luca grinned fiercely and continued, "It means taking care of you the way you take care of me. Whether you're bandaging my feet or making me stay inside because I'm a helpless city git who'd get lost in a blizzard alone." His voice softened, eyes lidding, as he rested his hand to Imre's chest. Slim fingers threaded through the curls of Imre's chest hair, and he couldn't help sighing at the feeling, melting to the touch, to Luca's quiet words. "You said we look out for each other. So we look out for each other."

"Hm." Imre considered once more, then shrugged. "I cannot argue that logic."

Luca snorted. "Why are you even trying to?"

"I really don't remember, little cat." Imre leaned around him and reached for the washcloths he'd piled on the edge of the bath, and the bar of black lava soap in the dish. "We are supposed to be getting *clean*."

"That requires moving. I like where I am."

"The water will get cold sooner or later."

Luca beamed. “We can run more.”

“Brat. Here.”

Imre offered Luca a washcloth, but Luca only folded his arms over his wet-slicked, glistening chest and shook his head. Imre arched a brow. So it was going to be like that, was it? Little monster. With an amused, heavy sigh, Imre dropped one of the towels back on the rim, wrapped the soap in the other, dipped it in the water, then worked it in his palm until deep grey suds foamed through the terrycloth, the pleasantly pungent aroma of volcanic stone rising to mix with the soothing scents of rose and teak in sharp counterpoint. When he curled his fingers against Luca’s throat, the cloth-wrapped soap pressed between his palm and that slick skin, Luca’s eyes widened; against Imre’s fingertips, his pulse jumped.

“Imre…?”

“Hush.” Smiling slightly, Imre traced the cloth softly down Luca’s throat, leaving a trail of soapy foam that gleamed against smooth flesh. Luca swallowed hard, shifting against Imre, his body moving warm and wet and bringing Imre a deep, lazy pleasure as skin glided to skin while those long, slim thighs and Luca’s gently rounded ass shifted against Imre’s hips, his cock. Silence built between them as Imre savoured each touch, painting a path of suds over Luca’s shoulders and the delicate arches of his collarbones; in the silence each soft musical *plink* of water droplets falling back down into the bath became a strange ticking timer, counting second after second of slow and aching tension.

Imre lingered on the path of his fingers, lingered on how pale and smooth Luca was under the dark, coarse sweep of Imre’s touch, but as the towel drifted down over Luca’s chest he sucked in a sharp breath, chest swelling hard under Imre’s palm. The towel had just barely skimmed the edge of one pale pink nipple, but Luca began to tremble, and when Imre looked up his eyes were almost too wide, his lashes shivering, his lower lip suffering under the abuses of worrying teeth. Imre met those wide eyes, then deliberately and slowly swiped the rough terrycloth over Luca's nipple, tracing the roughened circlet of darker flesh before grazing and stroking the tight central nub. Luca sucked in a breath, back arching, and ducked his head with a low sound caught in the back of his throat; a sharp dash of red streaked across his cheeks and the bridge of his nose.

"A-ah…Imre…"

Imre couldn't look away. Not from those sweet reactions; not from the lovely young man trembling in his lap. "Are you sensitive, angyalka?" he asked, then brushed the towel against Luca's nipple again. The round bud immediately hardened, thrusting against the terrycloth, and Luca made another strained, soft sound, curling forward. His fingers knotted against Imre's chest, clutching then relaxing—then digging again as Imre let the towel and soap fall, and caught Luca's nipple between his fingers. Slowly he rolled it, teased it, tugging lightly until Luca's breaths broke and hitched, then stroking it with the rough pad of his thumb until Luca whimpered.

"O-oh…*oh!*" Luca gasped out huskily with a little shake of his head. "Th-that…that shouldn't feel like…"

"Why not?" Imre asked, then stroked again just to hear that throaty, needy sound spill past Luca's lips, that sound that shot right down to his gut and pulsed hard through his cock.

"I…I-I'm…I'm a man, and…"

"You are," Imre agreed softly, and eased up for a moment, just taking Luca in. He was so flustered, so embarrassed, and fond warmth swelled in Imre's chest. "I'll spare you the science of nerve density and sensitivity, and simply say it's perfectly natural for this to feel good." He dipped his head to press his lips to Luca's other nipple, licking the water from his skin, lingering on the pebbled texture against his tongue and—when it instantly tightened, Luca's soft cry startled and rough—taking it between his teeth to tug gently. "And that," he murmured as he released with one last lick. "Not all men are so sensitive, but for the ones who are…"

He bowed over Luca's chest again, nuzzling underneath his tucked chin, wordlessly urging him to let Imre in. Let Imre close. Let Imre once more take that tight-roused nipple into his mouth, capturing it in his lips, sucking gently, flicking and taunting and circling with his tongue until Luca rasped out a cry, tangling wet fingers in Imre's hair, breathing so roughly his chest pushed against Imre's mouth with every gasp. If Imre let himself, he could lose himself in this moment: in Luca's breathlessness, his almost shocked reactions, the way he reacted as if no one had ever touched him this way before, and *God* Imre was terrible for hoping that no one ever had. That no one in Luca's early youthful fumblings had ever been allowed in this far, no Will or any other crude and tactless prat touching and tasting Luca in this way while Luca arched his back and keened softly under his breath.

"Imre…*Imre*," Luca whispered, as if in answer to Imre's unspoken demand. As if saying *only you, only you* with every utterance of his name, and inside Imre *burned*.

"Ah, Luca…" He let go of the damp little nub of flesh and nuzzled against it; the pink skin was reddened, gently swollen, and he fought himself not to torment it further, not to tease and bite and taste it until it was red and sensitive enough to make Luca scream with taut pleasure-pain. Slow, he reminded himself. Imre had set that rule, and he was already on the verge of breaking it. His breaths felt jagged, as he rested his brow to the centre of Luca's chest and closed his eyes. "You will shatter me, one day."

"I…I don't mean to…" Luca curled against him, his parted, gasping lips hovering near Imre's temple, his fingers still clutched shakily in his hair; his cock was just as hard as Imre's, nudging against Imre's stomach and ribs. Luca made a soft, distressed sound. "I'm sorry."

"No—don't be. Never be sorry." Imre slid an arm around Luca's waist, grasping him close as he kissed over Luca's chest, tasting beads of water on soft skin. "Perhaps I needed to shatter. Perhaps I have been too rigid in my ways for too long."

Perhaps I grew too accustomed to the idea of being ever alone, he thought, but would not say.

He wasn't alone now. And even if this moment had far too short a lease, he could take it while he had it. He kissed the tender, vulnerable place just below Luca's jaw, then let his touch stray downward: careful, testing, just barely brushing his fingers over the head of Luca's cock, the skin burning-hot beneath his fingertips and slick-smooth in the most entrancing way. Luca jerked with a tiny sound and Imre buried his face into his throat, breathing in that sweet scent mixed with lava soap, feeling the wild throb of his pulse as Imre slowly wrapped his hand fully around Luca's cock.

"May I?" he whispered, and Luca rocked his hips upward, sliding the hard length of him against Imre's palm.

"Imre," he strained, almost unheard. "Please…yes, *please…*"

That *yes* was everything Imre needed and all the things he hadn't known he'd wanted until now. Luca writhing; Luca begging; Luca *willing*, and grasping at him fiercely as Imre stroked over his full length, taking his time exploring the shape of that warm, throbbing cock, toying his fingers over every detail, stopping when he found every little place that made Luca's entire body tighten against him and turned those soft, almost restrained whimpers into high peaking cries.

Imre lifted his head to watch him, captured by the lost expression on Luca's face, transforming his pretty, catlike features into a portrait of tormented pleasure. He was so *responsive,* grasping at Imre's shoulders as Imre trailed his fingertips beneath the sensitive flare of his cock head, Luca's nails digging in with pleasant points of mildly burning pain as Imre tightened and released his grasp rhythmically, alternating pressure with faster and faster strokes until Luca's thighs quivered against his lap and he rolled his entire lithe body up to meet each downward stroke.

If he could have held this moment endlessly, Imre would have. The newness of it; the wonder of seeing Luca undone for the first time, and realizing that with each new facet of Luca that Imre discovered, he only grew more and more beautiful. He had seen Luca the scarred and wounded young man; Luca the sharply intelligent provocateur; Luca the dedicated worker; Luca with the kind, gentle hands and a natural touch with the animals; Luca the pleading and lovelorn; Luca his *friend.*

And now he saw Luca the lover, a sweet thing who gave himself over so fully to his pleasure that it sang in every motion of his body.

Friction built in burning caresses of skin to skin, slicked by heated water and fragrant oils. Imre kept his gaze locked on Luca's face as with every stroke Luca's voice rose higher, his arms wrapping desperately around Imre's neck, his body growing more and more tense until he was a guitar string drawn taut and ready to quiver with a building, resonant note of pleasure.

And then it came—that moment, that shocked and grasping and gasping moment, Luca frozen, his eyes snapping wide open then squeezing tightly shut, his voice seized, his fingers knotted in Imre's hair. That peak of tension…and then that note Imre had been waiting for, *aching* for spilled past Luca's lips in a shivering, breathless cry as a hard shudder moved him against Imre's body, and warm wetness joined the water and oils slicking their skin as Imre slowed his strokes.

He could hardly breathe, that sweet moment when Luca had lost himself hitting Imre deeper, harder than a blow to the chest.

As Luca sank against him, Imre eased off and then let go with one last stroke to the tip of Luca's cock, rousing a boneless half-shudder before Luca went limp again. And when Luca tucked his head under Imre's jaw and curled against him, Imre was more than content to enfold him in his arms and sink deeper in the steaming water, eyes closed, breathing in the scent of sated relaxation rising off Luca's body and the damp tendrils of his hair.

He'd crossed a line, he thought. Perhaps that line had been crossed the moment Luca had first kissed him and Imre had fallen into it for those few heady moments before pulling away. But before this moment—before those quiet cries on Luca's lips—Imre could, perhaps, have turned away. Refused to acknowledge how deeply Luca drew on him, and how much these weeks of denial had made him ache. Yet now?

If he was to be damned, he was to be damned, and he would not be ashamed of making his angyalka happy.

Luca sighed softly, nosing into his throat, tickling against Imre's skin. "Imre."

Imre cracked his eyes open. "Mm?"

"That…was okay?"

That soft note of insecurity coaxed a smile. Imre held Luca that much tighter for it. "More than, angyalka." He pressed a kiss into Luca's hair. "You were lovely."

Luca hunched his shoulders, almost burrowing against Imre, hiding. "You kept…you kept *looking* at me…"

"I enjoy looking at you." He frowned as a thought struck him.

"Was that why you were so quiet? Did you hold back because I was watching?"

"…well I didn't want to be yelping about like some yappy pup, now did I…" Luca mumbled sullenly.

"You don't need to be embarrassed." Nudging his knuckles under Luca's chin, Imre coaxed his gaze up, looking into green eyes that glimmered with uncertainty. "Not with me. You don't have to hold back." He grazed his thumb over the yielding curve of Luca's kiss-swollen lower lip. "I love the sound of your voice raised in pleasure, Luca. Don't deny us both."

"Oh God, you're fucking *terrible*." Luca jerked upright sharply, that dreamy, lost, vulnerable look replaced by a glare that couldn't quite manage ferocity when he was blushing so deeply, even the tips of his ears a bright coral pink. "I never thought you'd actually fucking give in, and when you do you spend the whole bloody time making me blush like a virgin."

"You are a virgin," Imre pointed out.

"*Shut it!*" Luca hissed. "Seriously, you're supposed to be all stiff and grave and stuffy. Not suave."

"I am not suave," Imre pointed out again.

Luca screwed his face up, then drew himself up. His voice dropped to a deep rasp, coming out in a rather comical growl as he set his mouth in a hard line and mimicked, "'I love the sound of your voice raised in pleasure, Luca. Don't deny us both.'"

Oh, for the love of— Imre scowled. "I do not sound like that."

"The hell you don't."

Luca laughed, settling back down against him again—but then he caught a soft sound in his throat, eyes first widening, then half-closing, as his bottom shifted against Imre's lap. The brush of friction and sweet flesh against his cock sucked the breath from Imre's lungs, catching in his throat as his fingers reflexively tightened, his control straining at its leash. Luca looked up at him with that damnable lower lip twisting and plucked and soft between toying fingers, as he drifted his other hand down Imre's chest, his stomach, raising ripples of tension, tightness flexing and heating in every muscle that delicate touch caressed.

"Mnh…Imre…"

Imre almost let his body get the better of him, but God, he was still reeling. Still needed time to process this, and he couldn't if he let himself fall headlong into hedonistic pleasure without thinking about how this would affect both of them. He shook his head, swallowing back and forcing himself to move, to catch Luca's wrist and gently lift his hand, kissing each of his fingertips.

"Shh," he said. "You don't have to. It can be just this, for now."

Luca's face fell. "But…you…"

"I take pleasure in giving you pleasure." Imre leaned in and kissed that soft, sulky mouth until it relaxed for him, until Luca sighed and relaxed against him once more. With one last brush of lips to lips, Imre withdrew. "Again, I will remind you: slowly, slowly."

Luca sighed, but offered a small smile. "You're going to drive me up the wall with 'slowly, slowly.' You've been moving slowly since I came here."

"I have been moving backward since you came here. But your magnetism always drew me forward." And yet he couldn't bring himself to cross that line, even when Luca only *looked* at him, the question and the wanting so clear in his eyes, that silent pleading that tugged Imre's heartstrings into knots. He just…he needed *time.* With a sigh, Imre leaned forward, resting their brows together. "Luca…"

"It's okay, Imre." It came out as a brittle half-laugh, words spilling through the cracks. "I know it's…it's just this. And it's over soon. I won't ruin things between you and Dad."

So you would let me ruin everything between us, instead?

Imre searched those earnest eyes, and thought yes. Yes, Luca would let him break him, break *them*, because so very long ago Luca had made a sweet, innocent promise and would do anything if only Imre would make him feel like that promise was a possibility.

Guilt was a bitter taste in the back of his throat, the undertone of shame resting foul on his tongue. What was he *doing?* Letting Luca be so desperate he'd take whatever scraps Imre gave him? It wasn't fair. It wasn't equal, no matter how short this relationship might be. It wasn't *right*, letting Luca feel like Imre held all the power here, that everything was so very one-sided.

But he didn't know what to *do*, either, when he was afraid of…of…

Too many things.

He closed his eyes, taking a deep breath, then let his hands fall away.

"Come. Wash up," he said, and handed Luca a towel. "There's something I wish to show you."

63

LUCA WASHED UP IN SILENCE. He didn't know what to say, after that. Part of him was ready to burst apart in a shower of fizzy sparks, his heart on fire; Imre had *touched* him, and it had been better than anything he'd ever expected. Better than Will's clumsy fumbling, better than his own palm and five fingers.

It was almost mortifying how deeply he'd responded to those coarse hands on his body, that coaxing touch that had lit fire under his skin. He'd probably be more embarrassed after his first time like that with anyone if Imre hadn't, as always, been so patient, so gentle, so calm. Luca's parents had never really had the birds and the bees talk with him. Sex was something chavs jeered over or people joked about on TV, uni students Luca's age went wild with, and everyday people were so practical about that it just wasn't something anyone talked about. Have a good rib with your friends, yeah, but when it came down to having a real conversation…

He'd never, with anyone. That one fumbling kiss with Xav had been couched in prodding and teasing, and when it was over Xav had punched him in the arm and grinned just so Luca knew it was okay.

And yet Imre had so calmly, clearly said *It's all right. There's nothing to be embarrassed about. You were lovely.*

What they did together was lovely.

If only Imre would let Luca touch him back.

He watched Imre from under his lashes while Imre scrubbed his shoulders off, the two of them manoeuvring around each other in what was luckily an Imre-sized bath or they'd be all knees and elbows. It might almost be cute, the two of them covered in suds, if Luca wasn't still aching and deliciously sensitive from Imre's touch; if Luca couldn't still feel Imre's cock against the small of his back. Even if Imre seemed content to act like it wasn't even there, Luca couldn't help how his gut tightened every time the hard, slick cock head slid against the small of his back and nudged into the groove of his spine.

But Imre had said *slowly*, and wanted to show him something.

Luca only bloody well hoped that *something* would sort why Imre was perfectly willing to touch Luca, but still wouldn't let Luca touch him. He knew Imre had his boundaries, but…

Keeping things one-sided like that wasn't all that fair, either.

Imre draped his washcloth over the edge of the bath, then lightly rested a damp, dripping hand to the top of Luca's head. "Ready to get out?"

Luca nodded, curling his arms around himself. "Mm."

"Don't squirm too much, then. You're slippery."

Before Luca could ask what Imre meant, Imre wrapped his hands around his waist and lifted him out; that wild sweet vertigo gripped him, as if he was all feathers and Imre all stone, and he laughed as Imre settled him lightly on his feet, the tile cool against his soles and the steam-filled air licking at his damp skin. Everything smelled like roses and something soft and smoky, and Luca thought for the rest of his life he would remember, every time he caught the scent of roses, the way Imre looked sprawled naked and gleaming in the bath, his powerful body languid and at rest, grace in the damp fall of his hair and the splay of his fingers and the casual spread of his legs. Roses, to him, would always be the day Imre had held him in his lap and whispered *You will shatter me, one day* with that soft lush beard teasing against Luca's jaw and that deep husky voice in his ear and those wicked hands turning him every which way.

Imre cocked his head, gripping the edge of the bath and pushing himself up with a rippling flexion of thickly corded biceps, water sheeting down his hips and thighs. "Everything all right?"

Luca blinked, then shook himself, clearing his throat. Look at him, fucking staring like a soppy overemotional knob. "Fine," he said, and snagged a towel to scrub it over his body before wrapping it around his hips.

A second towel draped around his shoulders from behind, and for a moment Imre wrapped him up in heat and safety, his lips hot against Luca's nape. "Let the water out, dry off, and get dressed," he murmured, rumbling against Luca's back, and Luca's stomach went hot and liquid and trembly in the most wonderful ways. "I'll meet you upstairs. My room."

Then he slipped past Luca and, dripping and unabashedly naked, thighs and ass flexing, strode from the bathroom and left Luca alone with his breaths coming shaky and his skin feeling too deliciously tight. Speaking of unfair…

It really wasn't fair that Imre could strut around like that when he had Luca so fucked up.

He forced himself to breathe, exhaled on a shaky laugh, then leaned over to pull the stopper from the tub. For a moment he lingered, watching the water swirl out, then raked a hand through his hair and padded from the bathroom up the stairs.

In his room, he tugged on a t-shirt and a pair of boxers, took half a second to drag a comb through his hair, then headed down to Imre's room. He held back for a few breaths just around the door; he felt like an overeager puppy, wanting to be where Imre was, wanting to be close, wanting just the slightest touch even if it was only a brush of hand to hand. *Stop being silly*, he told himself. Imre wasn't going to push him away again just for being eager.

He pushed you away before, the ugly voice of his doubt whispered. *He won't let you touch him.*

Yet, he countered fiercely. *Yet. He…he said he wants to go slow, and that's okay. So…so maybe he just…maybe what he did tonight was for me…if that's how he wants to, then…*

His doubt had no answer, but there was something distinctly amused about its silence.

Luca shoved his errant thoughts down, shook his hair out of his eyes, then stepped through Imre's bedroom doorway. Imre had laid the fire in the hearth, and the entire room glowed in shades of gold and deep-burnished wood polish. Imre, too, glowed where he sat on the edge of the bed, slouched casually in a pair of loose, low-riding grey pyjama pants, their hems dragging against the floor around his bare, spread feet. The nightstand drawer was open, and Imre paused, caught reaching inside, and glanced up at Luca. His eyes warmed with a subtle smile.

"Come. Sit with me."

Luca pulled at his lower lip, then made himself let go—even if his fingers immediately found a home twining nervously together as he drifted into the room, then sank down on the edge of the bed a few inches away from Imre.

"What do you have there?"

"A moment," Imre murmured, and withdrew a small carved wooden box from the drawer, no longer than the breadth of Imre's hand from fingertip to the base of his palm. Darkly stained, unpolished rosewood glimmered softly in intricate curves and hand-carved patterns in Roma designs, concentric florals and mandalas surrounded by smooth borders. Imre passed one broad hand over it almost reverently, then flicked the simple brass hook latch and flipped it open.

Inside, the little keepsake box was full of tangled odds and ends. Two old dog collars, and as Luca leaned closer, peering curiously, he glimpsed Cirikli and Gullo's names on the tags. Old, creased bits of faded paper with scribbled handwriting. A thin cord of red string with a brass coin tied to one end. Several small, bent, battered, wafer-thin silver coins. A key. And a lump of something wrapped in tissue paper, perched atop the rest.

Imre carefully plucked the ball of tissue out, then set the box on the nightstand and delicately peeled the tissue away, one layer at a time. Inside rested a slim loop of braided grass, dried stiff and brown with just the faintest edge of green, the little overlapping chevrons meticulous yet still as irregular as only a child's clumsy hands could make them. The loop closed in a little frayed knot, and Luca remembered closing that knot and fumbling with it and feeling like his stomach was in every twist and pull and tight careful tug.

His stomach twisted now, then dropped out as his heart skipped and stumbled over its next few beats.

"You kept it?" he whispered, staring at the brittle thing resting in Imre's palm.

His ring.

The ring he'd given Imre, when he'd promised *I'll always love you, Imre.*

"You made it for me," Imre said, and there was *something* in his voice, something in darkened cobalt eyes, that Luca didn't understand, but it warmed inside him and swelled his heart to bursting. Imre gently lifted the ring out of the tissue paper, set the paper aside, and cupped the circlet of grass in his palm as if it were a fragile and precious thing. "I take promises, even wee promises, very seriously."

Luca had started to reach for the ring—but stilled at those words, drawing his hand back and curling it against his chest. He stared at Imre, an odd numb tingling in the tips of his fingers and the pulse of his lips and the curl of his toes. Did Imre know?

Did Imre know Luca still loved him?

"Imre…"

"I…" Imre looked down at the ring, then away, his breaths loud and shuddering. "I don't know what I'm saying. Forget that."

He picked up the spread tissue paper, deposited the ring gently in the centre, and began tucking it away inside cocooning folds again—but Luca pushed closer, reaching out desperately to stop him, one hand on his arm, the other covering Imre's hand, curling those rough fingers to a standstill cupping the little grass ring.

"I can't forget it," he said, and suddenly nothing was more important to him than this moment, this now, the words he wouldn't say to Imre's face and that ring in his weathered hand. Luca looked up at him, heart in his throat, his eyes stinging and he didn't understand *why*, only that all his emotions were braided into that damned silly childish ring. "Will you wear it for me?" he begged. "Please?"

Imre looked at him with that quiet stillness, his gaze softening with something like regret as he shook his head. "I can't, angyalka. It will break. Time has dried it until it would crumble the moment I closed my fist. Don't ask me to destroy this."

"Then I'll make you another one!" Luca flared. "And another and another and another, over and over again, no matter how many dry out and break!" Why did this *hurt* so much? Why was his heart seizing, its seams splitting? He shook his head, tightening his hand around Imre's. "I'll make you one that won't break," he swore, and then the fucking tears were coming, why the *fuck* was he always crying now, he didn't need this, didn't need to fall apart right now with the taste of salt in his mouth when…when… "I need it to not break, Imre…I just…I need *something* to not break…”

“Angyalka…” Imre pulled his hand free from Luca’s and set the box aside, taking an agonizingly long moment to set the ring reverently against the lid before he was back and his arms enfolded Luca in heat and warmth, pulling him against the solidity of Imre’s chest and the rumble of his voice. “Come here,” he said roughly, and then his breath was hot in Luca’s hair and his hair and beard flowed in a mix of silk and scratch against his cheek. “I won’t let the ring break, Luca,” he swore, a strange fervent edge in his voice. “I promise.”

But you’ll let us *break,* Luca thought, and buried his face against Imre’s chest, his shoulders shaking hard enough to hurt his spine and ache his ribs as he struggled not to give in to the dry, soundless sobs heaving his chest. *Just like Mum and Dad.*

If there’s even an us *to break.*

64

LUCA DIDN'T REMEMBER FALLING ASLEEP. He must have, because he woke curled close in Imre's arms, tucked under the covers and cradled against the curve of Imre's body. The last he remembered was feeling like his heart was going to break at the sight of that ring, sitting there dried and fragile but still whole, cherished precious and close after all these years.

It was still there now, sitting atop the keepsake box—a shadow in the darkened room, the near-dead fire casting just enough light to make the very edges glimmer. It must be well after midnight, for the fire to be so low and yet the light still so dark outside, though all he could see when he pushed up enough to peer over Imre's shoulder was a sheet of white out the window. It could be midday with that whiteout and he'd never know it, if not for Imre enveloping him like flesh forged from iron-wrought bands still hot from the flame. Luca gave him an hour, two at most, before he was up and moving and *doing* things again.

For someone so graven and slow-moving and still, Imre was bizarrely restless. Luca didn't think others saw it; he wasn't sure Imre was aware of it himself. It was as though, if he stopped moving, he'd have to…

What?

Luca lingered on Imre's sleeping face. Even in sleep his face was all hard planes and angles, barely softened by the edges of firelight; his grace was the grace of mountains, his beauty the beauty of raw and unfinished things. Luca gently threaded his fingers into Imre's beard, stroking down until he touched the fierce line of his jaw. Imre exhaled heavily in his sleep, his arms tightening around Luca, his head turning subtly toward the touch, but he didn't wake.

What was he hiding from, with that quiet desperation to always be doing *something?* Even when sitting still he had to be reading, or working on spreadsheets, or thumbing through his almanac and making notes. Maybe Luca was reading too much into things. Just because Luca had perfected the art of being a shiftless fucking sod who did nothing for days on end didn't mean that was normal, and it didn't mean Imre was hiding from jack shite.

But that nagging feeling…

That nagging feeling that had only gotten stronger, when he'd seen that ring. He'd never thought Imre would remember it, let alone keep it locked away and wrapped in tissue like some precious treasureling.

Had it really meant so very much to Imre?

Luca's mouth creased. He wanted…

He wanted to fucking destroy it.

That ring, that promise, belonged to five-year-old Luca—and he wasn't that boy anymore. He didn't want the person who lived in Imre's thoughts, that person who left smudged fingerprints on the glass walls of Imre's heart, to be *that* boy. If Imre still cherished the memory of that child enough to keep the ring locked away for so long…

Could he ever really see Luca as a man, or was this just pretend?

Was it all right as long this little dalliance was short-term, and he could pretend Luca was someone else, someone not connected with that child? Was he just—

"You," Imre rumbled through his beard without ever opening his eyes, voice heavy and deep with sleep, "think very loudly."

Luca froze, his mind screeching to a halt in the middle of another rabbiting circle. "Uh."

One eye cracked open. Imre peered at him through a fan of dark lashes, just a faint glimmer of drowsy blue. "You're working yourself into a tiff over something."

"Oh, *God*." Luca groaned and slumped against the pillows. "I'm sorry. I didn't mean to wake you, I'm sorry, I just—how could you tell?"

"Tense." Imre yawned—a deep lion's yawn, stretching and full and lazy—before opening the other eye, watching Luca steadily. "Want to talk about it?"

"No—no, you should just go back to sleep—"

"Can't. Awake now."

"Fuck. Sorry."

"Don't be." Exhaling heavily, Imre pushed himself up on one arm, warm gaze drifting over Luca. "My stomach would've woken me up soon anyway. We fell asleep without supper. But I'm not going back to sleep when you're upset."

Luca pulled the pillow out from under his head and dragged it over his face. "Mmph."

"Luca?"

"*Mmph!*"

Imre tugged at the pillow. Luca held it tighter, growling under his breath. The mattress shook with Imre's low chuckle, before he pulled at the pillow harder.

"Why are you hiding from me, angyalka?"

"Because I…I'm being daft. I'm waffling. I'm fussing. I'm worrying. This relationship is only forty-eight hours old and I'm worrying if I can even call it a relationship or if—"

"Luca?"

"Nngh."

"…I've not a clue what you just said."

Oh, bloody hell. He'd just confessed all that to the pillow and that was just—so bloody pointless and—why did he even—

Typical Luca.

Heaving a deep sigh, he reluctantly dragged the pillow down just enough to peek over it, looking up at Imre. He was just shadow and edges of gold and silver, hovering over Luca and watching him with that quiet, gentle patience.

Luca dug his fingers into the pillow, then ventured, "…I'm afraid you don't see me."

His voice came out small, barely a whisper, but in the ensuing silence it could have been a scream. Imre tilted his head curiously, considering, then asked, "How so?"

Why, oh *why* couldn't he just vanish into the bed? Luca hunched into himself, hugging the pillow against his chest and skirting his gaze away. "The ring," he said, voice catching in his throat in a gritty whisper. "That…ring…a little boy gave you that ring. A little boy who didn't think about the things I think about you. That little boy didn't know the difference between friend love and romantic love. That little boy didn't know about kissing, or touching, or the way my heart sets on fire when you look at me like you *want* me." It all sounded so childish when he said it out loud. But it was out now, and Imre was still watching him, and he might as well finish. "I'm not that little boy. But you love that little boy, enough to keep that ring. And I'm…I'm afraid that you don't see *me*. Just…some shadow of a memory, and not…"

"The man you want me to see," Imre finished softly when Luca trailed off, the knot in his throat too large to speak, choking him miserably. "The man you want me to desire, while I say I want to move so slowly you're afraid I won't take a single step at all."

Luca nodded, trying to swallow and failing. He couldn't breathe, but he didn't even want to try, when right now he'd happily pass out just to escape this moment. Imre said nothing at first; he shifted to sit up against the headboard, his bare chest and pyjama pants hissing against the sheets until he settled. Gentle tugs coaxed Luca closer; Luca let himself be pulled for a moment, before he gave in and voluntarily settled himself against Imre, curling up and tucking himself into the dip of his waist while a heavy arm settled over his back and a warm hand drifted through his hair.

Imre made a thoughtful sound, but it was several more long moments before it formed words. "I can't see that boy in you, Luca," he murmured. "I may be a touch too vanilla for the kind of Daddy issues inherent in seeing you that way, in linking you with that memory. I've been asking myself who you are to me since the moment you stepped off the train. Memories are only that. Memories. The warmth of familiarity. The sense of home. That's who you are. Not the child I used to know, but the sense of home you bring with you always—that feeling that makes you my angyalka. This place…it stopped feeling like home, when you left. And now it feels like home again. *That* is what I see. Not a boy, but the man who makes Lohere feel like home."

That tightness in Luca's chest didn't quite ease, but it changed—from something jagged and cold to something blooming warm and squeezing him close; he uncurled enough to peer up at Imre. "Lohere…hasn't felt like home? Not for ten years?"

"No. It hasn't." Imre regarded him gravely. "You and Marco and Lucia were all I had, and then you left me."

Ah, *fuck*. That shouldn't sting so hard, shouldn't cut so deep. It hadn't even been his *choice*, that move ten years ago—but if the sins of the father were the sins of the son, he felt like everything his dad had ever done wrong was crushing down on his shoulders right now. He wished he'd never asked, never brought this up.

"I'm sorry," he managed to force out.

It didn't feel like enough.

"No, Luca. No. It's not your fault. Not at all. I never meant to say that." Imre cupped his cheek and tilted his head up into a soft, lingering kiss, warm as the balm of forgiveness. Sighing, Imre leaned in brow to brow, his breaths heating Luca's skin, his voice soft and intimate between them, scored by the occasional faint pop from the fireplace. "Sometimes lives simply go on different paths, and while Marco and Lucia are my friends, they had to walk their own paths. Those paths just happened to take them away from me."

"Is that why you never just…stop?" Luca ventured.

"Hm? Stop what?"

"Stop everything. Stop doing things. You never just…*sit*. Do nothing. Nothing at all."

"I hadn't realized that was what I was doing." Imre chuckled and brushed their lips together once more. "You notice peculiar things, angyalka."

"That's not an answer."

"It's a deflection to stall for time while I work out the answer for myself." Exhaling deeply, Imre drew back once more, settling against the headboard again but still keeping Luca close with one heavy arm. "You may be right. Perhaps I fill my time so I don't think about the emptiness of this house, and how it should be bright with laughter and warmth." His gaze unfocused, drifting across the ceiling as if searching for constellations in the dark blue stucco. "I am the last

Claybourne. When I am gone, there will be nothing. Nothing but a 'For Sale' sign on the lawn."

"I don't…I can't…" Luca shook his head as if he could deny it, make it not true, before burrowing into the heated, firm muscle of Imre's side and curling a hand against his chest. "I can't think of Lohere without you. You *are* Lohere."

"A lonely man in lonely halls?"

"Are you really that lonely now?"

"No. Not now." Warm breaths filtered down to Luca's scalp, warning just a moment before Imre kissed the crown of his head, lips moving in quiet words against his skin. "Do you want me to get rid of the ring, Luca?"

"No. Keep it." He curled his fingers tighter, knuckles tangled in the soft silver-black pelt of Imre's chest. "I just…wanted to know…"

"I'm not lost in the past. I promise. I'm not looking for you to be anyone but who you are now," Imre said. "We've both changed over the years. It only makes sense that we had to start over. To learn our new selves."

"Is that what we did? Started over?"

"After a few speed bumps, yes. I would say that we did."

"I never thought about you being different, too," Luca murmured. "But you are. You're…"

"I'm…?"

Luca shook his head. Words escaped him again; he wasn't *good* at this, at quantifying things he only knew as something nagging at the edges of his senses like fine prickling hairs. "More sad, I think," he ventured. Yeah. That sounded about right. "It really hurt you when Dad just took off, huh?"

Imre's shoulder went stiff under Luca's cheek. He made a low sound under his breath, then said, quiet and rough, "Yes. And that they could not even tell me themselves about their divorce." His lips thinned, before he relaxed. "But some hurts…there's no one really to blame. They just are what they are." He smiled slightly, gaze focusing on Luca again. "Am I so unbearably different?"

"No. Not unbearably." Luca grinned. "I think maybe now I'm just old enough to see the real you, and not my giant stone teddy bear."

"So am I still the man you—"

Imre stopped, cutting off mid-sentence so abruptly that Luca involuntarily strained forward as if reaching for those missing words that never came. But Imre only looked at him strangely, his brows deepening into furrowed lines, then looked away. He said nothing. Nothing at all, and Luca's throat tightened.

"Imre…?"

"Nothing," Imre said. "It's nothing." He pulled away, then, leaving Luca cold and feeling far too small against the massive breadth of Imre's bed as Imre rolled out of the bed, dragging a hand through his hair. "Come. After skipping dinner, we've earned an early breakfast."

"Sure," Luca replied faintly, but whatever peace he'd found with the answers Imre had given fell to bits, sharp little things that pricked him inside. But as he watched Imre move, prowling tense and restless toward the door, stopping only to snag a shirt from the back of the chair, Luca knew he wouldn't bring it up. This thing was too fragile, and would be over far too soon. And so, "That…that sounds good," he said.

When nothing sounded good at all, right now.

Nothing but shutting out the world, and hoping January would never come.

65

OVER SCRAMBLED EGGS, OVER LIGHT pleasantries that started forced and soon smoothed into that comfortable, natural ease that couldn't be suppressed for long, Imre wondered why it was so hard to ask a simple question. Why it was so hard to finish the sentence he'd started, rather than leaving the unspoken unsaid between them, Luca lingering on him with wondering looks, Imre refusing to look head-on at something he wasn't sure he could stand an answer to.

What would he do, anyway? What would he do if he asked Luca *am I still the man you said you'd marry one day?*, and Luca said *no*?

Even more, what would he do if Luca said *yes?*

God damn it. He swore to himself as he pulled on his boots and layered on thermals, jumpers, jacket, thick overcoat. Luca struggled with multiple pairs of socks, cursing and wobbling like a newborn pup as he balanced on one foot and tugged at socks and boots when there was a chair not two feet away. Imre smiled slightly, but bit his tongue. He seemed to be doing that quite a bit lately.

And if he was honest with himself, he was terrified of a twenty-year-old man so tiny Imre could pick him up in one hand.

Because he didn't think he'd survive the wreckage of solitude left behind, when Luca abandoned him again.

66

"NOPE," LUCA SAID. "I CHANGED my mind. We're not going out there. I'm not doing this."

He hung back from the open kitchen doorway. Snow spun into the house in sheets, dashing up against the wall of Imre's body and bursting into swirls. Even with Imre mostly blocking the door, the cold reached in with fingers of ice and grasped at Luca, digging in hard enough to knock the breath from him. He could *taste* it through the scarf wrapped over his mouth, a kind of strange hard-edged crisp flavour that he could really only describe as *cold*.

Imre looked back at him mildly. "This was your idea."

"And now I'm changing my mind. Visibility's like two inches out there! It's colder than Santa's dick!"

"Have you been fondling Santa's unmentionables lately, then?"

Luca flushed and scowled. "You know what I meant. Going out there is crazy."

"The animals don't get to opt out," Imre pointed out quietly. "So neither do we. I cannot trust that the barn heating or water pump have held up in the storm. But if you don't feel safe, stay inside. I told you I could do this alone."

"Nngh. God I hate when you're fucking logical like that." Luca breathed in deep, trying to acclimate himself to those biting gusts cutting into his throat, then exhaled. "Okay. All right. We got this. We can do it. Let's go."

"I'm waiting for you."

"…right." He eyed Imre. "Pull your hood up. You're going to catch cold."

Imre let out a short, startled laugh, grinning, white teeth flashing as he pulled up the wool-lined hood of his under-coat and tucked his hair away. "Yes, dear."

"Shut it!"

"*Yes, dear.*"

"I hate you." Grumbling, Luca yanked his knit cap down further, then pulled his own hood up and wrapped his scarf tighter until there was only a thin strip left to peer past. Okay. All right. He could do this. Maybe twenty minutes total with respites in heated barns. They had the walkways; the only hard part would be the orchards. It'd be fine.

…frostbite was treatable in the twenty-first century, right?

"Ready?" Imre asked with a pointed lift of his brows.

Stop stalling, he meant, no matter how gentle and good-natured it might be. It wasn't hard to read between the lines. Luca lifted his chin and marched forward, pushing past Imre with a mutter.

"You're paying for my prosthetic fingers."

"…what?"

Any response ripped from Luca's lips as he stepped into the cold and a wall of snow blasted into him, carried on a driving wind and smashing at him like a frozen fist. He gasped, but his breaths were only pain, sliding icicles down his throat to cut his lungs. There was only a thin gap between the back door and the wood-walled walkways, but that gap only narrowed and focused the wind. Luca thrust himself forward and into the relative shelter of the walkway; the wind still cut through the open gaps near the overhang, but the siding blocked the worst of it even if the weight of piled snow bowed the walls inward until they creaked and threatened to collapse.

Luca doubled forward, grabbing at the necks of his layered coats and pulling them up, pressing them hard against his nose and mouth and breathing through the extra layers until the slicing pain in his chest eased. Dimly, he heard the door close. Then Imre's hand on his back, rubbing in slow circles.

"Are you all right?" Imre shouted over the wind, words muffled behind the high collar of his coat.

Luca couldn't talk. His mouth didn't want to cooperate, his breaths too thin, but he managed to straighten, squinting at Imre through the stinging snow-grit slapping into his watering eyes, and nodded. Imre did this every damned day. Luca could do it, too. Rather than try to move numb lips, he just tossed his head, then turned to trudge down the walkway, crunching through the miniature drifts of snow that had blown past the tops of the walls to accumulate in the narrow passage.

It was only two minutes to the smaller horse barn, but by the time they ducked inside Luca's fingers were numb, his ears scouring and burned, and the wash of heat from the barn's furnace hurt like dipping his face in boiling water. Gasping, he stomped the feeling back into his feet and joined Imre in mucking out Zsofia's and Andras's stalls, filling their feed and water buckets, tending to the chickens, and checking the generator lines and ventilation. Then it was right back out into the snow and the walkway to the big barn. The smell of goats in rut was overpowering in the thick heat billowing off the furnace, and Luca gagged, turning his face into his hood.

"Remind me of why I used to love this place so much?"

"Your parents made you stay in the house during breeding." Imre chuckled, raking his hood back and shaking snow out of his hair in a silvery tumble. "You holding up all right?"

"Be better when I'm out of this stink."

"Think I need to turn the heat down a bit. Let's get this place cleaned up."

They set to work, crowded by bleating, butting goats, and by the tenth time Merta shoved her nose under his hand and squinted her eyes up with pleasure as he scratched, Luca was laughing enough not to care about the smell. But he left the fussing with the does in heat to Imre, even if he couldn't help cackling when an overeager buck rammed into Imre's stomach and knocked him arse over elbows into the hay. Luca draped his arms over the pen.

"Need a little help in there?"

Imre tilted his head back to give him a disgusted upside-down look. "So you actually intend to get your hands dirty?"

"Can't say I minded the outcome last time." Luca grinned and offered his hand. "C'mon."

Imre grasped his hand—then yanked, pulling Luca right over the fence. He let out a *most* unbecoming shriek as he tumbled over, only to land sprawled atop Imre, face buried in his chest. That chest moved under him in a rolling laugh, shaking his entire body.

"Don't say it," Imre said. "You hate me."

"Fucking right I do!" Luca pushed himself up with his hands braced against Imre's chest, glaring, but his anger melted at the sight of Imre's unrepentant grin. As quiet as Imre was…that grin, mischievous and cocky, broke through his pensiveness with the strength of the first spring wind on a winter's day, and Luca melted. Hmph. Fucking dickhead. He looked away, then leaned down and brushed his lips tentatively across Imre's. "Let me up. Arse."

"So fickle. Weren't you just implying—"

Luca blushed hotly. "I know what I was implying, but not when there's a goat fucking another goat practically on my head."

"No appreciation for nature." But Imre let him go, waiting until

Luca scrambled up before he levered himself up out of the hay and brushed himself off. "Does it really bother you? The goats."

Luca shrugged, squinting down at his feet and curling his toes inside his boots, scrunching up his triple-layered socks and focusing on the texture against his skin rather than that question. "It's just…weird? I mean I know it's normal and clinical and all that shite, but like you go into Sheffield and we're joking about Hameron fucking a pig and out here it's just another day's work helping goats have a quick shag, eh?"

Imre snorted. "Country life and city life are very different. Do you miss city life?"

Luca considered, then shook his head with a smile. "No," he said. "I don't think I do."

And he settled quite contentedly into country life as they fed the goats and finished cleaning out the pens, working comfortably side by side with Imre. Once they'd done, he washed in the water pump and hovered over the furnace to dry and warm his hands; wouldn't do to freeze his fingers together because he went out wet. Imre emerged from the barn's storage room, a hefty coil of rope looped over his shoulders, a frown on his lips. His mouth moved in soundless murmurs as he turned the coil over again and again; looked like he was marking off lengths. He shook his head.

"This is about twenty metres; it's a good fifteen to twenty to the storage barn. This'll do us to get out there even if we won't have much slack, but I'm not sure there's enough rope in the storage barn to spool out to the orchard."

Luca bit his lip and pulled his gloves back on. "What do we do if there's not? We can't just leave the bees. You said if they die, everything dies, right?"

"Aye. They pollinate everything from the clover to the apples."

Imre frowned deeper, then shook his head. “No sense making more trouble for ourselves than we’ve already got ‘til we see what we’re dealing with. I want you to hold on tight to me out there, understood?”

“Thought we were going to tie ourselves together?”

“We can, but I still want you to hold fast. I’m not losing you out there, Luca.”

Something about the way he said it left Luca shaky, his gut in knots. He nodded, pulling his hood back up. “You won’t. I promise.”

“Then let’s go get this done and then get inside safe. Lift up your arms.”

Luca dutifully complied, and held still while Imre looped the end of the rope around his waist and cinched it in place, sucking in his breath when it pulled a little too tight. Imre left several feet of excess on the end of the rope, and he circled that around his waist and tied it off, keeping the rest coiled over his shoulder. When he wordlessly reached back for Luca’s hand, Luca took it, lacing their fingers together and telling himself his hands weren’t trembling. He wasn’t afraid. It was just out to the orchard and back. They wouldn’t get lost.

They wouldn’t.

Nonetheless, when Imre pushed the barn door open on howling white winds over a sky of black ice, Luca shivered with more than the cold. There was nothing out there but endlessness in every direction. People could walk in circles for hours in this until they died.

“It’s all right,” Imre said softly, as if he could sense Luca’s thoughts in his shaking hands. “We’ll be all right.”

“Y-yeah. Okay.”

Together they edged out into the buffeting storm. Imre set his shoulder to the barn door and heaved it closed, then unslung the rope from his shoulder and tied the other end off around the handle, triple-knotting it. Then, taking Luca’s hand again, he nodded and stepped out into the storm, forging toward the dim shadowed shape of the storage barn.

The trek through the covered walkway couldn't prepare Luca for walking blind out into the full teeth of the storm. Every step was an effort of will, pushing against a wind that shoved back relentlessly and endlessly, a wall of force when he was just a leaf struggling to hold his place. He clutched at Imre's hand, and God he was weak but he couldn't have done this without Imre's bulk shielding him. Imre cut the wind around him and made an isolated pocket of safety that Luca huddled in, pressing to his back and clinging to the rope and struggling not to whimper when the cold slid its licking tongue through every gap it could find in his clothing, turning his flesh to pure winter where it touched.

He'd never seen anything like this. A white darkness that made the world formless and groundless—no sky, no earth, no up or down, until steps lost meaning and time faded away and he only knew gravity existed because of the slight incline pushing up against him as they ascended the hill toward the storage barn. He'd read ghost stories as a kid about people losing themselves in snowstorms when reality twisted around them, vanishing into the hungry wind.

He could understand, now, how that could happen. With every step, he felt as though he fell farther away from reality and into some strange null place where the only thing concrete was the terrified, overwhelming thump of his heart, so loud it turned the storm into a thunder in the sky.

Then the relentless driving snow stopped. The wind cut, only a whistling cry keening past to either side. When he took a breath it flowed past his lips, rather than snatching from his lungs. Panting, Imre leaned hard against the side of the storage barn. His fingers gripped Luca's hand so hard Luca thought it might hurt if he could feel anything other than numb, frightened dread. Imre's gaze cut to him, just a bright slit of blue beyond his coat and hood, before he ducked around the side of the barn, flung the door open, dragged Luca inside, then slammed the door closed. The hard *slam* tore Luca from that timeless trance and he let out a strangled yelp, his heart rising up his throat.

"Are you all right?" Imre wheezed, bending forward and rubbing at his chest.

Luca stared at the door, just a dim shape in the darkened barn. Somewhere in the back of his mind, the storm had become a living thing—a wolf prowling the night, skulking just beyond the perimeter of safety, waiting for them to go outside again so it could swallow them up. They weren't going to make it back to the house. They wouldn't—

"Luca." Imre took his shoulders firmly and gave him a little shake. "*Luca.*"

Luca blinked. Clarity snapped on, the light switch in his brain flicking. He stared up at Imre, then laughed shakily and pulled his hood back, shedding snow. It was still frigid in the unheated barn but a million times better out of the wind, and he needed to *breathe.*

"Sorry. I—I'm sorry, I'm being a ninny."

"You're not." Imre exhaled a cloud of frozen breath; a band of red, scoured skin marked where his coat and hood hadn't covered his face. Dark blue eyes searched, pinning Luca. "Are you afraid?"

Luca winced and dropped his gaze. "…aye. I just…I had heard storms like that played tricks with your brain, but it wasn't real until I was out in it."

Imre swore softly, then dragged Luca close and into his arms. "I shouldn't have let you come."

"Knowing you were out in this alone would've been even

worse." Luca burrowed into him—into his comforting warmth, his safety, his *reality.* Imre was real. The wolf howling in the storm wasn't. "I can handle it. I can. I want to be here. Two of us are less likely to get lost."

"Or twice as likely," Imre said dryly, letting out a hoarse laugh. "But the sooner we're done, the sooner we can get warm. Check up in the hayloft for more rope. I'll mix up a sugar solution for the bees."

"Aye."

Luca fumbled at the knots on the rope around his waist with numb fingers, then stopped and let Imre handle it with surer, more capable hands. Once they were both free of their tether, Imre pulled the barn door open just enough to let in a shaft of whistling wind and swirling snow while he looped the end of the rope multiple times through the door handle, then tied it off.

Luca clambered up the ladder into the hayloft and flicked the dusty, swinging overhead light on. The pale, washed-out white light cast everything into stark shadows. He picked his way among neatly organized boxes and hanging racks of tools and spare supplies to several lengths of rope hanging from the wall in tight coils, draped over massive nails. Several were old and thin and frayed, and Luca frowned as he fingered them before dragging down a massive coil of thick-twined hempen rope. It was *heavy*, heavier than he expected, and he grunted as he wrestled it over his head and shoulder before looping on a few more thin-but-strong nylon cords in bright colours.

Getting down the ladder was a bit more precarious with the weight of the rope dragging him, and he let himself fall the last few rungs to land in a crouch on the barn floor. Imre glanced up; he stood next to a small steel refrigerator, working at a table with several litre jugs of water lined up next to a tin of sugar. He had half a dozen of those bottles Luca remembered from chemistry class, couldn't remember for fuck-all what they were called, only that they were soft-sided, squeezable plastic; the long, slim, right-angled spout on the cap made squirting chemicals easy without spilling. Imre had taken the caps off and was ladling sugar into each, a few spoons at a time.

Luca dumped the piles of rope off a few feet away, then leaned against the table, watching Imre work. "That's everything sound that was upstairs. Few of the others looked frayed enough to break."

Imre glanced at the heap of rope, then back to his hands as he started filling the squirt bottles from the litre jugs. "That should do. We'll have to do it a bit differently, as the beehives aren't in a neat straight line where we can just run a rope and follow it from the orchard fence. We'll run a rope to the fence, then run a rope from the fence to you, then run a rope from you to me. That'll give us both a working radius."

Luca eyed him. "You mean it'll let you put yourself in more danger by working farthest out."

"I won't be in danger. You'll be keeping me safe." Imre flashed him a warm, promising smile, then capped off the last of the squirt bottles. "Now here. Let me show you how this works. There's a well on the right side of the hive, just inside the box. There's a small hole drilled just large enough to insert the spout, toward the front and underneath the lip of the box's roof. You might have to brush the snow away to find it, but not too much. The packed snow is actually insulating heat for them. Find the hole, slip the tip in, and squeeze. Gently." He demonstrated, just barely depressing the sides of the bottle, and a little sugar water squirted from the tip in a glittering arc. "Each hive gets a third of a bottle. Once you're done, pack the snow back over it so the hive doesn't lose enough interior warmth for the sugar solution to freeze."

Luca picked up a bottle, squeezing it lightly just to test the resistance, then nodded. “Got it. Yeah. I can do that.”

“Then bundle up and we’ll get moving. The sooner we’re done, the sooner we can curl up with a warm fire and a mug of hot cocoa.”

“And your laptop. And your spreadsheets.”

Imre arched both brows, then chuckled. “No. Just you, me, and something to keep warm. I’ll be still, Luca.”

“Tenner says you’re fidgeting in fifteen minutes.”

“Hard to make a bet without any money.”

“Then it’s a good thing I’ll win.” Luca grinned, and Imre rolled his eyes.

“Wretch.” Imre caught the edges of Luca’s hood and pulled it up over his head, mussing his hair until it fell into his eyes. “Let’s go.”

“Oy!” Luca grumbled, swiping his hood back and smoothing his hair before pulling the hoodie up again and fixing his scarf. “Arse.”

Imre only laughed that low, rumbling laugh that chased the cold from every inch of Luca’s body to leave him too warm, simmering through his skin. Imre’s hands on his body didn’t help, burning him in handprint-shaped patches of stomach-fluttering warmth as Imre roped him to one of the nylon cords, then looped another out to tie him to Imre with a good eight to ten metres of slack between them. Imre gathered the coils of the main lead rope and led Luca to the door.

“Ready?”

“As I’ll ever be,” Luca strained, when what he meant was *not at all*.

At least this time he knew what was coming. They bundled up the bottles inside their coats, three each, and pushed out into the storm, stepping into the full force of a buffeting blast that felt twice as cold for the few moments’ relief inside the barn. Luca huddled behind Imre while Imre secured the end of the rope to the handle of the barn door, tugging it twice against the knot before leading the way into the gale.

Luca kept himself focused by curling his fingers in the back of Imre's coat and counting their steps. Fifteen steps to the edge of the barn. Forty-three skidding, low-crouched steps down to the bottom of the hill, crunching through snow up to their knees. Fifty-six numb-toed steps from the bottom of the hill across a featureless plain of white with no sense of direction until they were stumbling into the fence, fetching up against upper planks that barely peeked above the dunes of snow.

The rows of trees cut the wind somewhat, and offered a touch of shelter from the driving, stinging snow. Luca blinked ice crystals from his lashes and, breathing hard, helped Imre tie off the main guide rope to the fence, then knotted their tether next to it.

"You take the two rows closest," Imre called above the wind. "I'll take the three farthest."

Luca shook his head fiercely. "You have farther to go," he hissed, getting a mouthful of his scarf and spitting it out. "I'll take the closest three. You take the farthest two."

Imre looked as though he might argue, then thought better of it. Thank God; Luca wasn't going to stand out here freezing his bollocks off so Imre could be the big tough man. Imre worked his jaw, then nodded, fished one of the bottles from inside his coat, and pushed it at Luca.

"If you get confused, lost, or frightened, trace your rope back to the fence and wait for me," Imre said.

"But the bees—"

"You're more important than the bees," Imre said firmly. "Let's go."

"Okay," Luca said, stuffing the bottle into his coat and hugging it to his chest. "Okay."

They set out together, making for the first beehive in the rows spaced between the neatly ordered apple trees. Imre showed Luca where to brush the snow away, where to fit the spout of the squirt bottle into the wall of the hive, how to pack the insulating snow back in—and then he was gone. A heavy, gloved hand to the top of Luca's head, a silent, promising look, and then he turned and walked off between the snow-crusted trunks. Three steps and he was just a dark shape against the snow. Six steps and he was gone, vanishing into the swirling walls of white, just a nylon rope stretching into nothing and the faint tugs of his movements pulling at Luca's waist.

Luca swallowed roughly; his heart felt tight and strange and scared, but he ignored it as best he could and trudged to the next beehive, the snow sucking at his feet and pulling him into the deep-piled cover until every step was a labour. Everything was fine, he told himself. As long as that rope tied them together, as long as he felt those tugs of Imre's steps, everything would be all right.

He'd finished the four hives in the first row and started on the second when the rope tied to his waist went slack.

He froze. The bottle dropped from numb fingers. He scrabbled for the ropes; the one stretching back to the fence still had tension, but the one tied to Imre fell straight down his hips to the snow, laying there in a snaking cord of blue. It didn't move, didn't tug, and when he pulled at it gingerly it slithered back toward him with no resistance.

As if there was nothing on the other end.

Nothing and no one at all.

A scream tried to rise in his throat and came out as a tinny whimper, frozen into tiny brittle pieces. He jerked on the rope again, hoping to fetch up short, but it gave easily, pulling toward him. His lips trembled; his heart encased in ice, frozen slivers stabbing into his chest.

"Imre?" he whispered, staring down at the coils of nylon clutched in shaking fingers, then lifted his head and stared out into the white wall of snow. "*Imre!*" he cried.

No response. No tall, looming shape forging toward him through the snow; no deep voice cutting through the wolf-howl of the wind, because the wolf in the wind had eaten Imre and left Luca out here alone and Imre was out there cold and stiff in the snow—

Stop it.

"Imre!" he called again, pitching his voice as loud as he could. Imre was fine, he told himself. Imre was fine—but if Luca shouted loud enough, Imre would find his way back. He dropped the rope and cupped his hands around his mouth, sucking in a breath full of frozen razors, then screaming as loud as he could. "*Imre!* Where are you?"

He stopped, chest heaving, listening for a response. Nothing. Tears prickled in the corners of his eyes, froze, crackled against his skin. He drew in another deep breath, swelling out his chest.

"Imre—Imre, please, please—*Imre!*" But the silence only screamed back at him, taunting him in mocking swoops of laughter, this was his idea and now Imre was lost and freezing to death because of Luca and his arse-headed plans. "IMRE!" he screamed again, choking off on a sob and shaking his head, stepping back until his back hit the wrapped trunk of one of the apple trees. "Imre, Imre, Imre—"

"Luca!"

Barely a whisper, teased on a curl of wind, skittering over Luca's eardrums and then flitting away. Luca whirled, searching the whipping whiteout, pleading he hadn't imagined that.

"Imre?" he gasped. "Imre! I can't see you—"

"Here."

And then Imre was there—looming out of the snow, first shadow then colour them warmth as his arms wrapped around Luca, dragging him close into the smells of snow and man and safety. His voice rumbled against Luca's cheek, steady and reassuring.

"I'm here," Imre said. "I'm right here."

"Oh my God." Luca buried against him, clutching at his coat. "Oh my God—Imre, don't scare me like that, Imre—"

"Shh. Hush. Hush, love." Imre stroked the top of his head, solid and warm even through the layered hoods. "My rope came loose, and I lost my grip and got disoriented. I felt my way along the fence until I found the guide rope, and traced it back to you."

"You could have—you could have been—"

"I'm fine," Imre rumbled, then took a step back, drawing Luca with him. "Inside. We'll talk inside where it's warm. Stay with me."

Luca bit his lip, looking up at Imre. "But the bees…"

"Will survive. We've ensured that at least enough of them will survive to repopulate, but they're tough little things and even the hives we didn't get to have a fighting chance." The crinkle of Imre's eyes told Luca he was smiling, underneath the protection of his high collar. "I'm more worried about you. Let's get you out of this snow."

Luca looked over his shoulder at the faint mounded shapes of the beehives. He didn't feel right leaving them, but he felt even worse thinking about losing Imre in the snow again, and this time maybe never finding him. He nodded, but curled his fingers tighter in Imre's coat.

"Just stay close," he whispered. "And don't let go."

67

IMRE WOULD NEVER ADMIT ALOUD just how terrified he'd been for those few directionless, lost minutes in the snow. Not for himself.

For Luca.

All he could picture was the two of them separated, both fumbling blindly back to the house, but only one of them making it. In his mind's eye it was always Luca huddled in a frozen ball in the snow, his lips blue and his fingers frozen to his arms where he'd curled into himself to try to conserve his warmth in his last moments, too frozen and weak to even call out Imre's name even as Imre scoured the snow for some sign of him for hours on end.

Don't, he hissed to himself. That hadn't happened. It wouldn't happen.

Nonetheless, he kept one hand on Luca and one hand on the guide ropes at all times as they trudged back to the barns, then into the relative safety of the walkways, and finally back into the house.

The warmth of the heated house was blistering after over an hour out in the icy blast, making Imre's eyes water. He stomped snow off his boots on the mat and shrugged out of his jacket, then ripped his cap and scarf off so he could *breathe.*

Only to get the breath knocked out of him as Luca flung against him once more, burrowing close and clutching surprisingly tight for such thin, willowy arms.

Imre choked out a grunt, rocking back, then gathered Luca

against him. Luca was trembling, shaking all over as if he'd fly apart at one harsh look.

"Shh. Shh," Imre soothed. "We're home. We're safe."

"But we almost—"

"Nothing. Almost nothing. We were safer than you realize, angyalka. If a mishap were to happen, we were in the best place for it. Even without a rope, we could only go so far in any direction before hitting the orchard yard fence."

Luca pulled back, looking up at him with his eyes wide under the shadow of the hoodie. "So I wasn't a reckless fucking prat who almost got us killed with his daft ideas?"

Imre choked on a laugh and tugged Luca's hood back to kiss his forehead. "No. It was a good idea. The ropes made that much easier than it has been in past winters."

"Even though past winters were milder?"

"Even though past winters were milder." Imre frowned. "If this weather keeps up, I don't think you're going back to Sheffield in January."

Luca went oddly still, like a rabbit that might dart away into the bushes at any moment, his voice strangely neutral as he said "Yeah?"

Imre held his tongue. In moments like this reading Luca was a difficult thing, and he didn't want to risk saying anything that would break that fragile glass heart. Not when the idea of Luca staying was so very fraught, and if anything the snow only brought a reprieve and not a stay of execution.

One way or another, Luca would have to leave. Even if he returned to Harrogate to apprentice with Mira, Imre couldn't risk pursuing more, *wanting* more, unless he wanted to completely destroy his relationship with Marco. Lucia, he thought, would understand, but Marco…

God, he really had ended up stuck between the father and the son.

He met those wary, guarded eyes, lingered on Luca's stillness, before sighing and tearing his gaze away. "Let's get out of these clothes and wash up and get something warm into our bellies."

"Oh," Luca said in that same strange, neutral voice. "Aye."

They washed up separately this time, Luca in the upstairs shower, Imre stealing a quick and shallow bath downstairs. Imre was almost grateful, when the thought of the snow lifting and tearing Luca away from him made him wonder if he could even trust himself with Luca pressed close and naked, tempting him to forget everything that made him want to take this as slowly as he could without letting it slip through his fingers entirely.

By the time Imre towelled off and dressed, Luca was already curled up on the couch, small in his usual oversized t-shirt and boxers. He'd stoked the fireplace and made two mugs of cocoa, the rich chocolatey scent blending with the deeper tang of woodsmoke; firelight flickered over him, reflecting in unseeing eyes as he stared into the fire over the rim of the mug clutched in both hands.

Imre settled down on the sofa; with one hand he picked up the second mug from the coffee table, and stretched the other arm along the back of the couch, leaving the invitation open. After long moments Luca took it, scooting over to tuck into a ball against his side, moulding himself against Imre's body and guarding his mug like a squirrel with autumn's last nut. Quiet settled, save for the firelit crackle and the wind's haunting cry. Normally, for Imre, silence was comfortable.

But when Luca wouldn't look at him, resting tense against his side, silence became a wall he didn't know how to climb.

He let it stretch until they'd both finished their cocoa, empty mugs rimmed in remnants of foam resting on the coffee table. After

Luca set his mug down, he tucked himself back against Imre, saying not a word as he pressed his face into Imre's side and burrowed in so close he practically bruised Imre's ribs with the pressure.

All right. This had gone on long enough. "Luca." Imre sighed, leaning into the warm pressure of Luca's body. "Talk to me. You know what happens when these silences take control."

"I know," Luca mumbled into Imre's side, lips ticklish through his shirt. "I just…don't want to talk about it."

"What is 'it'?"

"Answering that would be talking about it." Luca lifted his head and blew shaggy hair from his eyes, then smiled thinly. "I promise it's nothing. Or if it's something, I'll talk about it when I'm ready. I just need time to think."

Imre studied that smile. It wasn't like anything he'd ever seen on Luca's face before, even when he was sad or angry and trying to hide it. Imre didn't like it. Something about it, strained and fatalistic, made him feel odd.

"Is it something I did to upset you?"

Luca shook his head. "No."

"Something I didn't do?"

"No." Luca laughed quietly. "You really worry too much." Slim hands braced against Imre's chest, faint pressure, and then Luca pushed himself up and pressed soft lips to his cheek. "It's sweet."

Imre turned his head to catch that teasing mouth in a light kiss. "I can't help it," he grumbled. "For someone who wears his heart on his sleeve, you are an utter enigma at times."

An odd expression flickered across Luca's face; pale eyes ticked back and forth, searching over Imre, and Imre wondered just what he was looking for. "I should be saying that about you," Luca murmured.

"If we two are filled with such mysteries, can we ever truly know each other?"

"I think we can. We *do*." That strange smile eased into something sweeter, and Luca leaned in, his warmth and soft, shower-fresh scent falling over Imre, his shadow blocking the light. "I think there's a part of us that would always know each other. We could die and come back as different people in different bodies, and we'd still know. We'd still find each other, no matter what."

Even if Luca wouldn't talk to Imre about what was bothering him, something in the way those pale green eyes watched him seemed to beg for…something. Imre didn't know what, didn't know if it was something he could even give, but he could at very least *be here*—and he caught Luca's face between his hands, tipping him up so that he might steal that raspberry mouth in a slow kiss. With every stroke of lips and teasing flick of tongue he tried to say *I'm here. I'm here if you need me, and I'm not going anywhere.*

And when Luca melted for him, lips slack and parted and so sweetly giving, Imre gathered Luca into his lap and enveloped him in his arms as if he could keep him forever.

As breath drew short, as the ache in his chest drew too tight, he let go, taking one last taste of plush lips caught between his teeth and glistening with that ripe fullness he loved. Exhaling heavily, he rested his mouth to the slim slope of Luca's neck. "That is a lovely thought, angyalka. Impractical, but lovely."

"I'm full of impracticalities. They're what I specialize in." Luca chuckled, husky and soft, and traced his fingers down Imre's chest, walking them in ticklish little patterns. He circled a single fingertip, then slid and trailed it down over Imre's stomach, painting prickling fire over his skin as his touch teased lower, lower…then hooked in the waist of his jeans, tugging them out. Luca turned his head, sweet wet mouth brushing Imre's ear. "I'd like to be a little impractical right now."

Then his hand slid between Imre's thighs, cupping him. He was half-hard already, the warm pressure of Luca in his lap and the aftertaste of his lips hot in his blood, but when that slender hand moulded over the shape of his cock and stroked, a hard surge of need throbbed, pulsing the full length of his cock. He hissed, lifting his hips, groaning as his head fell back against the couch.

"Luca…Luca, I…"

He trailed off as that touch firmed, teasing the rasp of fabric and hard ridges of denim against his cock; a low growl rose, feeling like it rumbled in the pit of his tightening stomach and then clawed its way up his throat.

"*Fuck.*"

"Please," Luca whispered.

Imre opened his eyes, looking dazedly up at the boy leaning over him, teasing him with that steady touch, that kneading stroke that worked and toyed and caressed his flesh until his cock *ached*, straining against his jeans. Pale eyes watched him with a mixture of hunger and quiet, vulnerable pleading, cutting into him with a single sweet look.

"I want to touch you the same way you wanted to touch me," Luca said. "Am…am I allowed that? Am I allowed to want you the way you want me? Even a little?"

There was something more in that question; something more in those glimmering eyes. Something like the fear that had frozen Luca's face when he'd screamed Imre's name into the snow. This was about more than just desire, Imre realized, even if desire was more than powerful enough to make him weak, make him pliant, until those slender hands tamed him like the lamb taming the lion.

This was Luca needing to touch, to feel, to know that Imre was really *here*.

Imre forced himself to move when that stroking touch made him want to melt, boneless; forced himself to push up just enough to brush his mouth over Luca's, to taste him.

To give his assent, with a single quiet "Yes."

Luca let out a soft, almost frightened sound, leaning into him, kissing him sweetly, breathlessly. Yet only for a moment, before he pulled away. That softly teasing hand slid from between Imre's legs, relieving the building pressure that made his blood pound. That second's relief was short-lived, though, as Luca slipped down his body, slender frame stroking against him, soft whispers of skin and cloth as Luca stepped off the sofa.

And dropped to his knees, angling his body between Imre's thighs to push them apart.

Imre's mouth dried as he realized what Luca wanted. As Luca caught the button of Imre's jeans in his fingers and snapped it open. As Luca looked up at him through his lashes, almost demure, a shy smile tugging at the corners of his mouth as he dragged the zipper of Imre's jeans down with a too-loud rasp and tugged the denim down just enough. Just enough for it to slide down Imre's hips; just enough that when Imre lifted his hips, his cock slipped free from his boxer-briefs. His cheeks burned. He was embarrassingly hard, nothing but soft touches and sweet kisses to leave his breaths burning in his chest and his cock aching. He didn't think Luca realized: he had Imre on a tether, and even the lightest touch pulled so hard on his leash until every atom of his body aligned toward Luca and Luca alone.

And the hunger that roused, tightening in his gut, was almost shameful as Luca wrapped his slim fingers around the base of Imre's cock and leaned in, his soft breaths gusting over Imre's skin and making him shudder, biting back a groan at the delicate tease of sensation.

Luca flushed a fetching pink, tongue darting over his lips and leaving behind a wet sheen. The unsteady stroke of his fingertips from the base to the tip of Imre's cock burst through him like a shower of sparks, and he hissed and bucked upward. Luca's shaky breath rose audibly between them, as he leaned closer still.

"You'll have to tell me if I'm doing this right," he whispered. "I've never done it before."

Before he pressed his mouth to the head of Imre's cock, that plush flesh yielding against his hardness, wrapping around him with a luscious, wet, sucking softness.

Need crashed down on Imre with the weight of a thousand tonnes of stone, crushing him beneath a breathtaking, binding pleasure. It held him captive, frozen, watching in near-stunned silence as Luca tasted, tested, working his lips over the head of his cock and flicking his tongue out in tentative, experimental little licks that struck sharply as a whiplash, scoring deeper and deeper with every caress of that rough, damp, heated tongue. Imre's eyes tried to close, but he forced them open, groaning, breaths coming shallow. He wanted to watch—*needed* to watch, when Luca's mouth was so red and wet and pretty with how it stretched around the head of Imre's cock. Luca's movements were clumsy, exploratory, as if testing how Imre fit in his mouth, but he didn't need to be sure of himself to set Imre's blood on fire.

But when Luca gripped his cock to steady it and dipped forward, sliding his mouth down around the shaft of Imre's cock and taking him deeper, Imre couldn't stop his eyes from slamming closed as he arched against the couch, digging up handfuls of the cushions to either side of his hips to keep from reaching for Luca and clutching him so hard the lovely thing might break.

Break like he was breaking Imre, with the sweet innocence in his every touch.

Damp, gripping warmth enveloped him, surrounding him in lush, yielding flesh and the rough stroke of Luca's tongue. Pleasure arrowed through Imre's body, liquid and bright, melting him in sharp surges and making his thighs tighten and tremble. It took everything in him to hold still, to let Luca find his way, dragging each gentle sucking lick out into an agony of careful, hesitant touches and fluttering contact that spiked Imre's breaths into great deep gasps torn from him in erratic bursts with every unpredictable touch.

And then came the soft moans of pleasure, muffled and thick and vibrating against his cock, the most erotic sounds Imre had ever heard. He caught a growl in the back of his throat, once more cracking his eyes open, watching Luca with a sort of dazed, riveted wonder as Luca gave himself to what he was doing completely, closing his eyes and absorbing himself with breathy, hitching little mewls. The look on Luca's face was almost more arousing than the heat of Luca's mouth, and Imre watched transfixed as that glistening, full red mouth moved over his cock, pulling him into a steady, drawing rhythm that contracted and gripped around his length with maddening friction.

"Luca," Imre whispered, only to strangle off in a hoarse groan as the tip of Luca's tongue flicked just under his cock, finding those sensitive spots just under the head and jolting him so hard his hips rocked up, beyond his control, pushing deeper into that intoxicating mouth. Luca jerked, nearly pulling back, but then braced his hands against Imre's thighs and leaned *into* it, taking him deeper until he was nearly strangling Imre with the heat and tightness of his mouth, this perfect well of lush, soft wetness that Imre wanted to bury himself in again and again, if only those sweet licking touches and that steady, needy pressure didn't *stop*.

Luca tasted every inch of him as if learning him through the touch of mouth to flesh, as if making love to him with his mouth in a deep, drawing kiss. Where his lips didn't touch, his fingers took control, stroking and exploring over Imre's flesh with a curiosity and hunger that undid him. Imre was entranced: Luca on his knees between Imre's thighs, his mouth drawing wide and soft and abused to stretch around his cock, his expression rapt and lost, dark hair falling in soft, silky washes over Imre's thighs.

Beautiful. Fucking beautiful, and Imre drank him in with ravenous eyes even as that brutal tight fire coiled at the base of his cock, that hard deep burn that warned he wouldn't last much longer. Not when Luca had him so wrapped up in every moment of this, not when that curling tongue teased and tormented, not when every swift rush of suckling lips over his cock matched the beat of his heart, the throb of his pulse building in his inner thighs and thumping into that hard-clutched seat of his desire.

And when Luca moaned low in his throat, kneading his fingers feverishly against Imre's thighs…Imre lost himself. He was weak, powerless, and when Luca's pretty mouth demanded he might as well have taken the leash he had on Imre and *pulled*. Imre's desire wound tighter and tighter inside him, his self-control shredding, his back arching away from the couch and his head falling back against the cushions. He couldn't breathe. He couldn't breathe, couldn't think, his chest seizing up tight, his thighs bunching, his gut locking, every muscle in his body seizing in an iron clasp.

"L-Luca," he begged, trying to warn him, trying to tell him to *stop*, but he couldn't find words, knew nothing other than the taste of that name on his lips. "*Luca!*"

He clutched Luca's shoulders. Luca licked and swirled his tongue around the head of his cock, watching Imre in *just that way* through his lashes.

And the pleasure building inside Imre unravelled, tumbling

through his body in a spill as if he'd come apart at the seams. He choked on a snarling cry, closing his eyes, his cock throbbing, jerking, needling bites of pleasure savaging as he spilled in one, two, three sharp bursts. Luca made a soft, startled sound, his fingers digging harder into Imre's thighs.

Imre remained rigid for trembling, overwhelmed moments, only for his muscles to go loose and drop him, panting, back to the couch. He opened his eyes, letting his head roll to the side, gaze finding Luca dazedly. Luca watched him with a sort of wide-eyed uncertainty, a mixture of shy question and pleasure in his gaze, liquid in the firelight. His lips were slick, gleaming with droplets of white that dripped down his chin, and he met Imre's eyes for an unsteady moment before ducking his head with a sheepish smile and wiping at his mouth with a delicate touch.

"Messy," he teased softly, his voice strained and husky and hoarse.

Imre wanted to hear his voice like that always, dark and raw in the aftermath.

He couldn't find words, his mind still coming down from the fog of desire, but he managed to move to drag his jeans back up as Luca crawled back up onto the couch and snuggled against his side. Imre zipped up, then slid his arm around Luca's shoulders, gathering him close and turning his face to press into his hair and breathe him in.

Luca made a soft, pleased sound and pressed his face into Imre's ribs. "Told you you wouldn't be able to hold still," he teased, then trailed off into a whisper, muffled against Imre's shirt. "...was that okay?"

"God, angyalka." Imre found his voice in a chuckle. "Do I really need to answer that?"

Luca peeked up at him. "No," he said, then let out a little

embarrassed laugh. "I guess not. I…thank you. For letting me."

"You shouldn't have to thank me." With a sigh, Imre rubbed his cheek to Luca's hair. "I'm sorry if I'm moving too slowly for you."

"It's okay. I understand why."

Luca draped his arm across Imre's stomach, but Imre caught his hand, lacing their fingers together and lifting his hand to kiss Luca's wrist. That fragile flutter of his pulse was wild against Imre's lips, a swift and fascinating drumbeat under Luca's skin. He watched Luca sidelong, lingering on the curl of his body, the blush in his cheeks, the way his breaths hitched as Imre pressed kiss after kiss to his skin.

"Luca," he murmured. "Do…you want…?"

Luca coloured deeper, ducking his head. "I…not right now?" he ventured, something in his voice as if he was afraid of being struck down for saying *not now*. "I'm…I don't…need anything like that. I just wanted to feel close to you. Wanted to know you that way. To see you like that."

Something about the hitch in his voice caught Imre. He frowned, using that captured wrist to tug Luca gently closer. "…Luca."

Luca made a muffled sound and hid his face against Imre's chest. "Mm?"

"What you were afraid of today…"

Imre sighed, then just gave in to impulse and gathered Luca into his lap, pulling him into a close-held bundle and wrapping him up in his arms. Luca squeaked, clutching at his arms, and looked up at him with wide eyes. Imre leaned in and rested their brows together, brushing nose-tip to nose-tip.

"It didn't happen," he murmured. "I'm here. You're here. We're alive."

Luca's shoulders slumped. He closed his eyes and slipped his arms around Imre's neck. "I…I was trying not to think about it."

"It's not a bad thing, to want to be closer to someone you care for after something frightening." Imre stroked Luca's back in slow circles, until that tense body went lithe and soft and quiet against him. He nuzzled Luca's shoulder, letting his eyes slip closed. "But it's not a bad thing to talk about it, either."

Luca tucked his head under Imre's jaw, nuzzling into his neck. "I just couldn't stand if anything happened to you, Imre," he whispered, voice thick.

"Nothing will happen to me."

"Promise?" Luca pleaded.

Imre opened his eyes, watching the fire flickering in the hearth over Luca's shoulder. He couldn't promise that. Not when he was nearing fifty, and even if he still felt young and vital, he wasn't immortal. One day his time would wind down, and he wondered idly if, at his funeral, Luca would be there, his eyes red-rimmed, his shoulders stiff in a crisp suit, still so very young while Imre was old and wrinkled and shrivelled in his coffin.

The morbid thought chased away the lazy, post-orgasmic lassitude to leave him cold. He'd been trying not to think about it—that spectre of death, of the years separating them and the inevitable fact that he was so much farther down that marching road than Luca. That weighed on him heavier than even the possibility of Marco's censure, his rage.

Even if he could keep Luca for ever and always, his *always* had far fewer miles left in his road.

But Luca wasn't asking him that, right now. He needed reassurances, soft affirmations, a promise that at least for this game of pretend they played, Imre would keep himself safe.

So, throat tight, he answered "I promise."

And hated himself for the lie.

68

DECEMBER WAS VANISHING FAR TOO quickly for Luca's tastes.

The past few months had felt timeless, but now he felt every minute, every hour that passed as if it scraped his palms raw with how hard he tried to hold on to it. He counted every kiss shared—over breakfast in the mornings, stolen between chores, traded in lazy evenings on the couch, reading or watching Netflix by firelight until Luca couldn't stand it anymore and slid into Imre's lap and kissed him until the rush of their breaths became a torrent and one or the other of them gave in to stroking fingers and caressing tongues and hitching sighs.

Slowly, Imre said, and yet Imre was never slow to tumble Luca onto his back and touch his body, explore him, taste him, and let himself be touched and explored and tasted in return. Luca had no idea what he was doing, but Imre didn't seem to mind—and it nearly filled Luca's heart to bursting every time Imre gave in to his touch, his kiss, and shuddered for him like a great and growling beast, his starkly beautiful face lost in the pleasure Luca gave him as he tested, learned, explored to his heart's content.

He wondered how those men who had loved Imre before could see him this way, this great and graven thing of caged power and quiet sensuality, and ever think he wasn't *enough*.

If anything, he was too much. Too much for Luca to endure; too much a *part* of Luca, until he didn't know what he would do when he had to let go.

These days should have been everything. Everything he'd ever wanted; everything he'd wished for in the darkness of his dreams.

But instead they were only a bandage over the ever-bleeding wound of his love, soaked through and through with the crimson of his heart's blood.

Let me stay, he almost said, each night as he tucked himself into Imre's bed, into his arms, and took shelter in the heated tangle of their bodies. *Let me stay.* It howled in him with the same scouring desolation as the storm winds outside, and he wished the storm would never lift, that he could lock them here in a moment in time, winter-bound and wrapped together in a shroud of frost.

But that was as impossible as the idea that Imre could ever want him for always, and so Luca said nothing.

He had this, now.

And he couldn't endure if Imre pushed him away for what time they had left, just because Luca had pressed.

Yet when he woke a week after that frightening episode in the orchard, he thought for a moment he'd gotten his wish. He was *freezing,* not even the embers of the hearthfire enough to warm him, and against him Imre's stone-heated bulk wasn't much help when his skin was cool to the touch. The only part of Luca that felt warm was his feet and lower calves, something heavy draped over him that drowsy familiarity told him was Vila and Seti. He groaned, cracking one eye open, and peered across the darkened room blearily.

"Imre…?" he mumbled. "The dogs are on my feet."

Imre rumbled softly, his chest vibrating under Luca's palm. "…don't wake me up. If I wake up, I have to be cold as bollocks."

Luca choked on a laugh, then yawned and dragged the blankets up to cocoon them both closer, trapping meagre body heat. "Is the furnace out?"

"More likely the power's out, and the boiler for the furnace radiator is electric-powered." Imre made a weary, drowsy sound. "Generator should have kicked in."

"Is it bad that it didn't?"

"Probably just needs a good wallop." Imre yawned deeply and looped an arm around Luca's waist. "We'll bundle up and go check it out, and check the barns as well. Might be a day or two before the power's fixed. Snow probably took out a power line nearby."

Luca whimpered. "I don't want to get up. *Cold*."

"…sooner we get up, sooner we can get the gennies running and into a hot bath."

"Bath?" Luca perked, bracing his hands against Imre's chest and pushing himself up. "Together?"

Imre arched both brows, looking up at Luca flatly. Like this, his hair spread across the pillow, his mountainous shoulders rising above the quilts, his eyes darkened by sleep, Imre looked like a centrefold: artlessly lazy, perfectly dishevelled, gracefully disarrayed and utterly unaware of his own appeal.

Even when he snorted sceptically and said, "Bit eager to get me naked and wet again, are you?"

Luca just grinned. "Am I that transparent?"

"Subtlety is not one of your greater talents, angyalka."

"Never claimed it was." He leaned down and stole a kiss, then pushed himself up again to tumble out of bed, hissing when the frigid stone floors bit his skin through his socks. "Bloody *hell*. Come on, before we freeze to death."

"Get back here."

Imre levered himself out of bed, moving with lazy ease, then caught Luca around the waist and dragged him close so effortlessly his heart flipped. And flipped again, tumbling into leaping somersaults as Imre leaned down and captured his mouth, kissing him with a slow and quiet possession, an ease that made Luca ache for this to be his every morning, his every night, his everything. He clung to Imre's arms, stretching up on his toes to meet him, parting his lips and trying to tell Imre with every gasp, with every sigh:

I'm yours.

I will always, always be yours.

But it was over too soon, Imre drawing back with a languid, gentle smile, knuckles brushing to Luca's cheek. "Feel warmer already," he murmured, then turned away to stride toward the wardrobe, leaving Luca weak in the knees and watching him dazedly.

Cocky *git*.

And yet Luca loved that Imre felt comfortable enough with him, with *them*, to kiss him with such casual, sleepy warmth.

He watched Imre for a few moments, lingering on the easy strength in his every movement, until the simple gestures of tossing a few logs on the fire and opening the wardrobe door were acts of quietly controlled power. When Luca tore his gaze away, the dogs were watching him from their tumbled pile on the bed, as if they knew exactly what he was thinking.

He stuck his tongue out at them, then laughed and slipped out into the freezing hallway to his room.

After bundling up tight in layers, he met Imre downstairs for a fortifying mug of tea and a promise of a hot breakfast when they were done, before stepping out into the cold. After days, nearly weeks of whiteout conditions blocking all light, the glare of the sun against endless plains of sleek, glittering snow nearly blinded him; Luca winced and turned his face away, shielding his eyes.

"*Bright*."

“Try not to stare at it too long. It’s possible to get snow blindness.” Imre turned to lead the way around the house, his boots making crunching noises as they broke through an upper crust of snow only for the soft pillowy stuff underneath to crumble away, leaving a path for Luca to follow in his wake. “Looks like the storm finally blew itself out last night.”

Around the back of the house, the generator huddled up against the rear wall, nearly buried in the snow. Luca hung back and watched while Imre brushed snow away from the control panel and checked the fuel tank. He felt useless just standing there, dancing from foot to foot and watching his breaths puff out in clouds, but there was nothing he could do while Imre checked wires and breakers, fiddled with something, pumped a lever a few times, then tested the power. The generator grumbled, shaking, emitting a faint scent of petrol before settling into a steady, humming whine. A distant answering whine came from inside the house, and in one of the upstairs windows a light switched on, glowing against the glass.

“Relay had frozen over,” Imre grunted. “Wasn’t able to switch from the main grid to the generator feed. Should be fine now.”

He tossed his head, and together they trudged toward the barns. The secondary generators had kicked in, at least, and the barns were almost stiflingly warm—warm enough that Luca shucked layer after layer until he was sweating into his t-shirt as he helped Imre muck out and feed the horses and goats. But he chilled again rapidly enough as he bundled up once more and headed out back to the house, and took pleasure in sneaking his hand into Imre’s as they walked, curling their gloved fingers together. Imre faltered mid-stride, glancing down at him, before letting out an amused, indulgent snort and continuing on.

But he squeezed Luca’s hand tight, and didn’t let go.

They were almost back to the house when they passed a patch of bare earth, dark against the endless fields of white. Luca drifted to a halt, frowning down at the dead scraggles of browned, crisped grass sticking up in tufts from the damply naked soil, saturated into a slurry of thick mud.

"The snow's already starting to melt?" Something so simple shouldn't strike so deep, hitting hard at the ache below his ribs, sliding between the third and fourth like a dagger aiming straight for his heart. He swallowed back, jerking his gaze away and fixing blankly across that eye-searing horizon of glimmering white snow dunes. "So much for hoping I'd be snowed in past January."

"We get a few warm days here and there before the snow comes down even harder." Imre shrugged. "It's only a temporary reprieve."

Somehow that stung even worse—the bland neutrality in Imre's voice, the calm and casual dismissal. When the snow and Imre's will were the only things keeping Luca here, the only thing worse than the threat in that patch of bared earth was Imre's casual response.

Luca tugged his hand free from Imre's. "Is it?" he bit off bitterly, then pulled away from him and turned to trudge through the snow toward the house.

It was long moments before Imre's footsteps followed after him, but Luca only shoved his hands into his pockets and walked faster, pushing against the cold until he reached the house and thrust through the door into the kitchen, kicking snow off his boots onto the mat. Imre caught him just past the doorway, ripping his scarf down from over his mouth and shaking snow out of his beard before gripping Luca's arm gently and drawing him back.

"Luca."

Luca jerked on his arm, glaring mutinously at the floor. "Don't." He didn't want to hear Imre's platitudes, his calm reasonable responses, the gentle neutrality in his voice.

But instead Imre's voice was ragged, hoarse, as he repeated, "*Luca*."

And captured Luca's face in his gloved palms, crisp granules of snow melting against Luca's cheeks as Imre coaxed him to look up, to meet wet-glimmering blue eyes that stared at him with something stark and raw and haunted in them.

"I don't want the snow to melt," Imre strained out. "I don't want winter to end."

Fuck. Luca leaned into him, digging his fingers into the lapels of Imre's coat, begging with everything in him, feeling like his entire body was a bundle of taut-strung threads of *wanting*. "What are you saying?"

"I don't know." Imre closed his eyes, leaning into Luca just as hard, resting their brows together. "Don't ask me right now. I need…I need to think. To work things through for myself." His mouth brushed against Luca's, and Luca realized his lips were *trembling*, his breaths shaking as he whispered, "I don't want to think right now."

Luca pressed his mouth to Imre's, kissing him deeply, fiercely, tangling his hands in snow-strewn silvered hair and winding it around his fingers. The fever in him was desperate, needy, his love a broken mirror reflecting back Imre and only Imre and yet too sharp-edged for Luca to touch. He couldn't stand this. Couldn't stand that his hold on Imre was as tenuous as winter's hold on the land, and he kissed him as if he could fill himself up on the taste and scent of Imre, as if he could brand himself with the full, firm pressure of heated lips.

"Then don't think," Luca breathed, and traced the tip of his tongue along Imre's upper lip. "Don't think, Imre. Just be with me."

"Ah, *God*."

Imre let out a near-helpless groan, his hands falling to curl, rough and heavy, against Luca's hips. His beard dragged harsh against

Luca's cheeks as he kissed him again: hard and swift and needy, raw about the edges with a hunger that left Luca dizzy, gasping.

Breaths coming thick and fast, Imre tore back. "This…might not be wise."

"Why not?" Luca begged, and Imre opened his eyes, watching him with that stark, desperate gaze. Honest, so very honest Imre was, and his honesty was in his eyes, on his lips, tearing Luca to pieces.

"The thought of losing you," Imre said, "leaves me particularly un-inclined toward self-control."

"Then don't control yourself." Luca stroked his fingers back through Imre's hair, trailing down to curl against the back of his neck. "If you won't keep me, at least have me."

Imre stilled, going quiet, gaze searching. Until, after long moments: "Don't say it that way."

"What way?"

"That I won't—" His voice broke. His jaw tightened, and he turned his face away. "That…I…" A short, sharp shake of his head, followed by an aching, almost agonized breath of "*Luca…*"

"This hurts, Imre." Luca's throat closed. He stretched up on his toes, pressing his cheek to Imre's, rubbing his jaw to that soft, luxuriant beard of silver and iron that he loved so very much. "I won't make you choose between me and Dad. I won't. I'll…I'll still be your friend when this is over. I promise that." He pressed his lips to Imre's cheek, tracing that taut, weathered skin, and wondered how he could do this again and again. How he could keep throwing himself against the wall of Imre's implacable calm, and expect anything but heartbreak. "But I need to be something other than your friend right now. I need to feel like you…like you…"

Nothing, save for Imre's deep, rasping breaths. But slowly those heavy hands tightened on Luca's hips: possessive, needy. Slowly Imre turned his head, the tip of his nose brushing Luca's. Their breaths mixed and curled, and the terror and need and love and longing in the pit of Luca's stomach twisted themselves into a single perfect knot of tension that threatened to shatter, and break him forever.

"Like what, angyalka?" Imre murmured huskily, darkened blue eyes capturing him, consuming him.

Like you love me, Luca thought.

But "Just kiss me," he said, and crushed his mouth against Imre's as if he would never, ever have this again.

As if this kiss would have to last the rest of a long, lonely life, when after Imre he would never be able to stand the touch of another man.

Touch branded him now, as if the sun's cruel fire was in the palms of Imre's hands. He caught Luca up hard, kissing him so deeply that Luca went weak, overwhelmed and clutching tight. *Please*, he begged with every mating lock of their lips, every rushed, needy, tangled breath, every feinting dart of tasting tongues and grazing touch of nipping teeth. They kissed as if trying to tear away the boundaries that made them separate people, searching deeper and deeper into each other in the desperate search to touch heart to heart.

Luca's heart was breaking, and if Imre touched it, it would crumble in his hands, the glass walls cracked beyond hope of ever salvaging.

And when Imre lifted him up, Luca clung to him, never letting go of that bruising, hungry kiss. Never letting go of Imre, fingers buried in his hair, body pressed close. He hardly realized Imre was carrying him forward: across the kitchen, through the foyer, up the stairs, that fifth step giving an agonized cry before they were down the hall and Imre stepped into his bedroom and the world turned topsy-turvy as he tumbled Luca down onto the bed.

Their lips parted, leaving Luca gasping in great, aching breaths that tore at his chest. Imre stood over him, looking down at him with something dark and haunted in his eyes, something so at odds with the desire that kindled in every raking look. Broad shoulders heaved as though Imre fought some great struggle in that single frozen moment, before he tore off his coat, flinging it to the floor, followed by his henley. The shirt rose up over the powerful sculpture of his body, baring the thick, tightly packed muscle of his waist and stomach, the massive barrel cage of shoulders and chest, the sheer size of him somehow hitting harder in this moment, the raw strength in every corded, taut-veined muscle that threw back the firelight's quiet glimmer with a molten bronzed edge. He hardly looked like a man, in this moment—instead some primal godlike thing that had been on this earth before mankind, a wild force of nature greater than humanity that every shallow copy afterward had struggled to imitate.

He took Luca's breath away with the power of such beauty, such strength, caging such a gentle soul.

Luca reached for him—but Imre caught him by the wrists, stilling him. His heart twisted, his stomach drawing tight, as Imre drew him up and pressed his lips to Luca's knuckles, first one hand, then the other, beard lush and caressing against his fingers, lips warm.

Before Imre pushed him back down, stretching his arms above his head, hands gliding upward to press palm to palm and lace their fingers together while Imre pinned Luca to the bed.

Luca arched against that rough hold, but Imre's grip was immutable, immovable, only making him feel smaller, more helpless, something delicious and hot kindling inside him. For long moments Imre watched him with that unreadable, burning gaze before sinking down over him, weight pressing him into the mattress, dwarfing him under Imre's bulk. A single gentle kiss pressed to the peak of Luca's chin.

Then Imre slid down his body, nuzzling his jacket open, nudging his shirt up with the tip of his nose, before pressing his searing, sucking mouth to the sensitive skin of Luca's stomach. Luca's stomach jerked in as little sparks of heat rained down on him, one kiss after another after another, each ending in a slow, careful bite that drew his flesh into Imre's mouth and bit down just wonderfully hard enough to make his toes curl, his thighs spreading, his hips twisting. He wanted to clutch on to Imre, but with his hands captured he could only whimper and writhe as each kiss travelled higher, teasing him to new heights of gasping anticipation.

And when Imre's mouth closed over his nipple, drawing it into warmth and wetness and suckling, drawing pressure, Luca cried out, jerking off the bed and wrapping his thighs against Imre's waist and sliding against him with a raw and shameless need.

"Imre," he gasped. "*Imre!*"

"Shh, angyalka," Imre soothed, and rose up his body to rest against him, fitting so perfectly between his thighs. Where hips pressed to hips there was no mistaking Imre's arousal, the thickness of his cock pressing hard through their jeans and teasing at Luca with every minute motion that ground their hips together and made his breaths catch between his teeth. Imre's lips brushed over his, kissing him gently. "Do you love my name so dearly, to cry it so?" he whispered.

I love you, hovered on Luca's lips. *How can you not see that?*

But he only pressed his mouth to Imre's, stealing a taste of him, taking what he could when Imre had him so thoroughly pinned. Imre groaned, almost submitting to him, his full, richly red-lipped mouth going warm and molten as Luca tasted, delved deep, stroked every crevice he wanted to claim as his. That solid weight crushed down on him harder and he went boneless, so tangled up in this, knotted so deeply with Imre that every pull of his threads threatened to snap him in two.

As he released Imre's lips, Luca traced them with his tongue, capturing that perfect taste they made together, before letting go with one last nip. "Give me more reasons to say it," he breathed, and silently begged Imre wouldn't stop as he had so many times before.

Imre shuddered—a full-body thing like some great stone engine coming to life, deep and trembling into Luca's body. His grasp relaxed on Luca's hands, stroking downward over his wrists, his arms, before curling in the collar of his jacket and hoodie, gripping…and ripping them to either side, that raw strength handling Luca like a doll as Imre peeled him out of both outer garments swiftly, only to grasp the hem of his shirt and tear it upward, dragging it almost hungrily over Luca's head and leaving Luca falling to the bed breathlessly, staring up at Imre and suddenly feeling far too exposed when the man watched him with something rough and burning igniting behind an unwavering, consuming gaze.

"I-Imre…?"

"That's one," Imre said softly, then flicked the button of Luca's jeans open.

Next thing he knew he was naked, those sure, capable hands on his body and stripping away his shoes, his socks, his jeans, his boxers, to leave him shivering underneath Imre as the winter chill brushed over his body. Quickly those large, rough hands chased the cold away with their heat, stroking over Luca from shoulders to hips as if shaping him, moulding him, caressing him into the form of a man. A man who arched for Imre, as Imre dipped his head and rubbed his cheek to Luca's inner thigh, the scratch of his beard teasing sensitive skin. A man who sucked in a rough breath as Imre caught him under his knees, lifted him up, spread him open, hooked his legs over broad shoulders that stretched and bared him almost beyond enduring. A man who sucked in a sharp breath as Imre's breaths curled over Luca's aching, throbbing cock.

And a man who gasped *"Imre,"* eyes slamming shut, when Imre's lips danced over the head of his cock, tongue flicking out to taste.

"Two," Imre growled, then took Luca's cock into his mouth.

Luca lost all words as gripping heat enveloped him, a stroking, deviant tongue searching over every inch of his cock and finding every perfect spot that pulled pleasure into concentrated, vibrating knots in that delicious place just behind and below his cock, a place that seemed deeper than flesh, this darkness inside him where every sensation collected in pools like dripping, heated honey, shimmering with their own breathless light. He knotted handfuls of the quilt as he moved with every draw of Imre's mouth; even in this Imre was utterly sure of himself in every stroke of firm lips, every tracery of a fiery and flicking tongue, his unshakeable confidence giving him complete and utter control over Luca's body, his flesh, his breath, his life.

But when Imre traced the thick vein on the underside of Luca's cock with his tongue, Luca strangled off a sharp cry, tossing his head back against the bed, every muscle in his body locking. His pleasure built in a rapid, cresting wave, threatening to break and crash down.

"*Imre,*" he gasped, barely finding his voice. "I…I-I'm going t-to…"

He couldn't hold it back. But Imre drew back quickly, that maddening torment easing, the overwhelming rush of sensation calming and leaving Luca sprawled dazed and helpless, hovering just on the edge.

"Three," Imre practically purred, soft and satisfied, and braced his hands to either side of Luca's body, slipping free from his thighs to lean over him. Silver hair spilled over Imre's shoulder, draping and flowing against Luca's shoulder and throat. "You don't want this to be over yet."

Luca reached up, brushing his fingers to Imre's glistening lips, his heart beating violently. "How do you know what I want?"

"Body language, angyalka." Imre smiled—a slow, confident thing that nearly stopped the violent throb of Luca's heart in its tracks. A smile that promised, if Luca trusted him, Imre could handle Luca's body with the same surety with which he handled the horses who responded to him as if he was part of them and they a part of him, the words on his tongue the same he'd teased Luca with that day he'd fallen off Zsofia over and over again only to get up with his body bruised and his blood wild. "Body language."

Imre sank down once more, trailing a path of shivering kisses against Luca's inner thigh, then leaned away and drew the nightstand drawer open. The keepsake box still sat atop the nightstand, the faded green of the ring resting atop it, but Imre brushed past that to delve inside the drawer and withdraw a small glass bottle of clear liquid. Luca stilled as he realized what it was, his eyes widening, breaths catching in his throat and hitching tight in his chest. For all the things they'd done, tumbling each other back over and over again, they'd never gone that far.

And when Imre flicked the cap on the bottle open and slicked the thickly viscous, glimmering liquid inside over his fingers, Luca swallowed back hard, pushing himself up on his elbows, already tensing thinking of those thick, coarse fingers inside him, a strange hot empty feeling building as his imagination supplied phantom sensations of rough skin, stroking fingertips.

God. This…this was happening. This was really happening.

Imre wanted him. Imre *needed* him, the way Luca had needed Imre for his entire life.

"Imre," he whispered, heart hot and light.

"Four," Imre added with a softly rumbling chuckle, and set the bottle aside. He shifted farther up onto the bed and stretched out on his side, his heavy weight indenting the mattress, drawing Luca closer to him like gravity. He held himself up on one elbow, looking down at Luca with an utterly shattering warmth in his gaze, his slicked fingers curling against Luca's thigh. "Are you afraid, Luca?"

"Y-yeah. A little."

"It's all right to be afraid. And it's all right to stop me at any time."

Imre's touch stroked higher, leaving warm, slick trails against Luca's trembling inner thigh. He captured Luca's mouth, melting him with a slow, sweet kiss, and Luca realized Imre's lips were *trembling*, his breaths ragged, that quiet calm masking a depth of emotion that built between them with the tight tension of a building electrical charge waiting to explode. Luca leaned into him, curling his hands against the breadth of Imre's chest, threading his fingers into the soft pelt of salt-and-pepper chest hair. A whisper of breath, a flutter of his heart, a sigh of *ah, Imre,* and God he wanted Imre to know he understood, he felt it too—that this *mattered*, that this was more than just sex, that this *meant* something.

But all he could do was whimper, as Imre teased into the depths of his mouth and caressed him until his lips felt like wet silk. As Imre gathered him close, capturing him against the power and heat of his body. As Imre's touch slipped higher between his legs, and ghosted against the cleft of his ass, working gently between. When callused fingertips brushed against his entrance, Luca gasped, tensing, arching against him, unfamiliar shocks of sensitivity making his gut clench.

"Five," Imre whispered. "You tell me when enough is enough, angyalka. You tell me when too much is too much."

Then one finger pressed against Luca—gently at first, then harder, and he arched his hips with a broken, choking inhalation as that moment came when pressure became penetration and Imre was *inside*. His voice tried to rise in his throat, but strangled into a faint nothingness as that finger eased inside him slowly, gently, touching him with a sweet and caressing intimacy and care. He curled his fingers against Imre's shoulders and hid his burning face against his chest, breathing in short, sharp gasps. It was too *much*, being with Imre like this. Feeling him *inside,* as deep in Luca's flesh as he'd always been inside his heart.

"Relax." Soft words breathed against his ear, coaxing, warm, reassuring. "Let me in."

I can't stand it. Luca whimpered, trembling and pressing closer into the comforting heat of Imre's body. *I can't stand it when you're already so deep inside me. Any more and I'll love you too much. Any more and I…I…*

I won't survive leaving you.

Yet he couldn't deny this, couldn't resist it, and he wrapped his arms tight around Imre's shoulders and buried his face against his throat and strangled his soft, keening cries in his throat as Imre pressed again, sinking deeper, opening Luca in a way that nearly flayed him raw with the vulnerability of it, the newness of it, the strangeness and sweetness and intimate invasion. Slick oil licked against him from within, warming and soaking into him in a pleasant burn that melted through his bloodstream. Slow, steady, Imre thrust his finger inside him, drawing out each stroke languorously, tracing his fingertip against sensitive inner walls. Luca writhed, unable to stop the mewls escaping his throat, the only sound in the room save for Imre's ragged, deep, growling breaths.

And when Luca whimpered "Imre" and slid against him, body to body, Imre's arousal pressing against Luca's belly and his painfully hard cock, that finger twisting inside him…

The low, burning whisper of "Six" that ghosted against his ear was so erotic it nearly undid him.

When a second finger joined the first, he dug his nails into Imre's shoulders. When a third finger joined the second, stretching him in unnerving and wonderful ways, turning him molten inside with new and strange sensations, he bit down on Imre's throat to keep from screaming, his breaths coming short and never seeming enough, his chest growing tighter and tighter. It *hurt*—but the pain was satin and fire, and every time those taunting fingers drew out he only wanted *more,* wanted them back, wanted the shapes of Imre's knuckles printing against him from within and the lightest flirting touch with one bright-bursting spot of sensitivity that made his blood light up and tightened every muscle in his body and pulsed in the base of his cock. Every time Imre almost brushed it, then pulled away on the next stroke, leaving Luca straining into him, begging with whining gasps as if he could reach for that feeling that hovered always out of reach, denying him with every caress.

When Imre's touch withdrew, Luca almost screamed with the loss. He was strung so tight, built so high, and he couldn't stand this slow and deliberate torment another moment—yet he trembled as he looked up at Imre, met molten, quietly simmering eyes, understood the power of desire burning there, open and naked and offering an understanding he hadn't grasped before.

Imre hadn't waited because he didn't want Luca.

Instead, Imre had waited to savour the pleasure of wanting Luca more and more.

He'd never been looked at in such a way before—as if he was something to be devoured, to be worshiped, to be loved, to be defiled. As if he was the heart that made the blood flow in Imre's veins; as if he was the breath that filled his lungs. As if he was beautiful.

As if he was everything, and the man who mattered more to him than anything else in this world finally, truly *saw* him.

Imre's gaze flicked over Luca's face, and Luca's heart turned over, rocked hard. Rough knuckles brushed his cheek. "Are you ready, angyalka?"

Luca wet his lips, tried to find words, but could find nothing. Nothing to say *yes*. Nothing to say *with everything in me*. Nothing to say *please, I need you, please, I'm frightened, please, I can't stand to wait.*

So he only nodded, then closed his eyes and leaned into Imre when beloved lips touched against his, kissed him tenderly, tasted him with heat and fire and possession.

"Turn over for me, love," Imre rumbled against his lips.

Luca's body almost didn't want to obey. Almost didn't know how to do anything but melt in boneless submission, but after several trembling moments he managed to gather himself enough to turn over, moving like molasses, heavy and slow and warm, giving Imre his back. Coarse knuckles brushed his back, followed by the rasp of a zipper and the scratch of denim against cloth. Then Imre's heat enveloped him, pressing against his back, naked skin to naked skin, and Luca sucked in a soft breath as the hard ridge of Imre's cock pressed against his ass, slipped against his spine, burning-hot. Thick arms enveloped him, gathering him close into the comforting curve of Imre's body and shifting him with Imre, moving them both to curl on their sides, fitted so perfectly together. A callused palm stroked fire over his stomach, glided over his cock in a caress of thrills, curved over his inner thighs.

"Tell me you want me," groaned against his ear, shivers on every breath.

"I want you." Luca let his head roll back against Imre's shoulder, breathing in the heady rush of his scent, giving himself to this: the anticipation, the fear, the pleasure, the heady and drowning emotion. "I've always wanted you, Imre."

That powerful body shuddered around him. "Seven," Imre sighed, his stroking touch nudging Luca's leg forward, bending him, opening him so gently, baring him.

Then his cock pressed against Luca's sensitive, stretched entrance, hot flesh against hot flesh, sweet wild pressure, the groan in Imre's chest rumbling against Luca's back. Pain: a bright, searing flash, a thickness no fingers could prepare him for, an invasion of slow depth and aching penetration, a fullness so bone-shaking he could hardly breathe for the fire and fever and wonder of it. He curled in Imre's arms, those hands so rough on him, holding him and claiming him and drawing him into Imre as hard burning slickness and pressure sank deeper, *deeper*, the pain choking him, the pleasure destroying him from the inside out.

"*Imre!*"

But that building peak of pleasure burst as the head of Imre's cock nudged deeper than his fingers had ever reached, the flare and stretch of it opening Luca with such pervasive, undeniable intimacy. That moment of sweetness his fingers had flirted with became a whitefire rush, melting through every inch of Luca's body in trembling lashes, sizzling friction. His muscles went loose, lax, and in that instant Imre let out a low growl and jerked his hips forward sharply, pulling Luca back into him and sinking in fully.

"Eight," ghosted ragged and sultry against his ear, damp and burning lips tracing his throat, his jaw. Imre's hand spread over Luca's stomach, massive and spanning the breadth of his body, and pushed down gently, just enough for Luca to feel the pressure and overwhelming fullness of that cock throbbing inside him in rhythm to his breath, his pulse, his life. "You feel so good, angyalka."

Luca melted back against Imre, sinking into the stone-forged heat of his body, surrendering utterly to this. To the feeling of being filled with Imre; to the overwhelming intensity of Imre's possession, his complete and utter claim on his body. He burned inside, eating away at his control, at his senses, until he sank into a cloud of slow pleasure, like drowning in a sea of warmed oil. He felt *everything* too deeply, too intensely, gasping out as Imre's lips grazed his shoulder, shuddering with the sharp cool shock as the silk of steel-grey hair slithered against his back, his neck, the scrape of Imre's beard against his spine, every cool blue bead a raindrop kiss.

His senses were tuned to the key of Imre, to the resonance of his rough palms stroking over Luca's stomach and upper thighs, to the hum and vibrato of his hungry, quietly growling breaths, to the shiver-whisper of hot, weathered skin slinking over corded muscles, to the deep bass rhythm of Imre's heart pulsing against his back.

He could stay like this forever: not moving, not parting, joined with Imre flesh to flesh, captured in the perfection of this moment. Yet with every stroke of his fingertips Imre grazed closer and closer to his cock, until long fingers wrapped around Luca's length and he cried out as a bolt of sensation shot liquid to his centre, making him clench and shudder and draw up in a rigid, trembling arc as every contraction of muscle made his body grip tight against Imre's cock, made him hyper-aware of that shape stretching him from within, moulding him to fit, pressing every inch of Imre against his inner walls. He clutched at Imre's forearms helplessly, keening in the back of his throat.

"Come for me, Luca." Soft words, barely heard, mouthed against his skin in lingering, drawing kisses that left brands on his flesh. "Like this. Just like this."

Long, strong fingers shaped him with knowing strokes, plying and teasing and exploring every inch of his cock as if kneading pleasure into his flesh, sinking it into him one firm, compelling caress at a time. He soaked it up like soaking up the sun, basking in it, writhing for it, gasping to every teasing flick and delicate tracery and gripping draw that pushed him closer and closer to falling apart. Imre's teeth in his shoulder, Imre's utter control over his body, the scrape and stroke and twist of Imre filling him and working inside him in liquid-silk ways every time Luca twisted his hips, the shudder and tension of tightly corded muscle that whispered Imre was just as close to losing control, to losing himself, to melting into Luca until they were one and the same, lost and found and lost again.

It came on him before he could stop it: sharp, unexpected, breaths dragging over his tongue with a thick and heady texture like flesh, a sharp snap of sensation and the parting of needy lips, the bite of his fingernails into the unyielding steel of Imre's forearm, the tension of a whip poised to crack. He tried to hold back, but that whip snapped, lashed him, bit deep into his flesh and scored all the way down to his core. The knot of darkness inside him burst, bloomed, radiating out in a liquid rush. His thighs tightened and trembled. His inner walls contracted around Imre's cock, sliding and sucking and stroking inside against that place that tore him to pieces.

And he ripped like so many paper scraps, falling apart with his voice a thing swimming deep in his throat, his body a vessel shattered and spilling in a flooding wash.

Imre touched him sweetly, softly, as he spent himself in quiet shudders, as the flame inside him melted into embers. Dazed, he fought for breath. His fingers hurt. He had Imre's arm in a death-grip, and he peeled his hands away, joints aching as they unlocked. He felt wrung to pieces, scraped and sanded until the raw edges of his desire became smooth and soft.

But Imre was still hard inside him, stretching the soft malleable warmth of his body until Luca couldn't help but feel every inch of him in the quiet, simmering sensitivity that came in the aftermath.

"Imre," he sighed, turning his head enough to rub his cheek to Imre's beard.

"Nine." It came out on a low, satisfied rumble. "Are you ready for more?"

"More?" Luca whispered hazily.

"I want you to feel this."

Imre caught Luca's hand and guided it up to his stomach, pressing his spread palm over his own flesh. And then Imre *moved*—a slow and liquid undulation of his hips, his cock gliding and twisting inside Luca, sparking hot rushes of lingering sensitivity, rolling over him and dragging him deep. When Luca was already spent, his entire world narrowed to the sensation of Imre within him, taking his body with deep and lazy thrusts, working his flesh with precisely controlled strength and deliberation. He *felt* every raw burst of friction, every kiss of flesh to flesh, every time his body caught and tightened and gripped and held on to Imre as if he could keep him, catch him, never let him go.

And every time, under his palm, the shape of Imre's cock moved against his stomach and teased against his palm, as if his body had been made to bend and bleed and mould around the shape of Imre's flesh.

"No distractions," Imre purred, nuzzling the curve of Luca's ear, breaths rough and broken. "Nothing but this. I want you to feel me in you. Every moment of it, angyalka."

"Ah—*ah*, Imre!"

"Ten." Imre's sigh was soft, contented, so deeply pleasured, erotic. "Stay with me, my angel."

And then he tore Luca's world apart.

Every thrust was a timeless moment, consuming, catching Luca up in the fullness of it, in the slow, satisfying feeling of Imre sliding into him deeper, deeper, flooding into every empty crevice and easing the drawing, aching pull inside. He fell into the rhythm of Imre's body with a synchronicity as raw and sweet as sugar, rolling back to meet him, caught up in the ebb and flow they made between them until together they were the music, the melody, the striking notes of Luca's overflowing, breaking heart.

He'd never known it was possible to feel this close to someone: utterly absorbed, transfixed by the smallest touch, the smallest breath, the most perfect, trembling detail. The slick of sweat binding skin to skin. The perfect tangle of their legs. The press of Imre's brow to the nape of Luca's neck. The luxuriant flexion of raw masculine power flowing from Imre's shoulders down his entire body to roll into Luca, sinking deep. The way Imre's fingers laced with Luca's, clasping together over his stomach and holding against that mark of possession, that ridge swelling out his stomach each time Imre filled him.

And the way the hitch in Imre's breaths, the soft sounds catching in the back of his throat, betrayed that he was just as overwhelmed as Luca.

Nothing should feel like this. This blending of self to self, this invasive oneness, this utter immersion. There was nothing for Luca but the stroke and sigh between them, the ache and burn of his body, the enveloping fire of Imre's embrace. He rode the high and came crashing down again and again and again, until Imre shuddered against him. Until Imre clutched him, pressing them so close he couldn't breathe.

Until that beloved voice, deep and gritty and raw with desire, with something Luca didn't dare wish for, whispered "My Luca" against his ear as, with a low growl, Imre spilled into Luca's body, molten heat that teased and licked and filled him in ways that left him flushed, gasping, an answer of Imre's name on his lips.

And an etching of Imre's name upon his soul, graven as deep as heart's blood.

69

LUCA'S SKIN TASTED OF SWEET sweat and the quiet, heady musk of desire, and Imre thought he could kiss that flavour from his flesh for hours.

He pressed his mouth to the back of Luca's shoulder again and again, and again, taking his time over each, savouring in the lazy aftermath. Luca was nearly asleep against him, his entire body sheened with a layer of misted sweat that made him glisten pale as pearl, his damp hair spilling against the coverlet. His body was hot around Imre's spent cock, their legs still twined, fingers still clasped, just a soft, lax tangle of boneless man in Imre's arms.

Exactly how Imre wanted him.

He'd never known anyone who responded as beautifully as Luca did, so open and receptive and *with* him in every moment. As if they could read each other in touch; as if contact and body language were all the words they'd ever need. The sound of his name on Luca's lips was addictive, the whisper of Luca's quiet cries a heady drug that injected deep in Imre's veins and spun him into a dizzying high.

And the way he flowed, the beauty of his body in the faint glow of firelight, the stretch and pull of silk and sinew…

Imre closed his eyes, resting his cheek to Luca's shoulder and gathering him closer. He never should have done this. He couldn't imagine how he'd waited as long as he had. Conflict tore painfully inside him, and yet it couldn't ruin the deep, satisfied languor that left him warm and melted and so contentedly tired.

Luca. He traced his lips against Luca's nape. *Beautiful, beloved Luca.*

Luca stirred sleepily, sighing out a soft, "Mm…?"

Imre chuckled, nosing into his hair, breathing in more of his scent. "Are you all right?"

"Mm…yeah." Luca's smile was in his voice, drowsy and warm. "I feel good. I feel like melted sweets."

Imre couldn't help chuckling. "Sweets?"

"Sweets." Luca turned one softly glimmering eye over his shoulder. "Like toffee. Pulled and stretched until it's warm and just right."

"Imp. Is it how you thought it would be?"

"Better." Luca closed his eye again and rubbed his cheek to the sheets. "I wasn't expecting you to…not like *that*."

"Were you expecting the perfect simultaneous orgasm?" Imre grinned and caught Luca's earlobe in his teeth, biting down and tugging gently, only to let go. "How much pornography do you watch, angyalka?"

Luca gasped. "Not that much! Not *any!*" When Imre remained silent, Luca scrunched his nose up in that lovely way he had. "…some. I just…"

He fell still, silent. Imre waited him out, letting Luca think, letting him gather his thoughts. He was content with this, close and tangled and intimate and silent and giving Luca all the time he needed.

Finally Luca murmured, "The idea was that it would always be this fast, intense, harsh thing. Messy. Urgent. Kind of clumsy and desperate. But you…" His voice quieted, softened. "You made it gentle. Soft. Intimate. You made waiting worth it."

Imre was grateful that Luca faced away from him, and couldn't see the heat burning in his cheeks. "Anticipation can be as heady as gratification."

"Does that mean you're going to make me wait two more months before we do this again?"

"I don't think I can wait two more days now that I know how it feels to have you."

Luca tensed, before letting out a spluttering laugh. "Imre!"

"Ah—" Imre hissed as tight flesh gripped and clutched around his cock. "Be still or you'll be finding out in two minutes." He took a deep, steadying breath, nuzzling into the crook of Luca's throat. From the corner of his eye, it was hard to miss the race of pink flooding down Luca's pale cheeks. "Blushing now? What happened to the bold little cat who begged for reasons to scream my name? Fourteen, by the way. If you thought I stopped counting."

"You shouldn't have *started*." Luca grumbled sulkily. "Don't be awful."

Imre bit back a laugh. He didn't want to prick his prideful little cat's feelings. "You wouldn't care for me if I wasn't."

"If you think being terrible is part of your appeal, you have another thing coming," Luca huffed, then trailed off, making a thoughtful sound before adding, "I like you because you're *not* awful. You think I haven't turned men down before?" He made a bitter sound in the back of his throat. "They were…they were so caught up in all this swagger about what it means to be a man, rude and aggressive and arrogant in all the bad ways." He turned his head enough to look at Imre over his shoulder, that sweet throaty burr making whiskey out of his shy words. "I…I think it takes a bigger man to be gentle than it does to be cruel. That's what I like about you."

"Luca."

Imre had no words. So often he was silent while he sought the right words, but there were no words for the ache in his chest at the utter raw sweetness of Luca's honesty, his shy and breathy confessions. And so Imre gave not words, but touch: catching Luca's chin gently, leaning in, capturing his lips. He didn't have words for the things he loved about Luca, so he showed him in the worship of his lips, in the desperate need to taste him and mark him and make him Imre's forever when forever, for them, might only be a few short days.

Perhaps that was why, when their lips parted and Luca snuggled back against him with a little purr, Imre couldn't bring himself to part their bodies. They couldn't sleep like this, even if part of him wanted to. He needed to look after Luca's body, give him something for the soreness, make sure his little cat was comfortable and safe and happy.

In a minute. Soon.

For now, he needed this.

He needed to feel like this moment wouldn't end.

And so he pressed his cheek to Luca's hair and held him close—while beyond the bed, outside the window, the day clouded over in drifts of white.

"It's snowing again," he murmured.

"Yeah," Luca said, and sighed, deep and slow. "It is." He tightened his grip on Imre's fingers, their hold laced sweet and true. "I just hope it never stops."

70

LUCA WASN'T SURE HOW CHRISTMAS Eve crept up so quickly. One moment he'd been watching the snow come down on his twentieth birthday, and the next his world was full of the taste of Imre's lips and the roll and sway of his hips. With the power unsteady and the heat fritzing on and off when the generator iced over, some days it was all either of them could do to get up, make breakfast, check the animals, and tumble back into bed.

And if, in bed, they found other ways of keeping each other warm…

Luca wasn't complaining.

Even if some days, after Imre had spent hours teasing him open and leaving him full more often than not, walking could be something of a trial.

He woke early in the evening on Christmas Eve; the house was warm for once, at least, and he sprawled languidly in the blankets, stretching against the sheets just to feel them, luxuriant, on his naked skin. The bed was empty, but Imre was probably up and being restless again. The scents rising from below said "up and being restless" likely involved supper, and in response Luca's stomach growled heavily. He groaned, rolling over and burying his face in the pillows.

Up. Right. Up.

Up meant time with Imre.

Even if he was trying not to think of that ticking countdown, hanging always over his head.

But it was hard to forget, as he padded across the hall with a quilt wrapped around his hips and rummaged in the drawers for something to wear. Even if he spent half the day and every night in Imre's room, in his bed, Luca still had his *own* room, his things separate. Hauling his kit and baggage into Imre's room might imply something like permanence.

And they couldn't make that mistake, now could they.

He pushed the bitter thought away, slipped into a pair of jeans, and tugged on a t-shirt and socks before padding down the stairs. He peeked into the kitchen, but there was nothing but a pot bubbling on the stove. The living room yielded better results: Imre with a number of boxes scattered about on the floor, including one with a neatly folded artificial tree and another burgeoning over with tinsel. Vila pushed a silvery ball of something across the floor with her nose only to jerk back and sneeze, shaking her head, while Seti watched her with sceptical patience. Imre lifted out delicate, shimmering ornaments in varied shapes, painted with intricate designs in thin lines of white against bold colours.

Luca leaned in the doorway, watching Imre quietly in this unguarded moment before Imre might notice him. He loved watching Imre's hands work, loved the way he handled even the most fragile things with such precision, putting as much care and consideration into something as simple as unpacking ornaments as he did into everything else.

Imre untangled the glittering silver strings of two ornaments, then paused, glancing up. His gaze landed on Luca, and he smiled—a slow thing of pure warmth like the dawn breaking, casting soft light over the crags of his features, falling to dwell in his eyes. That smile coaxed forth Luca's own, rising up from inside him with unstoppable joy. He couldn't help himself, not when Imre looked at him that way, making his stomach flutter and tighten.

God, Luca was such a silly little nit in love.

"So you finally decided to wake up," Imre said.

"You weren't in the bed with me. I had no reason to stay." Luca pushed away from the door, lacing his fingers together behind his back and drifting closer. "What are you doing?"

"I haven't put a tree up for the holiday in years. I suddenly felt like it." Imre lifted one of the dangling ornaments, a heart covered in beautifully stylized fine line art of holly berries and leaves. "Would you like to help?"

"Yeah."

Luca drifted closer and reached out to take the ornament. He remembered ornaments like this, glimmering in the light of the fireplace. He remembered Christmases stuffed full and happy and lolling on the sofa, while Imre sang those soft Romani and Hungarian songs to the faint strumming of the guitar, and Luca's parents drowsed together.

He remembered happy Christmases, instead of separate meals and an awkward, perfunctory exchange of gifts.

He thought he'd like to have a happy Christmas again.

"I think it'll be nice," he said, and grinned. "And this time you won't have to lift me up to put the angel on top."

"Who says I won't anyway?" Imre pushed to his feet and hooked an arm around Luca's waist, spinning him into Imre's arms with that little thrilling rush that made Luca gasp every time. "You are still very small, angyalka."

Luca curled the delicate ornament against his chest to protect it, the other hand gripping at Imre's arm as he looked up at him with a laugh. "No, you're still too obscenely large."

Imre's eyes glimmered. "You are baiting me into saying something terrible."

"I am not." Luca pushed up on his toes, draping his body against Imre's solid bulk, rubbing his cheek into that thick beard and brushing his lips against his ear. "If you say something terrible, I'm going to want you to do something terrible."

"Ah?" Imre chuckled, turning his head into the touch of Luca's lips, their cheeks brushing. "If I do that, there'll be no tree. Just a mess everywhere, and Christmas Eve dinner ruined."

"How hungry are you?"

"You're still baiting me, little cat."

Thick fingers wove into Luca's hair, stroking his head back, gently tilting his head to kiss him—all he wanted, all he needed in this moment no matter how he teased. Imre's kisses dissolved him into sweetness, made him feel like a wholly new Luca, someone who understood the deep, quiet pleasure of sensuality more and more every day, someone who discovered his body with every new secret Imre teased from him, teaching him things he'd never known about himself even while Imre made himself an open book for Luca's exploration. He knew every line of Imre's body, now. Every scar ridged against his skin, every dip and rise of sinew, the shape and silhouette of them and how they fit into the flow of Luca's palms.

And the perfect sound he made every time Luca caught his lower lip in his teeth and nibbled until Imre groaned, his grip turning rough, possessive, his mouth soft and slack and needy.

"Brat," Imre breathed, groaning as he brushed his lips open-mouthed across Luca's, then gently caught Luca's shoulders and parted with a last flick of a teasing tongue. "I'll make a mess of you later. Be good long enough to keep from scandalizing Szent Miklos."

Luca laughed, draping his arm around Imre's neck. "Maybe he'll want to watch."

"He can watch someone else." Imre growled, something black clouding his eyes. "I do not share."

Luca's smile faded. He lingered on that expression on Imre's face, fierce and firm. Possessive, Luca realized.

Imre was possessive enough to want to keep him to himself, but not enough to say a word about letting him go once the New Year had passed.

It's not his fault, Luca reminded himself. *You promised him. You promised you wouldn't resent him. You promised you'd still be his friend.*

Imre's brows knit. "What is it?" he asked.

"Nothing," Luca answered, finding his smile again and stealing one last kiss, light and sweet, before pulling away to untangle the cord of the ornament. "Nothing at all. Let's put up the tree. Maybe then we can talk about getting messy, aye?"

"Aye," Imre echoed, calm and agreeable.

Yet still, as they worked together to lift out the tree, Luca felt Imre's gaze on him, asking. Asking what was on his mind.

Asking things that Luca wouldn't say, because the moment he did he would break down and beg.

THE SMELL OF COOKING FISH told Imre, not long after he and Luca had finished erecting the tree, that supper was ready. He'd kept his own counsel, but something about that strange, withdrawn smile on Luca's lips had left him unsettled and quiet, and he wondered if he was in for another few days of the silent treatment while Luca worked through whatever was bothering him enough to talk about it. Stubborn, *prideful* thing, and Imre sometimes thought the long silences were less an inability to touch whatever raw thing was eating at him and more the long and endless hours it took to chip away at the walls of Luca's pride enough for him to unbend.

But Luca was all smiles and laughter, as they raised the tree and strung the tinsel. Warm, with those soft, idle brushes of affectionate contact Imre had grown addicted to, from the tracery of Luca's fingertips down his chest in teasing lines to the light brush of his lips, caught in a swift and stolen kiss. And that way Luca had of looking at him sidelong from under his lashes, green eyes glimmering and dark…

As if Imre wouldn't notice the way Luca took him in, lingering on his every movement until those hungry glances left Imre too hot, too needy.

As if Imre wouldn't understand the quiet desire in that gaze, begging for the moment when Imre would pin Luca to the bed and take him again and again until they were both spent, exhausted, sated and melted in each other's arms.

That was the moment that captivated him the most, that came to live in the halls of his memory and the chambers of his heart.

The way Luca fit into the curve of his body, the way their arms and legs tangled until they were a braid of brambles wound together, pricking each other's hearts with sweet, piercing thorns.

Only the smell of cooking food stopped him from taking Luca upstairs and making good on those slow, lingering glances. He stole one more kiss, then extricated himself and ducked into the kitchen to turn the heat down under the bubbling pot on the stove. Luca trailed after him, leaning over and watching while Imre lifted the lid off the pot and stirred the thick, pale soup inside. With the lid off, the scent was almost overpowering, rich and fishy and tangy. Luca whistled softly, mock-flinching away.

"Bit much, that."

Imre chuckled and took a quick taste of the savoury soup, testing the flavour, before offering Luca the spoon. "Do you remember this?"

Luca leaned in and sipped at the spoon delicately, and Imre caught himself watching those soft lips, sheened in a glistening skim of white, his thoughts drifting back to last night. Luca on his hands and knees, slim shoulders upthrust in smooth mounds, the dark shag of hair falling across his face, his lips wet and swollen as he moved over Imre's hips and tore his self-control to pieces with a teasing, stroking tongue. How he'd moaned with pleasure every time Imre's cock had hit the back of his throat.

And how his mouth had shone just like this, once he'd coaxed Imre to the edge only to slink up his body and kiss him with his lips still bitter and wet and gleaming with that salt taste shared between them, so utterly and innocently unaware of the sensuality in his every feline movement.

A hard jolt of need curled in the pit of Imre's stomach; if he said the burn in his cheeks was the stove he would be lying to himself. He sucked in a breath and looked away.

Luca made a thoughtful sound that trailed into one of delight. "Fish soup," he said. "Mum always complained about the smell when we'd come visit for Christmas."

"But she ate it anyway." Imre dragged his wayward thoughts under control, kept his hands busy so he'd keep them off Luca. He tried to focus on stirring the soup, setting the burner to simmer, reaching up to pull down earthenware bowls from the overhead cabinet. "There's stuffed cabbage in the oven, if you want to fetch the tray."

Luca snorted and pulled on oven mitts, navigating around Imre to pull the oven door open. "Only you could get me to voluntarily eat cabbage."

"It's a Hungarian tradition. I suppose that made it a Romani tradition, over time." He set out large plates in dark blue, speckled in white, with deep soup bowls to one side of each, then began ladling the soup into the bowls. Strange how this was so much a part of who he was, but trace back even five generations and these things would have been things belonging to gadje, outsiders, those not of his people. His lips thinned. "It's hard to know who we are, sometimes, when we scattered to the winds and the four corners, and became chameleons taking on the colours of the lands we settled in in order to survive." He stilled, resting the soup ladle against the edge of the pot, a frown making tension pull between his brows. "Everywhere we go, we make it a part of us."

Luca remained silent for so long that Imre finally looked up to find those frank green eyes watching him with an open and accepting warmth. Sweet Luca; silly Luca, who looked so much like everything Imre thought of as *home*, standing there with his slender hands dwarfed inside massive oven mitts and his hair falling into his eyes. After long moments, Luca cocked his head with a sweet little smile.

"If you made it yours, then it's yours," he said simply. "Does it feel like home, Imre?"

"It does."

You do.

Luca's smile broadened into a grin, his eyes glittering. "Then it belongs to you."

"Xav t'jo ilo," Imre murmured, unable to stop the words as they rose on his tongue, dwelled in his breath, beat in his heart.

Pausing, Luca fixed Imre with a searching look, his eyes softening. "I missed that," he murmured. "Hearing you speak Romani."

"I hadn't realized I'd stopped."

"You sound happier in Romani."

Do I?

How perceptive, his little cat.

And yet still Luca didn't realize one thing.

Xav t'jo ilo, Imre had said. *I eat your heart.*

To the Rom, those words meant *I love you.*

The English words hovered on his tongue, those words he never said and yet tried to show every time he tasted the silk of Luca's skin and drew their bodies together until they moved one to one, but he couldn't bring himself to speak them.

Saying them now would only make this that much more terrible later.

"Perhaps," he deflected, leaning down to kiss Luca's temple, "I only speak it when there are people here who make me happy."

Luca laughed, leaning into him with a nuzzle. "Sweet talker."

"Only for you," Imre said, and carried the plates and bowls to the table.

Luca pulled the oven open, releasing a medley of both bitter and sweet scents, and withdrew two baking pans with stuffed cabbage rolls on one and rolled, flaky pastries on the other. He deposited the pans on the stove just in time for Imre to return with a tin of powdered sugar to shake over the pastries, before lifting one to Luca's lips. Luca took a lingering, savouring bite, exposing the sweetened date filling inside; with a soft, appreciative sound, eyes lighting up, he stole the rest of the pastry from Imre to nibble.

"Kifli," Imre said. "You used to—"

"—steal them while they were cooling on the rack," Luca finished and laughed, popping the rest of the pastry into his mouth. "Do you remember the time I gorged myself bloody sick on these?"

"I remember. Your mother stayed up all night with you, stroking your hair, while you moaned and whimpered in pain."

Luca chuckled, leaning his hip against the counter, and stole another pastry. "You stayed up, too."

"Someone had to make you tea."

But Luca didn't respond. He only looked down at the pastry in his fingers, lifting it to his lips without biting in. Imre frowned, settling to lean against the counter next to him, arm to arm. What had he—oh.

"Are you going to call them today?" he asked gently.

Luca shook his head, quick and short and sharp. "I'm not ready, Imre."

"You don't have to be."

And in truth Imre wasn't ready, either. One day soon Marco and Lucia would say *come home, son, come home*, and this moment would melt like the last snowflake of winter losing its sweet fragile spires and delicate traceries to melt away and evaporate forever. Putting off that phone call put off that moment, delayed the sun, let them keep their secrets in their own private night for a little bit longer.

He lingered on those downcast eyes, on the delicate lines of Luca’s profile, then dipped and caught that sweet mouth in a kiss, lingering until the hard lines of Luca’s lips softened and the hurt went out of them with a soft and willing surrender.

“Merry Christmas, angyalka,” he whispered against Luca’s lips. “Boldog Káracsonyt.”

“Merry Christmas, Imre,” Luca sighed, and curled his fingers into Imre’s shirt.

And in the silence that followed dwelled such simple words, unsaid.

Always, always unsaid.

72

SUPPER WAS QUIET AND SLOW as supper always was, long silences interspersed with low murmurs and the occasional laugh, powdered sugar in Imre's beard when Luca tried to feed him kifli and the taste of sweetness on his tongue when he licked the last bits of sugar from Luca's fingertips. The warmth of tradition in a simple meal, things Imre hadn't bothered cooking for Christmas Eve in years.

Once the dishes were done and the leftovers put away, they settled on the sofa, basking before the fire with Imre sprawled on his back and Luca stretched atop him, his slight, warm weight seeming to pin Imre to earth. Imre wasn't sure how long they drifted like that, his gaze locked on the hearth, following the hypnotic flicker and spark of the fire, his thoughts circling around things he couldn't quite face just yet. Unnamed longings; a sense of things unfinished; the bitter, harsh voice calling him a coward.

And the desire to *do* something, something rash and impulsive and drastic, when that wasn't the man he'd been taught to be.

Luca sighed softly, stretching and rubbing his cheek to Imre's chest with a sleepy sound. "I'm so bloody stuffed," he murmured. "God, I just want to sleep."

Imre chuckled, idly trailing his fingertips down the back of Luca's arm. "In the bed this time. Your habit of falling asleep where you stand is becoming notorious."

Grinning, Luca folded his hands on Imre's chest and propped his chin atop his crossed wrists. "Maybe I do it just so you'll carry me."

"If that's what you want, you have only to ask."

Luca laughed, a wicked glimmer in his eyes, and pushed himself up to press his nose to Imre's. "Then take me to bed, Imre? Please?"

"Wicked." Imre cupped the back of Luca's head, threading his fingers into his hair, and drew him in for a kiss. "In a moment," he murmured against Luca's lips. "There's something I want to show you."

"Nnngh." Luca's sound was half laugh, half groan, as he nipped Imre's upper lip. "You're putting a bit of a wrench in my plans."

"Plans?"

"To take gross and filthy advantage of you."

Imre laughed helplessly. "I've created a monster."

"Nah. You've only figured out what a monster I already was to start with." Luca pushed himself up, shifting to straddle Imre's waist with his hands braced on his stomach. "What did you want to show me?"

Imre said nothing for long moments, lingering on Luca, heat kindling in the pit of his stomach. Those long, slim thighs had to stretch so wide to span his body, and his palms ached to catch Luca by the hips, slide his body just a little farther down, wrap those pretty thighs around his hips and let Luca feel exactly what he did to Imre.

God, years of celibacy were catching up with him in more ways than one.

Luca met his eyes, his stillness sudden and arresting, colour climbing in his cheeks. He ducked his head with a shy smile, watching Imre from under the fall of his hair.

"Tempting little cat," Imre murmured, cupping Luca's cheek, his skin so soft under Imre's palm, fresh-shaven and smooth. He grazed his thumb against Luca's lower lip, his gut twisting at how it yielded to his touch, such full, lush flesh. "Soon."

He pushed himself up, kissed Luca gently, dipped into his mouth to steal a taste of Luca and kifli and the tart mulled cider from supper. Then, just as gently, he lifted Luca off him, settling him into the corner of the couch before rising. He felt Luca's gaze following him with avid curiosity as he circled the room, turning off the lamps until there was nothing but the glow of firelight and the soft firefly pinpoints of lights floating among the Christmas tree branches. The firelight, too, shuttered as he stepped over the drowsing dogs and pulled the grate on the hearth until only a few faint flickers escaped, casting the living room into shadow with the faintest warm edges.

Imre fetched the small oil lantern he'd left on the corner of the hearth when unpacking earlier and set it in the middle of the floor, checking the oil and the wick before rummaging on a side table to pull a wide, thick sheet of black cardstock from beneath the stacks of his printed spreadsheets. He tugged loose one of the straight hairpins keeping his hair pinned back from his face, and used the blunt-sharp tip to carefully punch small holes into the paper, using it like a needle to dart and darn patterns in clustered scatters of dots.

Luca shifted to lean over the back of the sofa, folding his arms on the back and watching him with a small wrinkle in his brows. "Imre…?"

"Patience, angyalka."

Imre surveyed his handiwork, made a few more small holes, then slid the pin back into his hair and snagged the fireplace lighter, flicking it on to a small tongue of flame. He angled the nozzle carefully into the lantern and caught the wick, igniting the lantern into a glowing orb of glass, then knelt and held the paper over the lantern, shuttering its light.

Save for what bled through those pinprick holes, shining up onto the darkened ceiling.

"Look," Imre murmured. "My mother used to do this for me, when I was a wee thing."

Luca tilted his head back, looking up—where on the ceiling, tiny dots clustered and shimmered and sparkled into a galaxy. Imre lingered on the ceiling for long moments, remembering: remembering the way his mother would laugh as she did this, remembering his own joy, his chest tight, his eyes wide. This was what family felt like, he thought.

This was how Lohere should be, for now and for always.

"Oh," Luca breathed, hushed, awed. "Imre, it's…it's beautiful. It's like the winter sky beyond the clouds."

"Just so, angyalka," Imre agreed. "Just so."

Luca said nothing.

He only stretched one hand out, fingers splayed as if he would touch the stars, his lips gently parted on wordless sighs.

Imre couldn't look away. Where Luca saw galaxies, Imre saw only Luca, and a desperate need to see this every Christmas, every night, every year, for the rest of his life. And the wonder on Luca's face, the wrenching in Imre's chest, told him the decision he would have to make so painfully soon.

And the only choice he could ever have.

They watched their stars until the lantern guttered down, and there was only the stillness of night and the soft sound of the snow outside. Luca slipped off the couch and settled on the floor next to Imre, resting his cheek to his arm and filling him with his softness.

And when the dark came in full they rose together, fingers interlaced, and drifted toward the stairs.

But Imre paused as they passed the wide picture window in the foyer, looking out over the fields. Snow piled against the window pane, shaded soft in grey and blue, reflecting back the starlit night sky. He ran his fingers over the weathered windowsill, then smiled.

"Angyalka. Bring your boots."

Luca cocked his head, then perked, a slow smile spreading across his lips. "Shoes on the windowsill," he said. "I remember. You put your shoes on the windowsill, and when you wake up there's presents from St. Nicholas."

"Aye." Imre chuckled. "We should have done it on the sixth, but we were distracted by other things."

Luca brightened and disentangled their hands, dashing to the row their shoes made to one side of the back door and fetching his boots. With a laugh, he returned and plunked his boots down on the windowsill, making a show of arranging their laces before dusting his hands off.

"You have to put your shoes out, too."

Imre laughed. "I don't think St. Nicholas has anything for me."

"Do it?" Luca looked up at him with that wide-eyed, pleading expression Imre could never resist. "Please?"

Imre met that begging gaze, then sighed before trailing into a laugh. "All right, all right." He drew back and snagged his worn work boots, then propped them on the windowsill next to Luca's.

They immediately tried to fall off.

He caught them quickly, then gave Luca a flat look; Luca watched him with his fingers teasing against his lower lip, a stifled laugh glowing in his eyes. Little brat. Imre's shoes were too big, but he turned them sideways and lined them up one after the other, then stepped back, dusting his hands off.

"Happy?"

"Entirely." Luca beamed, then curled soft hands against Imre's arm, stretched up, and brushed sweet lips to his cheek. "Now take me to bed, Imre."

Such soft words, and yet they struck Imre hard as a hammer to an anvil—and God, did sparks fly. He caught Luca around the waist, dragging him close, relishing the widening of his eyes, the way his body went lax and soft and melted against Imre.

"Angyalka," he growled, as he stepped back, drawing Luca toward the stairs, "I have wanted nothing else for hours."

73

LUCA WOKE BEFORE DAWN ON Christmas morning, his breaths light with an excitement he hadn't felt in years, his body achingly, wonderfully sore; he could still feel the prints of Imre's fingers against his hips, and while he wanted to savour the feeling for a while longer, he also wanted to be out of bed and downstairs before Imre woke up.

He couldn't remember the last time he'd been happy on Christmas morning. The day was usually an awkward thing in the Ward house, gifts gruffly exchanged in passing, thrust at each other in the hallways, each on their way to somewhere else and never *there*.

His last happy Christmas had been at Lohere, ten years ago.

It was only right that his first in so long should be at Lohere, too.

Yawning, he rolled toward Imre's warmth. Just one more snuggle before he tiptoed out.

He fell into the warm spot Imre had left behind, the bed empty, though the wrinkle in the sheets and the heat of the fabric said not for long.

Still, Imre was already gone.

Half-groaning, half-laughing, Luca rolled onto his back, dragging his hand over his face. "…god *damn* it, Imre."

Fucking farmers.

He dragged out of bed, pulling on his boxers and shirt and socks, and bent to scratch over Vila and Seti's ears where they dozed before the bedroom fireplace. When he slipped out into the darkened hall, there was no sign of Imre, but a faint hint of firelight glimmered from below. Luca couldn't hear him, but then he rarely did. For such a large man, Imre moved with the same soft, floating silence as falling snow.

Luca tried to be just as quiet as he crept into his room and retrieved a small wrapped bundle of tissue, tucked it into his palm, and tiptoed downstairs. Skipping the fifth step, always skipping the fifth step, just like he had when he was a little boy sneaking down after midnight to try to catch St. Nicholas before he left.

There was no sign of St. Nicholas in the foyer, but Imre's shadow fell long from the bright open square of the kitchen doorway. Luca peeked around carefully, caught a glimpse of Imre's back, then jerked back. Holding his breath—as though that could make him quieter—he moved quickly across the foyer and dropped the tissue-wrapped bundle into Imre's boot.

Something wet pressed against his wrist, and he jerked back with a little squeak.

"Oop!"

A tawny-coloured head popped out of Luca's boot, little cleft nose twitching, paws curled against the ankle of his shoe, ears flopping, curious dark eyes watching him fearlessly.

A tiny little rabbit kit, its fur velvety and caramel-coloured, its ears almost too long for its itsy body.

Luca caught his breath with a joyous little thrill twisting in his chest.

"Who are you?" he whispered, reaching one hand out toward the rabbit.

"Yours, if you want," Imre said at his back.

Luca jumped, then looked over his shoulder. Imre leaned in the kitchen doorway, bare-chested and barefoot in his pyjama pants, a sleepy tumbled mess with his arms folded over his chest. He lifted his chin toward the rabbit, a faint smile playing at his lips.

"She doesn't bite. Or at least hasn't bitten me."

Luca grinned, stuck his tongue out, then turned his attention back to the kit. Carefully, he stretched his hand toward her, offering his fingers. He'd thought she would flinch back, but she only twitched her nose at his fingertips curiously, and held still for him as he carefully slipped his fingers into her dense, lush fur, stroking over the top of her head. She was so *soft*, and wonder poured through him in little rushing sighs as he traced down to the tips of her floppy ears and watched her eyes start to sink closed.

Tentative, he slipped his hand into the neck of his boot and cupped underneath her tiny body, and lifted her out. She lolled against his palm, so small she made the tiniest of caramel balls in the centre of his hand, all baby-fine fur and long, floppy paws with little perfect pink candy dollops for toe-pads. He curled her against his chest, then caught sight of the collar around her neck.

Less a collar and more a twine of coarse handspun ribbon, green, the bow a burst of yellow turning little fabric scraps into a flower. His heart nearly burst as he made the connection.

"Dandelion," he whispered, and couldn't stop himself from grinning until his cheeks hurt. He stroked his fingertip down the bridge of her nose, sighing with pleasure as she went limp and closed her eyes. She was Dandelion, just like in the book, a long-fond memory come to life. He lifted his head, looking at Imre. "When did you ever…?"

"You sleep rather late on winter mornings. I had time for a drive out to the Rosewaites' farm while you were unconscious. They breed pet bunnies and show rabbits."

Warmth flushed all the way down to Luca's collar, his heart throbbing roughly. How long had Imre been hiding this little darling away until the right moment? Luca looked down at her again, lifting her up to rub his cheek to her fur and breathe in her soft baby scent. "She's so lovely." He paused, then, pulling back, frowning at the bunny kit. "…she…is a *she*, right?"

Imre let out short, startled chuckle. "Better call Mira if you want to learn how to figure that out, eh?"

"After the New Year. I promise." At Imre's sceptical look, Luca tried to scowl, but could only laugh. "It's bloody Christmas day! I'm not calling her on Christmas day!" He broke off, then, as a warm, damp nose pressed to his cheek, snuffing and rubbing; he squinted one eye up. "Oh, that's *wet*."

Imre drifted closer and gently nudged his curled knuckles against the kit's jaw. "A wet nose is a healthy nose."

"I know that. I'm not completely dim." Dandelion continued nosing at him, her whiskers soft and feather-light against his cheek and lips, and he laughed. "Oh but it tickles!"

"Whiskers generally do," Imre said with that same sardonic, teasing pragmatism, and Luca laughed again.

"I love her whiskers." Luca buried his nose in her fur. "I love *her*. Thank you, Imre. I'll take care of her always." He stopped, then, stomach sinking. "If…I can. I can take her back to Sheffield with me, can't I?"

Imre regarded him gravely, something odd and dark in his eyes. "Likely. I'm sure your parents won't mind—but it's not your parents you're thinking of, are you?"

"No," Luca admitted, dropping his gaze, cuddling Dandelion comfortingly closer. "I'm…I'm thinking about a place of my own. Getting a job, and…and…" *figuring out life without you* "Well if most flats will let me have a cat, they'll let me have Dandelion. I'll be sure of it."

"There you go."

Silence fell. Silence filled with the promise of the days left between them, the wondering of *what if*, the soft tiny whispers of Dandelion's breaths that would be the only thing Luca had left of Lohere when Luca left and Imre let him go.

That was what hurt the most, he thought.

That Imre would just let him go.

His throat tightened. He dropped his gaze to the rabbit kit again, and rubbed his brow between her ears, closing his eyes, searching for something, anything to say to deflect this thick and awful silence, to fill it with some kind of noise.

"…she better not have taken a shite in my shoe."

Imre barked out a rather ragged laugh. His hand felt, heavy and warm and gentle, to the top of Luca's head. "I'll clean them for you, angyalka."

Imre's hand fell away, his body heat withdrawing. Luca lifted his head, opening his eyes, watching pensively as Imre moved toward the kitchen again.

"You should look in your boot," Luca murmured.

Imre paused, glancing over his shoulder. "Ah?"

Luca said nothing, skittering his gaze to the side and hugging Dandelion close. His gift for Imre was probably ridiculous, cheap and small and daft. His heart felt heavier than a lead slug, trying to beat and failing. He'd been happy a few minutes ago.

But now he was just afraid Imre would find his gift as meaningless as these last days of December.

Imre drifted closer, his warmth brushing against Luca's side. He delved a hand inside the boot and retrieved the little wrapped ball of crumpled tissue. His brows knit quizzically as he peeled it open, large hands handling it with careful finesse.

The layers fell away on a little round green ball of interlaced twigs almost like a decorative wicker ball—but made up not of wood, but clover stems, interlaced and woven into place to make a cage. Inside was a single stemless clover flower, white and soft and pure and preserved, both the bloom and the cage of stems gleaming faintly with their coating.

Imre's face blanked oddly, washed first with confusion before it settled into something Luca couldn't quite read, something soft and thoughtful as he touched over the little cage of clover stems with reverent care. Luca swallowed against the lump in his throat and ventured into the silence.

"It…it was one of the last healthy clover flowers before the snow."

"How did you keep it like this…?"

"I stole a little of your beeswax." He bit his lip. "Looked up how to coat and preserve it on Pinterest. Worked on it while you were out and I had to stay in."

"It is…impossibly beautiful, angyalka." Imre's voice broke; was that *wonder* in his eyes, for Luca's silly, pointless little gift? Imre cupped the caged clover flower in both palms, so tiny against his broad hands, then leaned closer and pressed his lips to Luca's brow, warm breaths stirring his hair. "Thank you."

Luca exhaled raggedly. His heart remembered how to beat again, racing to catch up for the struggling pitter-pat thumps it had missed, tumbling in joyous leaps. "Yeah, well…" He scuffed his feet and hid his face against Dandelion's side. "I don't have much money, so…I thought I'd make something."

"I have been thinking about that."

Luca peeked over the rabbit at Imre. "Hm?"

"This farm is my livelihood." Imre watched him with a

discerning gaze. "How I earn an income. You contributed to that income. Your help has been invaluable, Luca. And it would only be fair to pay you for your labour."

"Don't." He shook his head quickly, voice catching. "I…I like being here. I don't want to make it about money. I don't want it to be mercenary."

"It doesn't have to be mercenary."

Imre's shadow fell over Luca, bringing his warmth with it, as Imre transferred the delicate clover globe to one hand and used the other to draw him close against his side. Luca leaned into him, tucking into the curve of Imre's body and crook of his arm with Dandelion snuggled against his chest.

Imre rested his chin to the top of Luca's head, a gentle pressure and the wash of his beard. "It's part of recognizing that you're not a child. You aren't dependent on me, Luca. You're a partner. An equal contributor, one I respect." Warm lips pressed into his hair. "Allow me to show you that respect by paying you the wages you've earned."

Partner.

He wanted to be Imre's partner, but not like this.

Not in any way he could have, but the ache of it was so raw, so real, that he could almost see it. Imre in old-fashioned Hungarian wedding attire and Luca a dorky mess in a button-down and slacks he'd borrowed from his father because he was fucked if he had anything but jeans. And instead of shouting at them and disowning them both, his father could be there with his mother to smile and watch them both wistfully, eyes wet, and there would be bouquets of clover flowers everywhere—

His chest seized painfully.

He couldn't be an adult. An equal partner.

Not when he was still clinging to unrealistic, childish daydreams.

He forced a smile, tilting his head back to look up at Imre and shoving his thoughts away. “Yeah?”

“Aye.”

“Okay. Okay, then.”

“Very well, then. Next time we’re in town, I’ll cut you a cheque you can deposit at the bank.”

Imre leaned down, ghosting his mouth against Luca’s, and Luca strained into it even as he wondered how Imre couldn’t *taste* the stifled scream on his breaths, bottled up and waiting to break free.

But Imre pulled away as if he could taste nothing at all, a warm, easy smile on his lips as he looked down at the clover in his palm, then tugged Luca toward the kitchen.

“Come,” he said. “Breakfast.”

And walked away, leaving Luca standing there with a bunny huddled against his chest, his heart beating as fast as her little thumping feet.

74

TWO DAYS BEFORE THE NEW Year and the snow was still heavy on the ground, thick in the sky, and Luca was beginning to think someone, somewhere, was on his side.

He leaned against Imre on the couch, nested between his thighs and snuggled back against his chest with Dandelion in his lap. He'd had trouble putting her down for more than five minutes, and even though she had a proper cage and even a little artificial rabbit run she was more likely to be found cuddled in a pocket of Luca's hoodie or tumbled in front of the fireplace, napping with the dogs.

She dozed in the curve of his hip now, a boneless heap of fur with her paws twitching every time he stroked down her side, while Luca rested his head to Imre's chest and watched the snow fall outside the living room window.

"It's not letting up," he murmured, breaking hours of comfortable silence.

Imre's chest heaved against his back in a lazy breath. "Like as not."

Luca bit his lip. "…think the trains are running?"

Imre held his silence for so long Luca thought at first he wouldn't answer, letting that question and every unspoken implication fall between them. Sometimes their silences felt like a deep, dry river bed, and everything they *didn't* say was just another drop building up into a trickle, then a stream, then a torrent, then a flood.

Until one day there'd be nothing but raging river rapids between them, too far for either to cross.

He closed his eyes, pressing a hand over the ache in his chest, and parted his lips to speak—but Imre beat him to it, voice rumbling against Luca's back.

"Can hope not."

Hope. Luca exhaled softly. What was he hoping for? A few more stolen days?

"Do you want to check?" he asked.

"No."

"Will you just—"

Will you just say you want me to stay?

But he couldn't finish.

And Imre didn't ask.

He only shifted against Luca's back, sliding his arms around his waist, sending Dandelion flopping over to tumble against Luca's stomach. Rough beard and soft lips touched the back of his neck.

"Call him," Imre rumbled.

Luca stiffened. "Why?"

That hold tightened, barely soothing him. When had this become so tense? "To tell him the trains aren't running."

"But we didn't—"

Oh.

Oh.

That sweet flush running through Luca was bittersweet.

A temporary stay of execution was still an execution, nonetheless.

But he leaned away from Imre long enough to snag his phone off the coffee table, swipe the screen, then pull up his address book and his father's contact. He didn't want to do this.

But he wanted to pack his things and shove off into the snow even less.

He sighed, tapped the call button, then lifted the phone to his ear.

Somehow he wasn't surprised it took his dad six rings to answer. Marco Ward probably didn't want to talk to Luca any more than Luca wanted to talk to him. *Don't pick up*, he thought, pleading for voicemail, but the phone clicked over, followed by a breathless, "Hello? Luca?"

Just the sound of his father's voice made Luca's mouth crease bitterly. He fought it down and dragged out, "Hi, Dad."

"Hey." Awkward stillness, fumbling sounds, then, "It's been a while."

"Yeah. Like since the day you shipped me off."

"Luca," Imre murmured softly, and Luca shot a slit-eyed look over his shoulder. That patient chastising wasn't going to work on him. Not this damned time.

His Dad sighed. "You're still angry."

"Do you blame me?"

"I should." His dad groaned. "…I don't."

Luca said nothing. Inside he was practically vibrating, wanting to shout, wanting to rage, but he couldn't let it out. He was a bursting sack held closed by a zipper and straining at the seams, but nothing seemed to want to give to let the poison building inside him seep out.

He'd thought he wasn't so angry anymore. Thought he'd started to let it go, when no matter how shitty his father had been, it had brought him back to Imre, led him into this.

But he was just as angry as he'd been the day he'd left.

Marco Ward had dumped him off on Imre and left Imre to fix his shitty mistakes, left Imre to deal with the problem of Luca.

I made myself your problem so you wouldn't leave each other, he wanted to scream.

But all you did was abandon me.

"Luca…?" his dad said into the trembling silence.

"I'm not coming back," Luca blurted.

"What?"

"Not yet," Luca corrected quickly. *Not at all* he wanted to say, but that wasn't an option and right now he couldn't stand the idea of Imre's rejection when he still hadn't forgiven his father's. He took a deep breath, then continued, "The snow's bad. We're snowed in. I don't think the trains will run out of Harrogate right now, and even if they are…the bees are struggling. If Imre's bees die, the whole farm dies, and there's no one he can hire to help this winter. They're all busy with their own shite."

"Language, Luca."

"Fuck off," he retorted without thinking, and Imre burst into low, whispered laughter against his back, his entire body shaking and heaving.

"Behave, angyalka," he whispered, voice and breath hot against Luca's other ear; Luca shivered, pushing back against him, looking over his shoulder.

You behave, he mouthed. For fuck's sake, whispering in his ear when he was on the phone with his bloody dad!

His father sighed. "Was that all you wanted to tell me, then?"

"Yeah." Luca started to bite off something else, then stopped himself, looking down at Dandelion and gently fingering one of her velvety ears. "That's it. Maybe in a week. Maybe two."

"All right. Are you all right out there?"

"I'm fine." Luca shrugged as if his father could see him. "Just didn't want you to waste money on a ticket."

His father hesitated for a long moment, and sounded almost *hurt* when he spoke gain. "…it's not a waste."

Am I a waste?

But Luca only asked, "Do you want to talk to Imre?"

"Does he want to talk to me?"

Luca looked back again, arching a brow, pulling the phone away and offering it to Imre. Imre lifted his head, watching him through sleepy, half-lidded eyes shadowed by the tumble of his hair, then exhaled softly and took the phone, pressing it to his ear.

"Good evening, Marco."

Luca couldn't hear what his father said next, just a tinny burst of sound. Imre sighed, tilting his head back against the sofa. Luca eyed him—then tensed as thick fingertips idly walked down his thigh, to his knee. His eyes widened and he hissed, slapping at Imre's hand, flushing; bloody pervert!

Imre's expression didn't change, his gaze drifting to the ceiling as if he hadn't done a thing. "We're fine. The generators hiccup now and then, but for the most part everything's all right. We're well-stocked, just a bit buried." His gaze slid to Luca, a cunning glint in his eyes the only warning, followed by a slow, lazy smile as Imre stroked over his hip, shivering him through the thin texture of his worn jeans; the entire time Imre's voice never wavered in its drawling lazy calm. "No. No, he's been fine. I doubt I'd survive the winter without him." He paused, then chuckled, fingers curling inward to idly lift the hem of Luca's shirt and feather a touch over his stomach. "I'm serious. He's not misbehaved one jot."

"Imre!" Luca hissed under his breath, burning up to the tips of his ears, stomach tight. He pulled away, deposited Dandelion on the back of the sofa, and twisted to face Imre, kneeling between his thighs and glaring. "*The fuck are you trying to do?*" he mouthed. God, if his father heard him…

Imre met his eyes, smile widening slowly, and brushed his fingertips over Luca's mouth, then lifted his finger to his own lips, pantomiming *shh* before speaking into the phone. "No. It was a good year for apples, but did you really want to talk to me about apples?" he asked.

And promptly settled that heated hand on Luca's thigh again, his thumb stroking dangerously high over his inner thigh. Luca glowered, whispering through his teeth.

"Will you stop bloody teasing me while you're talking to my dad?"

Imre paused, arching a brow. "Hm? No, Luca's just talking to the dogs. And his rabbit." He stopped, then laughed under his breath. "I said rabbit." He cocked his head. "I gave it to him. For Christmas." That possessive grip on Luca's thigh squeezed gently, then relaxed. "Because I wanted to. I need a reason other than that?" Imre sighed. "Nothing's gotten into me. I'm simply not certain why you're so mortally offended over a rabbit." His gaze flicked to Luca again. "I don't think it'll be staying in your house."

"Imre!" Luca gasped, near-silent mouthings, eyes widening, his stomach dropping out. "Shut it! Fucking shut it!" Oh, *God*, if his dad took implications from that…

"He's already left," Imre continued with weary patience. "I didn't mean anything by it, Marco." His voice hardened. "I think that's a conversation you need to have with him."

Luca just closed his eyes, rolled forward, and thunked his forehead to the centre of Imre's chest.

Fuck.

Imre curled a hand against the back of his neck, stroking soothingly, gently, as he spoke into the phone. "Call him later. He's off in his room, and I'm not inclined to chase him down with his phone right now." He made an exasperated sound. "I know I am. Do try to calm yourself. Why are you so upset? …then why are you trying so hard to control him?"

Luca winced.

And didn't move when Dandelion tilted over, flopped, fell off the back of the couch, and plopped down between his shoulder blades.

At least Imre was covering for him.

And Imre sounded rather annoyed despite his mild tone as he said, "All right. I'll mind my business. …of course. Take care."

Then he was dropping the phone, gathering Luca and the rabbit into a tangle of Imre and Luca and Dandelion fur curled in Imre's lap. Luca let the soft, hurt sound welling in the back of his throat out, burying his face into Imre's chest.

"I'm sorry," Imre murmured. "That was tactless of me."

Luca muttered. "You were having a right fucking fun time there, weren't you?"

"I let relaxation make my tongue loose." Imre nuzzled his cheek. "But I thought you wouldn't want to talk to him further on the matter."

"You thought bloody fucking right." Luca pushed himself up and glared at Imre. "I wasn't ready to tell him I'm moving out."

"When did you intend to tell him?"

"When I had a lease and was already packed?" Luca winced, hanging his head, and slumped against Imre. Dandelion curled between them, making a warren out of the space between their bodies. "I'm not mad at you, not really," he murmured with a sigh. "I just don't know how to handle this." He wrinkled his nose. "He was really mad, wasn't he?"

"Rather perturbed, yes. I can't say I understand why."

"That makes two of us."

Luca twined his arms around Imre's neck, turning his head to nose into his throat, breathing in his scent—stone and steel and hay and clover and warmth, a sunlit day baked into bronzed flesh even in the dead of winter.

"I don't want to talk about him right now, Imre," he whispered. "I don't want his shadow hanging over our heads for my last time here."

There was no mistaking the jerk of Imre's shoulders, the haggard, hurt sound, the way his arms tightened around Luca. "Then what do you want, for your last time here?"

You know what I want. You've known what I want, but we never talk about it.

We just act like it's not there, like this is really okay.

He swallowed thickly, lifting his head, resting his brow to Imre's and curling his fingers in the silver and iron flow of his thick, lush beard, stroking deep, down to his jaw.

"To be as close to you as I can." He pressed his mouth to the soft dip of flesh just below Imre's lower lip, trailing to the corner of his mouth. "Be with me, Imre. As close as we can be."

Imre groaned, caught Luca up in a kiss like falling from the tallest mountains, dropping through the clouds toward a crash that didn't have to hurt as long as Luca closed his eyes and pretended he couldn't see it coming. A thick hand slipped between them, Dandelion's tiny weight gently lifted aside, and then the world was spinning and falling away as strong arms lifted Luca up. He caught a glimpse of the rabbit kit burrowing in with the dogs before the fire, before he closed his eyes again and nuzzled into Imre, clinging tight.

Imre carried him toward the stairs, quiet intent in every step, promise in the tightness of his hold. "Is that really all you want of me, angyalka?" he whispered hoarsely. Under Luca's palm, his heart beat sharp and erratic.

Luca only clung tighter, his body aching for the touch and taste and Imre, his heart aching that touch and taste alone could never be enough.

"Don't let me crash," was all he said, fingers digging in where he clutched. "All I want is that you…that you don't let me fall."

75

IMRE LAY AWAKE, WATCHING LUCA sleep with the faint blue light of moonglow on snow filtering through the windows to play over the soft lines of his cheek, the sharper knife edge of his jaw. In sleep that stubborn jaw was relaxed, his lips parted. His skin still gleamed with a fine mist of sweat, shining and as soft as it had been when that sweat had dripped down the channel of his spine and pooled there until Imre licked away its salt taste and shuddered as Luca made those soft, breathlessly needy sounds just for him.

Luca shivered, his brows knitting together, and curled in on himself. Imre pulled the blankets up higher, covering his naked shoulders and drawing that slim body into his arms, wrapping his warmth around him. He could protect him from the cold, from the dark, from all the little things…

But he couldn't protect him from whatever was riding him now, whatever made him strange and quiet and desperate and scared as he clung to Imre while their bodies plunged together, cresting and falling and tangling and knotting while Luca held on as if his small, soft touch could hold Imre in one piece.

He'd been so different, tonight. Trembling as if on the verge of tears, rushed and needy, wearing himself out only to collapse against Imre in a sleepy tangle with that tight heat still locked around Imre's cock and their bodies slicked together with a thin film of heat. Imre had waited until he was almost fully asleep to separate their bodies, soothing Luca's soft cry with slow touches until his little cat drifted into sleep.

He nosed into that soft, dark hair, breathing in the scent they made together—sex and soft quiet male musk and honeysuckle and something that was just *them*, just *right*.

"What are you afraid of, my angyalka?" he whispered. "What have I done, by giving you what you desired?"

He'd thought Luca was fully asleep, too far gone to hear him. But after a few moments he stirred with a soft, sleepy noise, looking over his shoulder at Imre through hazed eyes. "Mnh…? What was that?"

"Nothing." Imre smiled faintly and smoothed Luca's hair back. "Go to sleep, angyalka."

Luca yawned, wide and deep, then slumped down again, pillowing his head against Imre's outstretched arm, cool hair spilling in sweat-damp tangles against Imre's skin.

"Don't wanna. It's only…what…eight?"

"Around then, yes."

"Only old men go to bed at eight."

Imre closed his eyes against the rough, raw pain of that. "I am an old man, angyalka."

Luca tensed—subtle yet noticeable, when they were all skin and languid tangles and nothing else. "…you're not that old."

Old enough, Imre thought, but said nothing and only hoped Luca would sleep.

Sleep, and wake less troubled.

Luca remained quiet in his arms, but it wasn't hard to tell from his stillness, from the hard line his shoulders made, that he wasn't asleep. Imre pressed kiss after kiss over his shoulder, tasting the echo of sweat on his skin, breathing him in, silently asking with each touch of lips to flesh:

Talk to me.

Tell me what burdens you so heavily, my angel.

I will not force you…but please, talk to me.

Luca pulled away for a moment—but only to shift onto his back, skin hissing against the sheets as he twisted and settled, looking up at Imre. Clear green eyes studied him searchingly, and Imre wondered what Luca saw.

Perhaps someone who could even half hope to live up to the ideals Luca set for him.

Or perhaps just a washed-up, fading old man.

Luca pressed his reddened, kiss-swollen lips together and ventured quietly, "If I'm to apprentice with Mira, then…"

Then you'll be here, Imre filled in, and tried to ignore the painful, clutching squeeze of his heart. He couldn't. He *couldn't*. He'd set limits for a reason, and yet the thought of Luca alone in Harrogate, living his life as if Imre had never touched it, moving beyond him, without him, maybe *with* someone else…

It was only right. At Imre's age, he couldn't offer Luca more than half a lifetime, instead of the rest of their lives.

He couldn't hold Luca back that way.

But he couldn't look at him, either, dropping his gaze to the bridge of Luca's nose as he asked softly, "Then what?"

"Nothing." Luca shifted in Imre's arms, giving him his back, tucking into the curve of his body. "It's nothing."

Imre lifted his gaze, watching him. But Luca had closed his eyes, and if he wanted to feign sleep…

Sighing, Imre closed his eyes and pressed his brow to the back of Luca's neck, holding him close. They weren't any better than they were before, letting each other have their careful evasions and deflections while everything they didn't say slipped through their fingers.

Soon, he told himself.

He would have this conversation soon. Sit Luca down and not let either of them avoid it. When it was a choice, rather than the last things they said to each other as Luca stepped on the train back to Sheffield.

But *Ask me*, he begged silently, as he breathed in Luca's scent until it filled his throat and made it close, drawing tight.

If you ask me, I cannot say no to you. I could never say no to you.

But I cannot bring myself to something you will not ask.

76

THE NEXT FEW DAYS CAUGHT them up in the house, trapped and buried under once more. Luca had thought the snow had blown out, but after a clear, quiet Christmas and a day after, the clouds came down low again and spat their howling breaths over the farm.

Luca had been fine bundling up in the house, venturing out only to shove through that sloughing whiteout emptiness to check the animals in their barns. It was routine now and didn't even frighten him, though when he and Imre roped themselves together to check the bees, he always double and triple-checked every knot with his own two hands before he let Imre walk away from him.

He'd taken the idle time to try to train Dandelion to do tricks, but he might as well try to teach a cat. Luca sprawled in front of the living room fireplace, Vila and Seti flanked to either side—both dogs watching the treat he held between his fingertips intently, both dogs holding perfectly still. He lifted the little treat over Dandelion, trying to coax her to sit up on her hind legs.

She flopped her head, twitched her nose, and promptly bit down on the sleeve of the henley he'd pilfered from Imre, gnawing it between her front teeth.

Luca laughed, tugging back. "Oy, you. That's not food."

Imre laughed without even looking up from his book, stretched out on the couch with his reading glasses perched on his nose. "You'll never train her. Not like that."

"I've seen other people do it! People have their buns do tricks on YouTube."

"Then maybe you need a better incentive."

"It's alfalfa. Isn't that what they like?"

"She's a baby. She'd want something a bit closer to what her growing body needs. Babies have different nutritional requirem—" Imre stopped, brows knitting. He tugged his glasses off, looking toward the window, the arm of the glasses slipping between his teeth. "…huh."

Luca pushed himself up on his arms. "What is it?"

"Listen."

He cocked his head, frowning. "I don't hear anything."

"Exactly."

Then Luca understood what he meant: he didn't hear *anything*. Not the whistle of the wind, not its deeper, hoarser blow farther off, or the rattle of the eaves. Not even the soft *flump* of accumulated snow collapsing under its own weight and tumbling down from the roof to pile against the house.

Luca tumbled to his feet and to the window. Outside, the snow had stilled to leave a fresh sea of pure white, smooth as powder and rolling in dunes. The setting sun crowned each peak in shimmers of pink and gold, nearly blinding; Luca winced, shading his eyes with one hand and grinning.

"Bloody hell, I'd forgotten what sunlight even looks like."

Imre drifted to his side and folded his arms on the windowsill, leaning his shoulder against Luca's. "Just in time for the sun to go down."

"Just in time for the new year." It hadn't even clicked what day it was until he'd seen the sky, a clear glassy blue that, somewhere close by, would be lit up in bursts of fire against the dark fairly soon. He bounced on the balls of his toes. "Can we see if there'll be fireworks in Scarborough tonight? It's only an hour or so away, and it'd be lovely over the ocean."

Imre stiffened, his shoulder going hard against Luca's arm; even though he hadn't drawn away, it felt as though his warmth had been walled off behind glass. "I don't know, angyalka," he said, slow and careful. "It may not be wise."

"Why not?"

"People who see us together might talk."

"And? Scarborough's full of strangers. And I'm twenty, not twelve. Let them talk." Luca stared at Imre, hurt a tight and awful thing trying to fill him up so full it crowded out everything else, all his breath and blood and bone and silent, petrified heart. "You're ashamed to be seen in public with me."

"No!" Imre pushed himself up, straightening fully, hands flexing in helpless fists at his sides. "I simply…" He exhaled, raking his hair from his face, looking at Luca pleadingly. "I don't want to make life difficult for you, Luca. That's all."

God…fucking *damn* it.

Nothing had changed, had it?

Even now, Imre was just following the path of least resistance. The *safest* path. He didn't really want to be with Luca; he'd just gotten tired of fighting with him about it.

And in this moment, as Luca looked at the man he'd loved for his entire fucking life, he saw not the gentle stone giant, not the great graven god of earth and clay…

But a coward.

And he couldn't stand it. He couldn't stand to see Imre that way, when he needed Imre to be the one thing in his life that was as pure and good and honourable as he had always been.

“How is it difficult to go about in public with the man I’m—fuck, can we even really call it dating?” he bit off. “What should I call you? The man I’m fucking?”

Imre stopped so entirely that he seemed to stop breathing. His voice was a low, strained rasp when he spoke. “That’s painful, Luca.”

“Yeah. Yeah, it really is.” Everything that had been boiling up in Luca’s chest for weeks built to a volcanic head, swelling until he trembled with the effort to keep it inside. “But when you look at it in the cold light of day that’s pretty much all it is, isn’t it? Fucking because we’re trapped here together. Is that all it is to you?”

“Never.” Imre watched him steadily, almost sadly. “Angyalka. Please don’t be cruel.”

“I’m sorry, I just…I just…” Luca couldn’t meet those stark, wounded eyes. He felt like that cruel child in the Land Rover all over again, snapping at Imre to shut the fuck up, and he dragged his gaze away to glare out the window, forcing words past his knotted throat. “I’m just asking myself questions, that’s all.”

Imre’s warmth moved closer, but didn’t quite touch. “What kind of questions?”

“This…you just…” He shut his eyes against their blurring, burning. He couldn’t do this to himself, but couldn’t stop. Might as well clear the air once and for all. “You said you can’t touch people or sleep with them unless you’re—unless you really care for them, right?”

“Yes,” Imre answered softly, yet the neutrality in his voice might as well be a knife slid between Luca’s ribs. He dug his fingers against the windowsill.

“But…you touch me. You sleep with me.”

“I do,” Imre said.

And nothing else.

No quiet explanation of what he meant. No promise that Luca *meant* something to him.

Any idea that he would was just a childish daydream.

He opened his eyes—to the sight of Imre's back, walking away, shoulders stiff.

Luca's gut twisted. He clutched his fingers against his shirt, stepping after Imre, stopping.

"Imre…?"

Imre stopped. A powerful knot of tension rippled down his back. "I'm making supper."

"*Supper?*" Luca's voice cracked. *He* nearly cracked, right in half. "How can you say that to me and then brush it off with supper?"

But Imre was already walking away again.

"Imre!"

"Luca." Stopping again, Imre turned one weary eye over his shoulder. "Let it lie. Please."

"No!"

Before he could stop himself, he thrust himself forward, interjecting himself into Imre's path and glaring up at him, just a blur of bronze and blue and steel through the haze of tears.

"No, I won't let it lie," Luca rasped out. "Do you have any idea how much I *hate* this?" He drew in a ragged breath, choking on the taste of his own tears. "But I can't quit. I can't quit, because I love you." It hurt how easy it came out, this raw horrible truth between them, this truth Luca had been living since day one and trying to deny. "And you're supposed to be the one who can't live without love, but you're here fucking me and telling me there's a lease on it, and when that lease expires I'm fucking evicted."

Imre's eyes hardened, flinty. He parted his lips, but Luca cut him off with a shake of his head and a laugh that felt like swallowing shards of broken glass.

"No," Luca said. "I get it. My dad means everything to you, and I'm just secondary. You'll throw me away to keep him even though the first time he bothered picking up the phone to remember you're *alive* is to dump his problems at your door."

Imre's jaw tightened. "If you want to talk, we'll talk. If you simply want to say things to be pointedly hurtful, I have no intention of indulging that."

"Of course you don't. Perfect, patient Imre."

The worst part was that he could *see* the anger behind Imre's careful, stony façade, and Luca wanted it. He *wanted* it, because if he couldn't have Imre's love he'd have something out of him, something that said Luca affected him—and Luca didn't want to be that way, but he couldn't stop the small awful cruelties that just…

Just wanted to feel loved.

He shook his head, backing away. "I'm not patient like you. I'm *not.* I'm not made of the same stuff you are. And I'm tired of being everyone's problem to shuffle back and forth. I'd rather go it on my own than just be bounced between the two of you. I *need* to." He tore his gaze from Imre, wrapping his arms around himself, trying to catch enough of his raw edges to hold himself together and seal the wounds he was ripping open in himself. "I need to stand on my own two feet, Imre. And this isn't doing it."

"Luca…"

No. *No.* He wasn't giving in to the gentle pleading in that voice. Not this time. He turned away, giving Imre his back. "You asked me if I understood the situation," he choked out. "You never asked if I'm happy about it."

"I know you're not."

"But you never let me say that for myself." Luca dug his fingers into the sleeves of his shirt. Of Imre's shirt, even now wrapping him up in the scent and warmth of the man he loved who was too much of a fucking coward to love him back. "I love that you know me so well that sometimes I don't need to say anything. But sometimes I need to talk. And sometimes I need to be heard."

Imre's soft footsteps drew closer, before his hand touched lightly to Luca's shoulder. "I'm listening."

"No, you're not." Luca jerked away from that touch, jerked away from Imre, and moved quickly toward the stairs. He needed to get away before he did something daft, and before Imre tried to stop him. "I need some space. I'm going in to town."

"On foot?"

"Funny how I've toughened up out here."

Imre sighed, slow and deep. "If you wish."

Luca paused at the foot of the stairs, gripping hard at the railing, and closed his eyes. "…yeah. Of course that's all you'll say."

"What do you want me to say, Luca?" Imre asked, a sharp, almost helpless edge in his voice. "If you want to go, I won't fight you. If you want space, you deserve space. If you only said that to goad a reaction from me, I refuse to play such games."

Those words sank as deep as gunshots to the gut, blooming pain.

"No," Luca said. "I didn't. I meant it. Because I really don't want to be around you when you condescend to me this way."

Then, before Imre could stop him, he ran upstairs to change.

Because he couldn't stand to be in this house a minute longer, with its lies that made it feel like home.

77

IMRE STOOD FROZEN AT THE foot of the stairs, watching as Luca disappeared around the bend in the stairwell. He was bleeding inside—bleeding from a thousand cuts sliced by every razor-edged word. His angyalka didn't even know how easily he could plunge his hands into Imre's chest, grasp his heart, and squeeze it raw and bloody between bruising fingers.

How could he know, when Imre had never told him?

I can't quit, because I love you.

Over ten years since Luca had said those words to his face, rather than whispered in a secret dark.

And they'd been used to cut him open, and leave him dying from heartbreak.

He wanted to chase that maddening little cat upstairs, take him in his arms, shake him, kiss him until his lips no longer tasted like poison. He wanted to run from the house, plunge himself into the snow until he was numb and could no longer feel this. He wanted—he didn't bloody well know, but it kept him frozen, watching the stairs, locked in indecision and cursing himself for the most muleheaded bastard on the planet.

Within minutes Luca appeared at the stop of the stairs again, fully dressed and bundled up in layers of black, his hoodie drawn up and his earbuds dangling in his fingers as he fought them, glaring down at them with wet, gleaming, red-rimmed eyes. He clattered down a few steps, stopped on the fifth in a wooden scream of protest, jerked his head up, stared at Imre.

Then ducked his head and shoved past him, long, tense strides taking him toward the door in an angry jingle of zippers.

Imre found the will to move again, lunging after him, catching his arm gently. “Luca, don’t go. Not like this.”

Luca ripped violently from his grip, rounding on him with a fury that gave him a colour and fire Imre had never seen. “No. We’re not doing things your way this time. We’re not doing things the slow, quiet way. I’m angry and I want to fucking hate you and I can’t, so you’re going to leave me the fuck alone and let me be angry until I don’t want to hate you anymore.”

Imre let his hand fall, staring at Luca. That cavernous, horrible ache in his chest expanded, filling with echoes, reverberations that quivered louder and louder, harder and harder, until he thought they would shake him apart.

“Perhaps,” he dragged out, barely finding more than a whisper of sound crouching in the back of his throat, “it would be best if you hated me.”

“Fuck you for that, Imre.” Luca’s gaze kindled, smouldered, his jaw set in a stubborn line. “Don’t you understand that I fucking love you? How can you not see that? It’s not just some childish crush. If it was a crush I’d have given up after every time you told me you couldn’t because you still see me as a kid and all you care about is Dad. If it was a crush it would’ve gotten wiped out over ten fucking years without ever seeing your face. It’s not a crush, Imre.” He lifted his chin, staring Imre down almost challengingly, pale skin over that steel that had grown when Imre wasn’t looking, the backbone of a man who…

Who knew what he wanted, better than Imre knew himself.

"It's love, Imre," Luca said firmly. "It's real."

"You can't know that. You're only—"

"Twenty," Luca filled in flatly. "And twenty is old enough to figure out what I want to do with my life, but not old enough to know I love you, right?" He smiled—a bitter, hurting thing that never belonged on those pretty lips. "I was old enough to know that when I was five. And it was just as real then."

"And if you stay. If you love me." Imre clenched his fist, struggling. Struggling to explain the fear crouching on his heart, this horrid little demon digging its fingers into its walls and squeezing its every beat flat. "And then in a year or ten years, you realize that who you are is changing as you grow older, what you want is changing as you grow older…" Imre sucked in a shaky breath. "I don't want to be the mistake you regret when you realize you want something else, angyalka."

Luca stared at him, a strange expression on his face, wide-eyed and stricken. "You really just said that to me," he whispered, only to trail into a hiss. "You arsehole." He lit up again, crackling and bright with a snap of temper like a struck match, one hand flinging out in a gesture so sharp it rocked his entire body. "You fucking *arsehole!* You don't hit some magic age where you stop changing. People are always changing. You're changing. So maybe in a year or ten years you'll realize you don't want me, how is that any different?"

I'll never not want you!

"I wouldn't—"

"Of course you wouldn't. Because you don't really want me. Not that way." Tears spilled freely down Luca's lashes, coursed over his cheeks dripped from his jaw. "You're a liar." He swallowed hard, sniffling, then scrubbed his knuckles roughly against his nose. "You're a *liar!* You said all those pretty things about not being able to fuck someone unless you were in love with them, then you just…just…" He shook his head, lips trembling. "What? Was it a midlife crisis fuck? Was that all it was? You *liar*."

"Luca." Imre stepped quickly closer. He couldn't stand this, couldn't stand that his clumsy words were doing this, because he didn't know how to deal with conflict. Not like this, not when Imre moved slow and Luca was wildfire, and that wildfire was slipping through his grasp, burning his fingers every time he tried to grasp it. But still he caught Luca's arms, dragging him close, wanting to show him—to *show* him— "Luca, stop. Please. Let me—"

Luca shoved back so violently Imre had no choice but to let him go.

"Get away from me," Luca snapped out, low and even and sharp with finality. "Don't you touch me. Don't you ever fucking touch me again. Just leave me alone."

He ripped back out of Imre's reach, flung him one last glare, then yanked the kitchen door open and stalked out into the snow.

"*Luca!*" Imre cried.

But the door only slammed after him, cutting Imre off as he started after him.

Luca was gone.

78

IMRE SANK DOWN ON THE sofa and buried his face in his hands. Everything in him was screaming at him to go after Luca, stop him, make this right, but Luca had said *don't you touch me, don't you ever fucking touch me.*

And Imre wasn't going to make this worse by trying to force anything on Luca.

God, he hoped when Luca had cooled down they could talk this out. At the very least Imre could say he was sorry, and see if Luca was willing to listen. He just—he—

He'd blown this to hell and back.

And maybe Luca was right about him, if he was so weak he couldn't say *no* to a pretty young man but wouldn't say *yes*, either.

He sprawled back against sofa, staring up at the ceiling, rubbing at the ache in his chest where it felt as though a crack had been seamed down his papier-mâché shell, splitting him open and laying him vulnerable and bare and so easily broken…and waited.

He would wait as long as it took for Luca to come back.

To make this right.

But as the long shadows crawled through the windows to spread across the room, that sick ache of loss in his chest twisted into a nagging, frightened suspicion. Luca wouldn't really go into town. Would he? The snow was calf deep, the road buried under the top cover, and…

And Luca was a stubborn little cat Imre had driven out into the snow because he couldn't face the possibilities in every word Luca said.

Growling under his breath, Imre dug into his pocket for his phone and tapped Luca's contact before lifting it to his ear.

It rang and rang and rang, then went to voicemail without ever picking up.

Imre swore and tried again. He was a fucking arsehole. Luca could be out there buried in a snow dune and frostbitten. And when the phone went right to voicemail again, his heart turned colder than the snow, frozen in an icy cage of fear. He stared at the mantle, and at the delicate cage of slender clover stems more fragile and precious than threads of blown glass.

"Please answer, angyalka," Imre whispered into the phone. "You don't have to want to talk to me, but just let me know you're all right. I—" He balked on the words, large and jabbing their edges against the insides of his throat. "—I'm frightened."

He let the voicemail hang up, then fumbled out a text. Just one word.

Please.

But his phone remained silent, not even the buzz of a new message.

He dragged his hand over his face, blinking back the sting of frustration burning behind his eyes, then swearing under his breath and thrusting to his feet so hard the dogs and bunny started in their fireplace sprawl. He worked his jaw, hesitating for only a moment before beckoning to Vila with a sharp command. "Come."

She immediately bounced eagerly to her feet, intelligent golden eyes watching him inquisitively. He fumbled for something that would smell like Luca, and came up with a t-shirt that had been discarded and lost between the cushions when they'd torn at each other's clothing before dragging each other upstairs yet again, the memory momentarily grabbing at him hard and squeezing him so tight he couldn't breathe.

Luca golden in the lamplight and firelight, that pale skin turned to honey and amber, as glazed as his darkened, dilated eyes. Luca looking up at Imre with so much more than lust in his gaze, reaching for him with so much longing, holding fast through every moment and letting Imre take him again and again through every pleasure, every touch, every craving, every need when it had never been about sex. Never been about desire. Never been about flesh.

It had been about that moment when they knew only each other—when the world fell away, fell apart, crumbled to nothing and there was only dust and stars and the wheel and turn of the sky, binding them as one.

He curled Luca's shirt against his chest, closing his eyes, then knelt and gave it to Vila to sniff. Then he stood, shoved his feet into his boots, dragged on a coat, and clipped a leash to Vila's collar before heading out into the twilight snow.

Luca's path marked a clear trail, leading across the side yard and around the curve of the hill toward the road, footsteps crisp-edged as if he'd been stomping, lifting his feet high. Vila sniffed and nosed at the prints in the snow, straining at the leash, dragging Imre forward. He followed, heart in his throat, churning up snow in the wake of Vila's swishing tail as she whined and dragged him to the roadside.

Where Luca's footprints ended.

But the tracks of tyres stretched in either direction, cutting furrows in the snow.

Luca's footprints changed direction here, right next to a set of tyre tracks—as if he'd stopped, turned. One had a flaked edge, kicked as his foot had angled as he'd pulled it from the snow and up into a vehicle.

Imre closed his eyes, forcing himself to breathe slowly. Luca must have hitchhiked into town. Which meant he could be anywhere in Harrogate, but at least he wasn't off in the snow somewhere, lost and disoriented and unable to find a way back.

Imre detoured back just long enough to let Vila back in the house, feeding her a few treats for her troubles, before he locked up and slid into the Land Rover. Just a few minutes to let the engine warm up and the ice melt were a few minutes too long, and by the time the car was ready it took everything in him not to slam his foot on the gas and churn forward through the snow at breakneck, dangerous speeds.

He didn't know why he was suddenly so afraid. Luca could handle himself in Harrogate, was probably in a pub already nose-deep in a pint and calling Imre every name in the book.

It wasn't Luca's safety he feared for.

It was that Luca had meant it. *Don't ever touch me again.*

And if Imre didn't do something to make this right, Luca was never coming home to Lohere again.

79

HE MADE THE DRIVE INTO town in record time, slowing only when he saw the slightest shape in the dark, letting the headlights sweep over the snow to be sure it wasn't Luca abandoned on the side of the road and trudging his way home.

No Luca.

Just lonely trees, bales of hay, fence posts, weathered logs.

Fuck.

The streets of Harrogate were clear of snow, at least, the traffic light. People moved down the pavement in their winter coats, leaning close to each other, murmuring between them with warm familiarity. They looked so *happy*, Imre thought. Excited. Full of promise. He'd bloody well forgotten it was the new year, but the air swelled with portent, with joy, as if it would burst and fill the sky up with the collective lights of a thousand people's wishes.

Their joy only made the biting teeth of his fear more painful, as he cruised street after street looking for a familiar angry stride and shock of dark hair.

Nothing. He'd canvas every shop, every pub if he had to, but Harrogate wasn't a small town and he was better off looking for places Luca was likely to be. The only few popular gay pubs nearby were in Leeds, and the idea of Luca in one of those dark, soft-lit dives, other men slinking their greedy eyes over that catlike stride and wondering if he could belong to them for just one night… Imre's grip tightened on the steering wheel, his knuckles straining, before he let out a broken, self-mocking laugh.

Fuck. He was too much of a fucking knob to make Luca truly his, but he could bloody well get jealous over imaginary men easily enough, couldn't he?

He stopped in traffic at a red light, staring blankly at the faint spangles of Christmas lights still tangled in the roadside trees, at the small flecks of snow that were just beginning to wisp and swirl downward again. He loved Luca, didn't he?

Fuck.

He truly and honestly fucking *loved* Luca, deeper than this passing daydream they'd made for themselves.

Xav t'jo ilo. I eat your heart.

Because love was so needy, so voracious, so complete that it wouldn't be satisfied until it had consumed its object entirely. Until they had been taken in, made a part of body, blood, and soul, a piece of him so inseparable that even if Luca never came back, he would always live inside Imre, haunting him with what he'd been stubborn enough to let go.

He wasn't gone, he told himself. Not yet.

And he had an idea of where he might go first, if nowhere else.

The light changed and he spun the wheel, taking a U-turn at the next intersection. Street signs led him on, only traffic slowing his momentum, and with every puttering station wagon or little compact car that cut in front of him he ground his teeth harder and harder, digging his fingers against the steering wheel, swearing under his breath when he'd never been an angry driver a single day in his life.

Mira's house was off a lane at the edge of town, where the look of a city began to blend into the look of a farm town, houses along the outskirts often framed by smaller pastures. Mira's tall white frame house was old, with that pleasantly comfortable ricketiness, a barn of natural pine wood out back framed by trees and set against a glimpse of open field.

The lights were on in the front windows. Imre's heart beat harder as he pulled the Land Rover into the drive, crossed himself, and stepped out.

Mira answered on the third knock, fresh-dusted with snow and still unwinding her scarf, her tall snow boots pulled up over tights under her skirt and coat. She lit up with a warm, surprised smile.

"Imre," she said. "I'd not expected to see you."

"I'm sorry—I'm sorry to bother you on New Year's Eve," he said, and tried not to be obvious about craning ever-so-rudely to peer past her into the house.

She blinked. "Whatever's the matter? I've never seen you so mussed up."

"Luca," he ground out. "He left. Hitchhiked to town. And…" He made himself stop, really *see* her. The coat. The snow dotting her braids, her shoulders. The scarf clutched in her gloved fingers. He closed his eyes, sagging. "…and he's not here."

"I've not even been here, but I might have seen him." She touched Imre's arm gently. "I wasn't even sure it was him, at first. He blew past me without even stopping."

Oh thank God—at the very least, confirmation that Luca had been in one piece not too long ago. Now Imre just had to figure out where he'd gone, impossible as that may be. He took a deep breath and squared his shoulders. He wouldn't quit that easily. Quitting too easily, backing away from things, had made Luca look at him as though he'd somehow betrayed who he was supposed to be. Who he'd always prided himself on being.

Who he'd failed to be, when Luca needed him.

"Where did you see him?" he asked.

"Bus station."

"How long ago?"

Mira clucked her tongue. "It's been an hour, maybe two."

"And you didn't see where he was going?"

"I didn't get the chance to stop him." She tilted her head, dark eyes warm with concern, with sympathy. "What happened, Imre?"

Imre looked down at her. He hadn't realized how cold he was until the warmth of her hand burning through his coat, making him feel the chill of the snow, the night, Luca's absence down to his bones. "You told me to be careful," he said thickly. "I wasn't careful enough."

"Maybe you were too careful." Mira smiled, sweet and sad and understanding. "How much do you love that pretty thing, Imre?"

"So much that I can't breathe for it," he admitted rawly. "I don't know what I'm doing, Mira. I've never known what I'm doing, and now that's hurt him."

"Then you'd best find him and fix it."

"I don't know where he is."

"If you love him, you know him. Where would he go?"

Imre closed his eyes, trying to think. Lohere was everything Luca loved about Harrogate, but he'd loved the market too—but the market was closed for the new year. There were people gathering in the main town square to watch the fireworks…

Fireworks.

He opened his eyes. "He wanted to see the fireworks over the water at Scarborough tonight. We fought about it."

Mira chuckled and patted his arm indulgently. "That's a start." She stepped back, then, tossing her head. "Come in and warm up? The fireworks won't start for a while yet."

"I can't." He scrubbed his hands on his thighs, shaking his head, a sudden and restless agitation *pulling* at him. A need to be where Luca was, wherever that might be. "I have to go, Mira."

"Of course you do." She laughed, flapping her hands at him. "Go, you towering git. Get gone. And Imre?"

"Aye?"

"Tell that boy you love him, when you find him."

"I will," Imre promised.

If it wasn't already too late.

80

THE OCEAN AIR SMELLED LIKE brine and gunpowder, stinging Luca's nose.

That was why his eyes wouldn't stop prickling, he told himself. That was why his breaths burned. It was just the cold air, the smell, the sting of gunpowder from the floats out over the water, preparing for the new year and a light show that suddenly didn't seem worth shattering the last happy moments of his life.

He'd been out here for hours, watching as the sky turned from streaks of twilight marked with golden-edged clouds to a soft and pillowy purpled dark, then a deep and even blue dotted with stars. At least there wasn't too much cloud cover tonight, he thought wistfully. Nothing to ruin the fireworks.

Nothing but the fact that Imre wasn't here.

He sat on the sandy beach at Scarborough, hugging his knees against his chest, and stared out over the water blankly. He didn't care what he saw as long as he didn't look left or right at the happy families building bonfires or the couples leaning on each other, perched on their blankets together and whispering in the sweet and quiet dark. Everyone here was *with* someone, here to make a promise with the new year that what they were doing in this moment would be what they would want for the rest of their year, maybe the rest of their lives.

Was this what Luca wanted, then, for the rest of his year, the rest of his life?

Bitter and freezing and huddled alone, struggling not to cry just because Imre had confirmed what Luca had known all along?

He'd known what he was getting into. He *had.* It had always been temporary. A fantasy.

It had only gone wrong when he'd broken the fantasy and tried to force it to be real.

Fucking arsehole.

Fucking arsehole, going and falling in love with Imre for real.

Choking back a hiccup, he tilted his head back and looked up at the sky, picking out stars like he had when Imre had made stars on the ceiling. He guessed it was over now. He'd go back to get his things, and then Imre would ship him back to Sheffield and his father. There'd be a minute of confrontation, stiff disapproval, then Luca would stalk out of the house and go hide in Xav's dorm room until he could get a job and his own place.

And just like that, the last things holding Luca's life, his family, together would be over.

It had to happen sooner or later.

"Luca?"

Luca stiffened, his breaths stilling. He couldn't…that couldn't be Imre. He'd never told Imre where he was going, and even if he had, he'd torn Imre apart and then stormed off like a child, Imre would never—

"*Luca.*"

Scuff of footsteps on sand—and then Imre was *there*, wrapping Luca up, drowning him in every scent and heat and impression, dragging him into his arms with a choked, aching sound that tore Luca's heart like so much tissue paper as he suddenly, strangely, found himself enveloped in Imre, in everything beloved that made the world right.

He couldn't believe it.

He couldn't believe it, and with a hoarse, ragged sob as the bubble of pain in his chest burst, he buried himself into Imre and dug his fingers into his jacket and held on tight. "*Imre*. You came—you *came*—"

"You scared the bloody shite out of me," Imre gasped roughly, his hold so tight it *hurt*. Luca didn't *care*.

Imre had come for him. Imre was *here*.

Imre drew back enough to look down at him. He looked a haggard mess, his beard wild, his eyes red-rimmed and stark, his hair windblown and tangled. Darkened eyes flicked over Luca's face. "I've been looking for you high and low—I looked all over Harrogate, all over Scarborough—I texted your father, I called the bloody police! What were you thinking?"

"I—I—"

He didn't get to answer, as Imre swept him up into a kiss so fierce and desperate it melted the cold from Luca's bones and lit a fire inside him that would never die no matter how he tried to quell it, how he tried to smother it to nothing but the ash and embers of memories that should never be rekindled again.

Don't, he thought desperately. *Don't do this to me.*

Yet he couldn't pull away. Not when he needed Imre's kiss; not when he needed to know Imre *cared*, needed to know that even if this wasn't love it was *something*, it *mattered*, that these days that had meant everything to Luca wouldn't fade from Imre's memory as easily as the turning of the seasons, moving on and left behind.

And God, when Imre kissed him like this—deep, consuming, desperate, as ravenous as if he would devour Luca whole—he could almost believe it. Could almost believe he was as deep inside Imre as Imre was inside him, when he tasted salt on their trembling, mated lips and wasn't entirely certain those tears were his own.

He broke back when breath failed him, when his heart threatened to shudder to a halt, panting raggedly, brokenly, as he leaned into Imre and clung as hard as he could. "I'm sorry," he whispered. "I never should have run off, I shouldn't have been so awful and scared you—"

"I called," Imre rasped. "I called and called, why didn't you pick up?"

Luca winced. "…my phone died on the bus. I…I was listening to my music."

"Of course you were." Imre's lips creased in a pained smile, and he pulled Luca into him harder, gathering him into his lap. "If something had happened to you…"

"Imre…Imre, I…" He couldn't seem to stop touching over Imre's face, the trimmed edge of his beard beneath the saber thrust of his cheekbones, the wet trails glistening on his skin, the weathered lines creasing around his eyes and ridging between his brows. Familiar, beloved, just reminding himself desperately that Imre was *here*. "I'm sorry. I was upset, I wasn't thinking, I…I didn't think if I took off, you'd get in trouble with Dad."

Imre stilled. Naked hurt flashed so clearly across his features, as if it had been written in ink. "Is that why you think I'm upset?"

He cupped Luca's face in his palms, nearly dwarfing him, looking down at him with such intensity Luca couldn't stand it. That sheer unfiltered honesty was too much when it was turned on him with the full force of Imre's emotions, drowning him in them, pulling him into every raw ache in that penetrating gaze.

God, maybe he was lucky Imre couldn't love him.

Luca didn't know if he'd survive the sheer power of it, if he could.

"Luca. No," Imre said gently, and brushed heated lips to Luca's.

"Your father is my dearest and truest friend, and I dread the day he finds out what we've been about. But no. No." He shook his head, offering a faint, almost tentative smile. "I was afraid of losing you. Whether something had happened or you'd simply left, I was just afraid of losing you forever, angyalka."

"I'm sorry I got so mad." He dropped his gaze, shame making his cheeks hot, feeling as if his blush was captured against Imre's palms. "I feel like…like you see me as a child still, and…"

"Life would be easier if I could. But I've never been fond of the easy life." Imre coaxed him to look up, refusing to let him escape the dark depths of blue eyes. "I don't see you as a child, Luca. I've told you that. A young man, yes, but not a child. If I saw you as a child, I could not feel the way I do about you."

Don't make me ask, Luca pleaded. *Tell me something without making me ask. I can't take this anymore.*

But Imre was silent, something hesitant, almost frightened in his stillness. Something fragile, and it was then that Luca realized:

Imre was afraid to get his heart broken, too.

He swallowed roughly and brushed his fingertips to Imre's lips. His heart twisted itself inside out and right-side in again, struggling, labouring.

"How do you feel about me, Imre?" he whispered, and Imre closed his eyes with a groan kissing his fingertips.

"If I have not been so obvious in as many ways as I could, angyalka…then let me teach you a phrase in Romani."

Luca bit his lip, trembling. "Now? I…you can't even answer, I—"

A thick finger pressed to his lips gently. A warm smile flitted across Imre's lips, breaking that desperation, that hesitation. "This, I think, you will like. Xav t'jo ilo," he said slowly, then again, his husky voice lingering on the words as if he could feel them, taste them, sounding each one out carefully once and then again. "Xav t'jo ilo."

Luca tried, his tear-swollen lips and fumbling tongue clumsy. "Xav…xav tijo—"

"T'jo," Imre corrected gently, something thick and strange and aching in the word.

"Xav…t'jo…xav t'jo ilo."

Imre flushed deeply, a stark colour underneath his bronze skin. "Just so, angyalka," he murmured. "It sounds lovely on your lips."

"I…what did I say? What does it mean?"

"It means 'I eat your heart.'" Imre pressed his palm to Luca's chest, just over the wild sweet rabbit thump of his heart, a racing thing that fluttered and shivered against Luca's rib cage. "It means I love you."

Luca had to close his eyes again. He couldn't—he couldn't look at Imre or he'd break, he'd fall apart, those words etching on him like a tattoo. He'd never…thought Imre could, or *would*…not someone like Luca, useless and young and confused and just thrashing around making a mess of everything, and he was almost afraid to believe it because if it was real and true he'd want it so much he'd crush it trying to grasp on to it too much.

"You…you love me?"

"I have always loved you, in one way or another. It's simply changed, as you have changed." Even with Luca's eyes closed Imre was so overwhelming, surrounding him, cocooning him in warmth and the rumbling baritone of his voice, soft and coaxing and honest and sweet. "It's changed into something that consumes me, that demands I consume you. That is why we say 'I eat your heart.' Because love like this can devour all reason, all sense." His entire body shook with a deep, ragged sound, shaking Luca with him. "I am wild inside for you,

Luca. You're driving me mad, and I'm so afraid of hurting you—but I don't know how to let you go."

"Then let me stay," Luca pleaded, opening his eyes, looking up at Imre desperately. "How can you love me and just…just…if it's not about Dad, please…let me *stay*. I can't just walk away and move on like this never happened." He shook his head, struggling not to burst out sobbing. "I can't act like *you* never happened. It would break me."

But Imre faltered—a second's silence, but it might as well have clipped the strings of Luca's heart. "Luca…I don't know if I can."

"*Why?*" God he sounded such a right prat, but he didn't care. It wasn't fair. It wasn't *fair*, and he at least deserved to know why Imre had been jerking him around like this. "Why did you even come out here if it's just to tell me 'I love you, now shove off'?"

"That's not what it is!"

"Then tell me what it is." Luca set his jaw. "Tell me what you're afraid of."

"I…" Imre's grip loosened as he looked away, dragging his fingers through his hair. "I'm afraid of hurting you. In ways that only I can."

"Like you haven't been hurting me this entire time? Like I haven't been hurting *you?*"

"It's different." Imre's shoulders sagged. Weary eyes dragged back to Luca. "I'm twenty-six, nearly twenty-seven years your senior, Luca. One day, I'm going to *die*. And that day may seem far off now, but everything seems far off when you're twenty years old and the world is still new." There was something stark and desperate in his eyes, an open and bleeding wound. "What if I love you, Luca? What if I love you and keep you, only to leave you with nothing when your life's barely half over, and all you'll have to remember me by is those last feeble, decrepit years when I'm no good to you or anyone?"

Oh…oh that bloody *lunk.*

Suddenly Luca felt like the older one—older, tired, but God so much more sure of what he wanted than that haunted look in Imre's eyes would hint, even if Luca was just as raw and bleeding.

"Then I'll have those years to remember you by, instead of nothing at all," he said firmly, and found a smile from somewhere, even if it felt fragile as paper. "You can't know what will happen. You might live until you're a hundred and I'm seventy-something and wrinkled. Or I might get sick, or have an accident and die before you're even fifty. Something could happen to you tomorrow, or to me. So you can't look at one what-if and say that because of that one possibility, that I'll lose you before I even have a chance to get old, it's better to have nothing than to have weeks or years or *decades*." He threaded his fingers into Imre's hair, brushing it back shyly. "Nothing isn't better than something, Imre. I would live fifty years with the pain of losing you for just fifty days to *have* you."

Imre gasped out roughly, almost a sob, and pressed his cheek into Luca's palm, one heavy hand grasping at Luca's wrist and holding fast. "Luca…"

"Don't you *get* it?" Luca leaned into him, resting their brows together, breathing Imre in with everything in him. "How can you not understand how much I love you? How much I've always fucking loved you, you oversized rock?" He choked on a watery laugh. "I wasn't me, for all the time I've been away from Lohere. I've spent ten years growing up and that whole time, I wasn't me. I'm only me when I'm with you, and when I'm with you I'm everything I want to be." He kissed Imre's lips over and over again, stealing tastes of him between every word in case this was it, this was everything, this was the end and he would have to remember that taste for the rest of his life. "I love you. I love you so much I couldn't even see it because it's been a part of me so long it's like breathing, my heartbeat, the blood in my veins. I don't even need to do it consciously, I just…*do*. I don't realize I'm breathing until the breath's knocked out of me, and God, Imre…you take my breath away. You always have."

This was Luca's heart on the line, Luca's heart pulled out of him and offered to Imre in both hands, beating and bleeding and fragile. If their hearts were glass cages, Luca felt as if his must be burning so brightly, so blindingly, that it would set the world ablaze.

"Isn't there anything you love about being with me?" he begged softly, as he'd once begged *Isn't there anything about me that you could love? Even one thing?* "Anything at all?"

"Everything, Luca. Everything." Imre held him so close, so possessively. "You would not have my heart if I did not love you so, and every moment we are together."

"Then let me stay." Luca pressed himself into Imre as tightly as he could. "I'll do anything you want, just don't make me leave Lohere."

"Don't say it that way," Imre growled. "Don't say it like…like…"

"Like what?"

"Like you're only...how can you love someone if you're constantly begging for their approval? That's not love, Luca. It's…" Imre's brows drew together. "It's pain. It's nothing but pain, needing someone else so desperately you're afraid they'll thrust you away at the slightest provocation."

Luca smiled bitterly. "Won't you, though? You…you won't even let me stay…"

"No…I won't. And God, Luca, I'm so sorry if I've made you feel that way." Imre gathered him up as if he would hold all Luca's hurt, shattered pieces together in one place. "I'm not standing over you in judgment, waiting for you to balls everything up just because you're young and inexperienced. You don't stop making mistakes as you get older, angyalka." He laughed hoarsely. "I'm living bloody proof of that. You just…learn how to ride out the aftermath better, and rebuild from what you've broken. You're going to make mistakes. I am, too." Imre's expression was strange, almost wondering, his fingers gentle as they traced down Luca's cheek. "But a relationship isn't a relationship on uneven footing. I'm trying to meet you in the middle, not looking down from on high. If you want to stay with me…I need you to meet me, too."

If you want to stay with me.

Luca's entire body was one violent beating heart, shaking, throbbing. "Y-you…you want me to stay?"

Imre smiled—and even if it was raw with pain, with exhaustion, the emotion in it nearly cracked the last of Luca's fragile glass pieces to dust. "I want you to stay, angyalka. Damn Marco, damn what may come in ten years or twenty or fifty. I bloody well love you, Luca Ward, and I can't keep tormenting us both this way."

"*Imre.*"

Luca flung himself against Imre, laughing, hugging him so tight, clutching, clinging, he didn't even know where he was grasping, only that he needed to *hold on.* If he didn't he'd float away into the sky, explode over the night, bring in the new year with the fireworks of his heart, brighter than any moon or stars, brighter than the sun itself.

"Imre," he gasped again, his name a prayer baptised in tears, in laughter. "Imre, Imre, *Imre.*"

"Luca," Imre answered, only once, and yet the weight of it was crushing and enormous and wondrous and beautiful.

He didn't know when lips found lips. When they tangled up so close he could hardly tell one from the other, but it didn't matter. Luca sank into Imre wholeheartedly, willingly, yielding to every hard, breathless crush of Imre's lips, taking in kind when even if his heart had always belonged to Imre, Imre was just as much *his* and Luca wanted, needed, *craved* to leave the same kind of mark. He bit Imre's mouth until his lips tasted so sweet, so full, then licked and stroked and teased deeper, searching as if he could find the taste of Imre's love curled on his tongue like a drop of sweet clover honey, melting between them on every shared breath, shared caress, shared whisper of wordless things that needed no form to mean *everything*.

He was home.

Even sitting in the freezing cold on a beach in Scarborough…

As long as Imre was here with him, he was *home*.

Even when their lips parted, he couldn't speak. His throat was too tight, too full with emotion, and he only leaned into Imre, sheltering in the strength of his body, the firmness of his hold.

"Luca." Imre sighed his name, resting his chin to the top of Luca's head.

"Hm…?"

"Can you do that for me? Can you meet me halfway?"

"Mmn." Luca burrowed deeper into Imre. "I can try. I'm just…I'm afraid."

"What can I do to ease that fear, angyalka?"

"If you need time…I do, too."

God, he was more fucked up than he'd realized, when his chest stitched up tight in panic just at the thought of Imre looking at him like…like…

Like his parents looked at each other.

Glassy and not really seeing each other, looking through each other as if they were just dry bottles and everything they'd ever been to each other had spilled out a long time ago.

He swallowed, hunching into his shoulders. "I just…need time to believe you won't throw me out with the trash the second I fuck something up."

"Then I'll give you time, Luca," Imre said, and the quiet promise in his voice was everything Luca needed to ease that ache, that fear. "And I'll be here while you take that time. As long as you'll let me."

"Always, Imre. I'll always let you. Always need you."

Imre's gaze softened. "Always?"

"Yeah." Shyly, Luca pressed his lips to Imre's, stealing one more intoxicating kiss. "You're kind of a dick, Imre. But I love you."

"Lucky me." Soft words shaped against Luca's mouth, the pressure of a smile printed against his lips. "I love you too, Luca. And I think I always will."

81

IMRE HAD NEVER FELT MORE shattered than he did in these quiet moments with Luca in his arms, silent and watching the water, watching the sky grow deeper and darker as faint sparks of light out on the floats warned that the show would be starting soon.

Shattered, but maybe he had needed to break.

He only now realized exactly how safe his life had been. Slow, careful decisions, deliberate and keeping him at one remove from everything. Somewhere along the way his quiet withdrawal had turned into a shield, a cocoon, an excuse.

His father had taught him to be patient and kind and calmly reasoned.

He hadn't taught Imre to be a coward who hid from anything that might remotely threaten the safe shelter he'd built around himself for all these years.

He'd been so afraid of being abandoned again, afraid of people who couldn't understand the way he loved, that he'd become afraid of *love*, period. And when Luca meant so very much to him, it would have destroyed him if Luca hadn't been able to understand, wouldn't have cared.

So he'd been afraid. Afraid, and pushing Luca away.

When he should have been willing to fight for him through anything.

That was changing from this point forward. And even if he had to fight Marco Ward tooth and nail to get him to at least mind his own bloody business and let Luca and Imre's life be Luca and Imre's life…

He'd do it. He'd been stubborn enough to almost lose Luca to his own fear once.

He wouldn't do it again.

Even if getting in a shouting row like the old uni days with Luca's father wasn't quite the same as asking a man for his son's hand in marriage.

He couldn't help chuckling to himself, as he squeezed Luca tighter. Luca tilted his head back against Imre's shoulder, a tired yet so very sweet smile playing about his lips.

"What's so funny?"

"Just remembering how Marco and I used to fight in university, and thinking we're due for another quite soon."

Luca quirked a brow. "You. Fighting."

"If anyone could push me to it, it was Marco." Imre shook his head. "We'd get into right rows. Shouting all up and down the halls."

"Over *what?*"

"I don't even remember." Imre laughed. "It was usually the most ridiculous things. I'd spark his temper, he'd spark mine, and next thing you know we'd be going at it."

"I can't even picture you with a temper."

"I had my days. Probably worked most of it out of me going spare at him."

"Ah." Luca sighed, rubbing his cheek to Imre's chest in that catlike way Imre loved. "I hate that you even have to fight with him over me. He's got to cut the cord one day."

"Usually it's parents saying that about their children."

Luca snorted. "I'm not sure which one of us is the child here."

Not Luca, Imre thought. He thought perhaps even he hadn't been giving Luca enough credit—when Luca was the one with the clear head between them this time, the voice of reason who had talked Imre down from making the worst mistake of his life. Warmth bloomed in his chest, as he looked down at the sleepy man tucked drowsily against him. Warmth, wonder, and pride. This fierce, wild, brilliant little cat of a man was his. *Wanted* to be his, with such depth and longing and loyalty that he'd put himself out there more times than Imre even really deserved just to beg Imre to accept his love.

While Imre had been doing exactly what Marco was doing.

Refusing to listen, simply by his actions telling Luca he wasn't good enough.

I'm sorry, he thought, but he wouldn't ruin that sweet, drowsy expression by saying it, by making Luca talk through these things again. He'd just have to show it, one way or another. Every day, in every way he could think of.

An explosion of sound drew him from his thoughts. He looked up as light roared over the sky in a burst of pink and blue sparks, showering out in rays before raining down, only to fade into nothing but embers. He nudged Luca gently.

"Look."

Luca yawned, then opened his eyes and shifted to look up. Sparklight reflected in his eyes in brilliant colours as he watched the sky, while Imre watched him. Luca smiled faintly.

"Not exactly how I wanted to end up watching fireworks with you."

"But we made it here anyway." Imre caught Luca's hand, lacing their fingers together. "Happy New Year, my angyalka."

Luca's smile strengthened, and he squeezed Imre's hand tight. "Happy New Year, Imre." Then his gaze dropped, a shy downsweep of his lashes as he shifted about a bit more to face Imre. "Kiss me…?"

he asked softly, then made a stammering, nervous sound. "Only I…I know it's silly, but people kiss on the New Year. And they say what you're doing when the New Year rings in…"

"You're doing for the rest of the year." *For the rest of my life, if I have any say*. "Of course, Luca."

Yet still, he hesitated. This kiss, more than any other, felt like a vow—and as many times, as many ways as he had thought of doing this, it had never been like this: far from home, on a beach surrounded by a thousand other people doing the exact same thing. So much of anything that had meaning for him was tied up at Lohere, this sense of home, this sense of something he had built with his own two hands until he was soaked into the earth.

But if Lohere wasn't home without Luca, then Luca was home—and it didn't matter where they were, as long as Luca was there too.

And so he cupped Luca's face in his palms, drew his beloved to him, and kissed him as the night grew wild and bright and furious overhead.

He kissed Luca with everything in him—every quiet thing that had grown to raging in its deceptive stillness, everything that rioted through him until his silence became the roar of a heart that refused to be denied any longer. He kissed him as if he could make up for all the times he had smothered this love with his silence, kissed him as if the taste of Luca would light the darkness inside him with all the brightness of fireworks lighting up a still and silent night.

And when Luca melted against him with a soft, sighing moan of his name, slim fingers clutching so hard against his arms, Imre kissed him just to draw forth more of those sweet whispered sounds. Just to feel Luca's body move against him, fitting them so close, as if they had been made in halves so long ago and had been searching ever since to find that part of them that fit together just right, that once again made him whole.

His every breath ached, spearing down to the centre of his chest. His body burned. His mouth pulsed, tingling, his tongue hot with the taste of Luca and the sting of those taunting little nipping teeth. *Xav t'jo ilo,* he mouthed against Luca's lips, and felt Luca smile as he pressed deeper and deeper into the kiss.

The fireworks had begun to fade, trailing off into a last few bright, wistful shimmers, by the time they drew breathlessly apart. Imre's blood moved slow and hot, and he exhaled softly as he nuzzled at Luca's cheek, then paused, lingering on how ice-cold it was.

"You're freezing."

Luca's eyes drifted open, and he offered Imre a warm, lazily contented smile, almost drowsy. "I didn't think the beach would be too cold for just a hoodie."

With a chuckle, Imre shrugged out of his heavy leather coat and draped it over Luca. "Here."

"But you'll catch a chill—"

"It's just until we get to the car. I'll be fine." He tucked the jacket around Luca, wrapping him up in it until he nearly vanished into the folds of leather. "Let's go home, angyalka."

"Home?" Luca repeated, and there was something in his voice, in that soft note of entreaty, that said he was asking for more than confirmation.

He was asking if home truly was *home*, now.

"Home," Imre repeated firmly, and kissed the centre of Luca's palm. "We can send for your things from Sheffield first thing in the morning, if you'd like."

"Nah. Not that soon. Let's avoid the explosion for a few more days." Luca ducked his head shyly, peeking out at Imre from beneath his lashes. "But soon." He grinned, then, and nearly danced to his feet, tugging at Imre. “C’mon. Let’s go home.”

82

THE DRIVE BACK TO HARROGATE was quiet, a sweet silence that Imre settled into comfortably, broken only when Luca drifted over to tuck against his side, asleep within minutes. He must have really worn himself out, tromping around Harrogate and Scarborough. Imre smiled to himself, shifting to drive one-handed so he could drape the other over Luca's shoulders and stroke down his back.

He was taking his angyalka home.

Once they passed through Harrogate and onto the farm roads, Imre guided the Land Rover through the tracks worn into the snow cover on the road, even in the after-midnight dark finding his way home unerringly; he could drive these roads in the worst storm and always find his way back to Lohere. Luca didn't stir until the faint glow of the lights Imre had left on in the house pierced the gloom, golden rectangles swimming out of the dark and reflecting from the snow dunes piled against the high house walls. As Imre drew the car into the yard and killed the ignition, Luca yawned, slitting one eye open, peeking out from the tangle of shaggy hair and the leather coat bunched up around him like a blanket.

"Bed?" he murmured hopefully.

"Bed," Imre agreed. "Unless you'd rather a hot bath first. Your skin is still like ice."

Luca quirked a one-sided smile, biting down on one corner of his mouth. "…could warm me up in the bath."

"Impudent wretch." Imre pushed the door open and slipped out, offering a hand to Luca. "Just for that, you're bathing alone."

"Am not." Luca took his hand and hopped down, then smiled up at him impishly. "You love me too much to do that to me."

"You just want to hear me say it."

"I do." Luca's grin widened. "Right here, freezing our bums off in the snow. Tell me you love me again."

Imre sighed, yet his mouth wouldn't seem to stop dragging upwards at the corners, moving of its own volition. "I love you. That doesn't make you less of a wretch."

"Who ever said it did?" Luca sang, then turned and nearly sailed toward the house, dragging Imre unceremoniously behind.

Imre let himself be pulled, nearly stumbling over the threshold as Luca laughed and tugged on him. His laughter was infectious, and Imre found himself chuckling until the door swung closed behind them and Luca paused, staring wide-eyed at the coats strewn on the floor, the shoes tipped over, papers knocked from the desk in the living room and drifted into the foyer, scattered across the stone flooring.

"What happened?" Luca asked. "Did someone break in?"

Imre drew up short. He—oh. His neck grew hot, and he cleared his throat. "I may have left in a bit of a rush," he confessed. He didn't even remember knocking things over, but it wasn't hard to track his path from the living room to the door.

Those wide eyes turned on him. "You were that worried?"

"I. Ah." Imre grumbled it out, looking away. Bloody hell, he'd half wrecked the house charging through like a bull. It wasn't like him to be so rash, so impetuous. "…you ran off."

"I did." Luca's voice softened. "And you came for me even though I was such a brat."

"I gave you every reason to leave," Imre said, and dragged his gaze back to find Luca watching him with a sweet, wondering smile. “I wasn’t fair to you, Luca. I’m sorry.”

“Imre.”

With a happy little sound, Luca flung his arms around Imre’s neck, pulling himself up on his toes and clinging like a slender burr. Imre laughed, catching him around the waist and lifting him up, spinning him around; he still hardly weighed a feather, yet if he was light he was as light as Imre’s heart. And as he slowed, as he set Luca on his feet, the lightness in his heart turned hot and slow as pale green eyes caught him, asked a silent question that Imre was only too ready to answer. Luca drew himself up by handfuls of Imre’s shirt. Imre bent to meet him.

And their mouths crashed together like fire and wine, intoxication set aflame and leaving him drunk on its hard, sweet burn.

He couldn’t breathe. Not when every inhalation scoured his chest, swallowing sparks of need until they built up inside him into something roaring and wild as a love he could no longer deny. He was dimly aware of Luca’s hands on him, raking at his clothing, the moment of separation when his shirt tore off and spilled his hair everywhere and went flying to the side. Half cognizant, too, of fabric giving way under his raking hands until there was only soft, pale skin and the glow of firelight on smoothly toned, lean sinew as they fell from the foyer into the living room, shedding clothing with every step, their mouths a tangle of metallic bruise-taste and the sweet explosive sting of taunting bites and the flick of Luca’s tongue suggesting, inviting, luring Imre deeper into his mouth, his kiss, this consuming moment that was already too much yet could never be enough.

The last of their clothing fell away, Imre’s ankle still tangled in the leg of his jeans as they tumbled down onto the couch. Luca settled astride his lap, slim thighs flanking his hips, and Imre couldn’t help touching, gripping, stroking, digging his fingers into Luca's soft inner thighs just to leave his mark, just to drink Luca's cry from his lips. Heat fused them together skin to skin, pressed together everywhere their bodies could meet, clutching at each other as if they would die were they parted. Imre's heart thundered as he tasted Luca again and again, consuming that ripe strawberry mouth, searching deep, so deep, God he *needed* to be inside Luca, needed to touch and taste and devour his heart.

Haste wasn't Imre's way. Yet this thing building between them wouldn't slow, tumbling like river rapids, racing to the beat of Imre's pulse, driving them against each other in hard and hungry rhythm that made skin hiss and sigh together, that moulded the flex of his body to the flow of Luca's, that mated their hips until every movement slid his cock against Luca's in a rush of blazing, heated sensation, stroking hard and needy and igniting him with the craving for *more*.

He couldn't wait. Gasping, biting at the delectable sweat-salted slickness of Luca's throat, he fumbled for the couch cushions, searching for the bottle of oil that had fallen through the other day when reading on the couch had turned into that molten desire that never, ever seemed to cool. His fingers touched smooth glass. He managed to fumble enough to spill it over his fingers, then pressed them to Luca's entrance.

Luca rolled forward with a gasping, hotly thrilling cry that shot straight to Imre's cock, making it throb painfully, as he eased his fingers into Luca's body. He should take it slow, one at a time, but he couldn't stand another moment when some feral, carnivorous part of him needed this: needed the way Luca tossed his head back as Imre worked two fingers into him, needed the beautiful, tortured expression on Luca's face. The fire had died down to near nothing while Imre had been gone, and all that remained were glowing embers that licked their light against Luca's soft edges until he glowed like the first halo of sunlight cresting the morning. Beautiful. So fucking beautiful.

And Imre's, for all that he'd almost been cruel enough to let him go.

He worked his fingers inside Luca until he writhed like the little cat Imre called him, watching transfixed as he rocked back with that lovely body moving sinuous and sleek to meet the thrust of two fingers, three, four, and then Imre could no longer stand the suggestive pull of Luca's body, the bite of nails gouging into his shoulders. He pulled his fingers free, slicked his cock, then curled his hand around Luca's nape and drew him down, capturing that wet, panting, swollen mouth in a kiss.

"Xav t'jo ilo," he whispered, tasting the words shared on twining, slicked tongues as he curled his hands against Luca's slender hips.

"Imre," Luca begged, every bit of love he'd craved for ages in that soft whisper of his name. Imre groaned, kissing his name from Luca's lips, and started to draw his lover downward.

Only for Luca to sink down to meet him, hot flesh pressing against him, enveloping him, drawing him into a melting heat, tightness, softness that slid slick and silky against his cock, scoring him with raw talons of deep-digging heat.

He gasped, arching his back against the couch, fingers clutching at Luca's hips, but his angyalka didn't stop. With soft, erotic little sounds in the back of his throat, hitching and sweet, Luca worked himself down the length of Imre's cock, every twist of his hips jolting Imre with bursts of pleasure that built at his core until he struggled to breathe, his entire body aching with the force of the tension building inside him and locking his every muscle. Luca mewled, that soft begging sound that made Imre feel so very filthy, so very *hungry*, and buried his face against Imre's throat, clinging, sweat-slick skin to sweat-slick skin. He trembled in Imre's hold, sinking just a little further, then stopping, his quivering thighs tight against Imre's hips, his lap.

"Please," he whispered, throaty voice against Imre's ear. "*Please.*"

Imre gripped his hips tighter, unable to help the groan building in his chest, and dragged Luca down in one last hard thrust, lifting his hips to meet him and burying deep so fully that starbursts shot behind his eyes, fire sealing them together so perfectly. Luca gasped out a sharp, hoarse sound, curling into Imre, his every movement pulling and drawing at the tight cords of Imre's desire until it took everything in him not to lose control and just *take*. Struggling to rein himself in, he pressed his mouth over a pale shoulder, wrapping Luca up tight and just holding him, fighting not to give in to the rhythm of conjoined heartbeats moving through them both and making his blood sing.

Yet his blood *burned* when Luca captured his face, soft fingers threading through his beard, stroking his cheeks, and lifted him up to kiss him. That kiss tore him apart with its trembling sweetness, something so deeply, darkly enticing about the way Luca teased at his mouth, the plush give of his lips, the wet and taunting dart of his tongue. Imre thought he would lose himself right then and there; he felt as though his veins were threaded in bright, hot gold, pouring through him and tracing slow spidering filaments of perfect, shining warmth from his fingertips to his toes to that sharply molten place where body met body and they became not one and one, but a single gasping, shivering self.

So caught was he in the taste of Luca's lips, in the heady depths of his mouth, that Imre hardly noticed slim fingers trailing down his arms, feathering soft touches, curling against his wrists. Not until Luca gently pressed his wrists back, pinning his arms to the couch to either side of his shoulders, only to stroke his hands up to press palm to palm, fingers lacing between Imre's. Imre stilled, drawing back enough to look up at the sylph arched over him, that burn in the pit of his stomach deepening as he trailed his gaze over desire-darkened eyes and kiss-swollen lips.

Any question died on his lips, as he met Luca's eyes. As he saw the utter stripping focus in dilated pupils, how intently Luca looked at him. No lover had ever been able to make Imre feel vulnerable, exposed…and yet what he felt when Luca's gaze consumed him was more than that.

He felt…*seen.*

As though Luca knew him, understood him the way no one else ever could, and loved him for everything he was instead of everything he wished he could be.

Imre's heart trembled, and he tightened their laced fingers, leaned up, and brushed his lips to Luca's.

Do as you please.

Luca exhaled a shuddering gasp, leaning into Imre, his fingernails biting between Imre's knuckles. A soft whimper slipped past his lips—and then he lifted himself up, a mesmerizing ripple of tension flowing down his body, that gripping, sucking heat dragging along Imre's cock and rousing his own desperate, aching groan. But the sensation was nothing compared to the ocean of liquid heat that consumed him as, head rolling back on his pale, glistening throat, Luca plunged down again, taking Imre in with a willingness that nearly gutted him as much as the rushing flow of tight-contracting pleasure.

Never once did that intense gaze waver, as Luca lifted himself again, took Imre in again—holding Imre captured, spellbound, this pretty thing who hardly weighed a scrap keeping the entirety of Imre captive to his will. To his body. To this mercurial mixture of control and complete and utter surrender, as volatile and strange and wild and beautiful as Luca himself, as Luca freely gave his body into rolling, fluid undulations that made his flesh lick and tease and grasp so perfectly around Imre's cock, that made the shape of Imre's shaft press against his stomach in a mark of possession that pushed the fever in Imre's blood to the boiling point.

Endless torment. Endless pleasure. Silence, save for rushed breath and kissing skin. Every breath came shorter, came tighter, until Imre's chest ached and he thought he would shatter, the heat inside him burning him thin and fragile until he was fire caged in a translucent paper skin. Luca was everything, in this moment. Everything he'd ever wanted. Everything he'd never known he needed. Never again could he turn away from someone who knew him as intimately as he knew himself; never again would he deny the truth, the weight, the strength of Luca's love.

And never again would his bed be empty of that silken, writhing body that moved over him, pulling him closer and closer to the edge as inexorably as a waterfall's current rushing toward a cliff.

Luca's hips rocked faster, sharp and snapping, his breaths catching in little keens in the back of his throat. Imre strained toward him with a growl, this caged thing inside him desperate to break free.

"Are you close?" he breathed, watching Luca's bliss-transformed face raptly. "Are you close, my angyalka?"

Luca whimpered, tossing his head back. "Yes—yes, oh God, *Imre*, yes…"

"Then hold fast to me."

Imre pulled his fingers free from Luca's—then tumbled him forward, nearly breaking with the sharp movement as his cock shifted inside Luca as they re-settled with Luca sprawled on his back, pretty and perfect and spread open for Imre. Wide, startled eyes stared up at him above flushed cheeks; Luca's hair spread in coils over the sofa cushions, framing his face like a halo.

Angyalka.

Then his eyes snapped closed, as Imre moved—pinning him down, taking control, *needing* this moment when he could own Luca completely and utterly. He found the hard throb of Luca's cock, curled it against his palm, stroked it until Luca thrashed and struggled against him, fighting him to push into his touch, slim fingers burying in Imre's hair and grasping, pulling. Imre snarled in the back of his throat, giving himself over into it: into the pleasure of pinning Luca beneath his weight, the delicious sound of his cries, the decadent fire of a welcoming, yielding body that took him deeper on every thrust no matter how Luca writhed and whimpered.

Imre couldn't stand another moment; everything inside him was pulled too tight, drawn up into steel-hard knots, pressure building and yet still he held, he *held*, trembling to hold himself back until Luca suddenly stiffened, his neck arching, his chest rising and falling in sharp, shallow little gasps, frantic and needy. His thighs clutched at Imre's hips; his stomach tightened, and every clenching muscle inside him wrapped around Imre and crushed him with pleasure. Those trembling raspberry lips parted, tongue curling, then—

"*Imre!*"

—and Luca's body was jerking, arching, warm wetness spilling over Imre's fingers, tension catching and gripping Imre violently. Shuddering, gasping, Imre leaned down to catch Luca's mouth, taking the taste of his name from him again, shivering as he let himself go. He wanted it like this, this time—together, Luca's passion his passion, Luca's breaking his breaking, and he gave every ounce of himself into thrusting once, twice, again…

And then shattered, something inside him shifting as though the weight of mountains had moved with the force of the pleasure, the wildness, the emotion quaking through him.

He lost himself, for a few moments. There was nothing but the haze of a sore, aching body and the strange hyper-awareness of sweat cooling on his skin and that tight almost painful feeling of strain gathering in the base of his cock, too sensitive in the aftermath. Other feelings began to drift in, slowly. Luca's fingers in his hair. The slender body underneath him heaving with rapid gasps. Sluggish, contented, Imre turned his head, nuzzling into Luca's throat.

Luca made a soft, purring sound, then trailed into a hoarsely murmured laugh. "I'm going to run away every day, if you do that."

Imre exhaled a chuckle, struggling to catch his breath. "And I will drag you back every time, brat, but next time I'll take you over my knee."

"Sorry, not into that."

"Then what are you into?"

Luca sighed, and soft lips touched Imre's cheek. "This," he murmured. "Just this."

Imre smiled to himself, but said nothing; he only shifted to blindly seek out with one hand until his fingers caught in one of the quilts on the back of the couch. He dragged it down over them, then settled with both arms wrapped around Luca, nuzzling into his shoulder.

With a laugh, Luca gently thumped his shoulder. "Oy! You're not going to fall asleep like this, are you, you great ox?"

"Might," Imre answered, and nipped Luca's collarbone. "Comfortable."

"For you, maybe. I'm fit to wake up walking bowlegged!"

Imre fought back a laugh; laughing *hurt*, when Luca was still so tight around him. He pushed himself up, grinning down at his flushed, dishevelled little cat. "I suppose if I absolutely mu—"

He stiffened at the sound of the kitchen door opening, the jingle of keys. Who the hell? Imre jerked his head up, looking over the back of the couch.

Just in time for Marco Ward to come through the foyer door into the living room, dusting snow from his shoulders and his breaths clouded as smoke.

"Imre? Are you—" He froze, staring. "Uh."

Luca made a soft, panicked sound, eyes widening, and pushed himself up, fumbling against Imre and peering over the back of the couch. Marco went stiff, then pale—before a livid red flushed his face as his expression set grimly, brows lowering, eyes going flat.

"What the bloody rutting *fuck,*" he snarled, and Luca groaned, slumping down hard enough to pull on Imre's cock in all the wrong places at all the wrong moments.

"Oh," Luca sighed, dragging a hand over his face. "Oh, *fuck.*"

83

LUCA ESTIMATED APPROXIMATELY THREE SECONDS before the shouting started.

And he was lying here naked under Imre, his arse full of cock, and his father staring at them in fury and horror. Luca hadn't heard Marco Ward raise his voice in years.

He had a feeling that would change tonight.

God, he wasn't in the mood for this.

Wincing, he pushed himself up on his elbows, bracing his feet to either side of Imre's hips and pulling himself back, trying to separate their bodies. "Fuck fuck fuck fuck—ow ow ow *ow*—"

"I—what the *fuck?!*" his father spluttered. "Put some fucking clothes on!"

"I'm bloody fucking trying," Luca snapped, glaring over the back of the couch. "If you could turn the fuck around for a minute, eh?"

Imre let out one of those patient sighs that, right now, made Luca want to put his teeth out. He caught Luca's hips gently and separated their bodies in a single smooth movement that left Luca hissing and scored inside; he curled up and snatched at the quilt, wrapping it around his naked body, while Imre calmly settled to sit on the couch completely starkers, one arm stretched along the back.

"If the entire Ward contingent would just calm down, please," Imre rumbled.

Marco's entire face contorted into a mask of furious red ridges.

"Don't you fucking talk to me about calming down."

"Don't be rude, Marco."

"Rude? *Rude?!*" Marco's eyes bulged.

Luca covered his face with one hand. Oh, God, his fucking father was going to have an aneurysm right the fuck here on Imre's floor.

"You didn't knock," Imre retorted blandly, and casually leaned forward to snag his jeans off the floor. Luca's were tangled in them, and Imre separated them and his boxers out before offering them with an arched brow.

Marco flung a hand out. "I've never had to knock, I still have a key! And you never cared until you started shagging my—" He spluttered, a vein throbbing in his temple. "I sent my son here so you could raise him up, not core him out like a bloody apple!"

"Dad!" Luca gasped, heat suffusing his cheeks, fuck, his entire body. He snatched his things from Imre and wiggled into his boxers. "Christ, don't be naff."

"Look at that," Marco snapped. "He's such a wee babe he can't even hear this without blushing."

Imre heaved a slow sigh and started working into his clothing. "He's blushing because his father is humiliating him. Which you'd know if you would listen."

"Don't you lecture me. You text me that my son is missing and then I show up to find you fucking him?"

"Technically," Imre pointed out with a raised eyebrow, "we were quite finished fucking."

Marco's fists clenched, and he levelled a flat, deadly look on Imre. "Imre, if you think I'm too fucking old to punch you, you have another thing coming. What the fuck do you think you're doing? Did you not think for half a second that I would find out about this?"

"I knew you would." Imre's gaze shifted to Luca for a moment, blue eyes warm, before he rested a hand to the top of Luca's head and stood, hitching his jeans up his hips, then pulling away to round the sofa. He moved casually, as if the situation were utterly ordinary, as if he could quiet Marco with his own calm. "The question is why you're concerned that there's something to find out. You haven't even asked what this is."

"It's not anything, because my best friend is not fucking sleeping with my son!"

Imre bent to fetch first his discarded shirt, then Luca's. "I'm capable of many things." He tossed Luca's shirt over the back of the couch. "But traveling back in time to reverse what's already happened isn't one of them."

Luca snatched up his shirt and jerked it on, then stood to stuff his legs into his jeans. He couldn't look at them right now. Either of them. Especially when his father made a scornful, contemptuous sound and spat, "How could he possibly want…*this?*"

Closing his eyes, Luca turned away to smooth his clothing out, his heart a lump in the back of his throat. For fuck's sake, his father couldn't even—if he could speak to Imre that way, what kind of ugliness was Luca in for?

"Try asking him what he wants," Imre said.

"Like hell. Luca, come here. We're leaving. Now," Marco bit off, but Luca didn't even have time to snarl out a response before it was followed by, "Imre, *move*."

Luca opened his eyes and looked over his shoulder, fingers instinctively drifting to pick at his lower lip. He could hardly see his father for Imre's broad back, standing between Luca and Marco like the mountain of stone he was. Any other day Luca would have been grateful for that protective shield, but right now…

Right now he felt as though he was completely invisible to the two most important men in his life, while they fought over him as if he wasn't even there.

"Marco," Imre said softly. "I love you. You will always be my truest friend. But I will not let you railroad me on this. Have you ever actually listened to Luca?"

Marco stared at him. "What?"

"I know you love your son. But have you listened to him? Have you ever stopped to ask him why he's angry, frustrated, and lashing out?"

Is that what I'm doing? Luca's mouth tightened. *Lashing out?*

He couldn't stand this anymore. If he didn't say anything, he was going to *run*—and neither Imre or his father would get him to come back. Not to this. Not *for* this.

"I—" His voice broke. He tried again, turning to face them. "I can speak for myself, Imre. If everyone could stop talking about me like I'm bloody well invisible."

Imre's shoulders stiffened. He glanced back, visible eye dark with chagrin. "My apologies, angyalka."

"I know. You want to protect me. It's all right." Luca edged around the couch and rested a hand to Imre's arm. He tried to smile, but it was hard, so hard; he felt so tired, all of a sudden. So old. And he couldn't find it in him to even fake a grimace as he turned his gaze to his father, meeting his accusing, furious eyes. "Dad."

Marco drew himself up like he'd caught Luca pilfering from the biscuit jar after fibbing about it. "What do you have to say for yourself, young man?"

Luca only looked at him, but his father wasn't wavering. And in his eyes was reflected exactly how his father saw him: still a little boy, barely knee-high to a lampshade, incapable of having a single thought of his own that wasn't influenced by someone else.

Tired wasn't even a good enough word for the slow, sinking feeling falling through him. He shook his head.

"I'm not talking to you when you're like this," he said. "We can talk when you calm down enough to actually listen to me."

Marco blinked, brows twitching, before knotting up again. "Excuse me? What gives you the right—"

"The fact that it's my life and this was my choice." He'd let his father railroad him into coming out here. He wasn't going to let him railroad him into leaving. "You can talk to me when you calm down, or not at all. Never again, if you're going to look at me like I'm filth under your shoe for loving Imre." It should have felt good to say that. But it only left his throat raw, his chest tight, and *fuck* if he didn't want to be doing this, cutting those stitched-up threads that made them all a family. He took a step back, then shook his head again, pushing past his father and snatching up Imre's coat from the floor. "I'm done here."

"Luca—"

His father reached for him, but he pushed past him and out the foyer door and shoved his feet into his boots. He wasn't going far, not going to bloody run away to Scarborough this time, but he just needed some goddamned *air* that tasted like snow instead of like his own impending tears.

Imre's voice drifted after him. "Let him go."

"I don't understand," Marco replied. "I don't understand any of this."

"You don't have to," Imre said.

Then the door slammed shut, leaving Luca alone with the snow, the stars, and the horrid cold feeling of winter inside his heart.

84

IMRE SHRUGGED INTO HIS SHIRT, then leaned against the wall, watching Marco. That…could have gone better, really. Ripping the plaster off was supposed to make things easier, not worse. But Marco stood in the centre of the living room, hands flexing helplessly, looking like a wee lost babe who'd just learned there was no St. Niklaus after all, torn between confusion, pain, and pure, dismayed rage.

Imre supposed Marco had a right to feel that way, but he would not apologize for loving Luca.

"I…" Marco made an odd, glottal sound in the back of his throat. "What just happened?"

"If you would like a recap, you walked in on Luca and I post coitus—"

Marco let out a strangled growl, glowering. "I don't need to be reminded of that."

"—and then proceeded to throw a tantrum at your adult son for either his choice of lovers, or for exercising his autonomy. I'm not sure which."

Marco flinched. "Do you have to put it that way?"

"Am I wrong?"

"Mind your own business." But Marco deflated, looking away, his mouth thinning. A shadow of pain haunted his brow. "How *could* you?"

"Do you see it as a betrayal?"

"*Yes.*"

"Why?"

"I…I don't know." Marco wrung his hands. "He's barely a child, Imre."

Imre regarded Marco thoughtfully. There was a touch of desperation, almost a plea. He thought perhaps father and son were more alike than they realized: both afraid of losing what made them a family, both trying to hold on to it in ways that only hurt themselves and each other.

"He's more than a child," Imre said. "He has been for some time. He grew up when you weren't looking. Perhaps *because* you weren't looking."

"You make me sound like a terrible parent."

"No. Just someone dealing with life's complications." Imre folded his arms over his chest. "As am I. As is Luca. We're all only trying to make our way. We're all equals in this."

"Are you?" Marco threw his hands apart with a frustrated sound. "How *can* you be?"

"Maybe you would be better off asking him that."

"And if he—" Marco's voice rose into a shout, then choked off, came back again quieter, almost forlorn. "And if he won't speak to me?"

"Try talking to him without bloody well railing at him, and see if he'll listen."

"I…" God, Marco looked so lost, so young, in this moment. His Adam's apple bobbed in a swallow. "I don't know him anymore, Imre. And it seems like you do."

A smile twitched at Imre's lips no matter how he tried to stop it. "You tend to get to know someone while falling in love with them, yes."

"This is hurting my brain." Marco grimaced and raked a hand through his unruly mop of dark hair. "When did this start?"

"It's hard to say." Imre shrugged one shoulder, thinking back. A thousand moments. A million denials. Luca on his mind, his name on every breath. "Sometimes I feel like just yesterday. Sometimes I feel like I've been ignoring it since the moment he stepped off the train."

"Is that why he wanted to stay?"

"I told you. Ask him. Not me," Imre said. "I respect him enough not to speak for him."

Marco studied him discerningly, eyes the same pale spring green as Luca's but seamed at the corners by age, clouded by the weariness of life. "You're serious about this."

"Yes."

"Even with…how old you are?"

"All the more reason not to stall on important decisions, don't you think?" Imre glanced toward the door. He didn't think Luca would run off again, but he'd been out there for a while. Even if Imre's coat was warmer than that thin hoodie, it was still frigid out there. He frowned. "Would you like me to go see if he'll speak to you?"

"No," Marco said. "Let me." Then he dragged his hand over his face. "I don't know if I can deal with this. You being his lover."

"I *love* him, Marco—"

"And I believe you." Marco fixed Imre with a longer, steadier look—calmer, but there was something grimly fatalistic under his gaze. "But he's my son. This is between us. Let us talk it out."

Imre lingered on Marco. It wasn't his business. He'd told himself that a thousand times, but it became his business when he wanted to love Luca, to keep him safe, and Marco was one of the few people in this world who could damage his angyalka beyond recovery. He wanted to trust that his friend hadn't changed that much, that he wouldn't try to wilfully destroy his son, but…

Marco smiled wryly. "I know that look. I've known it my whole life. You don't have to glare at me that way. You want to protect him, I get it. And I'm glad, I really am. But if you really see him as an equal, let us talk this out without trying to shield him." He laughed shakily. "Though I might fuck this up, Imre."

"He'll still have a place to come home to," Imre promised softly.

"Good." Marco huffed. "That's the closest you'll get to my blessing."

"I never asked for it."

"Because you're a stubborn bastard. And don't think I'm not still angry at you. But Luca comes first." Marco hesitated, fumbling with the zipper of his coat, then asked haltingly, "Any pointers? Since you seem to actually *know* him…"

"Listen to him," Imre said without hesitation. "*Listen*, Marco. He's not you. He won't make your mistakes. He'll make his own mistakes. Perhaps I'm one of his mistakes, but you have to let him make them on his own."

"Fuck my life, this is weird." Marco squinted at Imre. "You're not like…projecting or anything? Going after Luca because it's like having me or something?"

Something cold hardened inside Imre—hardened enough to stab his heart right through. "No." His jaw tightened. "That's insulting. I was never in love with you."

The expression on Marco's face warred between embarrassment and relief. "Well that's a hole in my ego. Why not?"

"Because you were my friend," Imre bit off. "And an arrogant knob."

Marco just looked at him for long moments. Imre knew that look—knew it as well as Marco knew his silent glowers and body language. That look of lost, hopeless regret, a bloody kicked puppy who already wished he could take it back but knew he couldn't, and was working himself up to say the right words so Imre would forgive him because Imre always did, tactless sod that Marco was.

"I'm sorry," Marco said thickly. "That was callous of me. Selfish. Cruel to you." He smiled shakily. "Wee bit…what's the word? Homophobic?"

"Shitty," Imre said. "That's a better word for it. Apologize to me later." He jerked his chin toward the door. "Apologize to Luca now."

"I will." But still Marco lingered, watching Imre woefully. "But I do owe you more than an apology. Been thinking about it ever since we shipped Luca off, and I suddenly remembered how long it'd been since I'd seen you." He ducked his head. "We just…left. I was so busy thinking about my own life and my own family that I just left you behind. It was always 'next summer' that we'd come visit, and we never did." His shoulders slumped. "We left you alone, didn't we?"

"Life happens." Imre shrugged. He'd never expected Marco to have enough intuition to even suss that out without being told, but he wasn't quite ready to relent yet. Not after that great bloody wallop of an insult. But after a moment he added grudgingly, "…but you should come see Luca more often."

"I should come see both of you." Marco sighed. "You're the steadiest friend I've ever known, Imre. I never should've taken that for granted."

"Then why did you?"

"I…" Marco fell silent for a moment, then laughed weakly. "You know, I know it's that whole rose-coloured glasses thing, but…" Weary eyes fixed somewhere beyond Imre, distant and far-seeing. "My only memories of a perfect life were with you and Lucia back in uni. It felt like we made a promise, back then. That we'd keep feeling everything with just that much intensity. We'd always be that loyal, that passionate, that true to each other. All of us." His gaze sharped, focused on Imre again. "I felt like if I saw you, if I even spoke to you, you'd know Lucia and I already broke that promise ages ago. And the longer I stayed away, the easier it became to just *be* away." He looked down, staring at his worrying hands. "I don't know what's the worse betrayal. Abandoning you, or breaking that promise."

Imre growled under his breath. Marco had a unique way of pissing him off the way no one else could, but he also had a unique way of making Imre feel sorry for that sad, tired hangdog look. He wasn't one to hold on to his temper, but he'd like to just stay mad at Marco for five bloody minutes.

Even if right now he was less angry than aching inside, reliving those long, empty years after the only family he'd had left had walked away without looking back.

"It's only a betrayal if I felt betrayed," he replied, keeping his scowl by sheer force of will.

"Didn't you?"

"No." Imre sighed, then, letting his tension go, looking at Marco. "I just felt…left behind."

"I'm sorry, Imre," Marco said softly. "I can never be sorry enough."

Imre didn't answer, at first. He couldn't say *I forgive you*. Not yet. Not when so many things still stung, so many things he'd been trying to be patient and accepting of for years when sometimes lives just went in different directions, and there was nothing for it. But the ache of that wound was old, and deep—and one *I'm sorry* wasn't enough to heal it.

Not one.

But maybe, with time.

He was willing to give it that chance, if it meant not losing his friend.

His family, now in more ways than one.

"Your son is waiting for you," he pointed out after gathering his thoughts.

"No." Marco's lips quirked ruefully. "He's waiting for you. But I'll take care of things so I'm no longer in the way."

Marco turned away, heading for the door. Imre watched him go, then called, "Marco?"

Pausing, Marco glanced back. "Yeah?"

"I'll be wanting that key back before you leave."

Marco blinked, then laughed nervously. "Oh. Right. Sorry. Sure. When I come back." That nervous laugh turned almost frightened. "Luca's like as to kill me anyway, so no salt taking it off my corpse, eh?" He gulped. "Oh God. I can do this."

Imre couldn't help a faint smile. "Go."

"Yep. Right. Going."

"And Marco."

Another pause. An exasperated look. "What now?"

"*No shouting*."

"…oh. Right. Yes."

Marco took a deep breath and squared his shoulders, then straightened his jacket and marched out the door. Imre moved to the door and watched, through the window, as Marco trudged across the snow, following the trail of Luca's prints. Imre only hoped he wouldn't be consoling an upset, furious Luca when this was over—but this part, at least, he needed to stay out of.

He glanced back toward the stairs, frowning. He had to stay out if it, yes.

But that didn't mean he couldn't distract Luca with something better, once the explosions were over and the dust had setted.

85

LUCA SAT ON THE WALL atop the hill and watched the starlight glitter off the snow. Breathing shallowly of the cold air, he scrubbed at his cheeks. Little crackles of frost came, burning, off his skin, wiping free in streaks.

He didn't know what he'd expected. Maybe that if he went back to his father as this new, mature Luca, his father would recognize that it was time to cut the damned cord and let him be his own person.

Only now he understood that the problem had never been Luca at all. His father only knew one way to do things, and that was his way or no way at all.

Luca doubted that would change even when he was eighty.

Fine, then. He could go back to bloody Sheffield alone. Luca had said all he was going to say about it. It was between him and Imre and no one else.

His father could bloody well bugger off, and keep his nose out of it.

He heard the faint creak of the kitchen door, and listened for the sound of the blue Camaro parked next to Imre's Land Rover. Instead there came only the crunch of footsteps, slow through the snow and coming closer. Luca didn't want to look back.

He didn't want to look back and see Imre with that look on his face, that said he was sorry but he'd changed his mind because of some horrid thing Luca's father had said.

"Luca?" his father said at his back.

Luca stiffened, ice slipping down his spine, feelers of cold fury in his lungs. He tossed a glare over his shoulder. His father stood at the peak of the hill, hanging back a few feet, watching him with a forlorn helpless look that just made Luca want to sock him right in the fucking gut.

He turned away from his father, glaring across the fields. "Of course it's you. Why did it have to be you?"

"I wouldn't let Imre come."

Luca bristled. "You have no right—"

"I have every right when it's not his fight." His father's voice moved closer, then stopped at his side and just a little behind. "You're not upset with him. You're upset with me. So we need to talk."

Glaring straight forward, Luca hunched into Imre's stolen coat, pulling it up around his ears. "We're out of things to talk about."

"Are we?"

"Let's put it a different way." He shot a glower at his father from the corner of his eye. "I don't have anything to say to you, and I'm sick of everything you have to say to me."

Marco pulled himself up onto the stone fencewall, settling next to Luca with one knee drawn up to brace his foot on the edge. He sighed, icy clouds billowing from his lips. "What if I say I'm sorry?"

"I'd think you were lying."

"But I am. Sorry, that is."

Luca eyed him and edged away. He didn't buy it for one second. "For what?"

"Everything." Marco shrugged helplessly. "For not knowing what I'm doing. For being a shite dad." He closed his eyes, then opened them again, tilting his head back and looking up at the sky. "It's funny. Settling down is supposed to ground you, but it only made me feel like my life was spinning even further out of control. And in trying to control my life, I tried too hard to control yours." His lips remained parted, working on soundless words, before he continued, "I just didn't want to see you spinning the way I was, son. I didn't want you to be as lost as I am. And you seemed to be drifting. Directionless."

Luca said nothing. He didn't know what *to* say, when that was the most Marco Ward had said to him that wasn't a lecture in bloody effin' years. He didn't know what to do when his father levelled with him, talked to him man to man instead of man to recalcitrant, defiant child.

"I…" He wet his lips, considered. Fuck. He could only be honest, right? "I wasn't drifting. I was just trying to find true north. I'm not going to wank about doing nothing for the rest of my life, Dad. I just want to be sure that when I settle on something, it's something I love. That's all. I just needed a little more time to think about what I really wanted, and you wouldn't even give me that. You just saw me fucking around like a prat and thought that's all I was."

His father gave him a flat look. "You did crash a motorcycle into a church."

"Because you were being a prick," Luca retorted. "You're too old for a fucking midlife crisis motorcycle anyway."

"Don't talk to me about too old." Marco screwed his face up. "You're shagging my best friend. He's my age. He's *older*."

"Ew!"

"Imagine how I feel!"

Luca glared. "I'm not talking about my sex life with you!"

"I'd rather you didn't have a sex life at all, but God knows you can't keep teenagers celibate these days."

Wincing, Luca looked away again. "Not a teenager anymore."

"I…oh." Marco sighed. "I'm sorry I missed your birthday. I thought you wouldn't want to see me, and your mum agreed."

"Mn."

Marco made a faltering sound. "…you know about us, don't you."

"Yeah," Luca said bitterly. "I've known for a long time." But it was easier to smile after, even if it hurt, an awful feeling that crackled like the frozen tracks of tears on his cheeks. "It's okay, you know. I won't stop loving either of you if you move out into some dodgy singles flat or some such."

"I've a little cottage picked out on the north end of Sheffield. Closer to work. A little quieter than the old neighbourhood. Mum's keeping the house."

Something in his father's voice prompted Luca to look at him. Marco Ward sat with an odd, quiet stillness—as if he was just a seed husk with everything inside him emptied out, and if he moved the wind would carry him away. He looked so fragile, so tired, so empty.

And Luca couldn't help reaching for him, edging one hand over just enough that his fingers rested atop his father's on the stone ledge.

"You going to be all right?" he asked.

Marco's head lifted sharply, eyes widening, then softening as he smiled faintly. "I feel like I should be asking you that."

"Think I'm working my way toward okay. More than okay."

"Yeah?" Marco's smile strengthened. "Me too."

They lingered, then, quiet and watching the snow and the stars, and Luca thought…he could live with this. He could live with his father quiet and accepting, his father as broken as he was in his own way, both of them trying to find their own way. He'd wanted this for a long time. Wanted to be able to lean on his father, and have his father lean on him.

He'd never be the little boy his father had seen him as again.

But he hoped, perhaps, he could be his father's friend.

"Veterinary school," he murmured after a time.

Marco shook himself and glanced at him. "Hm?"

"I want to go to veterinary school. I really love working with the animals, and Imre says I'm good with them. There's this great vet, Mira—Ms. Landers, in Harrogate. She said she'll let me apprentice." He glanced at his father, biting his lip, his stomach knotting. "I think I'll really love it. It makes me happy, when I can help them. That's a good thing to build a career on, isn't it?"

Marco tilted his head, his expression awfully, forebodingly blank—before he smiled, easy and warm. "Yeah, son. Yeah." He squeezed Luca's hand reassuringly, and Luca's shoulders came down from around his ears. "That's a great thing to build a career on. I remember the Landers practice. Good people. Good work. You picked a school yet?"

"Somewhere close." Luca exhaled the tight, anxious breath that had bound up his chest. "I…I don't want to leave Lohere."

Marco cocked his head. "You're serious about this, aren't you?"

"Dad?"

"Yeah?"

"I've loved Imre since I knew how to say his name." The words were tight in his throat, until he could almost taste the red heart's blood of his own raw, aching emotions. "Is that fucked up?"

"No, Luca."

Luca wasn't expecting the hand that curled against his shoulder, or how his father pulled him close: fierce, fast, drawing him into a tight hug.

"No," Marco said, voice thick. "It's beautiful. I couldn't think of a better man to love."

Luca fought back the sting of tears. Fuck. He wasn't going to break down just because his fucking wanker of a dad was actually hugging him, *approving* of this, instead of shouting at him like a fucking lout. He curled his hands in the front of his father's coat, just pressing into him for a moment. He'd almost forgotten how he smelled. Like soft cotton and new leaves, that smell he remembered from being young and thinking nothing in the world could ever break his family apart until everything in the world finally did.

"I know it won't be easy," he whispered. "I know that. But I want it anyway. I want *him*. And I want you to be there for us, even if that won't be easy either."

Marco's body shook against him in a chuckle. "Nothing worth having is ever easy."

Groaning, Luca shoved away from him, dashing at his eyes with a shaky laugh. "No Dad quotes right now. Please."

"Okay, okay." Grinning, Marco held his hands up. "What about Dad puns?"

"*No*."

"Shame. Been storing up some good ones while you were away."

"Oy, fuck off. You've never had any good ones."

"Hey!"

The kitchen door creaked again. They both looked back to watch Imre step outside; from the look on his face as he looked up the hill, Imre half expected to find blood on the snow. A hard jolt of love and longing went through Luca at the sight of him; he wanted nothing more, right now, than to be in Imre's arms, and he tumbled off the fence, waving.

"Imre!" he called. "Up here!"

Imre cocked his head, a sheaf of hair tumbling across his face, then let the door bang shut and stepped forward to climb the hill. Luca flung himself down the slope to meet him, tripping in a spray of snow and falling forward only for Imre to catch him in strong, steady arms, looking down at him with that bland, quiet calm that barely hid the laughter sparking in his eyes.

"Are you a lemming now?" he teased in a gravelly rumble. "Throwing yourself off cliffs."

Laughing, Luca flung his arms around Imre's neck and pressed into him. "Came down to warm you up. You came out without a coat."

"Someone's wearing mine."

"Which is why I need to keep you warm." Luca couldn't seem to stop smiling, as he looked up at Imre. It took the sight of those intense blue eyes, deep and endless and as full of stars as the winter sky, to make him realize…everything really would be all right. His father had blown his top and simmered down. And Imre wanted him. *Wanted* him, instead of giving in to him. This was real, it was happening…and nothing was going to take that way.

As if he had caught on to Luca's thoughts, Imre's gaze softened. He pressed a chilled hand to Luca's cheek. "Everything all right, then?"

"Aye." Luca's grin widened. "Everything's perfect."

"What he means," Marco said, climbing off the fence and drifting closer, "is that I stopped being an arse."

"Not what I meant at all," Luca tossed over his shoulder. "Still an arse."

"Oy. You're not too old for me to spank you."

"Means something totally different when Imre threatens that, you know."

"*Oy!*" Panic briefly flitted through Marco's eyes, and he covered his ears. "I can't hear this!"

Imre let out a deep vibrato laugh. "Bloody hell, angyalka, stop terrorizing your father." His brows knit. He stroked his beard, his other hand settling on Luca's waist. "I suppose if we get married, that would make him my father, too."

"I'll not be your bloody damned father!" Marco spluttered. "You are not marrying my son, Imre!"

"Told you I wasn't asking you," Imre retorted, before returning his gaze to Luca. "Might just ask you one day, though," he said, a husky note darkening his voice.

Luca fell still save for his heart—his body a frozen thing but his heart frantically jerking against its cage. "I-Imre…?"

Imre chuckled. "Bit soon for that, perhaps. But keep that thought on the table until we find out if you can stand me in another six months. Until then, though…"

He fished into his pocket, and plucked out something delicate: a little braided ring in deep wine purple, almost identical to the dried ring of grass in Imre's keepsake box—but this one was made of ribbon shot through with subtle silver threads. Luca sucked in a breath, ribs tightening as if they'd squeeze his lungs to bursting, as he recognized it.

One of the ribbons woven into Imre's mother's sash.

Something so precious, passed through his family, and he'd…

His lips trembled, as Imre caught his hand and turned it over, stroking his thumb along Luca's knuckles as if trying to soothe his hand into no longer shaking.

"I know I said rings aren't the ending to everything, or the reason for anything," Imre murmured. "But I've owed you this one for a long time. Let me at least make things even."

Luca parted his lips, trying to find words, but they flitted away from him, born away on the tide of his racing pulse. His knees weakened, his stomach light and strange, as—never taking those penetrating blue eyes from him, holding him transfixed with the heat, the affection, the trust, the promise in that gaze—Imre gently slid the ring onto Luca's finger, the ribbon braid smooth as silk against his skin and fitting so perfectly, so snugly.

And when it settled into place, he felt as if the key had turned in the lock of his heart, unleashing a flood of emotion that he couldn't contain.

"Imre," he choked, and buried himself against him, clutching tight. This was too much. Too perfect, too *right*, and if Imre didn't hold him together he was going to fall apart.

Imre enveloped him tight, pulling him in close and surrounding him with the scent of Lohere, the heat of his body, the warmth of his love. "You remember what you said to me, all that time ago?" he whispered.

"I'll always love you, Imre," Luca recited, the words branded on his heart.

"I hope you meant it." A gentle touch nudged Luca to look upward, to fall into the depths of Imre's gaze. "Because I'll always love you, Luca."

"Don't kiss in front of me," Marco muttered.

Luca ignored him entirely. He smiled; he couldn't stop himself, not when his heart blazed as bright as the fireworks over Scarborough. "Xav t'jo ilo?"

Marco made a panicked sound. "*Don't kiss in front of me.*"

"Shut up, Marco," Imre said mildly, then whispered, "Xav t'jo ilo."

Luca leaned in closer, resting his hand—with its lovely braided ring, more perfect and more pure than gold or diamonds—against Imre's chest. "You meant always?"

"I meant always. Now," Imre said, as he drew Luca up and into a kiss that tasted of promises that could never be broken, “and forevermore.”

Epilogue

KIDDING SEASON WAS NEVER EASY, but Imre had never had one go quite as awry as this.

Normally the nanny goats at least staggered their births throughout late March and early April. He was accustomed to one or two birthings a day, three at most, making for a gruelling day of labour and birthing here and there but nothing he couldn't handle.

This season, however, the fractious, pregnant nannies had apparently come to a consensus.

And that consensus was that they would all kid in a single week, dropping baby goats like they were coming down a conveyer belt and leaving Imre working round the clock to make sure every one was born healthy and hale and as safe as could be.

He likely wouldn't have made it without Mira. She'd practically set up camp in his barn, refusing to even take one of the guest rooms when she wanted to stay with the goats, catching short naps here and there in a sleeping bag in the hay.

But even more indispensable—to his everyday life, to the animals, to everything—had been Luca.

Imre looked up from stroking the brow of a labouring nanny to watch Luca with one of the fresh-born babies. The squalling little thing bleated in his arms, sucking noisily at the nipple of a bottle Luca held so carefully, so tenderly. A few of the nannies' milk hadn't started yet with the early birthing throwing them off cycle, but Luca had been tireless in making sure that every last one of the kids was properly nourished.

Even now he wore his veterinary lab coat, twin to Mira's. Technically he was working; this counted as part of his apprenticeship, but Imre had a hard time getting him to take the bloody coat off even at home when he was so damned proud of the thing. Imre didn't blame him.

Imre was pretty damned proud of him, too.

And that pride swelled in his chest along with a love that had only grown day by day, as he watched Luca so utterly absorbed in the kid cradled in his arms. He fed the baby goat until its eyes began to droop, before he gently laid it into a nest of hay next to its dam—who, aided by an overeager Merta, began grooming the little baby intensely. Luca laughed, taking a step back, and nearly tripped over a few of the days-old kidlets who were already up on their feet, bouncing around like little horned kittens on spring-loaded hooves.

"Oy, oy," he said, laughing that sweet, throaty laugh of his with that husky burr. "You've got your own food. Go find your mums. You too, Leah," he chided one who clung when the others scattered, leaning down and scratching between a perky black and white kid's little nubby horns, then drifted closer to Imre. He met Imre's gaze for long moments, and the softness in those pale green eyes, just for him, made Imre's heart beat faster. He'd thought the effect would dull over time, yet it only grew stronger until his heart was a mighty machine roaring in his chest.

"Getting on all right with them?" he asked.

"Oh, ah," Luca answered with a merry little shrug, and sank down next to Imre, leaning shoulder to shoulder with him and stroking sure, capable hands over the nanny lying in the hay, so much more confident than he had been before. "How far off is she?"

"A few hours at most. She's the last." Imre glanced over his shoulder. "Where's Mira?"

"Snoring in her sleeping bag."

"And your father?"

Luca snorted. "Weeding clover, whingeing about going back to Sheffield, and swearing *he'll* go gay if he ever watches another goat give birth. Lazy tosser."

"We've not all got your knack for it. Your da'll be glad for the office again come Monday." Imre grinned, leaning in to nuzzle Luca's hair. "…so we've got a few hours alone…and free of afterbirth."

Luca eyed him slyly. "Do you ever bloody stop?"

"Not since you've moved in."

"And I've got the limp to prove it." Chuckling, Luca pushed up and kissed Imre's cheek, before his low whisper teased at Imre's ear, lips soft against its curve. "Tonight. We don't want to wake Mira."

Imre turned his head and caught Luca's mouth, stealing a taste, a nibble of those impudent raspberry lips. "It's just biology. She won't mind."

"So impatient."

"It's been a few days." Imre leaned harder into Luca, kissing him again, savouring how that sweet mouth went soft and yielding against his, how Luca moaned with such helpless surrender. He felt like a newlywed with how easily his angyalka could stir the embers inside him into flame, until Imre needed him every hour of each day, each night, without fail and without end. As if he could fill the years of loneliness in his life in a single instant, a single breath.

As if every time he kissed Luca, touched Luca, tasted him, took him…he reminded himself and Luca alike that Lohere was once again a home.

Even in five short months Luca had changed—more confident in himself, in his path, in his decisions, quieter and more considered until something sparked off an impulsively rash temper that only made him burn more beautifully, more brightly. That new confidence was there now as Luca curled his hands in the front of Imre's shirt and drew him down to kiss him with a lazy, promising sensuality, a taunt and a taste that said he knew exactly what he was doing to Imre—and exactly what Imre would do to *him* after days of holding himself back.

Imre groaned, snaring an arm around his waist, slanting to capture and claim that wicked mouth more thoroughly—only to draw up short as something went thudding against his side. He pulled back, arching a brow, and lifted his arm to look down. One of the kids had launched itself bodily against his side, headbutting him. He sighed and scooped the little off-white thing up, stroking his fingers through its short, stubby, soft fur.

"Someone's jealous," he said.

"Aye," Mira called groggily from her sleeping bag. "And it's me. I haven't seen my husband for a bloody week and the two of you are making out practically on top of me."

Luca tossed a laugh over his shoulder. "Go back to sleep so we can go back to it."

The only answer was a slim brown middle finger rising over the fence of one of the pens, before it dropped away.

Snickering, Luca pushed himself to his feet. "I'll go up to the house and make some sandwiches." He slipped a hand into the pocket of his lab coat and retrieved the little purple braided ribbon ring. It was still as smooth as the night Imre had slipped it on Luca's finger, when Luca cared for it as if it was the most precious thing in the world and took it off for safekeeping the moment it seemed like it might get damaged or stained. Imre's heart warmed to watch the care with which he slipped it onto his finger, but as Luca started to turn away he reached out, caught his hand, and drew it to his lips to kiss the ring.

"When will you let me replace this with a real one?" he murmured.

"Never." Luca leaned down and kissed their twined knuckles with a teasing smile. "This is real enough for me. I don't need a fancy ring."

Imre's eyes narrowed, and he dragged Luca closer with a playful little tug. "That's not what I'm asking."

"Then what are you asking?"

What *was* he asking? But then…what had he always wanted? Even when he hadn't known that Luca was and always would be the answer to that unspoken question, that yearning inside him…

He lingered on the ring, stroking his thumb over it, then lifted his gaze to Luca's. His heart was a quiet murmur, as if soft and holding its breath in anticipation. "Do you need me to say it?"

Luca's eyes widened briefly; a faint tremor of his lashes, a touch of colour in his cheeks. "No," he said softly, and in his voice was an understanding spoken in the language of silences that had built between them, a language in which they knew each other's thoughts by touch and each others' hearts in wordless sighs. "But if you don't need to say it, then neither do I."

"I want to hear it anyway."

Imre drew Luca down to him; the barn, the bleating goats, the world around them might as well have not existed—for all he saw was the pale, lovely man in his arms, watching him with those shy eyes the colour of spring and clear running brooks.

"Yes," Luca answered, barely a whisper, barely a shaking breath, and Imre's entire body trembled.

"Yes?"

"You knew that already, Imre." Luca leaned into him with a

smile like a secret between them, one they would keep forever. “You had to know.”

“Luca,” Imre said, and drew him in for another kiss as their fingers laced together with the slender ribbon ring between them, “I’ve known since the moment I saw you.”

The End

Discover Your Criminal Side

GET MORE OF THE THRILLING M/M romantic suspense serial everyone's talking about. Follow Baltimore homicide detectives Malcolm Khalaji and Seong-Jae Yoon as they trail a string of bizarre murders ever deeper down a rabbit hole—that, if they can't learn to work together, may cost them both their lives. **Full-length novels released once per month!**

Browse on Amazon and Amazon KindleUnlimited

https://www.amazon.com/gp/product/B07D4MF9MH?ref=series_rw_dp_labf

See the series on Goodreads

https://www.goodreads.com/series/230782-criminal-intentions

NORMALLY I WRITE LENGTHY AFTERWORDS to each of my books, breaking down important issues and themes in the story and how they relate to my experiences, as much of my work comes from #ownvoices perspectives in one way or another, whether by marginalization or by personal experience.

I don't have that for this one. Because this isn't an "issues" book.

This is a book I wrote just to be happy.

A book I wrote just to see two queer men dealing with normal life and relationship issues, and falling breathlessly, sweetly into an all-consuming fairy tale love. No coming out narratives. No homophobic parents. No tragedy. No abuse. No loss.

Just bright, euphoric love—love, and a friendship so deep it would have stood even if Imre and Luca *hadn't* ended up together.

Because being able to have that when it's been so long denied to our community?

Is as important as everything else.

-C

Get VIP Access

WANT STORIES AVAILABLE NOWHERE ELSE? Subscribe to the Xen x Cole McCade newsletter:

www.blackmagicblues.com/newsletter/

Get SOMETIMES IT STORMS (previously featured in IPPY Award-winning charity anthology WINTER RAIN), Red's story in PINUPS, as well as deleted scenes from A SECOND CHANCE AT PARIS and FROM THE ASHES – and deleted scenes, bonus content, episode soundtracks, and artwork from CRIMINAL INTENTIONS.

Subscribing also gets you release announcements and newsletter-only exclusives, including early access to new books, giveaways, and more. **Become a VIP!**

For Reviewers

INTERESTED IN ADVANCE REVIEW COPIES (ARCs) of upcoming releases? Apply to join Xen x Cole McCade's ARC reviewer team, A MURDER OF CROWS:

http://blackmagicblues.com/join-the-murder-of-crows-arc-team/

Acknowledgments

As always, I have many people to thank for the production of this book. My chosen family, sisters of my heart, who always give me somewhere safe to be human when such spaces are growing increasingly rare. My editor, who hasn't murdered me yet, and if you knew her you'd know that was more magnanimous than most people get, even if I'm pretty sure the only reason I'm still alive is to be her alibi.

Thank you, too, to my authenticity readers for double-checking this book meticulously, forgiving the little adjustments I needed to make for a primarily American audience, and introducing me to the delicious wonder that is Yorkshire Iced Tea.

And as always, hats off to the Fight Club. This talented group of writers keeps me moving like no other, and I wouldn't be here without them.

About the Author

COLE MCCADE IS A NEW ORLEANS-BORN Southern boy without the Southern accent, currently residing somewhere in Seattle. He spends his days as a suit-and-tie corporate consultant and business writer, and his nights writing contemporary romance and erotica that flirts with the edge of taboo—when he's not being tackled by two hyperactive cats.

He also writes genre-bending science fiction and fantasy tinged with a touch of horror and flavored by the influences of his multiethnic, multicultural, multilingual background as Xen. He wavers between calling himself bisexual, calling himself queer, and trying to figure out where "demi" fits into the whole mess—but no matter what word he uses he's a staunch advocate of LGBTQIA and POC representation and visibility in genre fiction. And while he spends more time than is healthy hiding in his writing cave instead of hanging around social media, you can generally find him in these usual haunts:

- Email: blackmagic@blackmagicblues.com
- Twitter: @thisblackmagic
- Facebook: https://www.facebook.com/xen.cole
- Tumblr: thisblackmagic.tumblr.com
- Instagram: www.instagram.com/thisblackmagic
- Facebook Fan Page: http://www.facebook.com/ColeMcCadeBooks
- Website & Blog: http://www.blackmagicblues.com

Find More Contemporary Romance & Erotica as Cole McCade

http://blackmagicblues.com/books-by-xen-x-cole-mccade/

Discover Science Fiction, Fantasy & Horror as Xen

http://blackmagicblues.com/books-by-xen-x-cole-mccade/

Made in the USA
Monee, IL
26 April 2024

57575553R00344